Praise for Jack Rogan

"*The Ocean Dark* demands to be a big, sprawling, bloody, brilliant thriller centered around a rising from the darkest myths and legends. Read it with all the lights on in the house. You've been warned!"

—JAMES ROLLINS,
New York Times bestselling author of *The Doomsday Key*

"A masterful thriller. *The Ocean Dark* is a big, sprawling tale filled with smart plotting and flesh-and-blood characters. It races from start to finish like an unstoppable vessel steaming full speed ahead."

—JEFFERY DEAVER,
author of *Edge* and *The Burning Wire*

"*The Ocean Dark* by Jack Rogan is a gale-force-ten thriller, blending furious suspense with brilliantly speculative science to create a riveting story of violence and mayhem on the high seas. Wow."

—DOUGLAS PRESTON, co-author of *Fever Dream*

"*The Ocean Dark* is a fantastic blend of horror and thriller. It has a great combination of character development and an intriguing story that will keep you turning pages. . . . Rogan's creatures are creative enough that they will have any reader look at any body of water at night with a bit more trepidation. . . . Fans of *Relic* by Douglas Preston and Lincoln Child or *Subterranean* by James Rollins would enjoy this creature thriller."

—Monster Librarian

"With enough story to keep the pages turning and enough description to keep the pages interesting and engaging, Rogan's first novel proves a successful thriller. And unlike so many authors of the genre, he has mastered the art of a loose-ends close, with enough pieces left open to carry characters into more novels, but not so blatant as to be too neatly pulled together or too set up for future scenarios. Hats off to you, Rogan, and here's to hoping we see more from you."

—Bookgasm

By Jack Rogan

The Ocean Dark

THE
COLLECTIVE

A NOVEL OF ADVENTURE AND SUSPENSE

JACK ROGAN

BALLANTINE BOOKS • NEW YORK

The Collective is a work of fiction. Names, characters, places, and incidents either are the product of the author's imagination or are used fictitiously. Any resemblance to actual persons, living or dead, events, or locales is entirely coincidental.

A Ballantine Books Mass Market Original

Copyright © 2011 by The Daring Greatly Corporation

Published in the United States by Ballantine Books, an imprint of The Random House Publishing Group, a division of Random House, Inc., New York.

BALLANTINE and colophon are registered trademarks of Random House, Inc.

ISBN 978-0-553-38519-9

Cover art and design: Jerry Todd

Printed in the United States of America

www.ballantinebooks.com

9 8 7 6 5 4 3 2 1

Ballantine mass market edition: July 2011

For my mother, Ann,
who always fought for her cubs

ACKNOWLEDGMENTS

Much love and thanks to my wife, Nicole, for her invaluable input. Thanks to my excellent editor, Anne Groell, for her unerring instinct, and to the following for their expertise and assistance: FBI Special Agent Dana Ridenour, David Kraus, and private investigator Jim Cobb.

Colonel Phil Greenlaw believed he had outgrown the nighttime fears of his childhood—right up until the day he became a father himself.

As a small boy, he had imagined endless horrors in the darkness of his bedroom. When the branches of the ash tree just outside the window scraped against the glass on stormy nights, he imagined the fingers of something dead and hungry. When the house creaked all around him, he recognized it as ghosts or intruders or rats in the walls. His parents indulged him by moving his bed twice—first against the wall because he felt too vulnerable, and then away from the wall because he was certain there were spiders hiding in the space between the bed and the wallpaper.

In time, of course, such fears had come to seem foolish. As a teenager he had thought of sleep only as a last resort, and bed as a place to collapse when exhaustion overwhelmed him. If, as an adult, he had nights when sleep didn't come so easily and the shadows of his bedroom took on a familiar ominous quality, he would remind himself that he wasn't a child anymore. He was a soldier.

Tonight he lay half-awake, listening to the sounds of his home and his sleeping family, wondering what had roused him. He turned onto his side and settled deeper into his pillow, soothed by the soft snoring of his wife, Carla, beside him. Drifting in the fog around the outskirts of sleep, he let the nighttime noises seep in. The hum of the cable box seemed strangely loud with the lights off. The air conditioner whispered through the vents. The little stone fountain Carla had bought at some New Age shop out on Sanibel Island burbled gently.

But sleep wasn't coming.

Phil opened his eyes again, brow furrowed with consternation. Had he actually heard something out of place? Ever since he and Carla had brought the twins home for the first time, he had not slept properly. Neil and Michael were adopted, but they had still been infants when they became Phil and Carla's children. Too many nights he had woken and wandered the house, checking to see if they were still breathing, or just standing in the half-open doorway of their room to watch them sleep. As the months passed, he had begun to relax a little.

So what was it tonight?

He slid nearer to Carla and put one hand on the curve of her hip. Sometimes just touching her helped him to get back to sleep. It was not something an Air Force colonel would ever have admitted to his colleagues, but he loved her fiercely. Bringing the boys home—seeing the joy in her eyes at finally becoming a mother—had been even more rewarding than his own happiness at becoming a father.

Inhale, exhale, let out the weird tension, and close your eyes against the shapes made by the shadows in the dark. Go to sleep.

But the tiniest of squeaks made him open his eyes again. Not a mouse. This had been a strangely metallic squeak. Another sound followed—a shifting of weight on wood, the creak of a presence that did not belong. A cold fear trickled through his heart and he propped himself up in bed, listening. It could be nothing . . . was probably nothing. Just the house, the wind, a shift in air pressure, the air conditioner, a towel finally dropping off a doorknob from which it had slipped by infinitesimal fractions over the course of hours.

He had climbed out of bed and checked on the boys dozens of times, had gone downstairs to investigate strange sounds hundreds of times before he and Carla had even had children. And he always made the rounds before going to bed, checking locks and shutting off lights before he carried two glasses of water upstairs—one for him and one for Carla.

But that peculiar metallic squeak lingered in his mind. And though he heard nothing more to alarm him, he could not erase it.

Then he heard a muffled voice, probably a moan, and he understood—Neil must be having another nightmare. The boy sometimes had bad dreams and would talk in his sleep.

Phil slipped out of bed, careful not to uncover Carla. The air-conditioning made her too chilly to sleep without the covers. He took a sip of water from the glass on his nightstand. Even with the A/C running, the ice had long since melted. The clock on the cable box glowed the time, 2:12 a.m. He waited half a minute but heard nothing more. Half-asleep, he scratched his head and thought about lying down again, but he had already committed to investigating the noise, and now that he'd sat up he felt a dull fullness in his bladder that urged him on.

Standing, he rubbed at the sleep in his eyes and shuffled toward the door. He would just peek into the twins' room. If he woke them now, especially if Neil had been having a bad dream, they'd want him to stay and he would end up asleep on the carpet between their beds. Carla would have to get up when his alarm went off, and he'd be stiff as hell from hours on the floor.

Gingerly, he drew open his bedroom door and stepped into the hall.

"Phil?" his wife said sleepily. "What are you doing?"

He turned and glanced back into the room. Her brown hair looked black in the dark, and it spilled across her face in a lovely mess.

"I thought I heard something," he said.

A drowsy, playful smile touched her lips. "Nudge me when you come back to bed."

Phil grinned, his anxiety vanishing. He had learned early in their relationship that Carla enjoyed the soft, tangled, dreamy intimacy of late-night sex. Sometimes she stroked or nibbled or licked him awake in the small hours of the morning.

"Guess I'm not the only one who's restless tonight," he said.

She arched an eyebrow. "Are you complaining, Colonel?"

"Not even a little."

"Then hurry back."

Brain buzzing with the anticipation of sex, he turned away, toward the boys' room. An unfamiliar shadow loomed in the hall, half-silhouetted in the twins' open doorway, and his smile faded. For the tiniest moment, Phil hesitated, presuming this was yet another in a lifetime of illusory nighttime shadows, but as he blinked, the shadow lunged at him.

His training kicked in along with his fear, but not fast enough. That tiny hesitation cost him his life. His skull slammed against the soft green paint of the corridor wall and powerful hands gripped his throat. He heard Carla screaming in the bedroom, heard her struggle to disentangle herself from the sheets as the footfalls of a second shadow rushed to attack her.

From the boys' bedroom, however, he heard only silence.

Alexandria's Old Town reeked of money and history. Gabled buildings overlooked tree-lined cobblestone streets where finely dressed men and women slipped out of expensive cars and into exclusive restaurants and boutiques. Many of the best and brightest of Washington, D.C., strolled through Old Town on any given night, enjoying the view across the Potomac from Virginia to D.C. and happy to be away from the capital for a while.

There were other facets to Old Town, of course—plenty of theaters and coffee shops and less expensive restaurants. Josh Hart had sometimes wandered through its antiques stores and bookshops. It would be hard to think of himself as a tourist—his apartment was less than half a mile away—but neither did he feel like a local. In the handful of months he had lived in Alexandria, he had rarely been at home for more than a few days in a row. Alexandria offered plenty of nightlife, but he had so little opportunity to take advantage of it that most of the time he felt like a foreigner. And he sure as hell didn't have time for a relationship.

The very idea of dating amused and wearied him. During the occasional flirtation, he had been called things like sweet and funny and charming, but there always seemed to be a distance between himself and women that he could not bridge. He made them nervous. Or maybe it was the job that created the uneasiness.

He liked to blame the job for his divorce. It was convenient. But he knew that a large part of the blame lay in his own hands. The only way to sustain a relationship was to effectively persuade a woman that she was more important than the job, and he had never been that good an actor. The job came first, always.

"So, you actually work for Homeland Security?"

Josh arched an eyebrow and smiled, studying the woman sitting across the table from him. Molly Bechtel, thirty-one. Never married, no kids. Shoulder-length blond hair, blue eyes, a few freckles, mouth a little too wide and nose a little too long, but the pieces all fit together into a very attractive whole. In fact, what he liked most of all was her spark, the feisty gleam in her eyes. It wasn't a small thing, considering he hadn't expected to like her at all.

"I do," he said. "Why, did you think Mikayla was lying to you?"

"I thought she might be exaggerating," Molly replied. "It wouldn't be the first time she's done so in order to get me on a date."

The waiter brought their salads, sliding them onto the table with an almost ghostly grace before vanishing again. Josh had chosen Hannah's for several reasons, the wait staff among them. The place was a little pricey, but unlike in similar restaurants he had patronized, the servers didn't hover. Perfect for a blind date.

Not that Josh was an expert. The last blind date he'd been on had been his sophomore year in college, and he'd ended up marrying the girl. But when Mikayla, one of the trainers at his neighborhood gym, insisted on setting him up with Molly, he had been unable to come up with a reason to refuse. He had been sure it would be a terrible mistake, but Molly had turned out to be anything but. With eyes full of wisdom and a playful smile, she had shocked him into foolish babbling for the first thirty seconds. They were only on the salad course, and already he wanted to see her again.

Josh took a sip of his wine. "So, have you been on a lot of blind dates?"

She relented, one corner of her mouth lifting in a playful smile. "No, actually. Just the one. It didn't go very well."

"And is this one going well?" he asked, watching her through the glow of the candle in the center of the table.

A sly smile stole over Molly's face. Josh liked the way that smile made him feel. She pretended to be thinking it over, but as she glanced past him, her expression faltered. Her brows knitted in curiosity, and whatever she had been about to say was forgotten. "Can I ask you a question?" she asked instead.

"Fire away."

Molly smiled again, but it seemed forced. "What does your ex-wife look like?"

"*Rebecca?* Why?"

"There's a woman sitting at the bar. Small, blond, mid-thirties, looks like she's in great shape. She came in a few minutes ago and she keeps looking our way, like she has something she wants to say."

Josh glanced over at the bar and saw the blond hair, not to mention the slight bulge at the small of the woman's back that gave away the presence of a weapon. Not sure if he was irritated or concerned, Josh pushed his chair back. "Excuse me a second."

"If it's your ex, just tell me now and I'll go. I like you, but I don't like complications."

Josh sighed. "She's not my ex, she's my partner."

Molly raised a dubious eyebrow. "And does she usually stalk you on your dates?"

"Not usually, no."

Leaving Molly behind, Josh weaved through tables to reach the bar, where Rachael Voss sipped at a strawberry margarita. As he approached, Voss saluted him with the paper umbrella from her drink.

"I *did* try to call," she said. "Bad boy, turning your phone off."

Josh tried not to smile at her gentle chiding, but couldn't manage it. "In case you hadn't noticed, I'm on a date."

"So you said. And I'll hand it to you, she's very pretty. I figured a blind date would be more like Quasimodo than Esmerelda."

"I'd remind you how long it's been since *your* last date, but I assume you didn't come down here just to tell me to turn my phone back on."

Voss slid off the stool and dropped a ten-dollar bill on the bar. Her expression softened as she looked at him. They were partners, yes, but she was also his best friend, and an electric current of temptation often crackled between them, daring them to become more than that. They had not succumbed to that temptation yet, unwilling to risk their partnership, but Josh was closer to Rachael Voss than to anyone else in his life.

"I'm sorry," Voss said. "It looked like the date was going well. I hope she'll understand."

"Shit." Josh glanced over at Molly, who watched him curiously and a bit suspiciously, perhaps thinking that Voss really was his ex-wife. "Where are we headed?"

"Florida. Quadruple homicide in Fort Myers with possible terrorist involvement; multiple agencies and police departments are en route to the site. The plane's already waiting for us."

Josh exhaled, nodding. "I'll meet you outside."

Voss started toward the door. She'd only managed three steps before she turned back. "Josh?"

He gave her a questioning look.

"Turn your phone on."

As she departed, Josh made his way to the table. Molly's curious expression had given way to disappointment. Josh figured she must have been able to read his face just as well as he could read hers.

"You're leaving?" she asked as he slid into his chair.

"I have to. I'm sorry to have to abandon you like this."

Her irritation flickered, then seemed to extinguish itself. "I guess this is why you don't date much, huh? Duty calls?"

Josh smoothed the tablecloth with his hands. "It is, and it does. Thanks for understanding. Maybe I can make it up to you when I get back?"

Molly smiled, but he could still see an edge of disappointment and annoyance in her eyes. "Give me a call when you're back in town," she said, "and I'll think about it."

Josh took out his wallet, slid out enough cash to pay for both dinners—though his would go uneaten—and left it on the table with a heavy water glass on top of it. For a second he felt like a john, leaving money on a prostitute's dresser before slinking home to his wife, and when he glanced at Molly he had the terrible feeling that she knew just what he was thinking.

He fought the urge to apologize again. Four people had been murdered and someone in authority thought there might be a terrorist connection. He shouldn't feel bad about having to leave. That was the job, and anyone who might even consider getting involved with him had to understand that.

But as he walked to the door, he knew he wouldn't be seeing Molly again.

The second he hit the sidewalk, he fished out his cell phone and turned it on. Voss stood at the curb, leaning against her aging blue Audi. Without a word, she went around to the driver's side and slid behind the wheel. Josh climbed into the passenger seat.

The quiet between him and Voss was the only intimacy in his life. Sometimes it felt like love and sometimes it felt like faith. Whatever it was, he knew Voss would take a bullet for him if it came to that, and the feeling was mutual.

It would have to be enough.

-3--

The guy beating the shit out of his wife looked lit up with violence, the way people said that pregnant women glowed. Six foot three, maybe two hundred fifty pounds of undrafted football goon, he had stormed out of Jillian's like he thought the paparazzi should be waiting. They weren't. This was Boston, not L.A.—no matter how many movies the state's tax incentives lured to shoot there.

There *were* cameras, but most of them were still inside the club. Local network affiliate news vans were parked up on curbs, the reporters mostly doing their jobs on the second floor of Jillian's. Three members of the New England Patriots defensive line were hosting a fund-raiser for a battered-women's charity—oh, the irony—attended by loads of other players, not to mention guys from the Red Sox and the Celtics and their wives, who seemed almost as famous as their husbands.

Cait McCandless sat behind the wheel of the Channel 7 news van and wondered if any of the Boston Bruins players were in there. Nobody had mentioned them, and it made her curious. Had they not been invited, or was there some political issue involved that she didn't know about? Not that she gave a damn about hockey—she was a football girl—but it was still an interesting question.

Supposedly there were actors at the party, too. Homegrown types—Matt Damon and the guy who used to star in *The Shield*. No Denis Leary, though. The guy loved Boston and did all kinds of charitable work with firefighters and such, but he was like an honorary Bruin or something, so maybe he was showing solidarity with his hockey brethren.

Cait was pretty sure Denis Leary would have knocked the wife-beater on his ass.

The Channel 7 news crew, on the other hand, didn't do a damn thing.

The washed-up football player had called himself A-Train when he'd played for Boston College—some kind of play on his real name, which nobody cared enough to remember anymore. A couple of ugly arrests and rumors about steroids had made him untouchable, but somehow he'd gotten an invitation tonight.

Or maybe he hadn't, considering how quickly he'd left the party. His wife—in a shimmery gold dress, with killer heels and her long brown hair in copper-highlighted ringlets—was just a few steps behind him. She had looked equal parts pissed and fabulous as she started turning right, heading off down Lansdowne Street, while he turned left toward the parking garage.

He hadn't let her go far, catching her by the wrist and hauling her alongside him toward the garage. She'd started screaming at him, feral and full of spite. When that got no response, she tried to pull away. And then she hit him.

The backhand he'd given her in return had knocked her to the ground. When she got up, her nose and mouth were bloodied, but she hadn't stopped screaming at him. Even now, after four more hard knocks, the curses still flowed. Though her voice was shrill and her Caribbean-island accent made the words difficult to follow, it seemed clear her husband thought she had been screwing someone behind his back—someone who must still be inside Jillian's.

Cait had never seen such a twisted dance in all her life. The wife would scream denials and counteraccusations at him, sobbing with tears and fury, not even bothering to wipe the blood from her lips and chin. He would threaten her, tell her to shut up, and when she told him to fuck off—the same words every time, only louder and with more blood flying with each new utterance—A-Train would belt her.

When she tried to hurt him, clawing at his face, he hit her with a closed fist. The meaty slap of impact echoed off the pavement as she went down to her knees and stayed there, quiet for the first time.

"Get up on your feet and go to the goddamn car right fucking now," A-Train told her, his voice not so loud now, though it still carried along the street.

Music thumped inside Jillian's. Lights flashed in the windows. People coming in and out of the party had stopped on the sidewalk by the front doors to watch, the same way they slowed down to check out a car accident. But this bit of wreckage was still in progress and nobody was doing a thing about it.

"Duffy, come on! This is nuts," Cait said, breaking a silence that had lasted longer than she could forgive herself for.

Mike Duffy, the new sports guy at Channel 7, had been running behind, pissed that he'd be the last to the party, but as Jordan had taken the camera out of the van, A-Train had come out of Jillian's and started in on his wife.

Cait had watched the whole thing through the open window of the van, face flushed with unspent adrenaline, hands gripping on the steering wheel though the engine wasn't running. On the sidewalk, Jordan had the camera rolling, getting the whole thing on video.

"Are we just gonna sit here?" she asked, addressing him through the open passenger's side window.

Jordan glanced at her, but only for a second. "You knew the rules when you took the gig, Cait. We spread the news, we don't make it."

Cait narrowed her eyes. During the Iraq War, Jordan and their friend Ronnie had watched her back, and she'd looked out for them as well. All three of them had made it home, and Jordan had been the one to hook her up with this job at Channel 7. It wasn't much—driving a van—but it was a hell of a lot better than being an unemployed single mother. She owed him for that, and she did know the rules, but it went against everything she believed in to do nothing.

She popped open the door.

"Caitlin," Duffy snapped, pushing past Jordan and leaning in through the window. "Do not interfere."

Cait glared at him across the front seat of the van. "Duffy, goddammit—"

"Jordan's right. We don't make the news, Caitlin," he said, chiding her.

He'd been making that mistake a lot, treating her like some whiny teenage girl just because she was cute and petite and had a button nose and a heart-shaped face and he probably wanted to bang her. But Cait McCandless had spent most of her twenty-six years making people regret underestimating her.

"No one is going to help her. Jordan, come on," Cait urged, still sitting in the driver's seat with her door halfway open.

Jordan looked uncomfortable. He'd been a soldier, and he was a gentleman. His instinct would have been to take on A-Train himself, but he had tried to make a clean break between Iraq and the civilian world. The job had rules, and though she could see him struggling, Cait knew he wanted to follow them.

"Duffy called the cops. They'll be here soon. There's nothing we can do. Let the proper authorities handle it."

Cait felt bile rising in the back of her throat. She didn't know what made her feel like puking more—the citizens out there in front of Jillian's watching like it was some kind of sidewalk performance, or the fact that she had already watched a two-hundred-fifty-pound football player strike his wife half a dozen times and still sat behind the wheel. She knew the rules of the job. They reported the news, they didn't make it. They weren't supposed to interfere. But there had to be exceptions.

"Fuck it," she whispered, and climbed out of the van.

"Cait?" Duffy said.

She ignored him. Instead, she focused on A-Train and his wife and the weird tableau they made in the yellow glow thrown by the lights just inside the parking garage. The woman had stopped screaming and even her crying had softened so it couldn't be heard above the dull thump of music from the club. A-Train stood over his wife expectantly, waiting for her to do as he'd told her, rage simmering.

Cait started toward them.

Duffy grabbed her wrist just the way A-Train had grabbed his wife's. But she spun on the sportscaster and shot him a look that made him let go.

As she turned back toward the garage, she saw A-Train

reach down and grab his wife's thin wrist, hauling the woman to her feet. Cait saw the spark of violence reignite in the air between them even before the woman lashed out. This time, Mrs. A-Train got the son of a bitch good, clawing furrows in the left side of his face.

A-Train roared in pain and caught her free hand so that he now held them both in his big fists. Then he must have squeezed, for she screamed, and Cait knew there would be broken bones.

She ran, cursing the silent watchers who had taken out cell phones and cameras to record the ugliness for later Internet posting, aware that she and Duffy and Jordan were no better.

Cait didn't shout at him to stop. The guy had gone critical; there'd be no turning back for him now. Maybe he'd carry his wife to the car and drive her to the hospital or maybe he would cave her face in with his fist in the next fifteen seconds. There was no margin for hesitation.

A-Train heard her coming, turned to look, and for just a second his rage faltered at the absurdity of this waif trying to interfere. Then he sneered and raised his fist, ready to belt his wife again just to prove there wasn't a damn thing Cait could do about it.

She snapped a side kick at the back of his leg, buckling his knee, and the bastard went down hard, smacking his head on the pavement. As he scrambled to get up, she danced in close and shot her hand down, fingers straight, jabbing his windpipe hard enough to hurt but not crush. Wheezing raggedly, A-Train reached for his throat. Cait waited. She'd chosen the angle of her initial kick carefully. The only reason she hadn't broken his knee was because she knew Jordan still had the camera rolling, and that was why she hesitated now.

But then he lunged for her, faltering a little on the injured leg as he came up. She took his arm, twisted, and used his own momentum to send him sprawling again before she waded in and stomped on his right wrist, hearing the bone crunch. Served him right.

A-Train started to rise again and she thought she would have to drop-kick him in the head, but then the sirens that had been growing in the distance blossomed into blaring, urgent life, and two police cars skidded into the intersection that separated Jillian's from the garage.

"Bitch," A-Train mouthed over the wail of sirens.

His wife huddled on the ground ten feet away, cradling her broken hands in her lap, staring at them in shock. Blue lights flashed across her face. Would she thank Cait for getting involved? *Probably not, but somebody had to.*

As the police rushed them all, Duffy ran over to explain. Several of the bystanders, suddenly finding their voices now that the bloody spectacle had ended, shouted to the cops in Cait's defense.

"Girl's a hero, man!" a fit, well-dressed young guy yelled. "She kicked his ass."

It made Cait sick to hear the word. Heroes didn't watch from the sidelines while head cases beat up their wives in public. She hated herself for how long she'd waited, but all she had been able to think about was what would become of her baby daughter, Leyla, if she ended up in the hospital.

And then she had thought about what kind of world she wanted Leyla to grow up in. And what kind of woman she wanted to raise her daughter to become.

A-Train was lucky she'd only broken his hand.

- 4 - -

Rachael Voss dreamed about retiring someplace like Fort Myers, Florida—provided she didn't catch a bullet first. She drove the rented Mercedes along a gently twisting road, seashells crunching under the tires. Even this late at night it was still too damn hot, but she had the windows cranked down anyway. Air-conditioning gave her more of a headache than the heat of Florida in August.

Her partner, Josh Hart, sat in the passenger seat swirling the remnants of his iced coffee around in a plastic cup. Music played low on the radio—the volume and station both still set to whatever they'd been when she and Josh had picked up the rental at the airport—but otherwise they traveled mostly in silence, only the breeze coming through the windows for company.

During the day, Josh would have bitched about the open windows and Voss would have surrendered and put on the A/C. They'd been partners for more than three years, first with the FBI and now as part of Homeland Security's new watchdog task force, the InterAgency Cooperation Division. The ICD consisted of one director, two assistant directors, and fourteen interagency case coordinators, Voss and Josh among them.

Delicious aromas steamed off of the vegetation, mingling with the ocean scent of the Gulf of Mexico, not far off. They rounded a corner and the road turned to pavement. The headlights picked out twisted tree limbs and the tall, thin trunks of palm trees, whose bark always reminded Voss of mummy wrappings. She slowed as she drove over a speed bump. A spotlighted sign announced they were entering Manatee Village, which made Voss roll her eyes. Manatees were the ugliest, laziest creatures in the ocean, the couch potatoes of the sea. They weren't cute like seals or sea lions—just big, fat things that lolled in the water like the cows they were named for, but without the benefit of providing milk or cheeseburgers.

"Who lives out here?" Josh asked.

"Good question," Voss said.

But the exchange had been rhetorical. They both knew who lived in Manatee Village—a development of faux-adobe-looking single-family homes with inground swimming pools and lanais that let the bugs in but kept the alligators out. Old people who retired to Florida lived in condo and townhouse developments, and people born and raised in Fort Myers couldn't afford homes like this. The last time Voss had been through the city's downtown, she'd been left with the impression of a place teetering between resurgence and total collapse, and neither fate seemed more or less likely than the other.

No, the people in Manatee Village weren't from here. They

were young professionals, mostly with families, who had moved to Florida for the sake of their jobs, working with startup companies when the economy had been surging and now hanging on by the skin of their teeth.

As they drove through Manatee Village, half of the pastel faux-dobe homes had either FOR SALE or FORECLOSURE signs in front.

Blue lights flashed ghost shadows against the houses at the corner of Periwinkle Lane. Voss turned right and let the Mercedes roll toward the riot of vehicles jammed up and down the block. Nearest were the news vans—only two for now, but in the days to come there would be many more.

"I'm surprised nobody's sent a helicopter yet," Josh said.

Voss guided the rental car between the vans. "I'm not. It's Fort Myers. Besides, it's dark out. If someone's going to pay for a chopper, it'll be tomorrow when the sun's up. They'll probably dangle Nancy Grace from a bungee cord with a microphone and let her prey on the neighbors."

"Stop. You're scaring me."

Neither of them smiled at the joke. When there were dead children involved, nothing was funny.

Just past the news vans, the road had been blocked by a pair of Fort Myers police cars parked nose to nose, each manned by a single uniformed officer. As Voss and Josh rolled up in the Mercedes, the cop on the left stood at attention, chin high, and strode over to them, rolling his shoulders like a boxer about to deliver the final blow.

"I'm sorry, ma'am—" the young cop began.

Voss flashed her ID. "Homeland Security. Let us through, please."

The kid managed to keep his composure long enough to take a closer look at her ID, then nodded in deference. "Yes, ma'am."

He stepped back onto the sidewalk even as he waved to the other cop to let them through. The man—a slightly older version of the tanned, fit kid who'd stopped them—jumped into his cruiser and backed it into a driveway to let them pass.

Voss almost expected Josh to make some innuendo-laden

comment about the young cop's obedience, but he remained silent, staring straight ahead. She was glad. He might actually have made her laugh, and it wasn't a night for laughter.

She guided the Mercedes past another Fort Myers police cruiser, then a couple of Florida State Police cars, and finally parked at the back of a cluster of unmarked sedans. The center of attention was 23 Periwinkle Lane, which looked indistinguishable from the other homes in the development. A brightly colored FOR SALE sign had been planted on the lawn, and Voss felt a pang of sorrow. The murdered family would never have another home.

FBI agents and state police investigators combed the yard with flashlights. In the open garage, gloved techs were going over a red Mustang like it had just crash-landed in Area 51. Half a dozen grim-looking men and women clustered in the driveway, engaged in a conversation that might have been an argument or just speculation about the case. Yellow crime-scene tape had been run along the white picket fence in the front yard, across the driveway to a palm tree, then along into the backyard.

"What's with the tape?" Josh asked. "Kind of overkill, right? Why not just do the front and back doors?"

"Maybe they found decent footprints and are going to make casts," Voss said.

They got out of the car and walked to the driveway, stepping over the yellow tape. A slender, attractive Asian woman in an FBI shirt noticed them first. She wore her hair pulled back in a severe ponytail and, despite her beauty, her expression—even in the moment she caught her first glimpse of them—was equally severe. She tapped another FBI agent, drawing his attention to them, and as the man turned around, Voss stiffened.

"You've gotta be kidding me," Josh muttered.

Voss felt her lips curve in a feral smile. "This should be interesting."

They had worked with Supervisory Special Agent Ed Turcotte once before, on the strangest and most terrifying case of their lives. She and Josh had been FBI agents themselves back then, doing ocean interdiction, dealing with gun smugglers and drug runners, mostly. Turcotte headed one of the FBI's counterterrorist squads and had tried stealing cases out from under them any number of times.

The last time, they had all nearly died.

But Voss and Josh didn't work for the FBI anymore. Turcotte probably knew that, which would have explained the confusion on his face as they strode up the driveway toward him. The man had gone bald enough that he'd shaved what remained of his hair down to a half inch of gray-brown stubble, and he looked about a decade older.

Turcotte and the female FBI agent stepped away from the group to greet them.

"Agent Turcotte," Voss said.

"What the hell are you doing here?" Turcotte replied with a scowl.

Voss produced her identification and Josh followed suit.

"Homeland Security ICD," she said as she flashed the ID. "Didn't anybody tell you we were coming?"

Turcotte gave a sardonic laugh. "I knew someone was coming, but nobody mentioned names. So you're Homeland's new Troubleshooters, huh?"

"Troubleshooters?" Josh asked.

The woman at Turcotte's side cocked her head, studying them. "That's what they're calling you at the Bureau. To be honest, there might be some sarcasm involved. Some people are wondering if you're going to ease troubles or cause them."

Josh glanced at Voss. "I like her."

"Me, too," Voss said, before focusing on the woman again. "And probably a little bit of both, since you're wondering."

The woman raised her hands. "Hey, I said 'some people.'"

"You did," Josh admitted, his blue eyes glinting with mischief.

"Special Agent Nala Chang," Turcotte broke in, "meet Agents Rachael Voss and Josh Hart, formerly FBI. Now, apparently, interagency cooperation coordinators for Homeland Security. Officially, our babysitters."

"Though *Troubleshooters* is growing on me," Josh said. "We'll have to bring that up at the next meeting."

"Good to meet you," Chang said.

They shook hands all around.

"So, what've you got?" Voss asked.

Turcotte frowned. "Weren't you briefed?"

"Only on the players involved and the general stuff—home invasion, four DOA, possible terrorist connections. They stuck us on a plane too fast to give us the details. Anyway, our job isn't to solve the case, it's to offer whatever help we can and to make sure all of you don't get in one another's way while *you're* trying to," Voss explained.

"And if we do? Get in one another's way, I mean?" Chang asked, with what seemed like genuine curiosity.

Josh and Voss exchanged a glance, but it was Turcotte who answered.

"Then they have the power to assume command of the investigation."

Chang stared at him. "You're fucking kidding!"

Turcotte glared at her, clearly not liking the profanity from a subordinate agent.

"I'm liking her even more," Josh said.

But Voss kept her gaze fixed on Turcotte. "Ironic, isn't it, Ed?"

"That's one word for it," he sniffed, then glanced at Chang. "Nala, run them through it, will you? Take them into the house and show them around. Then they can meet the rest of the folks they'll be babysitting."

"You're the boss," Chang said, turning and starting up a brick path toward the house. She glanced back at Voss and Josh. "You two coming?"

The sequence of events was off. Turcotte ought to have introduced them first and then sent Chang to give them the tour. Obviously, he wanted to warn the other lead investigators that the ICD Troubleshooters had arrived and to be on their best behavior—which in Turcotte's terms might mean not sharing all the information. Voss knew this, and it pissed her off, but she had expected as much the moment she'd spotted him. In the end, it wouldn't matter. She doubted the others would be foolish enough to go along with him when they knew it might cost them control of the case.

Josh headed up the walk after Chang, but Voss took a

moment to scan the property and the front of the house, trying to look like she was taking in the whole scene when in fact she just wanted a better look at the other investigators talking to Turcotte. Two of them—an attractive young Latino and a graying white guy—wore radios and guns on their hips, marking them as state police. She figured the tall black guy in the tailored shirt must be the officer from U.S. Special Operations Command that she'd been told would be in attendance—though why U.S. SOCOM had anyone at all responding to a murder case on U.S. soil, she had no idea. Each branch of the armed forces had its own special operations command, handling counterterrorism, special recon, unconventional warfare, and psych-ops, among other, similarly sneaky, badass tasks. U.S. SOCOM was the unified command, giving orders all across the top, so nobody stepped on one another's toes, but all of their operations took place on foreign soil.

The last guy was the one that bothered her most, though. He wore dark trousers and a red tie, hair perfectly in place despite the humidity, and looked like he never broke a sweat. His sleeves were turned up and she imagined he had left the jacket that went with his pants in the car, but he still looked like he would have been more at home in a corporate boardroom than at the site of a quadruple murder. He hung back from the others, listening to the conversation without contributing.

Voss caught up with Chang and Josh at the door and followed them inside.

"I assume I don't have to tell you not to touch anything," Chang said.

Josh gave her a look that said maybe he didn't like her so much anymore. "We've only been away from the Bureau for five months."

Chang paused in the foyer and smiled at him. "Yeah? How's the new job?"

"Better benefits, fewer people to answer to, and vast power to stomp on assholes who put their egos before their jobs," Josh said.

"Fun," Chang replied.

Jesus, Voss thought. *Is she flirting with him?* She wasn't jealous—or, at least, only a little. Josh was her best friend. They'd saved each other's lives more than once and shared an intimacy that had never crossed the line into romance but sometimes danced right on the edge. Still, she was amazed at the effect Josh so often had on women other than his ex-wife. Yes, his eyes were startlingly blue and he had his gorgeous days, but there were better-looking guys.

Okay, maybe a little jealous.

"Out of curiosity, Agent Chang, who's the suit out there in the driveway?"

Chang glanced around the foyer as though to orient herself. "Norris. Not sure if that's his first or last name. He's a consultant from Black Pine."

Voss was glad Chang didn't see the expression on her face. She frowned in distaste and turned to see Josh mirror her reaction. Black Pine Worldwide was a private military security and consulting firm who contracted with the U.S. government, among other clients, to provide everything from standard security to bodyguards to Black Ops, if the whispers were true . . . and she had no doubt they were.

"Why is he here?" Josh asked.

Chang turned to face them. "I'm gonna go out on a limb and say he's consulting."

"For who?" Voss said. "Who hired him?"

Now Chang got it and she frowned as well. "Actually, I'm not sure. You'll have to ask him."

"I will."

Chang shrugged. "Okay, on with the tour. You can go over the whole house yourselves if you want, but there was no sign of forced entry on the first floor. It all went down on the second floor, while they were sleeping. I'll show you the parents' room, but if you want to check out the twins' bedroom, you're on your own. I'll give you the lowdown, but I'm not going in there again."

"Twins?" Josh echoed, his face going slack.

"Three-year-old boys," Chang said, all of the spark gone from her eyes. "You didn't know?"

Voss felt sick. Her hands curled into fists as she started up the stairs.

-5--

Cait sat on the hood of the police car, legs dangling beneath her, slumped over and feeling petulant. Very few things made her crazier than being made to wait. Doctor's office, the chair outside the principal's office back in high school, stuck in traffic, the airport when her flight had been delayed. They were all hell, and this wasn't much different.

A glance at her cell phone told her eleven o'clock was fast approaching. All over Lansdowne Street, reporters were doing their thing, prepping pre-recorded packages for which they would do live introductions, talking both about the party inside and the violence that had taken place outside. But only her crew, from Channel 7, had the whole thing on video. Already the teasers running during commercial breaks would be pimping the exclusive, and once the clock struck eleven, Cait would turn into a local media star.

She wondered if the station manager would fire her.

Police lights flashed, throwing splashes of ghostly blue across the buildings. EMTs had treated A-Train's wife at the scene, temporarily immobilizing her hands and wrists and stopping the flow of blood from her mouth and nose before getting her on a gurney and hoisting her into the back of an ambulance with an oxygen mask over her face. The woman would be fine—as long as she could be cured of whatever illness made her want to marry someone like A-Train.

For his part, the washed-up athlete had also been treated by EMTs, but instead of an ambulance, he'd get to ride to the hospital in the back of a police car. He sat there now, twenty feet away, and Cait gave him a cheerful wave as she swung her feet like an impatient teen. A-Train mouthed abusive words through the glass, but she couldn't hear him. She hoped that the EMTs hadn't given him any painkillers and that the police made him wait a long time indeed.

The cop who had been assigned to babysit Cait—a surprisingly cute guy in a uniform so clean he had to be a rookie—had asked her to sit tight while he checked with his superiors to find out how long she would be detained. The rest of the cops were gathering statements from witnesses or talking to EMTs, and her rookie interrupted one of the plain-clothes investigators, who glanced at her, snapped something at the rookie, then came marching over.

"Ms. McCandless, I'm pretty sure one of the other officers asked you to be patient," the cop said. He was maybe forty, in need of a shave and a new workout regimen, but he still had a kind of brash charm.

She could have made a wisecrack, but thought better of it.

"Somebody did, Detective. But, honestly, it's been so long I can't remember which one. I'm starting to forget my own name over here," she said, trying for wistful and probably just managing bored.

"We're still going to need to talk to you—"

"I know, but I already gave a statement." She pointed toward the Channel 7 van. "Over there? Those are my co-workers. Technically, I'm on the job right now, only I'm not doing my job. In maybe twelve minutes, Mike Duffy's going to go live with this—hell, every station will be live at the top of the hour—and I'm over here, cooling my heels. The truth is, I'm probably in a shitload of trouble already, and I can't afford to lose this job. So if you're really thinking about arresting me, okay. But if not, could I please get back to work?"

The guy studied her grimly, sizing her up. He scratched his head, tracing furrows in his bristly salt-and-pepper hair, and she saw that he was not unkind, but also not convinced of her sincerity.

"How'd you get the drop on him?" the detective asked.

Cait blinked. "Huh?"

"Traynor," the detective said, hooking a thumb toward the next car, where A-Train cradled his broken hand against his chest. "I mean, I saw the video and I could hardly believe it, little slip of a thing like you. Okay, you can fight. Still, the guy saw you coming, so how did you know you had the drop on him?"

Cait shrugged. "Like you said, look at me. Guy saw me coming and reacted the way your windshield would to an on-coming fly. It's easy enough to get the drop on him if he assumes I'm no threat. And if you saw the video, you know that somebody had to step in. What would you have done?"

He gave a soft laugh. "Probably had my ass handed to me, but I get your point. Doesn't mean there might not still be charges against you."

"Not much I can do about that," Cait said.

The detective looked her up and down again, but there was nothing creepy about it. He was checking her out with a cop's eyes, not ogling her body.

"Where'd you learn to fight like that?"

"Iraq," she said. Half the truth had to be better than a total lie.

His eyes narrowed and he nodded, as if her answer explained everything. Maybe, to him, it did.

"Go ahead," he said. "Get back to work. Somebody will track you down if there are any more questions."

"Thanks." Cait smiled as she slipped down from the hood of the police car and hurried back to the van. The rear doors were open and, when she reached them, she found Duffy leaning into the back, busting Jordan's balls.

"Come on, man. We're out of time," Duffy said.

Jordan did not look up from the editing deck, where he was preparing the pre-recorded parts of their report for broadcast. His brown eyes were intense as he ran the images forward and backward, listening intently to the audio through big black headphones. Cait looked at the monitor and saw herself kick A-Train's leg out from under him, saw the man fall and his wife go scrambling to safety, then saw the whole scene run quickly backward.

"Come on!" Duffy said, and he banged on the door to get Jordan's attention.

Jordan snapped his head up, about to swear at Duffy, then hesitated when he spotted her there. Since the end of his tour, he had grown a thick, unruly beard that made him look almost Amish, but his smile still brightened her mood. Cait doubted she'd ever met a man as laid-back as Jordan. He had saved her life at least once in Iraq, and been her friend when nearly everyone else in their unit had turned from her.

Though, she had to admit, she did prefer him without the beard. It softened him a little, as if the hard man he had learned to be in Iraq, the capable soldier, was hiding from the world behind a fuzzy face. Cait found the man behind the beard more attractive. Not that her opinion counted, of course. They were friends and comrades, nothing more.

Duffy hadn't noticed her arrival, but Jordan's smile made him turn. The sportscaster looked like the kind of guy who spent far too much of his life playing tennis at a country club. Blond and blue-eyed, about thirty, the guy was a rising star. He was also a dick.

"Well, well," Duffy said, nodding in some combination of approval, sexual innuendo, and uneasiness. "If it isn't Boston's newest media superstar. Way to make the news. When A-Train and his wife sue the station, that'll be huge news, too."

Cait gave a disgusted snort. "You think she's going to stay with him?"

Duffy shrugged. "Happens all the time, women staying with men—especially famous men—who've beat them up. She'll make excuses for him, just watch."

"The guy is going to jail," Cait said.

"Doesn't mean they won't sue," Duffy replied. "Now get to work. We've got our live shot in about six minutes." He turned to Jordan. "You all set?"

Jordan nodded, climbed out of the van, then turned to Cait. "It's all cued up."

"Thanks."

"Don't sweat it," he said. "You did a good thing. I would've been in there myself in another second or two, and to hell with the job—"

"And he'd have kicked your ass," Cait teased him.

"I may not have your skills, but I can hold my own," Jordan said. "I did pretty damn well in hand-to-hand combat training."

Cait grinned. "He'd have kicked your ass."

Jordan smiled sheepishly. "No doubt."

Cait laughed softly, but her good humor faded. "Listen, should I be worried? You hooked me up with this gig and I don't want it to blow back on you."

"Don't think it for a second. First of all, Leyla's got to be your priority, not whether I get some collateral damage because you stepped in to help someone. Anyway, I'm sure you'll be fine. How would it look if they fired you?"

Though they were only words, they helped. She smiled as Jordan departed, and then climbed into the back of the van. She told herself Jordan was right. It had been a good thing.

But nothing good would come of it.

Duffy had picked up his microphone and was smoothing his tie, but now he glanced up.

"Almost forgot," he said. "Lynette asked me to tell you not to talk to anyone except the cops. No interviews until after they're sure that nobody's going to sue."

No interviews. That was fine with her. Duffy had probably asked if he could interview Cait for the segment, and the station manager—Lynette Alfari—had shut him down.

"Whatever," she said.

Jordan hefted the camera onto his shoulder, then headed around the front of the van to set up for the live part of the segment.

"Lynette also asked me to pass along a message," Duffy said. "She wants you in her office at eight a.m."

Then he was gone, following Jordan.

"Fantastic," Cait whispered to herself. "My best night ever."

-6--

•

His interrupted date with Molly had put Josh in a contemplative mood for the entire flight and the drive out to the crime scene. He wondered where the date would have led if work had not intruded, and pondered what kind of woman it would take to put up with a relationship in which she would always come second. Would any woman ever understand that? His ex-wife certainly hadn't.

Throughout the flight, he had let his edginess out with humor. He felt like being funny, a little caustic, and just letting everything roll off of him. Sometimes, that was the only way to get through the job.

But he didn't feel like being funny anymore as he followed Voss and Chang up the stairs. The whole house had been decorated in typical Florida coastal décor, all soft pastels and shell patterns. Even the framed photos of the family were shell-themed, but these had actual tiny shells behind the glass.

The father looked to have been in his late forties—ex-military, given the photos of him younger and in uniform—and the mother a lovely, dark-haired woman at least a decade younger. In most of the family photos, they were gazing at their twin boys with the kind of wonder only parents ever had. Josh paused to scrutinize one of the family photos more closely. The twins had dark tangles of black hair and deeply hued olive skin, even darker than their mother's. He wondered if they were adopted or the product of a sperm donor. With the father's fair skin and sandy hair, it seemed highly unlikely the boys were his biological children.

"Looks like the father was killed here in the corridor," Chang began as they reached the top of the stairs. She pointed to a place on the pastel green wall where the plaster had been dented. "There are no other signs of a struggle out here, but the crime-scene guys found hair caught in the cracked paint. They'll probably match it to the dad. His killer either slammed him into the wall or got him off balance so that he fell against it."

Voss had already taken a step past them, toward the open door of what appeared to be the master bedroom.

Josh studied the carpet under his feet. "No blood. What was the cause of death? Not the head trauma?"

"Strangulation," Chang said, catching up with Voss. Apparently she had told them all she thought they needed to know about the murder in the hallway.

Josh didn't move, staring at the dent in the wall. "What was his name again?"

Chang paused just outside the master bedroom. Voss had already gone inside. "Huh?"

"The dad. The colonel. Did he have a name?"

Josh already liked Chang. She seemed smart and competent and take-no-shit, and he admired all three of those qualities. And it didn't hurt that she had a firm, petite figure her boring FBI clothes couldn't hide, and lips that seemed on the verge of some kind of mischief. But when he saw the flash of self-recrimination that passed across her face in that moment, he liked her even more.

"Sorry. Of course he did. Philip Thomas Greenlaw, Colonel, U.S. Army, retired. Owns a cigar shop in Fort Myers, with another one supposed to open on Sanibel Island in October. His wife was Carla Jean, maiden name Santoro, and the twins were Michael and Neil."

Josh nodded, letting the names sink in, so he knew who he was working for here. In ocean interdiction, assigned to hunt and capture drug runners and gun smugglers, they had rarely come face-to-face with the victims of the crimes they were trying to stop. They wouldn't come face-to-face with the Greenlaws, either—their bodies had already been removed from the scene—but he had seen their pictures and now he had their names. As Troubleshooters, they were here to facilitate cooperation between agencies, not to solve crimes. But Josh was *on* this case, and he knew Rachael felt the same.

"Young to be retired," Voss said.

Chang glanced at her. "Fifty-one. He kept himself in good shape. Carla was forty-two."

"And the twins were adopted?" Josh asked.

"I thought you hadn't seen the file," Chang replied, frowning.

Voss gestured toward the stairs. "We saw the pictures. Not a huge leap."

Chang glanced between Josh and Voss as if she was appraising them anew. "No, I guess it isn't. The kids had been with the Greenlaws for two and a half years, but had only been their children legally for about five months."

Josh looked again at the dent in the wall. "And now this."

"Yeah. Now this."

Voss headed into the master bedroom and Chang hurried after her. When Josh walked in, Chang was standing at the foot of the bed and Voss had already progressed to just inside the bathroom door. Neither woman looked at him. Chang's attention seemed drawn by the tangle of sheets and the manner in which the pillows had been carefully arranged.

"The way we've got it figured, they were in bed together when they heard something out in the hall or in the boys' room. Colonel Greenlaw went out to investigate and one of the suspects killed him. The second intruder—right now we're going on the theory that there were two, but it could have been more—came into the room after Mrs. Greenlaw."

Voss had her back to them. "And she ran for the bathroom."

"Maybe she thought she could lock herself in," Chang suggested.

Josh crossed the bedroom to stand behind his partner. Over her shoulder, he could see the shattered mirror and the broken reflective shards that filled the sink and littered the expensive seashell-patterned tile floor. Spatters of blood were everywhere, but not enough to indicate a stabbing or shooting.

"Cause of death?" Josh asked.

Chang's nostrils flared in disgust. "Blunt trauma. Slammed her head into the mirror, then the sink. Caved in her skull."

"Jesus," Josh whispered.

Voss turned quickly, gaze dark and intense, and Josh and Chang both stepped out of her way as she strode into the hall again. They caught up to her quickly, but when Voss started farther down the hall, Chang held back.

"Sorry, I wasn't kidding. I'm not going back into the twins' room."

Josh glanced at her. "Don't worry about it."

When he entered Michael and Neil Greenlaw's bedroom, he expected blood, or worse—something gruesome. Instead, the bedroom showed no sign of the horror that had occurred. No blood soaked the sheets or painted the walls. The beds were rumpled and slept in, the pillows still carrying what might have been the impressions of the boys' heads. Toys and picture books were scattered on the floor and shelves. A Winnie-the-Pooh border ran along the top of the wall. A ceiling fan rotated slowly, perhaps forgotten in all of the chaos of the past few hours.

Josh stepped back into the corridor and looked at Chang. "How did the boys die?"

Voss, walking around the twins' room, perked up at the question, waiting for the answer.

"Actually, that was the entry point," Chang said.

"The boys' room?"

"They cut the screen just enough to be able to remove it. The window must have been open, and they locked it when they left. They even put the screen back when they were through, apparently hoping we'd be baffled as to how they got into the house."

Voss came out into the corridor and the three of them stood looking at one another.

"So the twins were killed first," Voss said. "And that was the sound their parents heard, the one Mr. Greenlaw came out to investigate?"

"Looks that way," Chang confirmed. Then she looked at Josh. "To answer your question, we're waiting on the M.E. to confirm cause of death on the entire family. I'm just telling you what we're hypothesizing at this point. With the twins . . . pillows were found over their faces."

"Suffocation," Josh said.

Voss leaned against the wall, her shoulder jostling a framed beach scene. "All right. We've had the tour," she said, studying Chang. "So what's the terrorist angle?"

"You'll get a full briefing," Chang said, "but the nutshell version? The house is for sale. I'm sure you saw the sign. Three days ago—that would be Wednesday—the realtor brought two men by to look at the property. The Greenlaws weren't supposed to be home—it's bad form when showing a house, right?—but Mrs. Greenlaw had sent the colonel to the grocery store while she took the boys out to buy them new shoes."

"And he came back early," Josh surmised.

Chang nodded. "And the potential buyers set off some alarms. Two men house shopping together could mean a lot of things, but he didn't get the impression they were a couple, and it troubled him that they didn't ask many questions. Saudi or Syrian, he thought, according to the call he gave us."

"Wait," Voss said. "He called the FBI because a couple of Middle Eastern–looking guys toured his house, looking for a place to live?"

Josh shook his head, studying Chang. "No, he called because he got a bad vibe, like maybe these guys were up to something or looking for a place to hide in plain sight."

"That's the gist," Chang agreed. "Colonel Greenlaw felt something was off about the men. On Thursday, he called the realtor and asked if their building had a security camera. It did. Then he called the Bureau to report his concern. With an ordinary citizen, we'd certainly have paid attention, probably even checked it out, and Colonel Greenlaw was a veteran officer with more than twenty-five years in the military. His last post was in Afghanistan. SSA Turcotte sent me to his place of business to talk to him, but Greenlaw hadn't shown up for work, so I came around to the house."

Josh studied her. "You were the one who found them."

"Yeah," Chang said. "Lucky me."

Now it made more sense, how the Feds had gotten onto the case so quickly. The state cops had been brought in because it was a potential terror plot. Somehow SOCOM had got word and stuck their noses in, maybe because of the army connection, and that triggered Homeland Security into sending Troubleshooters from the ICD.

"Are you investigating other possible suspects?" Josh asked. "Looking at a house that's for sale is a pretty thin motive."

"Agreed," Chang replied. "Obviously the state and local police are being thorough, but the Bureau is taking Colonel Greenlaw's suspicions seriously. The guy wouldn't have gone to the lengths he did, calling the realtor and the FBI, if he hadn't felt that these guys needed to be looked at more closely."

"So do we have video from the realtor's security camera?" Voss asked.

"We do. The photo images went into the database, and we've got other suspicious activity recorded for one of the two under a different alias. We think he's Saudi. And not only that, but we matched the address on their fake IDs to two additional men, both Iraqi. We're considering them KA at the moment."

KA. Known associates. Possibly other terrorists.

"Saudi and Iraqi together. That's unusual, isn't it?" Voss asked.

Chang shrugged. "Whatever their plans are, it's obvious these guys have shared goals."

"You think you have a terrorist cell?" Josh asked.

"The last two are legal residents, but both have traveled to Pakistan within the past two years," Chang acknowledged. "If Colonel Greenlaw's instincts were correct, I'd guess that those visits to Pakistan involved al Qaeda training camps. But that's all supposition at this point."

Josh glanced at Voss and knew that she felt the same way he did. Terrorists who murdered toddlers in their beds? If the various agencies and departments working this case started up any bullshit dick-waving contests that interfered with the investigation or slowed it in any way, they would be more than happy to use their authority and take the reins. Whatever it took to catch the bastards.

"Thanks for the rundown," Josh said, nodding at Chang. "Let's get to work."

"I thought you ICD guys were supposed to be observers."

"Didn't you hear your boss?" Voss asked. "They're calling us the 'Troubleshooters' now. Does that sound like we just observe? Now, introduce us to the brain trust out there."

As they started back down the stairs, Josh asked, "I assume you've got a team sitting on the address the suspects used?"

Chang hesitated, and Josh saw something flicker in her eyes. He swore, shaking his head in frustration. Voss read his reaction and understood as well.

"Seriously?" Voss said. "Turcotte is a prick, but I didn't expect him to play games like this."

"We don't play games, Agent Voss," Chang said. "SSA Turcotte and his team were about to leave for the suspects' address when you arrived."

Josh quickened his pace and Voss followed as he raced through the living room and toward the front door.

"Yeah," he said, as Chang caught up to them, "and giving us the leisurely guided tour before catching us up on the case—while he runs off to try to take down the suspects—was just him being cordial."

They left the Greenlaws' house at a sprint, racing for the rental car. There were plenty of cops still on-site, but Turcotte and the group he'd been talking to, including the guy from SOCOM and the man in the expensive suit, were gone.

"You've got this wrong," Chang said, as Josh flung open the passenger door and climbed in.

"This is a joint investigation," Voss snapped as she slid into the driver's seat. "Officially the FBI is leading the team, but we're not just here to make sure it stays a team. We're a part of it."

Josh looked out at her, his door hanging open. "And something for you to consider, Special Agent Chang. We weren't the only ones left behind."

He saw her hesitate and hit the button to unlock the back doors. "Plenty of room if you want to ride along."

Chang's expression softened, but her gaze was still tinged with worry.

"I've known Turcotte a lot longer than you," Voss said. "He'll be expecting us. And he'll be even more irritated if you're just standing here twirling your hair when we show up."

"Nala," Josh said, catching her attention with her first name. "We can help."

A smile flickered at the edges of her mouth. She locked eyes with him for a moment, cocking her head in a way that he found incredibly sexy. But she wasn't flirting—she was sizing him up.

"All right," Chang said. "I guess I'll go along for the ride."

She opened the back door and climbed in behind Voss. Josh managed to bite back the innuendo-loaded reply that had occurred to him, but mostly because Voss was sitting right next to him.

Nala Chang was intriguing. No doubt.

-7--

Voss pulled into a spot by the curb, a block away from where the police and FBI vehicles were clustered. "What is this place?" she asked, glancing at Chang in her rearview mirror. "Any idea?"

Chang said nothing. She'd spoken very little during the handful of minutes they'd been in the car. Voss wasn't sure if she'd been so quiet because she thought she might catch hell from Turcotte, or because she was ticked off at being left behind. Turcotte had introduced her as if she were his right hand, and maybe she'd thought that was true. But as far as Voss could tell, the jury was still out.

Josh glanced into the backseat. "You all right?"

Voss arched an eyebrow and shot him a sidelong glance.

Had he forgotten that Nala Chang worked for Turcotte and had just been part of an effort to shake them off? She glanced at Chang in the mirror again, thinking that she looked even more attractive when she was aggravated, and wondering if Josh had noticed.

Of course he's noticed.

"Let's go have a talk with Turcotte," Voss said, popping her door open. "We can remind him what happens if he doesn't want to play nice."

The three of them climbed out and headed toward the tangle of official vehicles that was now drawing attention from the locals. Most of the buildings along this block were storefronts—a few bars, a candle shop, a consignment boutique, a liquor store—but all seemed to have offices or apartments on the upper floors.

Uniformed police stood on the sidewalk and around the cars in front of an empty storefront that had last been a women's gym. Banners advertising membership deals still hung in the windows, but they were faded and one had partially collapsed. The door to the gym was still locked, a forbidding metal grate sturdy in its frame, but the authorities weren't interested in the gym. The dead giveaway was the gigantic FBI agent standing guard in front of the narrow door between the gym and the small pizza place beside it. Torn and cracked numbers above the door announced the address as 347, but Voss saw there was a digit missing.

"If Turcotte just found out about this," Josh said as they stepped onto the sidewalk, "how did he get a warrant so fast?"

"Good question," Voss replied.

Chang still wore her blue jacket with FBI emblazoned on the back. That must have been enough for the local P.D., because none of them—state police included—tried to stop them as they approached the massive federal agent. Voss had once known a Samoan of similar hue and build, and wondered if this guy shared that heritage. He frowned, making a noise in his throat as they drew near that reminded her of a dog guarding its bowl.

"Make way, Bode," Chang said. "We're going up."

"Who's this?" the giant Fed asked, indicating Voss and Josh.

Josh flashed his ID. "Homeland Security."

Bode looked him up and down, then gave Voss the once-over, too.

"Turcotte said no one gets past me, Agent Chang. And that means no one gets past me."

Voss smiled at him and stepped closer, inside what Bode probably considered his vast personal space. "Honestly, Agent Bode—" she began.

"Bode's my first name."

"I wish I gave a shit."

Bode frowned, nostrils flaring. "Listen, lady—"

"I don't want to upset you, Bode. Your boss gave you an order and you intend to follow it. That's admirable. But our mandate—and our authority—supersedes Turcotte's territorial interests. I'm going to ask you, only once, to please move aside."

Bode looked confused, glancing at Chang.

"Seriously, Bode," Chang said. "Get the fuck out of the way. If anyone squawks, I'll tell Turcotte I gave the go-ahead. But if there's going to be a dustup about who has jurisdiction, you don't want to be caught in the middle."

Bode gave a small shrug. "All right. It's on you, though."

As soon as Bode moved his bulk out of the way, Voss slid by him and hustled up the steps. Chang probably should have led the way—Voss knew that—but all the things she wanted to say to Turcotte were burning on the tip of her tongue.

Two federal agents stood guard at the top of the stairs, blocking access to the apartment, although the door was wide open. Forensic techs were already at work turning the place into a mini–crime lab, looking for prints and hair—any physical evidence—as well as the more obvious things like photos or ID, or a big map with an X on it along with written plans for the killers' next move.

Voss had her ID out as she approached the two guard dogs, but before she could start arguing with them about access, she saw SSA Turcotte walk past the open door.

"Ed!" she snapped.

Turcotte glanced over and a deep frown creased his brow. Then she could see him exhale, surrendering to the inevitable, and he mustered a smile.

"What kept you, Agent Voss?" Turcotte asked, coming toward the open door.

Voss pushed between the agents blocking the door and stood facing Turcotte, wearing a smile that matched his. She held out her arms.

"Ed, it's great to see you," she said, sliding into an embrace that he only offered out of sheer befuddlement. When she had him in close, she spoke in a low voice. "I don't expect you to be happy I'm here, but ditching us was pretty childish, don't you think? Kids are dead—"

Turcotte flinched and pulled back, breaking her hold. He frowned and glanced past her at Chang and Josh, who had just entered the apartment. If Turcotte was pissed at Chang for not keeping them at Manatee Village longer, it didn't show on his face. Mouth in a sour twist, he gave Voss a hard look. "Don't tell me my job."

Again, Voss kept her voice down. Many of the agents and techs in the apartment were already glancing their way.

"That's my point, Ed. I don't want to have to tell you your job. But if you want to pull schoolyard pranks when we've got terrorists—"

Turcotte held up both hands. "I give, all right?"

Josh and Chang came closer. The four of them made a small circle, excluding the others. Turcotte gave Chang a slight nod—a combination of appreciation for the job he'd asked her to do and forgiveness that she hadn't been able to do it well enough to keep them away.

"Listen, SSA Turcotte," Josh began, then hesitated and looked at Voss.

She gestured for him to go on.

"We're not here to interfere," he added. "Believe it or not, in the cases we've handled so far, having us around has made things go more smoothly. If a conflict arises between you and local authorities, or another federal agency, we'll smooth it over. We'll do everything we can to eliminate the bullshit so you can focus on your investigation. But the only way we can do that is by being *part* of the investigation. Work with us and we can be very helpful. Fuck with us, and you won't have to worry, because the case won't be yours anymore."

Turcotte grimaced, a muscle working in his jaw. He looked at Josh, studiously avoided looking at Chang, then turned to Voss.

"Simple as that, right? We're all friends now? On the same team?"

"That's up to you, Ed."

"Not much of a choice," Turcotte replied. "And it doesn't sit right."

"It's your call," Voss said with a shrug. "But tell me now and save us all a lot of bullshit that'll take away from the time we should be spending running these assholes down."

Turcotte pondered it for a few seconds, then nodded and stuck out his hand. "All right, Rachael. We're together on this. Let's see how it works out."

Don't call me Rachael, she wanted to say. Other than Josh, the only time she didn't mind men using her first name was in bed. But Turcotte knew she didn't like it and had done it anyway. And if she couldn't take a little ribbing, they'd never be able to work together.

"It'll turn out fine," she said, then gestured to the agents hard at work in the apartment. "What've we got so far?"

Chang nudged Turcotte. "Yeah, boss. I'm curious, too."

Her gentle chiding worked, and Turcotte gave her an apologetic smile. "Don't worry, Chang. I need you on this case. I just sent you on a little detour."

Chang looked like she wanted to say more, but Voss knew she wouldn't. Not in front of the others.

"All right," Turcotte said, glancing around as if to orient himself. "What've we got? Food in the fridge. Dishes in the sink. Dirty clothes in a laundry basket. But most of the drawers are empty, or nearly. They cleared out fast. Faster than they expected to have to."

Voss frowned. "I wonder what set them off? If they were going to commit a quadruple homicide, they had to know the hunt would be on."

"Maybe it didn't go as planned," Josh said.

Turcotte frowned. "What does that even mean? They thought they could kill all these people and not have it look like murder?"

"It's possible," Chang said. "Set it up to look like murder/suicide maybe? But things went wrong with Colonel Greenlaw and they couldn't cover it up like they wanted to."

They all pondered that for a few seconds.

"Maybe," Voss conceded.

"What else do we have?" Josh asked.

"In the pocket of a dirty pair of khakis we found the business card for the realtor who showed them the Greenlaws' house. We've got some junk mail with names, and we're running down the names on the rental agreement, but there's no doubt that all of them are aliases."

As he spoke, Voss caught movement from a bedroom off to the side. She glanced that way and stiffened when she spotted the two men who had been so out of place back in Manatee Village—the lieutenant from SOCOM and Norris from Black Pine. "What the hell are they doing here?"

Turcotte glanced into the bedroom. "Not my idea, but I have orders. Mr. Norris is a consultant from Black Pine. The guy from SOCOM . . . he seems decent enough, and you can understand why he'd want to learn how Greenlaw ended up dead."

"He's not supposed to be here at all," Voss said.

Turcotte smiled thinly. "Officially, he's not. Unofficially, he's just observing. It's ironic, though."

"What is?" Josh asked.

"You two worrying about other agencies interfering with my case."

Voss smiled. "It's what we do."

There was a commotion in the corridor outside the door, and then one of Turcotte's agents—thirtyish and bristling with urgency—slipped into the apartment and made a beeline toward him. He faltered for a second, noticing that Voss and Josh weren't wearing FBI insignia.

"It's fine, Barclay," Turcotte said brusquely. "What've you got?"

"We think we've found one of them, sir," Agent Barclay said.

Voss stiffened. "Where?"

"Talk to me, Barclay," Turcotte ordered.

"A newborn was abducted from outside a hospital in Bangor, Maine. Security cameras caught it all. The footage is grainy, but we're pretty sure the perp is one of our guys."

"Holy shit," Chang muttered.

"Wait, they're stealing babies now?" Josh said. "What the hell is this about?"

"And why Maine? The guy was in Florida last night. He must've gotten right on a plane," Chang said. "This doesn't make any sense."

"No, it doesn't," Turcotte said. "But it's going to be your job to make sense of it, Agent Chang."

"What?" Voss and Chang asked together.

"You were worrying about me not utilizing you on this case?" Turcotte said. "Well, as far as I know, we've got three suspects possibly still in Florida, so we've got to keep the investigation centered here. But we also need someone on this abduction in Bangor, trying to chase down the suspect there. That someone's going to be you."

Voss nodded. It made sense. They needed someone to set up a satellite investigation in Bangor, and Turcotte didn't want to assign someone out of a field office in New England. He wanted his people on it directly, so he didn't get secondhand information or someone else's assumptions.

Voss hated what she was about to say, but it was also the most logical conclusion. "Any objection to me sending Josh along with Agent Chang, to ride shotgun?"

"None," Turcotte said. "With all the agencies involved in trying to track an abducted child, it'll help to have a Troubleshooter along, to help cut through the bullshit."

Josh grinned at Chang. "That's what we do best."

Voss tamped down ruthlessly on a pang of jealousy. They were on the job. Personal stuff had to take a backseat.

"You're a little cocky," Chang was teasing Josh. "Has anyone ever told you that?"

Voss forced a laugh. "Has anyone *not* told him that?" Then she put her hand out to Turcotte and they shook for the second time. "Good to be working with you, Agent Turcotte."

"And you, Agent Voss. We'll get these guys."

"I have no doubt."

But inside she was not nearly so certain. One of the killers had abducted an infant. The child might already be in a shallow grave somewhere. Voss knew the job was to catch the killers, but more than that, she wanted to get them before there were any more dead children to bury.

-8--

When her son, Tommy, was an infant, Jane Wadlow would often wake in the middle of the night for no discernible reason. In the quiet darkness, she would listen for any disturbance in the house and then, met by silence, she would rise and go check on Tommy, just to make sure he was still safe in his crib and her world still spun on its axis.

Her son had long since grown to manhood and started a life of his own, and the house had more empty spaces since Tommy had gone off to film school in California. Tommy had grand plans for the future, and they didn't include ever living in Medford, Massachusetts, again. That was the bitter joy of parenting, Jane had learned. You spend all those years teaching children, nurturing them, preparing them to go. And then, damn them, they went.

But in recent months there had been many nights when the house breathed with new life. She babysat regularly for her niece, Caitlin, who worked as part of a news crew for the local NBC affiliate. Most of the time she worked the day shift, driving the news van for reporters working on stories for the midday or evening news. That worked perfectly, because it meant that Cait could be up early in the morning with her baby girl, and still have a little mother-daughter time before heading to work. But once or twice a week, Cait was called in to work the night shift, covering the eleven o'clock news.

On those nights, Jane and her husband, George, would put Leyla to sleep in her playpen in Tommy's old room, and it made more sense for Caitlin to crash there than to go home to her own apartment.

Shortly after two o'clock in the morning, the August sunrise still hours off, Jane found herself awake. The flickering glow and the low murmur of voices told her that George had fallen asleep with the TV on again. She sighed, knowing that if she didn't drift off within seconds it would be at least an hour before sleep claimed her again. Those seconds passed with no slumber imminent, and Jane lay in bed, wondering how late Caitlin had come in, and how the girl would ever find another man to fall in love with when all she ever did was work and play with her baby.

She doesn't want another man, Jane chided herself. *Not right now.*

Ever since Caitlin's father—Jane's brother—had died, the Wadlows had been Caitlin's guardians and closest family. Even while her father had been alive, Caitlin had been close to her aunt and uncle, and her only cousin, Tommy. She had practically grown up in Sweet Somethings, the fudge and chocolate shop that Jane had owned and run for decades in Medford Square. As Caitlin had grown older, she had helped Jane to mix fudge in the big copper pots in the back room and to put chocolates into the display cases. Jane had paid her, and in time Caitlin had become an official employee—until she'd graduated high school and gone off to college.

After her father's death, Caitlin had seemed to spend even more time at Sweet Somethings. Jane had sold the store six years ago and, though she was happy not to have to work the long hours anymore, she missed it every day. But she thought that Caitlin missed it more.

Jane smiled wistfully at the thought. She reached out and touched her sleeping husband's arm. At the moment, George lay beside her in their bed, snoring softly. He had fallen asleep during the baseball game and the remote control still lay on his chest, an inch from his splayed fingers. He always turned the volume down low, so it wouldn't disturb her. Now the late night news was repeating and she glanced at the weather forecast. She wanted to hear this, so she took the remote from her sleeping husband and turned the volume up slightly.

Other than a little rain shower, the attractive girl in the tight suit predicted a warm, sunny August week. That was good. But then the news returned to the same story that had been on right before the ball game, that of a baby stolen from its mother in Bangor, Maine, as she left the hospital with the newborn for the first time.

Grainy footage from security cameras in front of the hospital showed a nondescript man with dark hair striking the woman in the back of the head and snatching the infant car seat from her hand as she fell, then climbing into the back of a nearby van with the stolen child. The father had apparently gone to fetch the car to take his family home. The security footage showed him pulling up in his Buick only moments after the van pulled away. *A nightmare. I'd never have been able to live with myself.*

Beside her, George snorted a bit, then turned over to make himself more comfortable and fell into soft, easy breathing. Jane clicked the button on the remote that turned off the television and set it on her nightstand. In the deeper darkness and stiller silence, she listened for a telltale rustle or whimper that would suggest that Caitlin or Leyla might be having a restless night. She heard nothing, but old habits died hard. If she didn't get up and check on them, she'd never be able to fall back to sleep.

She ran her fingers through her hair, climbed out of bed, then padded quietly down the hall to peek into her son's old bedroom. Caitlin lay tangled in a single sheet, knees drawn up toward her chest and the pillow drawn down into an embrace. In sleep, her face was peaceful and soft, almost as if she were once again the teenage girl who had first come to live in this house, full of grief at the death of her father and anger at the world that had made her and her older brother orphans. But Caitlin wasn't that girl anymore. She'd been a soldier, and she'd fallen in love, and then the world had taken that away from her, too.

Jane had never met Leyla's father, Nizam, but in his pictures he looked handsome, serious, and kind. Jane had always loved photographs, and put a lot of stock in her ability to read people from their pictures. Cait tended not to talk much about Nizam except to Leyla, reassuring the baby that her father loved her and watched over her from heaven. But in those moments, the pain in Cait's heart was etched on her face. She'd found a good man and endured anger and resentment and prejudice in order to love him. Now she was an ex-soldier, a young widow, and a single mother trying to make a life with Leyla.

Quietly, Jane crossed the room and looked down into the playpen, where Leyla mewled softly, eyes still closed but fussing a bit. At seven months old, she might not be able to walk or talk, but even without words she had personality. She made people smile. Hundreds of times, Jane had been with her at the store or at the park and seen the way people lit up at the sight of her. Babies had that effect, she knew, but Leyla seemed to have it more than most. And when Jane explained the story of Leyla's birth—of her soldier mother and her Iraqi father, and of Nizam's death—a different light came into people's eyes, as if they had suddenly begun to understand something for the first time.

Jane knew exactly what it was. She and George had had the same feeling the first time they held Leyla in their arms. The beauty of this baby girl, with her Christian mother and Muslim father, reminded people that even those they saw as enemies could fall in love.

A cry arose from the playpen, as if the mere act of thinking about the baby had disturbed her. Jane glanced at Caitlin, then hurried to retrieve Leyla. Cait had worked late, and Jane didn't want Leyla waking her up.

"What's the matter, sweet pea?" Jane whispered as she reached into the playpen and began a comforting, rhythmic tap on the baby's back.

Leyla's eyes found her, and the baby made a kind of plaintive whimper, then went quiet. Seven months old, but she knew her auntie would take care of her. Technically, Jane was Caitlin's aunt, but she felt too young to be anybody's "great-aunt," so *Auntie Jane* would be just fine.

Her lower back protested as she lifted the baby into her arms, cuddling Leyla against her chest. Shifting her weight from one foot to the other, rocking gently, she started to pace the room.

As she rocked the baby, she glanced out the window and frowned. Badger Road was a quiet neighborhood. They didn't see a lot of cars parked on the street unless one of the neighbors was having a party, or the Mandells' daughter was having one of her high school sleepovers. So the dark sedan parked across the street and two houses down caught her attention for several reasons. First, it was after two o'clock in the morning, which meant even the Callahans, who loved a party, would have kicked any guests out hours ago. Second, the car looked brand new and expensive, which made it unlikely to belong to high school kids sleeping over at the Mandells' house. Third, the car was parked at the curb in front of the DiMarinos' house, two doors down, and the DiMarinos were on a cruise and wouldn't be back for more than a week.

Jane bent over a little for a better look out the window. She had never been great with makes and models, but she thought it was a BMW or Audi—something expensive, with dark windows. Then Leyla started fussing a bit, forcing her to stand up straight and rock her properly.

"All right, baby. Hush now," she whispered.

She relished the weight of the child in her arms, enjoying the smell and warmth of a baby. When Caitlin had first gotten her job at Channel 7 and begun fretting over how she would be able to afford daycare, Jane hadn't hesitated. She didn't have the chocolate shop anymore, so she had no job to prevent her from saying yes. No way would she let Leyla end up ignored and neglected in some germ-infested baby kennel. George had worried about how much work it would be—they were no longer young—but Jane had stayed firm.

Jane's younger brother, Rob, had gotten married right out of high school to a beautiful dimwit who had lasted five years before abandoning him for a lawyer. She had left him with two children, Sean—who'd been four at the time—and baby Caitlin, fourteen months old. Rob had been a strict father but sweet and loving with his kids, and they had respected and loved him in return.

Pancreatic cancer had killed him a week before Caitlin's junior prom.

Sean McCandless had been serving in the Marine Corps, stationed in the Middle East, when his father had died. The Corps gave him leave to come home, but only long enough for the funeral. Jane and George were named in Rob's will as Caitlin's legal guardians until she turned eighteen, and they looked out for her afterward, helping her sort out her finances and do her college applications, advising her in the sale of her family home since she couldn't afford to keep up with the bills.

Tommy might be the only child to whom Jane McCandless Wadlow had ever given birth, but Caitlin was the closest thing to a daughter she would ever have. The baby girl Jane cradled against her now could never be a burden. She kissed Leyla's head, and the baby shifted a bit. Her eyelids fluttered as though she might wake up again, then she gave a tiny sigh and nestled in Jane's arms. She was truly a beautiful baby, her skin a warm shade of cinnamon she had inherited from her father.

The yellow glow of headlights swept across the room and Jane heard the gentle purr of an engine as a car approached out on the street. She glanced out the window and saw a second car pull up behind the one parked in front of the Di-Marino house.

Then the first car started up, the headlights blinking on. Jane watched as it pulled slowly from its place at the curb and drove off while the new arrival replaced it, sliding into the spot. The new driver killed the engine and the lights winked out. In seconds, it was like nothing had happened. Anyone who had not seen the new arrival would likely have assumed this was the same vehicle.

Jane waited, swaying back and forth with Leyla, but though she watched for several minutes, no one got out of the car.

A stakeout, she thought. She had seen enough cop shows that this was the first thing that occurred to her, but quickly on its heels came another suspicion. What if somebody knew the DiMarinos were away and they were watching to see if anyone had been left to house-sit? The people in the cars could be burglars casing the house.

Okay, so maybe she had seen *too many* cop shows, but that didn't mean it couldn't be true. Something odd was going on down the street. What she had watched just now looked very much like a shift change, one car coming on duty and the other going off.

The question was, what duty?

A few minutes later, when she returned Leyla to her playpen and went back to her bedroom to find George snoring loudly, she was still wondering. Whatever those cars were up to, they made her nervous.

-9--

Cait woke to morning sunlight splashed across her legs and a breeze billowing the sheer white curtains. She stretched, her neck stiff and her eyes gritty with sleep, but she felt good. A glance at the clock on the bedside table—the same alarm clock her cousin Tommy had used all through his high school years—told her that it was early enough that anyone with a choice would still be asleep. But she didn't have a choice—not if she wanted to keep her job.

In spite of that, she rolled over, crushing the soft pillow, relishing the warm August morning and the comfort of the bed for a few extra moments. Then she studied the white mesh of the playpen that sat on the floor six feet away.

You must have known Mommy needed sleep, Cait thought. So strange, to think of herself as a mother, even seven months after she had given birth.

It had all started with Nizam. In so many ways, it seemed to Cait that her entire adult life had begun in the moment she had first seen Nizam. Her unit had been providing security for a group of outreach specialists who had been trained to interact with the civilian Iraqi community, trying to create good will amongst those who weren't already their enemies. Sometimes the outreach specialists would bring bicycles to kids in certain Baghdad neighborhoods, and that day they'd given out nearly a dozen bikes, all brand new and gleaming with metallic colors.

They'd been in a public square not far from the Kufa wall, with houses and apartments on one side, but mostly shops on the other. The thermometer had read 117 degrees and not even Ronnie—the wiseass in their unit—had made any jokes about it being a dry heat. That kind of thing had stopped being funny at the end of June. Now it was mid-July and Cait had sweat dripping into the crevices of her body—places she couldn't reach in uniform, draped as she was with equipment and weapons. They tried to smile, to be friendly to the civilians, but all they wanted was to go home.

When the last bicycle had been ridden away and the P.R. soldiers had gotten the last thank-you from a widow whose face was covered with burn scars, they all returned to their vehicles, smiling but wary. Cait could still remember the way the breeze seemed to still when they spotted the green bike lying on its side in the mouth of a small alley between a curry restaurant and an abandoned smoke shop. One of the outreach people, a handsome Arizonan named Griggs, started toward the bike, curious and not cautious enough by half.

Several voices from the unit called out for Griggs to halt, but the outreach team were the officers there. Cait's unit was only along for security. Griggs insisted, wanting to do his job properly, and a moment later Cait and Jordan were flanking the guy as he made his way toward the bike. Most of the people who had been in the square a few minutes earlier had departed, the children and their bicycles vanishing as though by magic.

Out of the corner of her eye, Cait caught movement. She could barely breathe the super-heated air and now her heart was pounding as if it might burst through her chest. She swung the barrel of her weapon toward the movement and saw a man standing in front of a faded apartment building. Tall and thin, he wore his dishdasha knotted up at the hips, with light cotton trousers underneath. His head was bare, without the traditional thagiyah most of the men adopted at a young age, and he stood with his arms crossed in front of him, idly smoking a cigarette.

But what struck Cait immediately were the man's eyes. They were wide and brown and gleamed with an intelligence that entranced her, even from twenty yards away. His gaze had locked on her and she had hesitated, wondering if she might be imagining that she was the sole focus of his attention. Then, as she watched him, he had given a single shake of his head, slow but emphatic, after which he had turned and vanished into the apartment building.

Jordan and Griggs had almost reached the green bike. Cait glanced back at the short convoy of vehicles, where other members of the unit stood guard, scoping the rooftops and balconies and alleys for any sign of danger. But she knew that the danger wasn't going to come from there.

Cait had shouted at Griggs, running toward him. The idiot had ignored her, but luckily Jordan had not. He grabbed Griggs by the arm and got him turned around, and then the three of them were running back to the convoy. The explosion, when it came, hurled her forward, searing heat slamming her against the cab of a truck. The impact knocked the wind out of her and left her with scrapes and bruises, but otherwise she was unharmed.

The man with the entrancing eyes had given her a warning that had saved lives . . . including her own.

That had been her first glimpse of Nizam. The second had come nearly two months later, after her unit had been assigned to protect truck convoys moving supplies and materials into and out of Baghdad. Most of those trucks were driven by Iraqis—who the U.S. military called "Nationals"—who were risking their own lives for a job in which they were constantly scrutinized and viewed with distrust. Insurgents targeted them for death because they were cooperating with occupation forces, but paying work was difficult to come by and there were always men willing.

Cait had recognized Nizam immediately, though she still did not know his name. She spotted him driving one of the trucks in the convoy her unit was escorting. When they reached the Green Zone, the protocol required a member of the unit to transfer from a military vehicle and ride along with the Iraqi National driving the truck, which was how she ended up sitting beside Nizam for the better part of an afternoon.

They talked a lot in those hours as she kept watch over his activities. She learned that he had been a taxi driver before the fall of Saddam, and that he had taken in his fourteen-year-old nephew after his brother and sister-in-law had been killed in the Ashura massacre, which meant that Nizam was Shi'a, though he considered himself progressive and Cait had to agree. His taxi business had been critically impacted by the war—fuel was incredibly difficult to come by, and hugely expensive if he could find anyone selling it. Driving a truck for the coalition forces was a temporary solution, helping him to feed himself and his nephew.

Cait tried not to let him see that he had touched something within her. She was a soldier, and he was a civilian whose allegiances had to be constantly questioned. And yet . . . he had taken in his nephew, just as her own aunt had taken Cait in when her father had died. His voice had a soft musicality that reassured her. Sometimes he let slip a lighthearted smile that charmed her, so different from the grave expressions of most Iraqi men. And though he hated the sectarian violence in his homeland, he was filled with pride in its history. Iraq, he claimed, had been the birthplace of civilization, "as well as of its ultimate expression."

She had frowned at him. "Which is what, exactly?"

Nizam had arched a playful eyebrow. "Poetry, of course."

"You like poetry?"

"I have no choice," he had replied, standing by the front of the truck while it was being unloaded, smoking a cigarette. "I am Iraqi. I am born with poetry inside of me."

Cait had wanted to laugh. Nizam spoke of poetry in an almost offhand way, but she could see the sincerity of his passion for it.

"You actually write poetry?"

He had put a hand over his heart, feigning insult. "You believe a taxi driver is not capable of creating poetry?"

Cait had felt stupid talking about it. Not that she didn't enjoy poetry, but in her mind, great poetry had been written by people who were now dead. She had always thought there was something faintly embarrassing about attempting poetry in the present day. And yet Nizam's love of poetry was so pure that she could never have mocked him.

"Don't worry," he had said. "I'm not about to begin reciting my poetry to you."

Cait had given him an uneasy smile. "That's probably for the best."

"But if you'd like, I could write one for you."

She did like. Very much.

In what seemed no time at all, she had fallen in love. But it wasn't the poetry or the kindness to his nephew or his surprising smile that had won her heart. It had been that first, wordless moment, the slow shake of his head—the warning that had simultaneously risked his life and saved hers. There were stolen hours of fierce lovemaking that could have had dire consequences for them both, followed by whispered plans for a future after the war, when they could find peace together. Nizam had spoken to his nephew, but the boy did not want to go to America, preferring to live with his aunt in Nasiriyah.

With the help of Jordan and Ronnie, Cait had managed to get Nizam enough fuel for him to begin driving his taxi again. Things were settling down in Baghdad. They could foresee a time when the fear and madness would end.

Then another bomb. Nizam had saved Cait's life with his warning that first day, but Cait had to live with the knowledge that she had not been there to warn him. An IED hidden in a van had exploded in a marketplace. Nizam had been cruising slowly, hoping for passengers, and his taxi had been only feet away. His fuel tank—full of the gasoline she had procured for him—had provided a secondary explosion that was the final nail in his coffin.

During the weeks of grief and anguish that followed, many

of the guys in her unit revealed themselves to be coldhearted bastards. If one of them had screwed an Iraqi woman, somehow that was all right, but they froze Cait out because she had fallen in love, and because she would soon be going home, pregnant with Nizam's child. Ignorance, jealousy, fear . . . she didn't care why the guys had reacted that way. The betrayal cut her deeply.

Only Jordan and Ronnie had stood by her, had defended her at every turn and held her when she felt the world beneath her feet opening up to swallow her. They had proven themselves true friends, both in Iraq and here on the homefront. She wasn't sure she would have made it home without their support. And now she had Leyla, and her world had again been forever changed, her heart filling with love for her daughter and beginning to mend.

But, *God,* how she missed him.

Surrendering to the inevitable, she sat up, swung her legs over the side of the bed, and reached for the jeans she'd been wearing the night before. Zipping them on, she walked over to peek into the playpen, only to find it empty.

Cait smiled. Auntie Jane must have come to fetch her the moment Leyla had started to fuss this morning, trying to let her sleep. Cait didn't know how she would have gotten through the past year without her aunt and uncle.

She went quietly down the stairs, knowing Uncle George was probably still asleep. A low murmur of television voices came from the kitchen, where she found Jane with Leyla on her hip. Expertly balancing the baby, she stole a sip of coffee and then went back to stirring a batch of pancake mix.

"Good morning," Cait said.

Jane looked up, her hair unruly from sleep. "Well, well, Leyla. Look who's up," she said, and then met Cait's gaze. "Your badass momma."

Cait's eyes widened. "Excuse me?"

"Come on," Jane said. "Did you really think I wouldn't notice my niece kicking the crap out of a dirtbag on the local news this morning?"

"They're still showing it?" Cait asked, sagging a bit at the realization that the previous night's events would be interfering with her life for days to come.

Jane laughed. "Of course they are. And they'll keep showing it. You'll be an Internet sensation by dinnertime. Scratch that; you probably already are. That was a pretty amazing thing you did last night."

Cait allowed herself a small smile. "He had it coming."

"He sure did. You're something else, kid."

"Well, nobody messes with Sean McCandless's little sister."

"Damn right."

Cait reached for Leyla, plucking her out of her aunt's arms and kissing her several times before propping the baby on her hip, just as Jane had done.

"You're making pancakes?" Cait asked.

"Anything special you want in yours?" Jane replied. "Bananas? Chocolate chips? I don't have any blueberries, but I'm going to the supermarket later."

"Actually, I have to deal with some consequences from last night. My boss wants to see me in her office this morning."

"They can't fire you for stopping a man from trying to kill his wife," Jane replied, harshly enough that the baby gave her a curious look. Jane smiled to reassure the child, and when she spoke again, it was in the special, loving cadence most people reserved only for infants, but the words were not meant for the baby. "You tell that Lynette woman that the *rest* of the press will eat her alive if she tries to fire you."

Cait smiled. That was a McCandless trait. There might not be many of them left, but damn if they didn't circle the wagons when trouble came calling.

"I doubt she'll fire me," Cait admitted, "but I broke the rules. She's got to at least give me a good talking-to."

Privately, she worried that Lynette might have something more punitive in mind, but she didn't want to say that to Jane—at least not until she knew exactly what she was up against. Driving the news van might not be the best job in the world—scheduled shifts often went into overtime and many days and weekends she had to be on call, ready to go in if they needed her—but the pay and benefits were decent, and watching the reporters and camera operators in the field was interesting. Jordan had promised to train her to use the camera and the remote equipment in the van, so at some point she hoped to move from behind the wheel to behind the camera.

"I've got to tell you," Cait said, "I wish I'd been in a position to buy Sweet Somethings when you sold the place. Making fudge and selling chocolates—being your own boss—is a much better way to live than this."

"Just imagine how much you'll save on Leyla's dentist," Jane said.

Cait laughed. "Hey, I didn't get *that* many cavities."

"Only because your dad was such a tyrant about you brushing your teeth," Jane reminded her.

"True," Cait admitted. Her father had loved Jane's peanut butter and chocolate fudge just as much as Cait herself had.

"I take it you need me to watch the munchkin while you go face the music?"

Cait nodded, shifting Leyla to her other hip. "I'm sorry. You've had her so much, and all night—"

"She's no trouble, Caitlin," Jane said, smiling at the baby even as she put a pan on the burner.

"I'm not working today," Cait added. "I should be back by ten-thirty, at the latest, and then we'll be out of your hair until Tuesday."

"No problem," Jane assured her. "Do me a favor, though? Before you leave, see if you can get a peek at whoever's sitting in that BMW, or whatever it is, down in front of the DiMarinos' house."

"Sorry, what?" Cait mumbled. She'd been playing with Leyla, blowing air into the baby's face to make her giggle.

"They're away," Jane said. "The DiMarinos, I mean. In the middle of the night there was this car parked in front of their house." She went on to describe what she had seen out the window the night before. "It's probably nothing, but I kept thinking, what if it's someone planning to break in?"

"Are they still out there this morning?" Cait asked.

"They were when I woke up," Jane replied.

As Jane started doling pancake batter onto the pan, Cait slipped the baby into her high chair and locked her in place.

"Where are you going?" Jane asked.

"To stick my nose where it doesn't belong."

"What about breakfast?"

"Save me some." Then she crouched down so that she was eye to eye with Leyla. "Take care of Auntie Jane for a few minutes, baby girl."

Her daughter gave her a toothless smile. Cait stood and headed out of the kitchen.

"Aren't they going to be angry if you interrupt their stakeout?" Jane asked.

Cait paused in the door frame, arching an eyebrow. "Stakeout? Next thing I know you'll be talking about skel informants and righteous shootings. They're in your neighborhood and not exactly hiding. You have a right to know what they're doing. This is America, remember?"

Jane's smile was halfhearted. "Sometimes I forget."

Cait didn't reply. They tried to avoid talking politics in the Wadlow house. George was a dyed-in-the-wool Republican, but Jane had turned her back on the party the moment the Patriot Act had been passed. Cait stayed out of it; she didn't much care who sat in the Oval Office. She had seen the faces of Iraqis up close, seen them laugh and seen them die, and they were just like anybody else—forged by the world they lived in. The Muslims who wanted to live in peace were no danger to America, and those who were willing to die if it meant taking American lives . . . well, they couldn't be stopped. As far as Cait was concerned, the best thing to do was just stay away from them. But that was why she had been a soldier, not a politician, and now she could only hope to never return to the Middle East.

Still barefoot, she went out onto the front steps and immediately spotted a silver Audi parked three doors down and across the street. At a quarter after seven on a Sunday morning, the neighborhood had a wonderful stillness about it. A door opened to her left and she glanced over to see a young bearded guy step out, shirtless, to retrieve his newspaper from the stoop. Other than that, the street was quiet.

She wasn't surprised Jane had thought the car out of place. The street consisted of small Colonials and ranches built in the 1940s and '50s. Any one of their driveways would have had room for another vehicle to park, including the absent DiMarinos'.

From a distance, and given the Audi's tinted windows, it was impossible to tell if the car was occupied.

Well, there's one way to find out.

She padded down the steps and across the front yard, enjoying the feeling of the grass under her bare feet. Once she hit the sidewalk, she stayed on her aunt's side of the street, not ignoring the presence of the car but not paying it any special attention, either. As she walked, she turned the whole situation over in her brain. The Audi sparkled in the morning sun. Really, it was too nice a car for undercover cops to be driving. Government, maybe, but what the hell would federal agents be doing in Medford? So maybe they were cops after all. On the other hand, some romantic entanglement—a cheating spouse, maybe—could easily put a private detective into play. She didn't know any private investigators, but doubted they could afford such a car.

A mystery, right here on Badger Road.

As she came abreast of the Audi, Cait stepped off the curb and strode toward the driver's side, the pavement warm underfoot. She put on her friendliest, most quizzical smile, thinking she would just rap on the window. Behind the tinted glass, she could vaguely make out the shapes of the driver and another man. But the engine growled abruptly to life, then softened to a purr as the driver threw the car into gear and pulled away, leaving her standing in the middle of the road, staring after it.

"Fine, be that way!" she called after the Audi, making note of the plate number and wondering if she really had just screwed up somebody's surveillance and, if so, who they might be surveilling. Was that even a word? She thought it must be.

As she headed back to her aunt and uncle's house, intending to write down the license plate number, an awful thought occurred to her. What if it wasn't something as simple as a cheating spouse? She had thought it might be a government vehicle. What if they suspected someone on the street of being involved in terrorism, or if one of the neighbors was a serial killer or something?

Despite the warmth of the August morning, Cait shuddered.

She had to jump in the shower and hurry if she wanted to get to Lynette's office by eight o'clock, but she couldn't just let this go. The odds were that the guys in the car were private detectives, but, just to be safe, she would put in a call to the Medford police as soon as she was out of her meeting.

-10--

The small plane that the Bureau had chartered to carry Josh and Chang from Florida to Maine touched down at Bangor International Airport just before nine a.m. The charter had been a necessity, as there had been no commercial flights departing Fort Myers for Bangor until late morning, and the clock was ticking for the abducted child. The kidnapper was a known killer and potential terrorist. Josh knew that the odds were against the infant being alive—this guy didn't seem the type to ask for ransom—but hope was all that they had. And if there was any chance the child *was* still alive, they had to work as quickly as possible to track the son of a bitch down.

A car was waiting for them on the tarmac. The agent behind the wheel introduced himself as Ian Merritt; with the halo of gray that was all that remained of his hair and the doughy, too-much-whiskey complexion, he looked more like an accountant on the verge of retirement than an FBI agent. Still, Merritt didn't balk at playing chauffeur to them, despite Nala Chang's youth and gender. Josh had known other agents from Merritt's era who would not have behaved so professionally, so the guy got points for that.

"The state police have agreed to let you guys set up shop in their Bangor barracks," Agent Merritt said as he put the

black sedan in gear, "but I assume you want to talk to the
TSA folks on-site before we head over there?"

"We do," Chang agreed. "Have they turned anything up
while we were in transit?"

Agent Merritt drove alongside the domestic terminal, the
vehicle eyed warily by an airport security agent standing by a
car parked between two gates. Like all U.S. airports, Bangor
International had a contingent of TSA agents on staff, screen-
ing bags and passengers and overseeing security. A typical
map of the airport would show gates and restaurants and
shops and checkpoints, but not the hidden rooms in which
TSA personnel monitored the comings and goings of passengers and staff. There were other rooms as well, where people
were detained and questioned, and sometimes searched.

Josh had done his homework. The Bangor P.D. maintained
a small storefront in a corner of the domestic terminal, but
while the local police would field complaints and help passengers as much as they could—mostly dealing with theft—
nearly everything that affected security fell within the TSA's
purview. Tracking murderers with potential terrorist connections had to be pretty high on their list of priorities, but that
hadn't stopped the guy from getting on a plane in Florida and
getting off in Bangor. Josh figured their suspect must be
on a no-fly list under another name—maybe a lot of other
names—but his picture hadn't set off any alarms.

All of that would change now. No way was this guy getting
on another commercial plane in the United States. But that
wasn't going to help them find the missing newborn.

Merritt pulled the car up to a nondescript door flanked by
armed TSA agents. These guys were not baggage screeners.
They were the rarely seen part of the Transportation Security
Administration—the ones who handled the enforcement elements of the job. But Josh wasn't paying much attention to
the guards. His mind was on the mother and father at Acadia
Hospital in Bangor whose infant had been taken from them
at the very moment they were to begin life as a family.

"I don't know their names," he said.

Agent Merritt turned off the engine and opened his door,

either not having heard him or correctly presuming the words hadn't been meant for him. Chang turned in her seat.

"What?"

Josh looked at her. "The parents—the people whose baby this asshole took. I don't know their names."

Chang frowned. For a second Josh thought it was disapproval, but then he realized that she had momentarily forgotten their names herself.

"Kowalik," she said at last. "The last name is Kowalik. The father is Richard, I think. The mother is Farah. That one I'm sure of."

"What about the baby?"

A glimmer of pain flickered across Chang's eyes. "They'd narrowed it down, but as of when I talked to Bangor P.D. before the flight, they hadn't agreed on a name yet."

Josh felt a fresh wave of hatred. The bastard had stolen a baby so new to the world that her parents hadn't even had time to decide on a name. *Kowalik,* he thought, committing the name to memory. *Richard and Farah.*

A Transportation Security Officer awaited them just inside the door. Lost in his own thoughts, Josh followed Chang and Merritt as the TSO led them through a long corridor, through two sets of locked doors, down another corridor, and into a room where monitoring equipment hummed quietly. Screens revealed live images from various security checkpoints and entrances in the airport, empty gates, and people waiting in chairs for their morning flights. Officers on monitor duty sat at several different stations, watching it all unfold, but Josh's attention was drawn to the rear of the room, where a Maine State Police lieutenant stood with a fortyish, hawk-nosed man in a suit. The cop and the hawk were looking over the shoulders of a young Latina in the TSA uniform as she worked the controls at her station, running back and forth through a particular piece of video surveillance.

The hawk in the suit glanced up at them, muttered something to the cop, and walked over to greet them.

"Agents," he said, holding out a hand, aiming directly at Josh. "Alfred DeLisle. Federal security director." That meant

DeLisle was the top TSA official at the airport, but he spent his days supervising the supervisors, distant from the actual work being done by his people.

Josh shook DeLisle's hand, but narrowed his eyes. "Josh Hart, ICD. But you really want to speak to Agent Chang."

DeLisle glanced irritably at Merritt, as if blaming the local FBI agent for not giving him enough information to avoid looking foolish. Then he smiled at Chang and shook her hand, as well, as if he hadn't just insulted her by assuming Josh was in charge.

"Agent Chang," DeLisle said. "We're at your service. Whatever you need."

Chang shook his hand, behaving as if she hadn't noticed the insult. "What can you tell us about the suspect's arrival in Bangor, Mr. DeLisle?"

DeLisle flinched at the word *mister,* probably offended at not being called "Director DeLisle"—or whatever he thought his proper title might be—but they weren't here to assuage egos.

"Well, your people gave us a fairly narrow window to search," DeLisle replied. "We examined video from all arrivals originating from the southeastern United States, beginning with yesterday morning and ending thirty minutes before the kidnapping from Acadia Hospital. I had three teams on it, but once we found what we were looking for, I sent them home."

It grated on Josh a little, the way DeLisle kept saying "we," as though he had done any of the work himself.

"What have you got?" Chang asked.

"He arrived shortly before eleven a.m. yesterday on a flight from Fort Myers, traveling on a Florida driver's license."

"Name?" Josh asked.

DeLisle pulled a piece of paper from his pocket, unfolded it, and read what he'd scribbled there. "Jamil Nassif."

Chang glanced at Josh. "Sounds Saudi, but that means nothing. It's got to be an alias."

"No doubt," Josh replied.

Agent Merritt had been listening to all of this in silence. "I don't get it. Why would this guy fly from Tampa to steal some random baby?"

"That's the question we need to answer," Josh replied. It wasn't Merritt's fault that he was playing catch-up.

DeLisle gestured toward the monitoring station where the state cop still loomed over the young Latina.

"I've had the video edited together. Come have a look at your suspect. There's no question it's the same guy from the hospital kidnapping."

They gathered together around the monitor and watched it all unfurl on-screen. The man calling himself Jamil Nassif had been flying coach, so he emerged from the gangway amidst a cluster of other people. He wore blue jeans and hiking boots and a white cotton shirt. Though he needed a shave, he was otherwise neatly groomed. His luggage was a small black carry-on suitcase, unobtrusively ordinary.

"Obviously, Nassif had gone through security at the time of his departure from Fort Myers," DeLisle said as they watched the man in the white shirt make his way from the gate, through the terminal, and then out the door toward where taxis waited for arriving passengers.

"We get it," Chang said. "Domestic passengers don't get a lot of attention when they're arriving. Why would they? You're not on the hook for this, Mr. DeLisle. But he's going to leave Bangor at some point, and if he tries to do it through this airport—"

"We'll detain him," DeLisle said quickly.

Chang nodded. "And don't be gentle about it."

As the tech ran the footage again, Josh studied the suspect closely. He moved with a calm determination. He knew precisely why he was in Bangor and what he had planned. A sick feeling uncoiled itself in Josh's gut—a cold certainty that they would never find the Kowalik baby, or if they did, the child would already be dead. He shuddered, watching the impassive face of the killer as he exited the terminal.

"There must be a camera outside, picking up the taxi stand," he said.

The state police lieutenant, who had been silent thus far,

grunted in agreement. "You'd think. But they relocated the taxi line in the spring and haven't gotten around to moving the camera." The cop gave DeLisle an aggravated look. "As for the Amber Alert, it hasn't turned up a damn thing yet, but I have people questioning all the cabbies who were on duty yesterday morning. At least we'll be able to find out where he went from here. It's just a matter of time."

Time the Kowalik child doesn't have, Josh thought. But he kept it to himself. These people were all doing their best.

"Thank you, Lieutenant," Chang said. "Agent Merritt tells me you're loaning us some space to work out of."

"We're setting up a command center for you, yeah," the cop said. "It's not much, but you'll have secure computer access."

"That's great. Thanks."

"Happy to do it," the cop replied. "We'll take all the help we can get on this one. I am curious, though. I mean, yes, if the guy takes the baby across state lines, kidnapping is a federal crime. But you're not waiting for evidence of that to get involved." He looked at Josh. "And Homeland Security . . . is this guy a terrorist or something?"

Josh looked at Chang, but she gave him a nod that indicated he should answer.

"Technically, we're not supposed to answer that," Josh said, looking at DeLisle and the tech before turning back to the cop. "And the truth is, we're not one hundred percent certain what we're dealing with yet. Whatever we find, though, you need to run it through Agent Chang and her supervisor before you discuss anything publicly."

"Of course," the lieutenant said, apparently irked that Josh felt the need to caution him. "I was just wondering. I mean, this sort of thing happens all the time. Not babies being snatched outside of hospitals, but kids being abducted. Parents snatch kids when they're unhappy with court decisions about custody. Perverts and crazies steal them off the streets. At some point, I'd love to know what makes this case so special."

So would we, Josh thought.

But the question stayed with him. Obviously the murders

in Fort Myers and the baby-snatching in Bangor were connected by the suspect, this man who called himself "Jamil
Nassif." But what if the cop's instincts were right and the
fundamental similarity between the two—the children—was
the more important connection? Was this actually about the
kids? And what did the kids have in common?

Josh would have to ponder the question, but he knew that
the place to begin answering it was Acadia Hospital, where
Richard and Farah Kowalik were camped out, waiting for
news of their stolen child.

-11--

Voss started Sunday morning with the biggest cup of iced
coffee in the world—at least according to a poster in the window of the café—laced with a double shot of espresso. The
night before had been a long one. The news had started running enhanced images of the two suspects who had approached the realtor to get a tour of the Greenlaws' house.
The murders at Manatee Village had become the hottest
story of the current news cycle, and the media vultures were
already picking at the bones. Voss knew it was their job, but
somehow could never quite forgive them for the way they
seemed to relish reporting the ugly news.

But fortunately, though the image from the security camera outside the hospital in Bangor showed his profile fairly
clearly, the abductor in Maine had not been identified by media as one of the suspects in the quadruple homicide in Fort
Myers. It wouldn't last, but for now they had a little breathing room in which to get their job done.

The news reports had included a call-in number for the
Fort Myers P.D. State and local cops were manning that line
together, but Turcotte had wanted to give the media an FBI
call-in number as well. He had spent the night butting heads

with a captain from Fort Myers P.D. and a Florida State Police captain named Wetherell, who hated the idea because it would tip reporters off to the terrorist connection, and he didn't want the people of Florida to panic—as if they weren't already panicking, thinking there were cold-blooded killers out there murdering families in their sleep.

With Josh in Maine with Special Agent Chang, Voss felt even more of an outsider in this investigation, and she fought the impulse to assert her authority at every step. Until Turcotte screwed up, it was his case to run. For the moment they had one suspect somewhere in Maine, and three others in the wind. The public had seen only pictures of the guy in Maine and one other, but thanks to the lease agreement on the place where the suspects had been living, they had now managed to track down aliases for and photographs of the other two. The two Iraqis had not only driver's licenses, but local gym memberships that required photo ID.

Amateurs.

But they were amateurs willing and able to murder children. The investigation had turned up only circumstantial evidence to suggest that these men were terrorists, and if they were involved in terrorist activity, she had no idea how that connected to the Greenlaws, or how they might benefit from abducting a baby in Maine. But at the moment, those were merely details. All Voss needed to know was that they were baby-killers.

Emerging from the café, she blinked the sun's glare from her eyes and lowered her sunglasses, gazing at the Days Inn across the street, where Turcotte had set up the command center for the case. Neutral territory. If he had tried to camp out in the break room at a Fort Myers police station or with the state cops, one or the other would have gotten their feathers ruffled. At least this way, they were all irritated.

And no one could irritate people as well as Ed Turcotte. As long as it wasn't her toes he was stepping on, she didn't mind at all. In this case, he had done exactly the right thing. Nobody came to Florida in August for fun, so there were very few guests at the Days Inn to be intimidated by the presence of so many cops, agents, and imposing guys in suits, and the management had been more than happy to fill its rooms with people paying on a government tab.

A crayon-orange convertible VW bug drove by and she stared for a moment at the silver-haired AARP member behind the wheel, then she raised her iced coffee in a silent toast. The sixtyish guy was tan and smiling, the picture of relaxation, and she envied him his contentment.

She marched across the road and up the drive. The hotel's electric doors whooshed aside to let her enter and the rush of cold, air-conditioned air seemed to reach out and carry her inside.

Uniformed police officers were locked in grim conversation, all of them under orders to avoid looking amused by anything, just in case reporters showed up. And Voss had no doubt the media would begin arriving soon enough. Despite instructions to the contrary, someone would leak the location of their command center before long. In fact, she would bet somebody already had.

"Good morning, Agent Voss," a state trooper said stiffly, nodding to her as she passed.

She gave him a sort of salute with her cup and kept walking. Most of the local police and a large number of Staties were in the field, following up on leads provided by the Bureau, which meant that the people lingering around the lobby of the hotel were mostly assistants and aides and other sorts of lackeys. Voss sighed in disgust, seeing no point in this waste of manpower.

The ice shifted in her cup and she took a long sip, wanting to finish the coffee before it became watered-down.

A junior FBI agent waited in the first-floor corridor outside the hotel conference room, looking like a high school kid sent to the principal's office. When Voss approached, he eyed her suspiciously. She took out her ID, flashing it at him as she reached by and turned the knob, pushing the door open.

"It's real," she told the guy. "And you should know by instinct who belongs on the other side of the door and who doesn't."

The young FBI agent frowned at this suggestion in the same way that teenagers did, thinking that a woman perhaps a decade older could not possibly have any counsel to share. It was an arrogance she had seen many times before, most especially in the mirror when she had come out of Quantico. But this kid would learn quickly. They all did.

The agent stepped aside and Voss entered. The conference room was filled with the smell of brewing coffee, and she spotted an urn on a sideboard laden with dishes of pastries, fresh cut fruit, and bagels. But for now, her own caffeine would do.

Files littered the conference table. Maps and photos had been taped to a couple of whiteboards that normally would have been used for business presentations instead of a quadruple homicide with potential terrorist connections.

There were half a dozen people in the room, including the heavyset, white-haired Florida state trooper she had seen the night before, two FBI agents sorting files, and the tall African-American guy who had been talking to Turcotte last night. The only difference was that today he was in uniform. She had guessed right; he was with SOCOM, and his stripes gave him away as a lieutenant. The other two people were in the back of the room, talking quietly as they leaned against the wall.

She wondered how Josh was faring with Nala Chang. The way the two of them had been talking together last night, right before their plane had taken off for Maine, had drawn Voss's attention. Josh and Chang didn't really know each other, but there had already been a kind of intimacy in their rapport. The thought made her uneasy.

One of the FBI agents, Michael Koenig, looked up from the files and nodded in greeting. "You didn't have to go out. We have coffee."

"But not the 'world's biggest cup of iced coffee.' Ed Turcotte's hospitality can't compete. Speaking of . . . where is he?"

Agent Koenig gestured toward the conference room door. "He's reaming out the locals. Seems their chief has an interview scheduled with CNN later this morning. Guess the chief sees this as his fifteen minutes and doesn't want it cut short."

Voss frowned. "I was wondering why we aren't already swarming with media."

Koenig's upper lip curled in disgust. "They know we're here, but they're all reporting live from the site. It's more horrifying to their viewers to see the scene of the crime. But don't worry, we'll be crawling with them soon enough."

"Lovely," Voss said. She glanced at the lieutenant, who had served himself a plate of fruit. "You know, I'm still not sure what brought SOCOM to the party."

The lieutenant paused with his fork halfway to his mouth, a piece of honeydew speared on its tines. After a moment's hesitation, he set the plate down and the fork on top of it, stepped over to her, and held out his hand.

"Marc Arsenault," he said, surprising her by not leading with his rank.

"Rachael Voss, ICD," she said, shaking his hand.

"You're right to wonder, Agent Voss," Lieutenant Arsenault said. "It's unusual for SOCOM to express any official interest in a domestic crime, even considering that the victim was a highly respected member of our armed forces. That's why there's nothing official about my presence. I'm here purely as an observer. If a decorated U.S. Army officer was targeted by foreign interests, whether they're terrorists or just mad dog killers, SOCOM wants to know who and why. But you don't need to worry about whether we're cooperating."

"Understood, Lieutenant," Voss said. "Though it could be the FBI will need your help with other known associates once they have legit ID on these guys. Even if SOCOM's not officially in the picture, that doesn't mean we can't all cooperate."

Lieutenant Arsenault nodded, but before he could reply, she added, "What confuses me is what Black Pine is doing here."

The lieutenant cocked his head, looking apologetic. "They're consultants."

"Yes, but someone must have asked for the consultation. According to SSA Turcotte, it wasn't the FBI, and we know it wasn't the Florida State Police. So who called them?"

"I don't know," Arsenault replied.

"Someone did," Agent Koenig said. "He's got clearance to be here and we have orders to keep him in the loop."

Voss didn't like that. Black Pine were civilians. They didn't have to follow the same rules that the government and law enforcement did.

The door to the conference room opened and they all looked up to see Ed Turcotte entering. He had a laptop under one arm and the moment Voss caught his eye, she knew that something had changed. He had a lead on the case.

"Gather 'round, kiddies," Turcotte said.

He set the laptop on the conference table, opened it, and tapped a button to make it come to life. While the screen lit up, he went back to the door and made sure it was tightly shut, then looked around the room as if confirming there wasn't anyone there he didn't want present. He seemed to hesitate on Lieutenant Arsenault.

Then a single knock came at the door and Norris entered. Turcotte's eyes narrowed. He obviously would have preferred not to have someone from Black Pine in the room, but he wasn't going to throw Norris out, which meant he had specific orders not to do so.

"What's going on, Ed?" Voss asked.

"As you know, we have names on all four of our local suspects, but they're just aliases. Or they were. But now we've got a positive ID on our babynapper up in Maine," Turcotte said as they all gathered around to get a view of the laptop screen.

"The Amber Alert for the baby has prompted the usual calls, but nothing concrete yet," Turcotte continued, glancing at Voss. "But Homeland Security has confirmed that the man in Bangor is definitely one of the guys who toured the Greenlaws' house."

"That's not news," a heavyset state trooper said.

Turcotte silenced him with a look that said he was dubious about allowing state law enforcement to take part in the investigation in the first place. Voss had no love for Turcotte, but she felt the same.

"We had grainy video before, and stills made from that. Now we've got confirmation from our analysts that it's the same guy. Better yet, we've got a name, and we think it's his real one. Or, at least, the one he's known by in the places that evil bastards gather."

He bent over, tapped a couple of buttons, and brought up the familiar grainy video showing the dark-haired man attacking the young mother in Bangor and snatching the infant car seat from her hand.

"That was last night," Turcotte said. "We've had our people working on it since then." He closed the screen and clicked on a different file. "Have a look at this."

The second version had been cleaned up considerably, the size and clarity of the image enhanced, and it had been slowed down.

"Gharib al-Din," Norris said.

Turcotte gave him a sharp look. "That's right."

Voss stared at him. "You knew who this guy was all along?"

"No," Norris said. "The video footage was too corrupted to get a decent look at him, both in Maine and at the realtor's office here. He could've been anyone. But my people have been working on this, too, and Gharib al-Din is known to us. According to our research, it's his real name."

All eyes looked to Turcotte then, and Voss saw his upper lip twitch with barely concealed fury. She decided it might be best for her to speak up first, before Turcotte did something to get himself into trouble. That was the whole point of her being there after all. Troubleshooting.

"By 'we,' I assume you mean Black Pine," Voss said.

"I thought I recognized him but I didn't want to say anything until I was sure. Black Pine has a file on him."

Turcotte nodded, his eyes clouded with distrust. "I'm going to need that file."

"Pertinent details are encrypted and on their way to you," Norris said. "Probably already in your e-mail in-box."

Voss stared at the two men. The subordinates in the room had the sense to look away, and it seemed Lieutenant Arsenault was making good on his promise to only observe.

"Explain 'pertinent details,'" Voss said.

A look of irritation flashed on Norris's face. "It means exactly what you think it means, Agent Voss. Black Pine's files are extensive. All of the details we think will be helpful to your investigation have been provided."

Turcotte laughed. "Mr. Norris, you're a civilian. You don't get to tell the U.S. government what is and isn't pertinent to an FBI investigation."

Norris picked a piece of lint from the lapel of his charcoal black suit jacket. "Actually, Agent Turcotte, we do. We're a multi-national corporation, and our clients depend upon us to provide discretion in all matters. The information we have sent you is a courtesy. Anything else would require a subpoena. And, as I'm sure you can imagine, any attempt to secure one would turn into a circus that would be embarrassing for you and still would not provide the further contents of that file, or anything else we don't wish to provide." He gave a small bow of his head. "Just to be clear, sir."

"You want clear?" Turcotte said. "How's this—"

"SSA Turcotte," Voss interrupted, "why don't we focus on the case for the moment? If Gharib al-Din helped commit a quadruple murder in Fort Myers the night before last, what was he doing in Bangor yesterday?"

Voss glanced at Arsenault, but the lieutenant seemed only to be waiting for the answers the same as everyone else. Norris had a smug look on his face that she wanted to erase with a baseball bat.

"That is the question of the day," Turcotte agreed. "If we can find the answer, we may be able to figure out how to track these bastards."

Voss opened her hands. "Just tell us how we can help. You're in charge of this investigation, Ed. Utilize all the resources you have, and if you need more, Homeland Security will provide them."

Turcotte nodded his thanks. They both knew that it might be his investigation, but it was Voss who held the real power in the room. And then, of course, there was the wild card—Black Pine.

"As for you, Mr. Norris," Voss continued, "I know I can speak for us all when I say that we appreciate Black Pine's assistance. And I know that we can count on your further assistance, even if Homeland Security must get directly involved with Black Pine's management. After all, the U.S. government is, I believe, your biggest customer. And the customer is always right."

Before Norris could reply, the conference room door swung open and a young Florida state trooper stepped in, excited and anxious.

"Agent Turcotte," the trooper said. "We've got one. Karim al-Jubouri."

"What do you mean, you've got him?" Turcotte demanded.

"Locals picked him up in Sarasota. Routine traffic stop," the trooper said, grinning like a kid.

"You're shitting me," Turcotte said.

"No, sir. Captain Wetherell's already on his way. The Sarasota P.D. has been notified to do nothing until you arrive."

Voss turned to Turcotte and found herself grinning at him. They weren't friends, but they both wanted the killers caught—and fast. Now maybe they would get some answers.

"Let's go get him," Turcotte said, starting for the door.

She let him lead the way.

-12--

Weekend mornings in the summertime, the highways north and south of Boston were jammed with people headed to Maine or New Hampshire or out to Cape Cod for vacation. Fridays were even worse, with the folks headed out of town just for the weekend. But getting *into* Boston on a Sunday morning in August was like driving through one of those post-apocalyptic movies. Last-woman-on-Earth kind of stuff.

The digital clock glowed on the dashboard of her old Corolla, warning Cait that she was going to be a little late getting into the station, so she nudged the speedometer up a bit. She didn't really believe Lynette could fire her for last night's scuffle, but she also didn't feel like antagonizing the woman.

As she drove south on Interstate 93, her thoughts lingered on the Audi. In her back pocket, she carried a slip of paper on which she had written the license plate number, and though she knew she needed to see her boss, solving the mystery of that car seemed like a much bigger priority.

Cait didn't like it, that car just sitting there, down the street from her aunt's house. In some ways, she was glad that Auntie Jane was taking Leyla to the supermarket. Uncle George would be home, probably working on some job or another in the garage, but Cait would rather her baby girl not be in the house today. Too many unpleasant possibilities had suggested themselves to her while she was trying to figure out who might be behind the wheel of that car. Some rich guy whose wife was having an affair with someone who lived on Badger Road? Maybe. But, then, who had been in the other car? According to Jane there had been two, working in shifts. And if they were cops or Feds, who were they watching? She would need to make some calls, try to find out what the car was doing there. And if she couldn't, her approach next time might have to be a little more aggressive.

Cait needed her job, and to keep it she needed Auntie Jane to look after Leyla, but she couldn't leave her little girl there if she had to worry whether or not the baby would be safe. If anything happened to Leyla . . .

A year ago, she would have laughed at the very idea of such parental paranoia, but she was a mother now, and even the hint of a threat to her child brought her defenses up.

Sometimes those feelings made her think of her own mother, and she wondered how the woman could have given birth to her and her brother, given them names, held them, and then just walked away as though her children meant nothing.

Cait thought her mother must have no soul. She had never spoken the words aloud, not even to her brother, but nothing else made sense to her. The woman had to have been entirely empty of love; otherwise, she could never have left. Cait had known from the moment of Leyla's birth that she would be willing to die for her daughter, and she had never felt that way about anyone before—not even Nizam, whom she had loved deeply.

Thoughts of Sean got her mind working. She twisted in her seat, straining against the seat belt as she fished her cell phone out of her pocket. With a quick glance at the road ahead, she flipped it open, skimmed her contacts list, and hit the call button. It rang and rang, and just when she expected the call to kick over to voice mail, her brother picked up.

"Hey, little sister."

"Hey, yourself," she said, smiling at the warmth in his voice. They'd done their share of fighting, but Sean had always looked out for her, no matter what.

"What's going on? How's my niece?"

Despite the tensions lingering from the night before and the weirdness of the morning, Cait found herself relaxing.

"Leyla's awesome, thanks. Getting bigger every day. And I'm good. But I had a little excitement on the job last night, so I'm going in to talk to my boss and make sure I'm still employed."

Sean asked for details, and as Cait drove she regaled him with the tale. Only now, talking to her brother, did she allow herself to truly feel the horror of watching the bastard beat on his wife, knowing how easily the violence could turn deadly.

"You did what had to be done," Sean said, grimly serious. He had no sense of humor where violence was concerned. "Those other people should be ashamed of themselves."

"I know, right? It's like they thought they were watching a show or something, like they didn't think it was real. I've seen enough ugly shit. I don't want any more, y'know?"

Sean hesitated for a heartbeat. To others, the pause would have been barely noticeable, but Cait knew him better than anyone.

"I do know," he said.

"I'm sorry, Sean. I know you're still *in* the shit—"

"I officially have no idea what you're talking about," he said, and now she could hear the smile in his voice—a lightness that was also a warning for her to tread carefully.

Four years ago, Sean had been discharged from the Marine Corps and gone to work at the Pentagon. Officially he worked in satellite surveillance, and Cait thought that was probably true, as far as it went. But within months of beginning the job, Sean had started to grow a beard he had never trimmed. It grew so bushy and wild that, with his black Irish heritage—black hair and dark eyes—he looked like a radical Muslim cleric.

Every few months, he went off the grid for a while. Last time it had been five weeks. And each time, he would call Cait beforehand with the same message: *I'm going out of town for a while. You won't be able to reach me. If you have an emergency, call Hercules.* She had never had to actually get in touch with Hercules, whose real name was Brian Herskowitz, but it was nice to know someone could get a message to Sean if there really was an emergency. She'd only met Herc a couple of times—he worked on satellite stuff with Sean and had a physique that made the nickname amusing—but she liked the guy well enough.

"Anyway . . ." she said.

"Anyway," Sean replied, "you'll be fine. Probably better than fine. Don't sweat it."

"I'm trying not to," Cait said, watching the signs for her exit.

"You're going in to see your boss right now, you said. An hour from now, you'll know one way or the other."

"Is that your way of brushing me off?" Cait demanded, feigning hurt feelings.

"Just being a realist. It's what I do."

"Yeah? When is the realist going to come home to visit? Leyla will be headed off to college by the time you see her again."

"You know it isn't as simple as that, Cait," Sean chided, obviously sensitive to the subject. "I can't wait to see her, and I'll get there soon. Before the year is out, I promise."

"You'd better," Cait said. "Look, I should focus on driving. My exit's coming up."

"You go, then. Call me later and let me know how it goes with the boss. And send me the video of you kicking the crap out of that guy so I can show all my friends. Actually, on second thought, I'm not showing it to them. Half of them might fall in love with a girl who can fight like you can."

"Yeah," Cait said. "That's the last thing I need right now."

-13--

The Library Café had been a little-known gem in downtown Alexandria, Virginia, for nearly forty years. Open for breakfast and lunch seven days a week, the place had a Bohemian flair, and always smelled of bacon and frying onions in the morning, and freshly baked bread and cinnamon in the afternoon. Their coffee cake was legendary. The walls were lined with books that customers were welcome to read while they relaxed for a meal or a cup of coffee, or to take home for as long as they liked. Just like a real library, some of the books were never returned, but according to the owner, Rose Whiting, most of them made their way back onto the shelves eventually.

Sean loved the café, and had made it his second home in Alexandria. Toni fixed a heavenly breakfast, and Rose always made it a point to wait on him herself, even when she had plenty of help. Sean had the same thing almost every time he came in—scrambled eggs with ham and cheese mixed in, eaten on top of wheat toast, with bacon on the side. A deadly cholesterol load, but twice a month he could spoil himself.

In the time since he had moved here to work at the Pentagon, he had dated a dozen girls, half of them more than once, but had yet to meet a woman with whom he would be willing to share the Library Café. It was his little Fortress of Solitude. He figured when he eventually met a woman he wanted to take out for breakfast here, she would be the one.

"How were your eggs, honey?" Rose asked as she topped up his coffee.

"You do 'em perfect. You know that."

Rose smiled. "That's Toni. She knows just what you like."

The woman added just enough naughtiness to her inflection that it would be impossible for Sean to miss the innuendo. Toni, a fortyish single mother, always flirted with him when he came in, and sometimes she used Rose as her go-between. The women made a little game of it, and Sean always went along. Most times he thought she was joking—that the flirtation was only surface—but on occasion he had wondered if there might be something more to it. The prospect of finding out tempted him, but his work was not conducive to long-term relationships, and he was too fond of Toni to treat her affection as something disposable. But innocent flirtation? That he could do.

He slipped some money into the leather folder with the bill Rose had left on the diner-style counter.

"Keep it warm for me," he said, sliding off his stool and heading for the men's room.

"I always do," Rose called.

Sean smiled to himself as he went into the restroom, but after he'd used the urinal and was standing at the sink, washing his hands, his thoughts went back to his sister. Cait had sounded off, and he didn't blame her. This afternoon, when he could steal enough time for a longer conversation, he would call her back. They might be adults now, but he knew he would never stop worrying about her.

When he came out of the men's room, Rose was wiping spilled coffee off the floor and there were napkins soaking it off the counter. A middle-aged suit with wire-rimmed glasses had taken the stool next to where Sean had been sitting, and now he was dabbing at coffee stains on his shirt. When he spotted Sean, his expression turned sheepish.

"You must be the guy whose coffee I just spilled," he said. "Sorry about that."

The guy had apparently slung his briefcase onto the counter. It sat on the stool beside him now, a few small rivulets of coffee dripping down the side.

"No worries," Sean said, grabbing some napkins and pitching in, wiping the counter. "Happens to the best of us."

"Especially if you're as uncoordinated as I am." On the counter in front of the man was a brand-new coffee in a to-go cup. He picked it up and offered it to Sean.

"Why don't you take mine? I just got it. Haven't even taken a sip. It's got cream in it, but if you want sugar—"

"He's sweet enough," Rose said, straightening up. She smiled and went around behind the counter.

Sean felt a little awkward, but he needed to get going, and the guy seemed to feel so sheepish that he hated to refuse.

"That's great, actually," he said, taking the offered cup. "You're sure?"

"Absolutely. It's the least I can do."

"Hey, I'm not the one who has to clean that shirt," Sean said, gesturing toward the stains on the man's clothes. "I got off easy."

The guy laughed, a little less sheepish now.

Rose dumped the napkins and paper towels in the trash, then took a clean cloth and gave the counter one more wipe down. Sean picked up a biography of Houdini, which he'd left on the counter. By some miracle, the pool of coffee had not reached it. He took a couple of long sips from the cup—hot, but not scalding. Perfect.

"Thanks again," Sean told the guy, raising his coffee cup. "See you soon, Rose. Give Toni a kiss from me."

"You could give it to her yourself if you'd shave that beard, or at least trim it back a little," Rose teased him, picking up the faux-leather folder that held the check and his money and slipping it into her apron.

Sean ran a hand over his bristly, close-cropped hair and then pushed his fingers through his tangled snarl of a beard. "I think it's distinguished."

"Hah! It's a rat's nest," Rose said with a laugh.

"That's no way to keep your customers coming back."

She winked at the clumsy, coffee-stained guy, then turned back to Sean. "You'll be back, honey. Where else are you gonna get such a warm welcome?"

Sean chuckled. "You win. No arguing that." He held up the Houdini book for her to see. "I'm going to borrow this one, if you don't mind."

"You know I don't. Enjoy it, honey."

"I already am," he replied. As he headed for the door, he glanced back. "Tell Toni I said good-bye."

The bell above the door chimed as he pushed it open and stepped onto the sidewalk, a smile on his face. The fans had been spinning inside the Library Café, but out here on the street it was warming up fast. The forecast called for a hot one today, but manageable. Tomorrow, though . . . the cute weather girl was predicting a scorcher.

Still sipping his coffee, Sean headed toward home, but not directly. Two blocks down there was a small market. He needed to pick up some OJ and a jar of peanut butter, and probably a loaf of bread as well, if they had anything decent. The bread stock at Taraji's Market was always a roll of the dice.

He hitched up his pants, glancing casually around to make sure he wasn't being observed as he adjusted the holster he wore clipped to his belt at the small of his back, his long shirt easily covering it.

As he did, he licked his lips, realizing he was suddenly thirsty. He took another sip of coffee, but then had second thoughts. Water would have been better. His throat felt so dry. And the sun . . . it was so bright that his temples began to throb.

Stupid, Sean thought, *having a big breakfast on a hot August morning.* He'd be feeling full and sleepy all day. Walking would do him good. Despite the pressure in his temples, quickly growing into a genuine headache, he picked up his pace.

He dropped the half-empty coffee into a trash can he strolled past, realizing that his throat felt even drier. He swallowed, felt it constricting, and frowned. *You'd better not be getting sick.* Actually, though it had been years since he'd had a bad one, this felt a lot like a hangover. His mouth felt stuffed with cotton, his lips swollen, and now he blinked, unsteady on his feet.

Sean froze, there on the sidewalk.

Oh, Jesus, he thought, as he realized what it was. This wasn't a hangover at all.

He turned to glance back at the trash can where he'd just dropped the coffee cup, then at the Library Café, thinking how stupid he'd been. Of all people, he should have known better than to take anything from a stranger. Bile rushed up the back of his throat and he dropped to his knees, vomiting blood and scrambled eggs onto the sidewalk. His stomach convulsed and he threw up again, unable to catch his breath.

Then the seizure started.

A good Samaritan, seeing him twisting in agony on the ground, shouted for someone to call 911 and raced to his side. By the time the man reached him, Sean McCandless had stopped breathing.

The Houdini book lay open, facedown, on the sidewalk beside him, blood and vomit soaking its white pages.

-14--

Cait stepped off the elevator at 8:12 a.m., late for the meeting to which Lynette had summoned her, but she had surrendered herself to fate. Whatever happened now would happen. She couldn't have gotten there any faster without risking a car wreck or a major speeding ticket. If the station manager wanted to make her suffer, then so be it.

The receptionist—a scrawny, twentyish Boho guy named Adam—waved to her as she crossed the foyer, chatting on his headset. The station was busy 24/7, but outside business hours, nobody got in without a magnetic key/ID card to swipe through the scanner. Adam split his job with a heavy-set Dominican woman named Linda, but since she had seniority, he was the one who had to work weekend mornings.

"Hey," Adam said as Cait pulled out her ID card.

She glanced up to see him covering the mouthpiece of his headset.

"You're my hero," he said. And there was none of the usual

laid-back coffeehouse demeanor in his tone. "Really nicely done last night. I fucking cheered when I saw it."

She couldn't help smiling. "Thanks."

Adam grinned, then went back to his phone conversation, which didn't seem to have anything to do with work. A quiet Sunday morning.

Cait waved her card at the sensor and heard the lock click open. She pushed through the door and went down a long corridor, past the restrooms, a conference room, and several storage closets, where she believed ancient videotapes were moldering to dust. A television hung on the wall straight ahead, the sound off, showing the current programming going out over the Channel 7 signal. There were other TVs in the office, some of them bulky, outmoded things that still sort of worked or that nobody wanted to go to the trouble of removing, considering how well they'd been bolted into corners or walls or the ceiling.

A right turn took her into a labyrinth of cubicles. Several people looked up from their desks as she passed, and she didn't think it was her imagination that they watched her go by with a new level of interest. One older woman, Janis, practically scowled at her, but everyone else either smiled or nodded in approval, and puffy-faced Bob Gorman actually gave her a thumbs-up.

Weird. It *all* felt weird to her.

On the far side of the cubicle maze was a junction. Off to the right were the executive offices, and the control room and studio were down the corridor to the left. As she reached the junction, the door to an editing suite swung open, and Jordan Katz stepped out, a cup of coffee in one hand.

Cait did a tiny double take at the sight of him. The cameraman had a laconic confidence that she liked, but the wild bush of a beard he had grown since their unit had been brought home from Iraq had always seemed wrong on him. At least her brother's beard was a part of his job and not a personal fashion statement.

Now, though, Jordan had clipped the unruly beard away, trimming it down to little more than stubble, and she could see the shape of his face again, not to mention more of the mischievous smile that matched the quiet twinkle in his eye when he spotted her. Without the beard, his features had a hard edge that combined with his soulful eyes to start an engine purring inside her that had been quiet for some time.

Stop, she told herself. *It's Jordan. Don't be stupid.* Yet she couldn't help wondering if a spark of interest in someone, a good guy like Jordan, might help her find the way out of her enduring grief.

"Hey, Cait," Jordan said. "Quite a morning, huh? Instant celebrity hell. Potential dates suddenly intimidated by your ass-kicking magnificence."

She laughed. "Nice. I hadn't even thought about the impact on my love life. Such as it is."

Jordan nodded solemnly. "Oh, yeah. Any guy sees that video's gonna want to do you."

Cait crossed her arms. "Who says I want to be *done*?"

He put his hands up in mock surrender. "I know, I know. Even the tiniest bit of sex or romance will ruin your plan to become the withered old crone who all the neighborhood kids think is a witch. You're right. It's a good plan. You should stick with it."

She couldn't help smiling—right before she punched him in the arm.

"Hey!" he protested. "Back off, lady. I've seen you in action. I don't want trouble."

"Just remember that," Cait said, shaking an admonishing finger at him.

Jordan probably knew better than anyone what Nizam had meant to her, and how much grief she still carried. Jordan and Ronnie had been there the night Cait and Nizam had met, had been the big brothers who watched out for her while she was falling in love with a guy everyone else looked at with suspicion, and Jordan had been the one who held her while she wept on the night Nizam had been killed. He and Ronnie made jokes about her love life as a way to drive back the shadows of her grief, though they all knew that it would not be as simple as that.

Someday, Cait would have someone in her life again. Nizam would not have wanted her to be alone. But for now, she reserved all her love for Leyla. She cherished her daughter, and whenever strangers asked about the little girl—as they often did, curious about her olive skin and foreign features—Cait never hesitated to tell her story. Even the bitter old woman at the supermarket deli had softened at the sight of Leyla. In a climate of prejudice and fear, Cait had watched bigots turn thoughtful and even kind upon learning of Nizam's death. One man, with a shaved head and tattooed biceps, had surprised her with a comment that touched her heart.

"Strange, isn't it?" the man had said, standing behind her in line at the bank, after she'd talked about Leyla's birth to the woman in front of her.

Cait had asked him what he thought was strange.

"Mixed-race kids," the man had continued. "They're always the most beautiful."

"Maybe that's the point," the woman in front of them in line had said. "Maybe it's not so strange at all."

And this man, about whom Cait had made some unpleasant presumptions, had smiled at Leyla and said, "Maybe."

If one little girl could start such conversations, Cait thought that one day she might be able to convince herself that Nizam's death had meant something to the world.

"Hey," Jordan said quietly. "You okay?"

Her smile had slipped. "Yeah. Sorry. Just drifting."

"I know that look." He gave her arm a comforting squeeze. "Come back, Cait. It's much more fun out here in the world than in the sad places in your head."

She exhaled, forcing her smile to return. "True. Just tired, I guess," she said, then cocked her head, studying him. "What are you doing here anyway? I didn't think you had to work this morning."

Much of the humor drained from his face and she instantly regretted the question. Without the smile, he seemed tired and even a bit sad.

"Spence is sick," Jordan said. "He's covered for me a couple of times, so when he called this morning, I figured I couldn't say no. But if I'd known what I'd be working on, I'd still be home in bed. Have you heard about these crib deaths out in the Midwest?"

Cait felt a sick twist in her gut. *Crib deaths.* Even the words were hideous.

"No," she said. And to herself, she added, *And I'm not sure I want to.*

"I guess the first one was in Columbus, Ohio. Well, the first time anyone noticed something weird anyway. Seemed to be SIDS, but then the parents saw that the screen in the baby's room was hanging loose, and when they checked, it had been cut. Someone had snuck in and then tried to put the screen back when they left, and now they're thinking the kid was suffocated, that someone murdered her."

Cait shuddered. "That's awful!"

"I know, right? So that started people looking more closely at some of these cases, and the Feds have put together a list of at least seven other incidents in Ohio, Kansas, and Iowa that seem like they were probably the work of the same person. A serial killer who suffocates babies in their cribs. I have a hard time just imagining the existence of somebody like that. I don't need that information in my brain, y'know?"

Cait nodded. "I do. Thanks so much for sharing."

Jordan frowned. "Sorry. I wasn't thinking. I've been editing stock footage and some reports from affiliates together for Aaron. I just needed some coffee before we start to dub in his voice-over."

"That's okay," Cait said. "I'm just glad it's far away from here."

"Do you want a cup of coffee?" Jordan asked.

"Rain check," she said. "I'm already late to face the dragon in her den."

Lynette kept her office impeccable. A flat-screen TV hung on one wall. Normally it would have been turned on so that she could keep an eye on their programming, but at the moment the screen was dark. Cait sat in a plush armchair, facing Lynette's desk, trying to pretend she wasn't worried.

"So," the station manager began, leaning back in her chair. "Some crazy night you had."

"Definitely not the night I expected," Cait replied, trying to read her tone.

"I talked to Mike Duffy last night," Lynette said. Her expression was grim, her eyes contemplative as she studied Cait. "He's pretty upset, actually. I'd go so far as to say that he's pissed off. He thinks you interfered with his story, that you should have waited for the police to arrive."

Cait stared, growing numb. "Look, I know I broke the rules—"

"The number one rule. We don't make the news," Lynette said.

"I know that. I get it. I guess I could argue that I'm new, that I haven't been in this very long, but that'd be a bullshit argument. I did what I did because someone had to—and under the same circumstances, I would do it again in a heartbeat. If you want to fire me because of that—"

"Whoa, whoa," Lynette said. "I have no intention of firing you, Cait. Yes, you broke the rules. But I wanted you to know about Duffy's tirade mainly so you can prepare yourself. He's going to be a baby about this for a while, even though I've told him to grow up. You want to know the truth? I think he's mainly just embarrassed that a *girl* did what he couldn't bring himself to do. I talked to Jordan Katz about what went on out there last night, too, and I've seen the footage, of course. It's possible you saved that woman's life, stepping in when you did."

Cait blinked, uncertain how to reply. Relief flooded through her, along with irritation with Mike Duffy and gratitude toward Jordan. Her old friend was still looking out for her. She owed him for that.

"No response?" Lynette asked.

"Sorry," Cait said. "It's just not what I expected. I figured you were calling me in here to read me the riot act."

"Every rule has an exception," the station manager said. "You did the right thing. It's possible not everyone is going to see it that way, but I think our footage is damned convincing. All of that said, though, there is one rule I'm going to have to insist you follow in exchange for me letting you off the hook."

"What's that?"

"No interviews to any other media source without my

consent—which, to be honest, you're not going to get. Local girl, single mom, war veteran—people are calling you a hero, Cait. We want to make it clear that you're Channel Seven's hero. You're off tomorrow, which is good, but I want you to take Tuesday off, too. We'll talk to the police, make sure no one's going to be able to make a case against you, and then Aaron will interview you on the air."

Cait fidgeted. She already didn't like the attention she was getting because of the previous night's encounter, and the last thing she wanted was to put herself any further into the spotlight. But she didn't see how she could avoid it.

"Not Duffy? It's sort of his story," Cait said. "Is he going to be pissed?"

Lynette grinned. "Let's hope so."

-15--

The hospital administrators were anxious for Richard and Farah Kowalik to go home. There was no medical reason for them to still be lingering there. They had been on their way home when Gharib had attacked Farah and stolen her newborn daughter. Farah had a minor concussion from a knock on the head she'd taken while trying to stop him, and she was inconsolable. Doctors had admitted her for observation because of both the concussion and the hysteria, but now it was their medical opinion that she ought to be discharged. But the Kowaliks did not want to go. Somehow, they seemed to think that their daughter might be returned to the hospital.

Normally, they would have been discharged regardless of their wishes. Insurance companies did not reimburse hospitals for putting up guests as if the facility were a bed-and-breakfast. But the administrators faced a dilemma. Several of the local network affiliates had reporters filing stories from the hospital during every major newscast, and the Fox

News people had somehow gotten wind of the fact that the Kowaliks were insisting they be allowed to stay. If the hospital kicked them out now, after their newborn was abducted practically on its threshold, the administrators would be crucified in the media.

Which was how Josh and Chang ended up interviewing the Kowaliks in Room 326 of the Timothy Spruce Wing of the hospital. Images flickered across the television in silence. Richard Kowalik—not Rick or Dick or Richie—had been watching some sports channel when they knocked, his eyes vacant and glassy from either grief or tranquilizers or both. Now he and his wife stared at Josh and Chang with that same empty gaze.

"Have you been shown the video of the attack?" Chang asked the Kowaliks.

Richard perched on the edge of the hospital bed. His wife lay beneath the crisp industrial sheet and blanket like a child who didn't want to get up for school. Josh couldn't blame her. He and his ex-wife hadn't had any children, but he couldn't imagine the anguish the couple must be feeling right now. They didn't just look lost. They *were* lost.

"They showed us only photographs taken from the video," Farah Kowalik said, her accent lovely and exotic. "They wanted to be merciful."

"But it's been on TV constantly," Richard added. He shrugged, his smile painful and ironic. "Everyone's seen it by now. I've watched it, wondering if I've seen the son of a bitch anywhere before." The man was tall and might once have been formidable, but now he had become small, somehow. Broken.

Farah took his hand and kissed it. "Richard thinks he should have been there." She squeezed his hand and he looked at her. "You were doing exactly what you should have been doing. You were being a father . . . taking us home."

For several long moments, their shared pain was unspeakable. Josh thought they might both crumple into tears, or just shatter, but then it passed and they exhaled simultaneously and returned their attention to the conversation.

"And you're sure you *haven't* seen him before?" Chang asked.

"How can I be sure of that?" Richard asked. "But I guess I'm as sure as it's possible to be. He doesn't look familiar to me, except that he looks like a thousand other people I've seen."

"And you, Mrs. Kowalik?" Josh asked. "Have you ever seen him before?"

She looked at him as if he were the stupidest man on Earth.

"I'm sorry," he said. "I know the police have asked you these questions before."

"Everyone has asked us," Farah replied. "But no, Agent Hart, I do not know this man. I have no idea why he would want to do this to us. Why anyone would want to do such a thing to us."

Neither do I, Josh thought, but he made a silent promise that he would find out. If the Kowaliks knew what their daughter's kidnapper had been up to the night before he had come to Maine . . . Josh didn't want to imagine their grief then.

He glanced at Chang, wanting only to leave. They weren't likely to learn anything helpful from these people. Instead, they needed to get out into the field, touch base with everyone helping to search for the kidnapper and the missing infant. They needed to take charge.

But Chang didn't seem ready to leave just yet. "Mrs. Kowalik, can I ask where you're from?"

"I am Persian," Farah replied, lifting her chin in almost childlike defiance.

"You're Iranian?" Josh asked.

In some parts of the world, Persia and Iran were used interchangeably. In the United States, the nation was sometimes called Persia by people who did not want to be associated with the stigma attached to Iran.

"I was born there, yes," Farah replied.

Richard squeezed her hand again, but now he stared at Chang and Josh with knitted brow. "What does this have to do with anything?"

Josh blinked, surprised it hadn't occurred to them. "Sorry, Mr. Kowalik. Mrs. Kowalik. But it can't have escaped your notice that the suspect appears to be Middle Eastern. He traveled here under a Saudi name that we're fairly certain is an alias."

"He could be from anywhere, really," Chang added.

Josh studied the couple. "How did you two meet?"

"I don't like the tone of your voice, pal," Richard Kowalik said.

Josh held up his hands. "I swear to you, Mr. Kowalik, all we want is to find your baby and bring her home alive. But it's our job to consider every possibility. If we don't, the odds of us figuring this out will suffer."

Richard took a breath, then nodded.

"I have lived in the United States for fifteen years," Farah said. "Richard and I met six years ago at a conference on green energy. I was a researcher for an international consortium, studying alternative fuels. Richard is a journalist. He was working on a magazine article about the conference."

She shrugged. "I cannot imagine any connection between my heritage and this . . . what this man has done. To assume that there must be some thread that connects us just because I was born in Iran . . . Well, I think it would be foolish and a waste of time."

"Not to mention racist," Richard added.

For a moment, none of them spoke. Josh hated the silence.

"Can you think of anyone who might want to hurt you? Either of you, for any reason?" he asked.

He wondered about ex-lovers, or maybe current lovers. Could Farah have been engaged in an affair? Was the baby even Richard's?

The Kowaliks hadn't liked the questions they had been asked so far, and they weren't going to like the next few any better. And yet Josh had a feeling he would be able to predict the answers. The Kowaliks were as broken and hollow as they were because they honestly had no clue why their baby had been taken.

The trouble is, neither do we.

-16--

Cait wanted to get home, not just to take Leyla off of Auntie Jane's hands but also to spend time with her daughter. It had been a busy week, and the thought of just snuggling with Leyla in the big chair in her living room was insanely appealing. But Jane had taken the baby to the supermarket, so Cait knew she had a little bit of time. Another fifteen minutes wouldn't make much difference, and she wanted to follow up on the Audi that had been parked on Badger Road this morning.

A quick stroll through the cubicle village revealed plenty of empty chairs. Only about half of the station's employees worked on weekends—essential personnel or flex-time staff—and she made her way to a quiet corner. At first she pulled out her cell phone, but then she saw that the charge on the battery was low. When she stayed over at Jane and George's, she never remembered to bring a charger. Instead, she picked up the phone on the desk she'd commandeered and tapped a button to get an outside line.

A call to information got her the number for the Medford Police Department, and she dialed quickly, glancing up at the clock. Just after nine a.m.

"Medford Police, your call is being recorded. This is Sergeant Bryce."

"Good morning, Sergeant. My name is Caitlin McCandless. This is sort of a weird phone call, I guess, because I'm not sure what you can do about it. I live in an apartment on Boston Avenue, but my aunt and uncle live on Badger Road. George and Jane Wadlow. Anyway, during the night and early this morning there's been a car parked on the street a few doors down, in front of the home of a family who are away on vacation. The driver stays in the car, almost like they're conducting surveillance, and during the night my aunt witnessed what she thought of as a shift change, with one car taking over from another. She's kind of unsettled by the whole thing, so I said I'd look into it for her. I went out this morning to try to talk to the driver, but as soon as I approached, the car took off. I guess my first question is whether or not you guys are conducting any surveillance on Badger Road."

The sergeant made a noise in his throat, a kind of "hmmm." Then he took a breath Cait could hear over the phone.

"I don't know of any ongoing surveillance, Ms. . . . I'm sorry, what was it?"

"McCandless."

"Are you a police officer, ma'am?"

"No. Why would you think that?" Cait asked.

"Just a tone of voice. But don't worry, it's a compliment," Sergeant Bryce said.

"I was National Guard, did a double tour in Baghdad, so I guess you learn how to give a report."

"That explains it. Look, I seriously doubt we've got anything going over there, but if you can hang on a second, I'll confirm."

"I'd appreciate it," Cait said, and then she waited.

She expected to be on hold for a while, but Sergeant Bryce came back on the line after a minute or two.

"Ms. McCandless, I spoke to the detectives on duty and, according to them, there is no surveillance operation in your aunt's area."

"In some ways, that's even more troubling. When I went out there earlier, the guy took off like a bat out of hell. They're not making much of an effort to go unnoticed, but he definitely did not want to talk to me. It felt wrong. My aunt lives there, but she also watches my daughter while I'm at work. I'd really like to know what these people are up to."

"Can you describe the car?" Sergeant Bryce asked.

"New model Audi. I got the plate number, actually," she said, slipping the scrap of paper from her pocket. "Do you have a pen?"

"I do. Shoot."

She rattled off the license plate number and then tucked the paper back into her pocket, just in case. Sergeant Bryce seemed competent and helpful, but she knew better than to rely on someone who had no personal interest in solving the problem. Maybe that was cynical of her, but she liked to think of it as merely practical. There were police who were very good at their jobs and took their duty as a sacred trust, and there were others who didn't care very much.

"All right," Sergeant Bryce said. "I'll send a car by there right now. If my guys don't see anything, they will do another pass tonight, after dark. Meanwhile, I'll run this plate number and see if I come up with anything. I'm on duty tomorrow, so if you want to give a call back then, I'll fill you in on whatever we come up with. In the meantime, give me a number where I can reach you."

Cait gave him her cell phone number—reminding herself to charge it—and her home number as well. He asked her to spell both her last name and Jane's.

"I really appreciate this, Sergeant," she said. "Thanks for taking it seriously."

"No worries. If some creep was sitting outside my house in the middle of the night, I'd want to know who it was, too."

"Thanks. Seriously. I'll talk to you tomorrow, if not sooner."

After she hung up, she sat back in the chair and smiled. As bizarre as the last twelve hours or so had been, Cait felt like she had people looking out for her. It was a nice feeling. She wasn't happy with the idea of being interviewed for the newscast, but she allowed herself to believe that the fallout might not be as bad as she feared.

A little instant celebrity, she thought. *Fifteen seconds of fame. What harm could it do?*

-17--

The first thing that alerted Voss to the fact that something had gone wrong was the helicopter. A chopper buzzed overhead as they drove toward the Sarasota police station, headed in the same direction. A glance upward revealed police tags on the tail, but she told herself that it could be anything. Maybe the chief of police had been at a conference and Sarasota taxpayers were content to fund transportation by helicopter. Or perhaps there had been a chase out on the highway and the chopper crew was returning from their job.

But then Voss spotted a news helicopter in the distance, moving toward the city's gleaming new police station, and she ran out of ways to pretend that this wasn't a bad sign.

"Are you getting the idea that this isn't going to go smoothly?" she asked, glancing at Ed Turcotte, whose grip had tightened on the steering wheel.

Turcotte swore under his breath and blew through a red light, banging a hard left that made the tires skid and squeak. Voss braced herself on the dashboard and said nothing more for several long seconds as they raced ahead.

The city had built a new police headquarters in the past few years—a contemporary structure of blue and silver, all clean lines. It looked more like the corporate headquarters of a TV network than a police station, but as Turcotte accelerated toward it, Voss had to admit the building was, at the very least, shiny. At the moment, however, no one would be paying attention to its architecture or the gleam of Florida sunshine off the windows. Sarasota police cars were arranged in a pattern all along the front of the building. Others had blocked off the street on either side. Still more vehicles—state police, Sarasota County Sheriff's Office, emergency personnel—were parked at the edges of the cordoned area.

Whatever crisis they'd happened upon, it was unfolding even as Turcotte pulled to the curb near the roadblock. Cops crouched behind their car, guns drawn, radios in hand. Tactical officers had been deployed on the roof. Voss glanced up and saw them hustling into position, the tips of their weapons visible, but she didn't know what they hoped to accomplish. Something was going on inside, and they weren't going to be able to do much from the roof, unless they had the equipment to rappel down and crash through the glass.

As she climbed out of the car she looked up at the roof again, wondering if that was, indeed, what they planned. If they had been in the building when it started, they couldn't easily get snipers into place on the roofs of nearby structures. They had to work with the hand they were dealt.

"Let's find out what this is," Turcotte said as he slammed his door, keys jangling in his hand.

Voss fell in beside him and they walked toward the cops manning the vehicles comprising the roadblock. She dug out her ID and Turcotte did the same.

"FBI," Turcotte told the young uniformed officer who stared at them as they approached.

"Damn, you guys are fast," the uniform said, wide-eyed.

Voss thought the kid was in shock, that when Sarasota P.D. built their glittery new station house, he'd figured it was some kind of impregnable fortress. *So much for that.*

"What the hell's going on in there?" Turcotte asked.

The young cop shook his head and gave a little laugh of disbelief. "Some guy we had in custody attacked one of our people and got his hands on a gun. From what I'm hearing, he killed at least three so far, including Detective Birnbaum, and now he's got hostages."

Voss ran a hand over her face. "Shit," she said, glancing at Turcotte. The second she had seen the chaos spread out in front of the building, she had known. "This is our suspect, isn't it?"

Turcotte nodded. "Most likely."

Voss scowled and led the way around the roadblock vehicles. She crouched low and ran toward a group of police officers who were behind a box truck with SARASOTA POLICE

DEPARTMENT emblazoned on the side. She knew a situational command center when she saw one.

Turcotte joined her when she was maybe twenty yards from the truck.

"Wetherell's with them," he said.

A quick glance confirmed it. Wetherell was the Florida State Police captain who'd been working the Greenlaw case with them. When the report had come in that Karim al-Jubouri had been arrested in a traffic stop and brought here, they'd had word that Captain Wetherell would meet them. But obviously the circumstances had changed.

A couple of the cops surrounding the command center got twitchy when she and Turcotte approached. Voss held her ID in front of her like a talisman and they cleared her a path. Wetherell spotted her, then saw Turcotte hustling behind her, and Voss saw him tap the shoulder of an aging black man in a uniform that identified him as a lot higher up the ladder than a street cop.

Through the open doors of the truck, she saw cops wearing heavy headphones and watching screens and monitors. They'd have remote access to the security cameras inside the building, and probably to the phone and Internet service inside as well. As Voss and Turcotte reached the truck, Wetherell and the man in charge came to meet them.

"Agent Turcotte," Captain Wetherell said. "This is Ron Lewis, deputy commissioner of the Sarasota P.D. Ron, meet Ed Turcotte, FBI, and Rachael Voss, Homeland Security ICD."

Deputy Commissioner Lewis had a firm handshake, but he was only half paying attention. Beads of sweat glistened on his forehead, and Voss didn't think it was just from the warmth of the day. He glanced toward the police station.

"Sorry the commissioner can't be here himself," he said. "He's otherwise engaged."

The grim tone had the air of gallows humor. Voss knew it well. Three of the officers under Lewis's command were already dead, and others might still die before the day was out. The man wiped a big coffee-brown hand across his face and then looked at them.

"I'd ask what I can do for you," he said, glancing from Voss to Turcotte, "but I'm more interested in what you can do for me."

"We'll do whatever we can, Commissioner," Turcotte said.

Voss glanced at Wetherell. "Are we assuming this is our guy?"

Wetherell's expression darkened. "We know it is. Security cameras caught it all. Street cops stopped al-Jubouri because the sticker on his license plate was out-of-date."

Details, Voss thought. *Always the little details.*

"The officers ran his license and registration," Lewis explained. "They got a hit—the BOLO you-all put out for him—and took him into custody on the spot. But while they were escorting him to an interview room, he went after one of the officers, managed to get hold of his weapon . . . and now he's got a lot of weapons and a lot of hostages."

"What does he want?" Turcotte asked.

Voss glanced at the building, then at the cops doing their job in the command center in the back of the truck. The tactical squad would be getting their orders from there, as would the rest of the officers gathered around. She and Turcotte might be talking to the men in charge, but while this conversation was going on, the situation was still unfolding.

"So far he's made only one demand," Wetherell said. "He wants a computer with Internet access and a camera."

Voss felt her heart sink. She looked at Turcotte and saw that he understood.

"There aren't going to be any more demands," Voss said.

"What do you mean?" Lewis asked. "He'll want a car or a helicopter. Safe passage out of here. He'll take at least one hostage with him. One of the detectives has already offered to be that hostage."

"That's not going to happen," Turcotte said. "With this guy's history and training, you've got to consider him a terrorist. He knows he's not getting out of there unless it's to prison or the morgue. If he wants a camera and 'net access, I'm guessing it's so he can go live, make some kind of statement. Whatever cause he represents, he wants to make sure he's a martyr for it. Publicly."

"That's not going to happen," Wetherell said, turning to Lewis. "You can't give it to him."

"What other option do I have? Send in the tactical guys? It'll be a bloodbath."

Voss stepped in a little closer. These men were all physically imposing, while she was petite and blond. Men who didn't know her tended to flirt, and sometimes she flirted back, just to fulfill their expectations. But these men reacted to her now because of her intensity. She might not be able to loom over them, but she could be formidable when she wanted to be.

"You're not thinking clearly, Commissioner," she said. "No offense. Under the circumstances, it's understandable. But right now I want you to listen to me."

She had their attention.

"This thing can only lead to more people dead. There's no way for it to go any other way. You said there are three dead already. If we're lucky, al-Jubouri will be the only new name added to that list. But odds are that he won't be. This guy is ready to die, and ready to pull the trigger. At some point, he's going to start killing people. The question you've got to ask yourself is, how good is your tactical unit? And can they save lives by going in now?"

The deputy commissioner's dark-coffee skin had turned café au lait. "I don't know."

Turcotte shook his head. "The answer's no. At least for now. Have your negotiators keep him talking. Promise him 'net access and tell him we're working on finding him a laptop with a camera. Buy us some time."

"Time for what?" Captain Wetherell said. "This situation is not going to improve."

Voss shot him a hard look. "Captain, SSA Turcotte here used to run one of the FBI's best counterterrorism units. He's going to get his own people in here."

Turcotte looked at Lewis. "Commissioner, all decisions from this point are going to have to come from the FBI. The Hostage Rescue Team at Quantico has been notified—"

"There's no time for anyone at Quantico to get here before this thing goes south," Wetherell said.

"I have an FBI SWAT team on the way from the field office," Turcotte said. "When they arrive, they will decide how to proceed in a manner that involves the least possible risk for the hostages. Meanwhile, your people are to maintain their current positions unless al-Jubouri surrenders or puts himself in the line of fire, in which case they are to shoot him."

"To wound, not to kill," Voss added.

"What?" Wetherell asked, incredulous.

Voss turned to Turcotte. "If at all possible, we've got to keep this guy alive."

"Not if it means giving him extra time to harm his hostages," Turcotte replied.

"Right now he's the only link we have to the Greenlaw murders, never mind whatever terrorist activities his cell is involved with," Voss argued. "And he may well be our only hope of finding that missing baby up in Maine."

Turcotte exhaled, then turned to stare at the police station in furious silence. The sun glinted off its glass and steel.

"Shit," he whispered. "There's no way this ends well."

Sometimes Voss hated being right.

-18--

The shopping cart had a squeaky wheel. Jane felt sure it had not been squealing when she'd first plopped Leyla into the baby seat and strapped her in, tucking her chubby legs through the openings in the mesh. The squeaking had begun about halfway through their sojourn amongst the aisles of Super Stop & Shop, and by then there had been too many things in the cart to switch it for another.

Not that Jane had been tempted to switch at that point. A little squeak was not so irritating, especially when she had Leyla there, blowing little bubbles and smiling, not to mention reaching out to grab something if Jane parked the cart too close to a shelf. Leyla made her happy enough that at first she had managed to ignore the squeak. The baby girl had that effect on a lot of people, drawing smiles wherever she went.

Now, though, with the cart full and the groceries paid for, the squeak had finally started to fray her nerves.

"Okay, you ready to go home?" she asked Leyla.

The baby gurgled adorably, which helped take the edge off. Jane sighed in amusement at her own agitation and pushed the cart along the front of the store. Having Leyla around had added a little to her weekly grocery bill, though she would never mention it to Cait. Her niece always brought diapers and baby food over, but it never seemed enough, so Jane supplemented that with purchases of her own. Tommy showed no signs of giving her a grandchild anytime soon, so if she spoiled Leyla a little bit—with the occasional toy or new outfit—she just considered it "grandma practice."

A couple of teenagers were coming into the store, bumping each other and snickering in the shared-secret way girls that age always seemed to have. When they saw Leyla, though, their eyes lit up.

"Oh, my God, she is so freakin' cute," one of the girls said, as her friend crouched to make faces at the baby.

"She *is* pretty adorable," Jane agreed.

"Except when she cries, right?" the girl said.

But then the crouching girl gave Jane an odd look—one she recognized. She had seen it many times before. "So, are you, like, the nanny or something?"

"She's my niece's baby, actually," Jane explained. "Her father is from Iraq."

"Oh," the girl said, obviously not quite sure what to make of that. But Jane saw a new curiosity in the girl's eyes.

Jane waited for them to move along and then she pushed the cart outside, strapped Leyla into her car seat, and then loaded the groceries into the trunk. The change in temperature rippled across her skin. She hadn't realized how chilly it had been inside the Super Stop & Shop with the air conditioner going full blast, but the August sun quickly warmed her. She thought that anyone who complained about the heat on such a splendid day ought to shut up come January, when the snow was hip-deep and the wind chill below zero.

At the moment, though, winter was very far away. She wore a blue cotton spaghetti-strap top, blue jeans, and sandals. In the supermarket, she had bought Popsicles and ice-cream sandwiches—George loved those, and had since childhood—but now she'd started thinking perhaps they ought to leave the snacks in the freezer and go out and get a decent ice-cream cone this afternoon.

Better yet, we should go visit Karen.

As she fired up her Accord and pulled out of the parking lot, turning toward home, she wondered how Caitlin would feel about a trip down to the Cape tomorrow. They could visit George's sister, Karen, spend the day at the beach in Chatham, and if they stayed late enough they might well miss most of the traffic. Even if George didn't want to make the drive, they could still go. *Girls' day out.*

She mulled it over while driving, but as she turned from Winthrop Street onto Badger Road, a chill went through her. While she and Leyla had been shopping, she hadn't thought about the strangeness last night and this morning with those cars across the street. Now she tensed, wondering if they might have returned. But as she drove up Badger Road, she saw no sign of the mysterious observers and she exhaled with relief, her smile returning.

"What do you think, Leyla?" Jane said, as she pulled into her driveway. "Do you want to go to the beach tomorrow?"

The car seat was rear-facing, but Jane could hear Leyla burbling to herself.

"I'll take that as a yes," she said as she killed the engine. "Just give me a second, babycakes," Jane added as she got out of the car.

She opened the back door to keep the heat from accumulating in the car. Leyla shook a ring of plastic keys at her. Jane grinned, then popped the trunk and surveyed her groceries. There were several plastic sacks, but most of the groceries were in reusable fabric bags with the Super Stop & Shop logo on the side. Some of Jane's friends teased her about being a twenty-first-century hippie; she tried to tell them that doing her part for the environment didn't make anyone a hippie these days, just practical.

She'd gather up a few bags, then take Leyla into the house with the first load, she decided. That way, the baby would be cool in the house while she collected the rest of the groceries.

Without the car's motion and the noise of the engine to lull her, Leyla had started to fuss. In another minute, the baby would start to cry.

"I'm coming, sweetie," Jane called as she juggled the bags into a more stable position in her arms. But when she went around to the backseat to collect Leyla, she let out a little yelp as she discovered a man standing just three feet away.

"I'm sorry," he said, smiling. "I didn't mean to scare you. It's just . . . you've got your baby there, and I thought I'd see if you needed help."

Jane laughed, embarrassed that she'd been so startled. But then she hesitated. Where the hell had he come from? Thirtyish and blue-eyed, he was handsome in a scruffy sort of way, but she didn't recognize him; he didn't live on Badger Road.

"Oh, she's not mine. I'm a little too old for babies," she said, studying him warily. "And I've got it. But thanks for—"

An engine roared, a gleaming black sedan skidded to a halt at the curb, and Jane turned, panicking as realization struck her.

Her blue-eyed helper punched her so hard that she staggered backward and banged her head on the open trunk lid, the bags dropping from her hands. Dazed, her mind whirling with questions amidst the pain and anger, still Jane reacted. She caught the bumper and forced herself up, even as her attacker gripped her throat with one hand and shoved with the other, trying to force her back toward the trunk.

"No, you won't, you son of a bitch," she grunted, fighting back.

As she tried to break the grip on her throat, she kicked out with one foot and felt sick satisfaction at the solid connection. The heel of her sandal struck his knee and the bastard swore, loosening his grip.

Jane reached up and slammed the trunk. No way was he getting her in there. He grabbed both her arms and drove her against the rear of the car. Pain shot through her back. She tore her right hand free, curled her fingers into a fist, and punched him with all her strength. Blood spurted from his nose, but he hit her back so hard she thought something cracked in her jaw.

She screamed as loud as she could, in both fury and alarm. As he grabbed her hands again, she pushed off from the car and started kicking him. He shielded his balls but she got him in the shin several times—all the while wishing she'd worn anything but sandals.

Leyla had started to cry, then wail, and then scream, face turning red. As she did, a man got out of the driver's side of the black sedan. Dark-skinned, hair clipped down to stubble, with a scar on his left cheek, he looked like a killer or a lawyer; it was hard to tell which.

"Stop fucking around and get the goddamn baby!" he snapped.

Jane turned to ice inside. She'd thought rape, murder— thought that the scruffy, blue-eyed man wanted to do terrible things to her—but they wanted Leyla.

"Not a chance," she hissed, reaching toward the open car door, and the baby.

That was her mistake. The guy twisted her hair in his hand and yanked back hard, hauled her around and drove her face into the back of the car. He lifted her by the hair, ready to do it again, but she stomped her heel down on his foot and drove her elbow back into his gut, and then she started to scream again.

"Help me! They're trying to steal the baby! Please, some-one—"

Jane heard the other guy shouting in alarm, heard the roar of another engine approaching, and she had a flicker of hope that her cries would be answered. But then the son of a bitch renewed his grip and drove her face-first into the back of the Accord, and she collapsed to the driveway.

She tried to rise, but the world tilted around her. She saw her attackers jump into the sedan, got a last glimpse of the African-American guy behind the wheel, and heard the tires squeal as it tore away. For an instant she wondered if she had blacked out long enough for them to take Leyla. But then a police car skidded to the curb and an officer jumped out, barking something into his radio as he came toward her, even as the bastards got away.

"Are you all right?" the cop called.

Jane tried to answer, but she had held on to consciousness as long as she could, and now darkness crowded at the edges of her vision.

Even unconscious, she could hear the baby scream.

-19--

Cait's cell phone had beeped twice while she was on the phone with Sergeant Bryce, but when she checked it before leaving the office, she found that it had died. In the car, she searched around for her car charger before realizing it was in the trunk, zipped inside her gym bag. She debated retrieving it, but decided that by the time she found a convenient spot to pull over, she'd be nearly back at her aunt and uncle's house. It gave her an odd feeling to be disconnected from the world, but Leyla was in good hands and, after all, people had managed to survive thousands of years before the invention of the cell phone.

Still, she hurried back to Medford, driving just a little faster than she had on the way in. Despite her rationalizations, she did not like being cut off, and a certain amount of trepidation had settled into her heart.

When she turned onto Badger Road and saw the police cars parked in front of her aunt and uncle's house, she felt all the blood drain from her face. Dread seized her, and yet somehow she found herself slowing down, letting the car coast, staring at the pair of police cars—one in the driveway and one at the curb. Despite the heat of the day, gooseflesh rose on her arms and the small hairs stood up on the back of her neck as she pulled to the curb behind a police car.

Trying not to panic, she thought back to her conversation with Sergeant Bryce. He'd get the Medford Police to send a patrol car by to see if the Audi had returned to Badger Road. Maybe they had stopped in to confirm her story with Auntie Jane and Uncle George. That made sense. Sergeant Bryce had been so nice—*Nice Bryce,* she thought crazily—that she could see them doing that, going the extra mile.

Or something awful had happened.

Cait slammed the door and bolted across the lawn and then the driveway, racing up the front steps. She yanked open the screen door and stepped inside.

An enormous bear of a man in a police uniform stood by the fireplace, holding Leyla in his arms. He had lifted her up so that she could see herself in the mirror, and both of them were smiling, the pudgy cop waggling his eyebrows at his own reflection, trying to make Leyla laugh.

Relief flooded Cait when she saw her daughter safe and smiling. But then she took in the rest of the tableau on display in the living room, and a knot formed in her gut. Jane sat on the sofa, her face swollen and bruised and her lip split. A bloody bandage covered most of her left cheek and a small butterfly bandage tugged closed a cut on her forehead. Her left eye had gone bloodshot red.

George sat next to her, holding her hand, even as he chatted with an auburn-haired woman in a dark suit who perched on the edge of the coffee table. A handsome, gray-haired man—also in a suit—sat in a chair opposite the sofa, and behind him stood a second uniformed officer. But Cait was so stunned by Jane's appearance that these other details made only vague impressions.

As she entered, all conversation ceased and everyone looked at her.

"Auntie?" Cait said.

"It's all right, Caitlin," Jane replied, her voice a mumble thanks to her swollen lips. "She's okay. I wouldn't let them—"

She began to stand, but George stopped her.

"Settle down, Jane. You need to stay calm," he said.

Cait glanced around at the officers and detectives—for the man and woman in suits were obviously police as well—and found that all eyes were upon her. Leyla had heard her voice and now reached toward her, starting to cry in frustration that the huge bear of a cop was not carrying her to her mother.

"What happened?" Cait demanded. "Oh, my God, what's going on?"

She crossed to the big cop, afraid for a moment that he would refuse to give Leyla to her, but then the man handed the baby over and Cait cradled her daughter against her chest. As she did, the auburn-haired woman stood up from the coffee table, picked imaginary lint off of her jacket, and fixed Cait with a grim look.

"Your aunt was assaulted, Ms. McCandless—" the woman began.

"They wanted Leyla," Jane said. "But I fought, honey. I wouldn't let them have her."

Cait clapped a hand over her mouth, feeling like she might vomit. Her breath came in short, stuttery gasps against her palm.

George rubbed Jane's hands, as though he was trying to warm them. It made no sense; the temperature in the house must be eighty-five, even with the cross-breeze from the open windows and screen door.

"A man attacked her while she was unloading the groceries," George said, looking at Cait. "Right there in the driveway. Another guy drove up in a car."

"I thought they wanted me at first," Jane said, staring wide-eyed at Cait. "But then one of them said something about the baby, and I knew, and then I . . ."

Jane started to cry, and that was when, finally, Cait felt her own tears begin to burn at the corners of her eyes. She kissed Leyla's head and cheeks and then rushed over to the sofa, where she sat next to Jane.

"Thank you, Auntie. Oh, God, thank you so much. But what about you?"

"The EMTs wanted to take your aunt to the hospital," the female detective said. "It's likely she has a concussion. But she refused to leave until you came back for your daughter."

A torrent of emotion flooded Cait. Fear for Leyla, gratitude, and worry for her aunt.

"Go!" Cait said. "I've got her now, Auntie. Please, go. I'll follow in my car. Or I can drive us all."

"Actually, Ms. McCandless, Detective Monteforte and I would like to ask you a few questions," said the male detective, speaking up for the first time.

"We'll be fine, Caitlin," George said. "You don't want to be sitting around the emergency room with Leyla. You should go home. Or wait here, if you like, until we come back."

"But—"

"I'm going to be all right," Jane insisted.

Cait blinked, trying to process it all. Auntie Jane would be okay. She could accept that. And, yes, she'd wait here for them to come home. But . . . the cops wanted to talk to her?

Of course they did. Someone had tried to snatch Leyla, and they wanted to find out if it was random or if they'd specifically targeted her baby. Thoughts tumbled through her mind in quick succession. With the mysterious surveillance on Badger Road and after her conversation with Sergeant Bryce, she couldn't help thinking that, for whatever reason, this hadn't been a random abduction attempt.

"Okay," she told the detectives. "Whatever you need."

Jane squeezed her arm, leaned over and kissed Leyla's head, and then kissed Cait's cheek before standing up.

"Officer Parker will drive you to the hospital," Detective Monteforte said.

The uniformed cop who had been standing behind the other detective responded to this, moving toward the door. George reached down to gently brush Leyla's thin hair with his fingers. Then he steadied Jane as they moved around the coffee table and followed Officer Parker from the room.

"I'll be here when you get back," Cait called after them.

Then she and Leyla were alone with the police. The burly officer over by the fireplace busied himself looking at family photos on the mantel while the gray-haired man gazed at his partner expectantly.

"I'm Detective Anne Monteforte," the woman said, taking a seat on the sofa. "This is Detective Jarman, and the sasquatch who had your daughter when you came in is Officer Grant. I think Grant's available for babysitting, by the way."

Cait smiled politely at this attempt at humor.

"Why don't you sit down, Ms. McCandless," Detective Jarman said.

He had strong features, and his skin was so dark his face looked carved from cherrywood. Though he'd said little, his very presence had a reassuring weight to it. Yet it did feel a little odd that he, a stranger, was inviting her to take a seat in her aunt and uncle's living room.

"Call me Cait, please," she said, as she settled onto the sofa beside Detective Monteforte and sat Leyla on her lap. The baby played with Cait's fingers, trying to bring them to her mouth to be gnawed on. She had a new tooth on the way.

"Cait," Monteforte said. "We've been over the day's events with your aunt. I want you to understand right up front that we've seen this sort of thing before. We're also aware of the call you placed to Sergeant Bryce earlier this morning. In fact, it's thanks to that call that things didn't go even worse here today. Bryce sent a patrol car to see if there were any suspicious vehicles parked on the street, and as Officer Grant came down the street, he saw the attack in progress."

Cait turned to Grant. "You saved them?"

Grant shrugged. "Right place, right time."

"Thank you," Cait said. She kissed Leyla's head. "Thank you so much."

"The odds are that this was a random thing," Monteforte continued. "Even if these guys were watching during the night and this morning, it's likely they were looking for a target, for a woman with a baby—"

"Why?" Cait asked.

Jarman shrugged. "I can think of a few reasons, all ugly. But the point is that we also have to consider the possibility that it wasn't random. So we need to ask you some questions."

"Shoot."

Jarman leaned forward in his chair. "Your uncle told us that the baby . . . that Leyla's father is deceased."

Cait nodded, grateful that she wouldn't have to tell the story. "Yes."

"What about his family? Is it possible that any of . . . I'm sorry, what was his name?" Monteforte asked.

"Nizam Qadir."

"Right." Monteforte went on, "Is it possible any of Mr. Qadir's relatives might think they ought to have custody of Leyla? Grandparents? Anyone?"

Cait glanced back and forth between the two detectives, blinking in surprise. This had never even occurred to her, and the idea startled her. On her lap, Leyla had managed to get the knuckle of her mother's right index finger into her mouth and nibbled it hard with her single tooth.

"I really don't think so," Cait said. "I mean, Nizam's parents and brother are dead. As far as I know his two sisters are still alive, but they're all in Iraq. His younger sister and I write letters. I've sent pictures of the baby, but she's never said anything."

"So it's not impossible," Monteforte said, glancing at Jarman.

"I guess not. But I'd say it's pretty unlikely."

Jarman sat back in his chair. "I agree it's far-fetched. So let's talk about A-Train."

Again, the line of questioning mystified her.

"A-Train?" she said, hearing the emptiness of her own voice. "You've gotta be kidding me."

Cait felt sick. Someone had tried to *take* her child. The thought filled her with a horror she had never before experienced—not even in Iraq. She could endure any physical torment that left her alive, but the idea that someone had tried to take Leyla was ripping her apart. And the cops were going off on tangents that seemed useless to her.

Monteforte cocked her head to one side, studying Cait. "You humiliated the man last night. It's obvious he's capable of violence—"

"Capable of convincing two other guys to beat the shit out of a middle-aged woman and try to snatch a baby? My aunt saw the video from last night. She'd have recognized A-Train if he was one of them. And, yeah, the guy's capable of slapping his wife around, definitely, but what was he going to do if he got my daughter? Kill her? Blackmail me? I don't see it. You need to focus on those cars. I tried approaching the one this morning, and it took off, but I got the plate number. I gave it to Sergeant Bryce. He was going to run it."

"He's still working on it," Jarman said.

"Hang on," Monteforte said, rising from the sofa. "I'll check in with him, see what he's turned up."

She went into the kitchen, leaving Cait and Leyla alone with Jarman and the silent Officer Grant. Leyla had started to fuss. Cait kissed her daughter's head, shushing her, and bounced her a little on her lap.

"We're not going to keep you much longer," Detective Jarman said.

Leyla started to cry, and Cait was relieved for the excuse to get up.

"Sorry, Detective, but it's time for her bottle."

When Cait had started working, she had pumped breast milk for Jane to give the baby, but within days of taking a bottle for the first time, Leyla had started to lose interest in breast-feeding. The milk didn't come fast enough for her and she'd grow frustrated and cry, refusing to latch on. Cait would have liked to nurse the baby longer, but with her schedule and Leyla's fussing, she'd had no choice but to move entirely to formula just to keep up with the baby's demands.

As she stood, Detective Monteforte stepped back into the room, just completing her phone call. Leyla would have to manage without her bottle for a couple of minutes longer.

"Thank you, Sergeant. Yeah, good. Much appreciated," Monteforte said. She ended the call and palmed her cell, gazing first at Cait and then at Jarman.

Cait could see the doubt in her eyes, mixed with confusion and disappointment.

"Anything?" Jarman asked.

Monteforte addressed her reply to Cait. "I spoke with Sergeant Bryce. He ran the license plate that you gave him but he came up with nothing. There's no plate with that number in Massachusetts or New Hampshire."

"It's a Mass plate. And the number I gave him was off that car. I'm a hundred percent sure of that."

"Maybe you wrote it down wrong?" Jarman suggested.

Cait shook her head. "I didn't."

Monteforte clipped her phone into the leather sheath on her belt. "That's a problem, Cait. There isn't a car on the road with that plate number."

Cait held Leyla tightly. The baby seemed to weigh more, as if she had somehow become more solid. She tried to let the anger flow out of her, breathing evenly, not wanting to upset her little girl.

"There is," she said, biting down on the words. "I saw it. Unless the plate was a fake."

Monteforte and Jarman glanced at each other, and Cait wanted to scream.

"I know what I saw," she said. "When the Audi tore out of here this morning, I got a face full of exhaust fumes. I can still smell them. And I wrote the number down correctly. The fact you can't find the registration should get you *more* curious, not make you assume I'm delusional."

"We're not discounting what you're saying, Cait," Monteforte replied. "But as we explained, we've got to investigate every avenue that might lead us to the answers we're all looking for."

Cait took a deep breath and let it out. "I hope you do, Detective," she said. "Investigate every avenue, I mean. We're not imagining all of this. And the A-Train thing . . . that's a waste of your time."

"And yet we have to talk to him," Jarman said.

Cait uttered a sound that was half sigh and half chuckle. "Great. Have fun with that. Are you going to have someone watching for these cars, in case they come back?"

Jarman narrowed his eyes, nostrils flaring. She had apparently pushed his buttons, but she was glad. Maybe it would wake him up a little.

"Officer Grant will be in his car, right out front, for a couple of hours. If you decide to go home during that time, he'll follow you and enter first."

Cait frowned, unconsciously rocking Leyla, the way she did whenever she wanted the baby to take a nap.

"Do you think I should be afraid to go home?" she asked.

"We're not saying that," Monteforte jumped in. "Not at all. Detective Jarman was just offering, in case you were concerned."

Cait glanced down at Leyla. "We'll be fine."

"Okay," Jarman said. "We'll have patrol cars drive by this house and your apartment building every few hours for the next couple of days, and you can always call if you see anything suspicious."

He stood, reached inside his jacket, and then handed her a business card. Cradling Leyla in one arm, Cait took it but did not bother to look at it. Monteforte produced her card as well.

"My cell phone number's on there, too," the female detective said. Then she glanced at Leyla, and her expression softened. "We're not ignoring you, Cait. I'm going to drive by tonight myself, see if one of those cars is parked down the street. But we don't have a lot to go on, which means we have to follow up on what we do have."

Cait just wanted them to leave so she could be alone with her daughter. "I get it, Detective. And I appreciate your help."

-20--

Voss stood inside the Sarasota P.D.'s command center vehicle, watching a blue screen and waiting for something to happen. The cop sitting at the computer in front of her was named Boyd, but she didn't know if that was his first name or his last. There were hundreds of computers inside the new twenty-first-century police station. Given the price tag on the construction, which she'd heard more than one cop muttering about, she was surprised they hadn't skimped on the tech. But it had been simple enough to locate a laptop in the building that had a camera built in, and to get an officer to volunteer to deliver that laptop to the windowless third-floor interview room where al-Jubouri had moved his hostages.

The guy might be a murderer and a terrorist, and he might be forgetful enough to drive with an expired registration, but it turned out he wasn't stupid. The non-hostage civilians inside the building had been evacuated, and most of the cops had gathered on the third floor, weapons ready, praying for an opportunity to kill the son of a bitch who had already shot three of their own. Of the three victims, two were DOA and one—earlier thought dead—had turned out to be alive, but in critical condition. The dead had already been retrieved, and the third victim had been taken out by EMTs. Voss had been told he was in surgery already, but nobody was making any promises about him pulling through.

The shooting had taken place in a corridor, and al-Jubouri had held a gun to the head of a fourth officer, threatening to kill him if the others didn't put their weapons down. Then he had directed the remainder of his hostages into the interview room, at gunpoint.

"Are we sure this is going to work?" Turcotte asked.

Voss glanced at him, then over at Deputy Commissioner Lewis and Captain Wetherell. Neither of them looked like they had an answer.

Boyd looked up from his computer. "It depends on how tech-savvy this guy is. If he goes to open a browser and it opens, and he's happy with that, we should be fine."

A tech on the inside had worked on the laptop before it had been delivered to what was now called the "hostage room." They had been trying to figure out a way to give al-Jubouri what he was asking for while still maintaining control of what he did with the computer once he had it. Voss figured in the post–Patriot Act era, the FBI must have a better way, but al-Jubouri knew there were computers in the building. He wasn't going to wait for some FBI geek squad to show up.

So they'd given him a laptop with one modification. The software used by the department—and millions of other people—allowed for remote access from another computer. If your laptop or PC was having serious problems, you could

contact a tech nerd or your corporate I.T. guy, and give them
access via an e-mail that was essentially a web link. All the
I.T. guy would have to do was click on the link and he'd be
able to remotely control your computer, move files around,
and do whatever else he wanted. You'd be sitting at your
desk, watching all the action on your own monitor or laptop
screen, as if the computer was doing everything by itself.

What the Sarasota P.D.'s tech guy had realized was that they
could reverse the process. Before giving al-Jubouri the laptop,
they had set it up as if the user—al-Jubouri—was the I.T. guy.
Everything he did on the laptop was actually him remotely
controlling an outside computer—in this case, the one in front
of Boyd, right there in the command center truck. So whatever
al-Jubouri did, they could see it. Every word he typed, every
link he clicked, anything he accessed, they could watch it all—
and they could cut him off at any point in that process.

It wasn't a perfect plan. If they cut him off, that would create its own problems. Certainly they could spin it, claim
something had gone wrong and they weren't interfering, but
he would only demand that they resolve the problem, and
then they were right back where they'd started. But for the
moment, at least, it would buy time for the FBI SWAT team
to get there, or for al-Jubouri to do something stupid, let his
guard down so the cops inside could get to him.

"He's on," Captain Wetherell said.

They all looked at the monitor, where the face of the terrorist looked back. His jaw was bruised and his beard matted
with blood. Al-Jubouri's eyes were wide with zeal. His face
loomed for a moment, as if he were looking right at them,
and then he backed away, leaving a young woman in a Sarasota P.D. uniform sitting in front of the camera. Her lips
trembled, but she didn't cry or scream. Al-Jubouri stood behind her with a gun in each hand—one aimed at her skull and
the other at the people not in view of the camera. Their shadows shifted and some of them muttered.

"Quiet!" al-Jubouri shouted, aiming at someone offscreen.

The female cop closed her eyes and tensed, waiting for the
shot, but it didn't come. After a moment she exhaled and
opened her eyes, but her terror had not abated.

Son of a bitch, Voss thought. She had been forced by circumstances to take a human life a handful of times in her career and those deaths haunted her, no matter how despicable the people might have been. But after the slaughter at the Greenlaw house, she didn't think that killing al-Jubouri would haunt her. It was letting him live that would get under her skin.

"This is risky," she said. "We should've waited for the FBI SWAT unit."

"If we didn't get him that laptop, he'd already have started killing them," Turcotte argued.

No one else spoke up; apparently they agreed.

Voss watched al-Jubouri in the background of the camera's view. The guy was twitchy, but he seemed excited instead of terrified. That didn't bode well. She didn't know if it was luck or planning that had led him to choose an interview room that didn't have one-way observation glass. If he had taken his hostages into one of those rooms, others would have been able to see in without him seeing out. They might already have ended this thing. As it was, he had disconnected the camera in the corner of the room so no one could see what he was up to.

Now that had changed. He had *asked* for a camera, given them a window through which to watch the scene unfold. In addition to seeing whatever he might see on the laptop screen in front of him, they could spy on him through the laptop's camera. Employers sometimes used the software to make sure their work-at-home employees were actually working.

"Log on to Skype with the account I gave you," al-Jubouri told the female cop.

Every person in the truck fell silent as they watched her terrified features while she did as he asked.

"I'm in," she said.

"Bastard," someone growled offscreen. "You know you're never getting out of here."

Al-Jubouri smiled. Despite the temperature inside the truck, heated by the sun outside and the equipment within, Voss shivered. The killer didn't reply, but she could almost hear him speak the words. *I know.*

"We've got his Skype account," Boyd said, tapping keys. An image appeared on another monitor, off to the right of the first. "This is what he's seeing on the laptop."

"Call Jamil," al-Jubouri said.

She tried. Voss watched Boyd working the keyboard in the truck. Jamil Nassif had been the alias that Gharib al-Din had used traveling to Maine. If they could find him . . .

"If anyone answers on the other end, I'll try to disconnect them without disconnecting the slave link between the two computers," Boyd said. "He might suspect we're interfering, but more than likely he'll just assume it's problems with Skype or with the connection."

Turcotte sighed. "A lot of trouble just to buy us an hour or so."

"We're looking for an opening to take this guy out," Lewis said. "Another hour is an eternity of chances for him to give us that opening. And by then your tactical team will be here."

Turcotte nodded. He knew that, just as Voss did. But they didn't know what this guy really wanted, which meant they couldn't predict how he would behave from moment to moment.

The female cop with the laptop tried to get through on Skype several times, but al-Din didn't answer.

"See if there's any way to track that," Voss said.

Boyd glanced at her. "Nobody answered. Not a chance."

In the background of the camera shot, al-Jubouri grew more and more agitated.

"Keep trying," he snapped, glancing back and forth between the laptop and the other hostages—half a dozen cops and a civilian office worker—who were off camera.

"Anything?" he demanded.

"No," said the hostage cop he had chosen as his proxy. Voss thought she looked like she was trying to come to terms with the idea of dying.

"This is going to blow up in our faces," she said.

"Damn it, Voss, we had no way of knowing he wouldn't be able to get through!" Turcotte snapped. He dragged a hand across his mouth like a drunk in need of a bottle. "Fuck!"

On-screen, al-Jubouri came closer to the woman with the laptop. He peered over her shoulder, glancing back at his hostages every second or two. The guy was still twitchy.

"We've got to go in," Voss said.

"Not yet. Let's just see what he does next," Lewis said. "I can't risk the lives of my people."

Voss spun on him. "They're already at risk!"

Turcotte had his cell phone pressed to his ear, demanding to know how long until his tactical team arrived.

"Call him!" Wetherell said. "Have the negotiators get him on the phone. See what else he wants. Anything to distract him."

Boyd threw up his hands. "If we do that, he could twig to the fact that we're watching him."

"If we don't—" Captain Wetherell began.

Al-Jubouri's voice interrupted him. "You know how to make a video on that thing?"

The female officer—Voss hated not knowing her name—gave a little shrug. "Not really. I don't . . . this isn't my laptop."

Al-Jubouri smiled thinly. He trained the gun in his right hand on the offscreen hostages and seemed to ponder a moment, as though deciding whether or not the time had come to kill them. Then he glanced back at the female cop—this nameless woman whose terror burned itself into Voss's subconscious. And maybe her conscience.

"How old are you?" the killer asked.

The woman blinked and glanced away from him. "Twenty-four."

"Twenty-four," al-Jubouri echoed, "and you have never made a video on your computer? Not for Facebook or the YouTube? I don't believe it."

"I—"

He put one of his guns against the back of her head, watching the offscreen hostages warily, still training the other gun on them.

"I do not believe you," al-Jubouri said. "You will prove me right, and we will make a video, you and I. Or you will prove me wrong, and you will die, and someone else in this room will take your place."

"You piece of shit," said the same gruff voice they'd heard from off camera before. "If you pull that trigger, they're coming through the door after you. You know that. You're a dead man."

Al-Jubouri raised his eyebrows. "Are we not all dead men? It is only a question of when we deliver ourselves to death."

Voss knew it then. She had suspected it all along, but now she saw the cold certainty in al-Jubouri's eyes and there could be no denying the truth. He intended to die. Al-Jubouri knew it was his only possible exit. He had wanted to get a message to someone, some kind of visual, but with Skype not working, he needed to make a video. Maybe he meant to post it, as he'd said, on YouTube or Facebook. Or maybe he wanted to make some kind of jihadist speech before he died, to show the world he had taken these hostages. But thus far he had not said a damn thing about Allah or Islam, never mind al Qaeda or any other cause or belief.

"Video," al-Jubouri said, pushing the barrel of the gun against the back of the female cop's head.

"Leave her alone, asshole," the gruff voice snarled.

Al-Jubouri rolled his eyes. Whoever that gruff voice belonged to—uniform or detective—the guy was pushing al-Jubouri too far. Voss watched the glint in his eyes go dull, and the way he sighed, exhaling in surrender. And though he didn't say the words, she could see the *fuck it* sentiment in his face. He was done.

"Go," Voss said. Turcotte looked up at her. "Damn it, Ed! Go!"

Turcotte picked up his radio and gave the order. "Go, go, go!"

Al-Jubouri pulled the trigger. Someone shouted in pain— the gruff-voiced man. There were cries of fear and shouts of fury, along with the sound of people hitting the deck and diving under tables. A uniformed cop rushed at al-Jubouri, who shot him in the face—and all they could do was watch.

The female cop with the laptop jumped up, searching for someplace to run. Al-Jubouri shot her, but he only had half his attention on her and the bullet punched through her shoulder. She spun around and fell out of the frame. A drop of blood obscured much of the camera's view, smeared in a veil of red.

The door blew open. Gas canisters clattered, clouds of smoke erupting in the room. Cops in Kevlar burst into the room. The first one took three bullets, at least one of which hit flesh instead of Kevlar, because the cop clutched his throat and collapsed, letting the others jump over him.

Voss didn't see any more. She ran, thinking about the guy with the bullet in his throat and the young woman in uniform whose name she wished she knew. She jumped out of the truck, barely aware that Turcotte was behind her. As she bolted through the police cordon and raced for the entrance to the building, shouting for the Sarasota cops there to open the door and let her through, she spotted a black BMW off to the right, parked near the car she and Turcotte had arrived in. Norris, the asshole from Black Pine, stood leaning against the hood, talking on his cell phone. His ankles were crossed and his free arm was across his chest. He looked casual and bored, cavalier about the violence erupting inside, and she couldn't help wishing he had been one of the hostages upstairs.

Cops got out of her way. Others didn't, maybe those who had friends or partners in the hostage room. She followed them into the stairwell, footfalls echoing off the walls, sharing their collective held breath as every one of them wondered how many people were going to die in the building today.

Behind her, Turcotte called her name, trying to keep up. Voss ignored him, running upward until she burst into the third-floor corridor along with a dozen others.

It was already over. Cops were milling around, weapons still drawn but dangling at their sides, wearing crestfallen expressions. One old detective who should have been retired by now wiped tears from his eyes. The cop who'd been shot in the throat sprawled half-in and half-out of the interview room. His blood was so fresh that the crimson pool around him was still spreading, but his eyes stared glassily at the ceiling. There was no hope for him.

Gun in her right hand, Voss dug out her ID with her left. "Homeland Security," she announced, and they let her pass.

She stepped into the hostage room. Someone knelt by the female cop, pressing a jacket against her wound, but she was sitting up. She'd be okay, despite the fact that the laptop had been sprayed with her blood. The civilian aide in the room, a fiftyish woman with stylish glasses and a crisp, short hairdo, had been grazed on the thigh. She, too, would be all right.

Of the other five hostages, two were dead. Voss felt certain one of them had had a gruff voice.

Cops crowded the room, weapons trained on Karim al-Jubouri. The wounds in his chest were bubbling and his breath hitched as he bled out. His eyes were glazed but they kept moving, as if he was trying to see into the next world, the afterlife he thought would be waiting for him.

"Talk to me, you son of a bitch," she said, dropping to her knees in the blood beside him. She felt Turcotte arriving behind her but didn't take her eyes off of al-Jubouri. "What do you want? Why did you kill the Greenlaws? Where are the others?"

Nothing.

"Who the hell *are* you people?"

His breath hitched again, but she thought it had been partly a laugh. Voss wanted to scream. She bit back her hatred for him and leaned closer.

"Don't you have any remorse at all?" she demanded.

"Did . . . did Herod have remorse?" he asked, coughing bloody spittle. "No. He did . . . what had to be done. This is the . . . the Herod Factor. Those who would . . . surrender . . . their beliefs for peace . . . must never be allowed to . . ."

He never finished the sentence. His last sound was a wet, burbling death rattle, and then he was still. Voss sat back, staring at him, and then she turned to look up at Turcotte.

"What was that?"

"No fucking idea," Turcotte said.

Frustrated and pissed off at herself and the world, Voss got up and looked around, shaking her head. After a second, she walked over to the female cop, who was on her feet and being helped from the room.

"Hey," Voss said. "You did just fine. You did what you needed to do."

The woman just nodded.

"What's your name?" Voss had to ask.

The cop looked at her oddly, eyes glazed from shock and blood loss, and let herself be led from the room.

Voss wasn't going to grieve for Karim al-Jubouri—she had no tears to shed for terrorists and child-killers—but she wished he had lived long enough to give her the answers she sought, and which he would now take to the grave.

-21--

After the police had gone, Cait sat on the sofa giving Leyla a bottle, relishing the feeling of holding her daughter close. Afterward, Leyla fell asleep, but Cait did not put her down for a nap. Nothing made her feel more at peace than when Leyla slept in her arms. When she was a little girl, Auntie Jane's chocolate shop had been her safe place, where she felt nothing could go wrong. But Sweet Somethings had been gone for years, and Nizam's death had unmoored her, made her feel that no place was safe . . . until Leyla had been born. Moments like this, cradling her sleeping child, this was her safe place. And today she had more reason than ever before to want to keep her daughter close.

She shifted her a little to the left and reached down to dig into a pocket for her cell phone. Only when she had slid it out did she recall that the battery had died, and her charger was back at her apartment. The nearest phone was on the kitchen counter. The last thing she wanted to do was get up from the sofa, but there was no way that she would be napping with Leyla today. Her thoughts whirled. The need to act, to do something, burned inside her, but she had no idea what that something might be. What could she possibly do, except be prepared in case whoever had come after Leyla tried again?

She froze. Would they do that? Try again? It seemed improbable, almost absurd, but she supposed it depended on why they had wanted her daughter in the first place. If they were organized, some kind of group that sold babies to desperate couples who longed for a child, or to pedophiles for their depravity, then certainly they wouldn't risk making a second try for the same child. The police were involved. To try again would be foolish.

But Cait could not pretend to understand the kind of people who would abduct an infant, so she would be on her guard.

Who are you kidding? You'll be on your guard for the rest of your life.

She stood and carried the baby into the kitchen. The phone lay on the counter, discarded by whoever had used it last— George, getting a call from Jane when the EMTs were patching her up? Cait picked it up and dialed Sean's cell number. She had needed to take care of Leyla first, to calm herself down, reassuring them both that everything would be all right. Now, though, she wanted to talk to her brother.

"Hello?" a man answered. The voice did not belong to Sean McCandless.

"Um, hi? Who is this?" she said.

"Can I help you?" the voice asked.

"You can help by telling me who you are and why you're answering Sean McCandless's phone."

The pause angered her. It had to be one of Sean's friends, either being presumptuous or trying to be funny, but Cait had little patience for anything today.

"If you'll tell me who's calling, I'll pass along the message, and someone will get back to you within twenty-four hours," the man said. From his voice, she guessed he was fairly young—early thirties, maybe—and not entirely used to stonewalling.

"This is Caitlin McCandless, Sean's sister. Look, all right, you won't tell me who you are. I get it. Secrets are part of his life, but I really, really need to talk to my brother. Is he away again? Is he going to be gone long?"

The pause again, and then a kind of sigh.

"Yes, he's away again. Someone will get back to you within twenty-four hours."

"Please. It's really important," she said.

One thing she had never gotten used to about cell phones was that, unlike conventional phones, there was no click when the call became disconnected, only that strange, flat nothing. Sometimes it took her a few seconds to realize that the line had gone dead. This time, she felt sure that the man had not hung up right away. Seconds went by.

"Hello?"

And now she heard that flatness, that nothingness. The call had ended. Maybe she had been mistaken and he had hung up after his last reply, and not been listening to her breathe.

She ought to call Sean's friend Brian Herskowitz. Sean had always said if she had an emergency when he was away, she could reach him that way. But the man on the phone had said someone would get back to her tomorrow, and Sean had not told her he was going away . . . had not given her the usual instructions to call Hercules. Maybe he was only gone for the day.

More troubled than ever, wishing for the soothing sound of her brother's voice, she carried Leyla back to the sofa. They lay down together and, though Cait was confident that her anxiety would keep her awake, she fell asleep within minutes, curled protectively around her baby, guarding her, even in her dreams.

The creak of the screen door woke her.

Cait inhaled sharply as she pushed herself up on one elbow. Leyla had already begun to stir, a bit of drool on her chin, so she didn't worry about waking the baby. Instead she scooped her up from the sofa and stood by the coffee table, tensed to run. But then the front door swung inward, and Uncle George entered, keys jangling in his hand. He reached back to help Auntie Jane into the house.

"I'm fine," Jane said.

"You have a concussion," he chided her.

"Caitlin?" Jane called, even as she turned to look through the doorway to the living room.

"I'm here," Cait said, hurrying toward them, even as Leyla stretched and yawned in her arms, beginning to scramble upright and looking around.

"I hoped you would be," Jane said. She smiled and reached for Leyla. "How's my sweetie doing?"

As Jane took the baby, Cait wiped her own mouth, realizing that Leyla hadn't been the only one to drool in her sleep. She smiled to herself.

"She's fine. We just woke up from a nap. More important, how are you? You have a concussion?"

George dropped his keys on a little table in the front hall. "A mild concussion, but that doesn't mean she can ignore the doctor," he said, even as he reached out to take Leyla from his wife. "You need rest, Jane. I'm going to insist."

Jane smiled and made a little pout, but she let George have the baby. Cait liked seeing her uncle with Leyla. He looked like the sort of man who wouldn't know what to do with a baby, but when he held Leyla he seemed to soften.

"Go up and lie down," he said to his wife. "I'll fix you some lunch."

But Jane wasn't quite ready to be still. As tired as she looked, and in spite of the cuts and bruises and swelling on her face—which had gone down quite a bit, thankfully—she turned to Cait.

"What about you and Leyla? Have you two eaten anything?"

Cait had started to shake her head before the first word was out of her aunt's mouth. "No way. I wanted to stay and make sure you were all right, but I'm not putting any more burdens on you. You've had a hellish day. I can feed Leyla at home. I'm going to change her diaper, and then we're out of here."

Jane frowned. "Caitlin, really, I—"

"Need rest," George finished emphatically. But he held Leyla to him as though he did not want to relinquish her. "Caitie, Jane's not the only one who's had a hell of a day. And you had quite a night last night as well. I hate the idea of you and Leyla being back at your apartment alone, and I'd be happy to make lunch for all of us." He turned to his wife. "But one way or another, Jane, you are going upstairs right now."

"I couldn't," Cait said quickly. "Really, we'll be fine."

"If you're sure," George said.

Jane smiled at him, her bruises making her wince. "I love you."

"I love you, too," George replied. "Now go."

He kissed her forehead, and then Jane bent to kiss Leyla. "We'll have to play tomorrow," she told the baby.

"No way," Cait said. "You relax tomorrow. I'll come by first thing Tuesday morning with coffee and bagels. Turns out I have the day off."

"All right," Jane said. "Tuesday it is."

Cait gave her a little hug and then watched as she went up the stairs, holding the railing with every step.

"She's going to be fine as long as she rests," George reassured her, once Jane was out of earshot.

"She deserves a long rest, and anything in the world she could ever wish for," Cait said, turning to her uncle. She watched Leyla playing in his arms. "I'm so sorry, Uncle George."

"You didn't do anything, Cait. And I don't want to hear *sorry* again."

Cait took Leyla from him. "A fresh diaper for my baby girl," she said, "and then we're gone."

-22--

"Herod? Are you sure that's what he said?"

Voss rubbed at the spot between her eyebrows, where a dull ache had been growing all day. She held the phone a few inches away, her partner's voice sounding strangely loud to her.

"Pretty sure," she said. "Something about Herod not feeling remorse for his beliefs."

She had returned to the Fort Myers hotel where they'd set up their command center for the Greenlaw investigation. A couple of Advil and a few minutes with her eyes closed had helped her headache a little, but she had not wanted to wait any longer to call Josh and fill him in on what had gone down in Sarasota.

"Christ," Josh said.

Voss uttered a small, dry laugh. "Are you being funny?"

"No. Sorry. Just my natural response. But it's crazy, right? Isn't al-Jubouri a Muslim? It seems pretty weird to have a terrorist worshipping some two-thousand-year-old Roman king—"

"Herod wasn't Roman," Voss said. She'd done a quick online search before calling Josh. "He was . . . I can't remember now. One of the Maccabees or something. Doesn't matter. He was a local ruler, and his people had been sort of absorbed by Rome, like a corporate takeover where they leave the CEO in place to give the illusion of stability."

"We're talking about the same guy, though?" Josh asked. "This is the Herod that ordered the execution of all the babies in Bethlehem, trying to kill Jesus?"

"First of all, it's biblical," Voss said, "so let's not confuse that with history. The story shows up in only one of the gospels. Matthew, I think. From what I read, it seems like it does refer to actual events, but the details are impossible to lock down. According to the Bible story, Herod heard a prophecy that the King of the Jews was going to be born in Bethlehem."

"And since he was King of the Jews—"

"Yeah. He didn't like the sound of that. He ordered all of the newborn males executed."

"And this is the guy Karim al-Jubouri holds up as his ideological hero when he's dying on the floor?"

"Yeah."

The phone line fell silent for a few seconds.

"You still there?" Voss asked.

"Just processing. I'm having some pretty dark thoughts about what this means for the Kowalik baby."

Voss massaged the ridge of her brow. "Yeah. I've had the same thoughts. They haven't named the baby yet?"

"No. I think the process was put on hold when the baby was taken."

Neither one of them mentioned that the Kowaliks might end up naming their baby only for the purposes of it being engraved on the newborn's gravestone. But Voss knew they were both thinking it.

"What do you make of the Greenlaw killings in light of this?" Josh asked.

"I don't know. Maybe it's all about the kids, but with Greenlaw's military background, that seems unlikely. And we can't jump to conclusions based on the ravings of one dying terrorist. We don't know that he was the leader of the cell."

"We don't know a hell of a lot, do we?" Josh said.

Voss leaned back in the hotel room desk chair, about to agree with him, but then there was a knock on the door.

"Hang on," she said, rising to answer it.

A glance through the peephole showed Ed Turcotte waiting in the hallway. She unlocked the door and hauled it open. Turcotte noticed the phone in her hand.

"I can come back," he said.

"No, you're good," Voss said. "I'm talking to Josh. Let me put him on speaker—"

"Inviting Turcotte into your boudoir now?" Josh teased.

If she'd been alone, Voss would have invented some kind of snappy comeback about the cobwebs and dust bunnies in her lonely boudoir. She and Josh often commented on the poor romantic prospects for people in their line of work. But even if she was working relatively comfortably with Turcotte at the moment, she wasn't about to talk about her personal life with him around.

She hit the button to put Josh on speaker and set the phone on the desk, then slid back into the chair, leaving Turcotte to sit awkwardly on the end of the bed.

"Say 'Hi,' Josh."

"Agent Turcotte. How are you holding up?" Josh asked.

"About as well as you and Agent Chang, I expect," Turcotte

said. "It's frustrating as hell being so completely in the dark. Especially since we had one of these guys in our grasp and fucking shot him."

"Can't get answers from a dead man," Josh replied.

"Exactly," Turcotte said.

Voss couldn't hide her surprise. Turcotte had once competed with her and Josh over certain cases, back before the ICD existed. Normally he kept them at arm's length, so it felt peculiar—even awkward—for him to be so open now.

Seeing her reaction, Turcotte smiled grimly. "Yeah. I know what you're thinking. It was a long night, and today's looking even longer. I did turn up something weird on this 'Herod' thing, though."

"Really?" Voss asked, intrigued.

"She's got you doing research now?" Josh asked.

Turcotte's grin was tired. Josh couldn't see it anyway.

"I went to my best researcher, back in D.C. She's been doing searches, cross-referencing files, trying to find anything that connects terrorist groups, murders, or Middle Eastern radicals with Herod the Great or, really, with any reference to the word *Herod*."

Voss arched an eyebrow. "She actually found something?"

"Not in our files," Turcotte said. "I've got her scanning it right now so we can read the whole thing."

"Wait, scanning what?" Josh asked. "If it wasn't in FBI files—"

"It's in an article from *Rolling Stone*," Turcotte said. "In May of 1971, they ran a long piece that included interviews with an FBI agent named Nixon—no relation—and an anonymous source he had supposedly been working with. The article apparently covered a lot of ground, ticking off the reasons why Vietnam was a clusterfuck, but in one section, Agent Nixon and this anonymous source talked about what they called the 'Herod Factor.'"

Voss narrowed her eyes. "The same phrase al-Jubouri used," she said. "What the hell does it mean?"

"According to my researcher, they claimed that—for lack of a better word, I guess—*breeding* between enemy cultures could help bring about peace."

"Gotta love *Rolling Stone,* especially in the seventies," Josh said.

"It makes a certain amount of sense," Voss said. "I mean, when people fall in love, that doesn't just connect them, it connects their families, and it impacts the people around them . . . the people who see them."

"It wasn't the relationships that these guys thought could influence the war," Turcotte went on. "They claimed that the babies born from those relationships actually had an effect on hostilities."

"Again—" Voss began.

"Wait, you mean on, like, a metaphysical level?" Josh interrupted.

"It's clear from the article that Agent Nixon was some kind of conspiracy nut. A fan of the Grassy Knoll," Turcotte said. "But, yeah, that's the gist of it. And remember, this was the time of the Vietnam War."

Voss exhaled. "Mrs. Kowalik is Iranian."

Turcotte flinched and stared at her. "You're not seriously—"

"Just pointing it out," she said. "This Agent Nixon obviously believed in this stuff. Is it so hard to buy that someone else might believe it, too?"

"There's always someone willing to believe, no matter how crazy something sounds," Josh said.

Voss massaged her temples. Her headache was spreading. "What happened to Agent Nixon? We should at least track him down."

Turcotte stood up. "He's dead. Heart attack in '73. The guy who wrote the article is also no longer with us."

"Which is going to make it hard to ID the anonymous source," Voss said.

"Unless it's somewhere in *Rolling Stone*'s files," Josh added, his voice sounding strangely far away on the phone. Voss wished that the case hadn't split them up, but they both had a job to do. "Something that confidential, I'd guess the writer probably didn't put it on paper anywhere."

"That's what I figured, too," Turcotte said, heading for the door. "But we'll look into it."

"You realize how unlikely it is that there's a connection

between some conspiracy nut from the Vietnam War and this case?" Voss asked.

Turcotte shrugged. "Given al-Juroubi's comment about Herod, we've got to look into it, and this is all we've got. But it's not like we're putting all our efforts into chasing ghosts from thirty-odd years ago. We've got real bad guys in the here and now. The second we get another lead, we're going to run them down. That's when we'll get real answers."

"Thanks, Ed," Voss said.

Turcotte nodded and left, pulling the door shut behind him. Voss picked up the phone and turned off the speaker.

"You doing all right up there?" she asked.

"Personally, yeah. Chang's good company. Though we're not as chummy as you and Turcotte."

"Funny guy."

"Listen, I just want to find this guy. And I want to find the Kowaliks' baby alive."

"Josh—"

"I know, Rachael. I know. But I can hope, right?"

-23--

Instead of making her feel safer, the police car in the rearview mirror made Cait more nervous. She glanced up again and again to confirm that it was still there, but she hated the idea that Monteforte and Jarman thought she needed the escort. Did they think that whoever had tried to snatch Leyla would make another attempt? It made no sense. If A-Train wanted payback, he would have come after her directly. And Cait couldn't really believe that Nizam's sisters had tried to abduct the baby, never mind the fact that they were too poor to hire someone to do it.

No, the men in their dark-windowed sedans had come after

Leyla for some other reason, and there was only one connection she could think of that made any sense. Sean.

Her brother was never able to speak plainly about the work he did for the government, but Cait knew he worked in intelligence, and she had the impression that his covert operations involved infiltrating terrorist organizations and training camps in the Middle East. If dark-suited men had come after Leyla in a car with untraceable plates—after watching Auntie Jane's house and looking for an opening—Cait figured it had to be connected to Sean somehow.

A strange unreality settled over her. The world looked different to her today. It even felt different on her skin. What would the police do now? If the canvass of the neighborhood turned up nothing, what *would* they do?

Before leaving her aunt and uncle's house, she'd retrieved her car charger from the trunk. Now, one hand on the wheel, she plugged in the phone to charge and called Channel 7, then asked to be transferred to Lynette's office. As she waited on the line, she glanced at the dashboard clock. Noon had come and gone, and she realized Lynette had probably already left for the day. On the weekends, she usually only worked mornings.

"Lynette Thompson."

"Good, you're still there," Cait said.

"Who is this?"

"Sorry. It's Cait McCandless. Listen, you wanted me to save the A-Train story for you. But I've got something else now, and it can't wait."

She told the story as quickly and succinctly as she could. Lynette stopped her only twice to ask questions—one about the untraceable license plate on the car out front and the other a more personal inquiry.

"Do you have anyone who can come stay with you?"

Was Lynette asking her if she had friends? The question troubled Cait, because she had no clear answer. Of all the kids she'd gone to school with, only a handful of those relationships had survived into adulthood. Of those, two lived out of state and one out of the country entirely. Miranda Russo had remained local, but had gotten married while Cait had been in

Iraq, and they had seen each other only once since she'd come home—an awkward lunch in which Cait had realized that they didn't really know each other anymore. Her best friend in high school had been a guy named Nick Pulaski; they had stayed in touch, but Nick had grown up to be an unreliable burnout who smoked far too much pot. There were only three people she still kept in touch with from her time at the University of Massachusetts Amherst, but those were e-mail and Christmas card relationships, far more about the time they'd spent together than the lives they now lived.

Then there was Jordan, of course. These days he was probably her closest friend. And in any inventory of the people she might call when she was in trouble, she'd have to include Ronnie Mellace. She and Jordan and Ronnie had been inseparable during their stint together in Iraq. But it wasn't like Ronnie lived down the street.

"There are people I could call," Cait told Lynette. "My aunt and uncle live here in Medford. But I'm fine."

Cait glanced in the rearview mirror at the police car, and then at Leyla's car seat. She could see Leyla's right hand, open and relaxed, and knew the baby had started to fall asleep.

"If you come into the office—"

"I don't want to leave my daughter with anyone, Lynette. Not right now."

"How about if I send someone to you? We can do the piece at your place. Who do you want to interview you? Aaron's off today, but you're friendly with Sarah Lin, right?"

"Yes. Sarah would be perfect. Do me a favor, though? Can you put Jordan on camera for this?"

"I don't think he's still here," Lynette said.

"He'll come in for it. I can call him myself, if you want."

"You've got enough to think about," Lynette replied. "I'll take care of it. We'll run it on the six o'clock broadcast, but we'll want to tease it at five. Does three o'clock work for you?"

"As soon as they can get here," Cait said.

She turned into the driveway of the house on Boston Avenue where she rented the first-floor apartment. The bright green VW bug in the driveway belonged to David, the Tufts graduate student who lived upstairs.

"Cait," Lynette said.

"Yes?"

"I won't try to tell you there isn't exploitation in what we do—you know better—but you're doing the right thing, publicizing it like this. We'll tell the story, and if anyone saw anything useful, they'll call in. Meantime, I'll do whatever I can to help."

"Thank you," Cait said.

They exchanged awkward good-byes and Cait ended the call. She killed the engine and sat in her car, listening to the engine ticking as it cooled. After several long seconds, she realized the car should not be so quiet, and she turned to find that Leyla had fallen asleep. Once again, her daughter's schedule would be messed up all day.

But she was safe, and beautiful, and alive.

-24--

Josh pushed back from the computer and rubbed at his eyes. Gray afternoon light filtered through the window, yet it felt like midnight to him. He needed sleep, but he wasn't going to get it anytime soon. The Maine State Police had given him and Chang more than enough space to work—a recently renovated room full of cubicles that hadn't yet been reoccupied. They were pretty much on their own. It was nice to have the privacy, but with the gray skies and the light rain that had begun to fall outside, and the quiet inside, he had to keep himself alert with coffee and a constant reminder that there was a child out there in the hands of a stranger. The Kowaliks would be horrified if they could see him looking drowsy behind the computer.

On the other hand, the search and the investigation continued at full speed. He and Chang didn't know the territory, so—thus far—the FBI had been put into a management position. Down in Florida, Turcotte had been moving state and local police around like chessmen, searching for the two remaining suspects now that Gharib al-Din was apparently in Maine and Karim al-Jubouri was dead. In Maine, with Josh's input, Chang was doing the same with state cops and FBI agents out of two separate New England bureau offices. They were questioning the hospital staff and checking surveillance cameras to see if they could track the vehicle that al-Din had used for his getaway.

And they had nothing. How could all of these departments and agencies be focused on these guys and not come up with anything truly useful? Even what little had been in the Black Pine file that Norris had turned over to Turcotte had given them next to nothing. Al-Din had been born in Basra, had been a militant Sunni since emerging from the womb, and was considered a jihadist. Big fucking surprise. He had dropped off the radar three years before, after a bomb had exploded in the London Tube, killing six people. Black Pine had connected al-Din to the bombing, but the file provided no supporting evidence.

And this was the FBI's case, not his and Rachael's.

When the offer to work for Homeland Security had first come up, Josh had been dubious, and his partner even more so. They had witnessed interagency turf wars too many times to think anyone could make it all run smoothly.

Then they had sat down with Theodora Wood, the director of the days-old InterAgency Cooperation Division of the Department of Homeland Security. African-American, forty-six years old, attractive and charismatic, but deadly serious about her job, Director Wood had convinced them both with one sentence: "You get to put an end to the pissing contests."

A noble cause. A hell of an opportunity. And a chance to put down roots in a community, though it would mean a lot of travel. But Josh knew now that one of the reasons Wood had hired them was that she trusted them not to exert the power of the agency unless all other alternatives had been exhausted. They had to wait for things to get completely screwed up before they could do anything to fix them. At first, Josh had been all right with that, but in practice it could become incredibly frustrating.

Like now, for instance.

They knew Ed Turcotte. The man had the capacity to be a gargantuan asshole, but he knew his job and he did it well. His deployment of his own people and the various law enforcement grunts showed that. He was totally on top of this case. FBI researchers were cross-checking a picture of every suspected terrorist and militant jihadists they could find to try to turn up real names for al-Din's surviving partners.

But it still wasn't how Josh would have done it. The first thing he would have done was throw Norris out. The guy had the best interests of his company, not his country, at heart.

Arsenault, too. The lieutenant seemed like a decent guy, but SOCOM had no place on this case.

The second thing he would have done was go back to the Greenlaw house and start over. They had to be missing something. Had the murders been revenge on Colonel Greenlaw? And if so, for what? Something he had done while in the service?

And how did that connect to the baby al-Din had abducted in Maine? The article Turcotte's people had turned up in *Rolling Stone* sounded like crazy talk. Certainly no one had taken it seriously at the time of its publication, despite *Rolling Stone*'s reputation. The FBI agent the magazine had interviewed—Nixon—had been fired shortly thereafter, according to Turcotte's researcher, leaving the writer of the article without a reputable source. There had been no follow-up story.

Still, he couldn't discount the possibility that somehow the kids—the Greenlaw twins in Florida and the stolen infant in Bangor—really were the connection.

Josh leaned farther back in the chair. The air conditioner hummed.

The computer screen went dark as the screen saver kicked in. Josh closed his eyes and pictured the interior of the

Greenlaw home. He wished he had the case materials in hand—crime-scene photos, floor plans, phone records, the contents of Greenlaw's hard drive—but sometimes the answers weren't to be found in the accumulated information. Chang was focused on the hunt for al-Din and the missing baby. She had FBI and state and local cops at her disposal, but Josh's mind kept going back to the Greenlaw home. Something had been off in that house . . . something more than the murder of a family of four.

The killers had taken a ladder out of the Greenlaws' garage and used it to climb up to the twins' second-story bedroom. They'd chosen an open window, obviously, so they would have known it was unlocked before they started climbing. They had cut the screen just enough to remove it and replaced it afterward to disguise their point of entry—

But what would it matter, if they were murdering the entire family? Had they done that just to confuse the police? It seemed a strangely contemplative choice for the fury of revenge.

Chang had gone to get them both some coffee, and to check in with the Bangor P.D. Josh could have just waited for her to come back, but his thoughts were moving fast now, so he got up to find her. He'd made it halfway across the room when the door swung open and Chang stepped in, a coffee in each hand.

She smiled. "Wow. You missed me that much, huh?"

Any other time, he would have welcomed the chance to flirt. Nala Chang was a very attractive woman, not to mention smart and competent, and the tired rasp in her voice was sexy. But he pushed such thoughts away. A family had been murdered. Children. That horror made any other concerns feel foolish.

"At the Greenlaw house," he said. "You were the first one in. Did you happen to take note of the state of the upstairs windows?"

"In what sense?"

"Which were open and closed, and which were locked and unlocked?"

Chang let the question hang for a few seconds, maybe running through the crime scene in her mind.

"Most of them were open, but even the ones that were closed were unlocked," she said. "The first floor had been locked up tight for the night, but upstairs . . . no. They weren't prepared for anyone trying to use a ladder to get in."

Josh frowned. He pictured the house in his mind. "The twins' window faced the backyard."

"Yes."

"But there were three other points of entry at the back of the house. The guest room, the bathroom, and the parents' bedroom. Do you remember if any of those windows were open?"

"All but the guest room, I think. What's on your mind, Josh? I can practically hear the gears turning in your head."

Josh exhaled, the grim weight of it bearing down on him. "There's no way we're finding this baby alive."

Chang shook her head, eyes full of hurt and anger. "Don't you dare say that. Until we find her, you've got to keep her alive in your mind. Once you stop hoping, you start to give up on her, in your heart. And I won't let you do that."

All the air seemed to have been sucked from the room, and the space between them felt charged with intimate electricity.

"You're right," Josh said, admiring her fierceness, and wanting even more of it. But he had to focus on the job for now. "And I'm sorry. But we're dealing with more than guesswork now. Follow me on this. Let's say you're al-Din and his buddy. The garage has a side door, okay, so you can get the ladder out without the noise of raising one of the main doors. Then you have to pick a point of entry. Obviously you go to the backyard to cut down on the chance anyone will spot you in the act. Now, there's no way to tell from the ground which windows are unlocked unless they're open, but you've got three possibilities. Bathroom, boys' bedroom, parents' bedroom. Which one are you going to pick?"

"The room with nobody in it," Chang said immediately. "Better chance of getting in without waking anybody up prematurely."

"Some bathrooms have windows much smaller than the others in the house. What about the Greenlaws' house?"

"A little smaller, maybe, but you could fit through."

"And if I'm remembering the layout of the property, the house is canted at a slight angle, right? The corner with Michael and Neil's bedroom is closer to the street, not to mention that the neighboring house on that side is closer. So wouldn't you say their window was more of a risk than either of the other two open ones?"

"So why go through the boys' window?" Chang asked. "Unless . . ."

"Yeah," Josh said. "Unless the boys were the target all along. They climb up the ladder, slit the screen, suffocate Michael and Neil, then put the screen back in place. If they're quiet enough, they can go right out the front door, put the ladder back in its place, and in the morning the parents will think they forgot to turn the dead bolt the night before, if they even notice in the midst of the screaming."

"God," Chang whispered. "I knew something was off. It didn't make sense to me that they would start with the children instead of the parents, who would be harder to subdue if they woke up. It would have made more sense to suffocate the parents—"

"If the parents had been their target," Josh said. "But if we're right, then they never intended to kill Mr. and Mrs. Greenlaw at all. If they hadn't woken up, the parents would still be alive. That's why the suspects had to clear out of their apartment in Fort Myers on such short notice, leaving so much behind. They didn't expect to have to blow town so fast."

"Okay, I'll buy it. But why?" Chang asked. "These guys are supposed to be terrorists, right? They've set up a cell in Fort Myers and obviously have some kind of operation in mind. But now they're killing kids in Florida and stealing babies in Maine. To what end?"

"Unless that *is* the operation," Josh said, cold dread forming a block in the pit of his stomach. Could these lunatics actually believe in what the now-dead Agent Nixon had called the "Herod Factor"?

He rushed back to the cubicle the state police had given him and tapped a key to clear his screen saver. He had already been logged on to the ViCAP database and now he maximized that window, bringing it up to fill the screen. He typed the keywords *child, suffocation, screen,* and the phrase *point of entry.*

"Why would Gharib al-Din abduct an infant from the maternity ward?" Josh asked. "That's what we've been asking ourselves, right? But let's narrow the focus. Why would he fly to Bangor from fucking Florida to do that?"

"He had orders from someone," Chang replied.

Search results filled the screen of his laptop, all of them with case numbers, dates, and the first couple of sentences of the report. The third result down caught his eye and he double-clicked to open the file.

"Columbus, Ohio," he said, glancing up at her.

"What about it?" Chang asked.

"Isla Rostan, nine months old, suffocated in her crib," he said, looking back down at the screen. "Investigators figured it was SIDS until small slits in the window screen were discovered, suggesting someone had entered the house. The baby was murdered, the killing made to look like just another tragedy."

Chang blanched. "Holy shit. It really is about the kids?"

Josh stared at the screen. "We need to call Voss and Turcotte. Right now."

-25--

Cait sat in the plush burgundy chair in her living room, listening for any chirp or whimper from Leyla's room, but the only sounds came from the breeze that flowed through the windows and the creak of floorboards in the upstairs apartment. Her second-floor neighbor seemed busy up there today, and she had decided he must be cleaning. Maybe he had a date coming over tonight, or maybe he had just gotten sick of living in a dirty apartment. Cait knew how he felt. She ought to be cleaning herself, but she knew that Leyla would wake up the second she started.

Whoever answered Sean's phone earlier had said she would get a call within twenty-four hours. The deadline was still far away, but she needed her brother more than ever, so she tried him again.

As she listened to the ringing on the other end of the line, a cold feeling of dread crept over her. The ringing continued and she began to wish she had counted the rings from the outset. After a time, the call simply ended, with no answer and no voice mail picking up.

Cait held the phone away from her face and stared at it a moment, then pressed END to clear the screen. Then she flinched when her ringtone started to play, the music much too loud in the quiet house. The display showed only *Unknown Caller,* but she felt a rush of hope as she answered.

"Sean?"

"Caitlin McCandless?"

The voice did not belong to her brother.

"This is she."

"Ms. McCandless, it's Brian Herskowitz."

"Hercules," she said, with a flood of relief. "Thank God. Listen, Sean usually calls me before he goes away, and he always tells me I should get in touch with you in an emergency. Well, he didn't call this time, but now I can't reach him. I was going to wait until tomorrow, but I really need to talk to him, or at least have you get a message to him. Can you do that?"

In the moment of his hesitation, she knew something was wrong. Hercules was supposed to be Sean's wingman. They were as much friends as they were co-workers—at least to hear Sean tell it. Hercules should have been warmer from the outset, friendlier, but he'd called her "Ms. McCandless" instead of just "Cait." The formality should have been a warning.

"Ms. McCandless—" he began again.

"Cait," she interrupted. "Call me Cait."

"I'm sorry, Cait, but I'm calling with awful news. Sean had a heart attack early this morning. He went out for coffee and had just left the café he always goes to, when he collapsed. The doctors say he died within minutes."

"What?" she said, telling herself she hadn't heard correctly, or that it must be some kind of horrible joke. "You . . . you ass-hole. Don't say that. It's not . . ."

Then the tears came, shuddering out of her in fits and gasps, and she held the phone against her cheek as if it were the only thing keeping her skull from falling apart.

Images of Sean flashed across her mind like playing cards in the hands of some magician—a brief glimpse and then back into the deck. Sean in a Batman costume one Halloween when he'd dressed her up as Robin; she couldn't have been more than seven. Sean making her lunch—peanut butter and jelly *and* Fluff, just like she wanted—on mornings when their dad had forgotten. Sean waking her up late at night to watch scary movies that Dad had forbidden her to see.

Her father had loved her, and had devoted as much time as he could to her, but for all intents and purposes, her big brother had been her primary parent. Dad had taught her to throw a baseball and to ride a bike, but Sean had taught her to throw a punch and drive a car. He had held her as she'd cried that day in the seventh grade when Mike Torchio had teased her because, at nearly thirteen, she still didn't need a bra, and told his friends in a voice loud enough for her to hear that he wouldn't dance with her even if she were the only girl in their class.

Sean had wanted to pummel Mike for that, but he had loved Cait enough to leave the boy alone, because she couldn't bear to see him hurt, no matter what he had done to her. As she got older, she had never regretted stopping Sean from beating up Mike, but she *had* regretted not doing it herself. Even back then, she could have taken him, because Sean had taught her how to fight.

And he had kept teaching her. The more he had learned, the more he had trained her. What she had learned about hand-to-hand combat in the National Guard had been next to useless in comparison to the skills and styles her brother had brought home from his training with the Marines, and then, later, from private instructors.

All to keep her safe.

"Tell me," she said, her voice hard and cold. "Tell me how it happened."

"Cait, listen. Sean and I worked together for a long time," Hercules said, voice halting and full of regret. "He was one of the best people I've ever known. And he won't be forgotten. I'm sure you're aware that he worked at the Pentagon. After his service in the Marines and his employment here, he's earned the honor of being interred in Arlington National Cemetery. His wishes have already been carried out, but—"

"Wishes? What are you talking about?" she asked.

It came at her too quickly. She could barely follow what Hercules was saying.

"Sean left explicit instructions about how he wanted his remains to be cared for in the event of his death. He's already been cremated. A non-denominational memorial service will be held at Arlington, but we can schedule that around your availability."

Cait could barely speak, but she forced herself to do so, if only to keep him from saying anything else to add to her pain.

"Cremated? Who gave you permission to do that?" she demanded, wiping at her tears, trying to make her brain work.

There would be no good-bye, she realized. Her brother no longer existed as anything more than ashes. She wouldn't even be able to see his body, to touch his hand and tell him how much she loved him. How much she needed him. How much she would miss him.

"I'm his next of kin," she said. "You can't just cremate somebody!"

Hercules seemed to hesitate. Cait thought she heard someone talking in the background and realized he wasn't alone. It had sounded to her almost as if he was reading from a script, and now she wondered if that wasn't close to the truth.

This wasn't a call from a grieving friend. It was Brian Herskowitz doing his job.

"Sean's wishes were very clear," Hercules said.

"Bullshit," Cait hissed. "He never would have done that to me. Jesus, I thought you were his friend. *Sean* thought you were his friend. What the hell is really going on? My brother works at the Pentagon, he grows that beard and runs off to the Middle East every couple of months, and now he's dead and you've turned him to ash before I've even had a chance to identify his body. Is he really dead, or is that just a story? And if he's dead, what are you hiding by cremating him?"

"I have no idea what you're talking about, Ms. McCandless—"

"It's Ms. McCandless again, huh?"

"Cait," Hercules corrected himself. "Sean and I worked together as systems analysts for the Pentagon. I know how hard this must be hitting you. I know your parents are gone. I know your baby's father was killed, and I can't imagine what—"

"Damn right, you can't imagine! You don't know me. We've met, like, twice. So stop trying to spin this. If these were supposedly Sean's wishes, I want to see the documentation where he requested it. And you'd better believe I'm going to look into the legality of you fucking cremating him before even notifying me that he was—"

Dead. The word wouldn't come. *Oh, my God. Sean is dead.* And then it hit her. Cars with untraceable license plates.

"Jesus," she whispered.

"Cait, why don't you take some time to recover from this, get your thoughts together, and then call me? You can figure out what you want to do about a memorial, and—"

"Wait." She felt sick, but her thoughts sharpened. "Listen to me. Sean couldn't talk about his work, but I always guessed. I always had an idea of what he was up to. And I don't believe a word of what you've said."

"It's the truth," Hercules said. "I wish it weren't."

"Shut up," Cait said, but without rancor. She was thinking. "Did Sean ever talk about our aunt and uncle? Jane and George?"

"I guess."

"Someone ran surveillance on their street last night and this morning. Earlier today, the same people attacked my aunt and tried to abduct my daughter. The local police are investigating, but they've got nothing."

"My God," Hercules said, his voice hushed, and for the first time Cait thought she was hearing the guy she had met before. Sean's friend.

"If you know anything about this—if there's something my brother was involved in that led to this—you've got to tell me."

Again Hercules hesitated. And in those few seconds, Cait felt like she would fall apart completely. How could any of this be possible?

"Cait, I swear to you, if I knew anything about someone trying to snatch your baby, I would tell you. You don't know me well but, through Sean, I feel like I do know you. There's no way I can possibly express how sorry I am to have had to tell you that we've lost him, but on top of that . . . I wish there was something I could do."

"There is," Cait said, the realization coming upon her suddenly. "I've got a license plate number from one of the cars that was in front of my aunt's house this morning. The police say it's not a registered plate, that they can't trace it. But I'm betting there's more to it than that. If I give you the number, can you look into it for me?"

She heard muffled tones, like Hercules had covered the phone and was talking to someone else. Then he came back.

"I can do that."

Cait got up and went to her bedroom, found the slip of paper, and read off the license plate number.

"I'll call you tomorrow," Hercules said. "Then you can let me know what you want to do about a service."

A service. For just a moment she had allowed her anger to cloud her grief, but now it came rushing back.

"Thank you," she said. The words tasted bitter on her lips. *Thank you for what? For lying to me?* Because she was absolutely certain that Brian Herskowitz had not told her the truth . . . at least, not all of it.

When she ended the call, she went in to check on Leyla and

was amazed to find her daughter still asleep. But she knew it wouldn't last much longer, so she walked to the kitchen and began to make some rice cereal, mixing it with jarred baby food. Leyla liked the plums best.

She wept silently, standing by the stove, her hands shaking. The tears were born of grief and sorrow, but also from the realization that she was not alone, even after all that she had been through. She had Jane and George, and she had her baby.

And she'd be damned if she would let anyone take Leyla away from her.

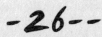

Josh stared out the passenger window of the dark gray Ford sedan, listening to the hush of the windshield wipers and wondering how Agent Merritt liked being relegated to the backseat of his own Bureau-issued vehicle.

If it troubled Chang that Agent Merritt might be sour about losing his driving privileges, she didn't show it. And that was for the best. Turcotte might be in charge of the overall investigation, but up here in Maine, Chang was running the show. If she wanted to be behind the wheel literally as well as figuratively, Merritt would just have to deal with it.

Chang turned down a narrow alley that bisected a strip of old brick buildings. A Bangor P.D. vehicle was parked at the curb, the officer watching the alley entrance, checking them out as they drove in. Either he recognized them, or had known to expect them.

Voss and Turcotte were even now on a flight bound for Maine. The FBI was still working with Florida State Police, hunting for al-Din's two surviving accomplices, but since the Bangor babynapping—as the press were calling it—represented the most recent sighting of any of their suspects, it made sense to move the base of operations here. There would be a meeting in a few hours, during which they'd put their heads together and figure out what to do next with the huge pile of nothing they had to go on.

Now, though, it looked like there might be one more piece to add to the puzzle by the time Voss and Turcotte arrived.

Another alley, much wider, ran behind the row of buildings, and beyond it was a chain-link fence rooted in a three-foot-high concrete barrier. In one place, the chain link had been cut away from a metal post and the mesh pulled back to create an easily passable gap. Beyond that barrier lay the Penobscot River. Two Bangor P.D. cruisers were parked in that back alley, along with a state police car. As Chang parked and they all climbed out, Josh glanced to the right, where he saw several other police cars farther down the alley.

A captain from the Bangor P.D. hurried toward them, a state trooper just behind him. The day hadn't gotten any brighter. Light rain pattered all around them and the gloom of the afternoon enclosed them like a shroud.

"Agent Chang," the captain said.

"Show us," Chang said.

The local guys led them off to the left, behind a Salvation Army store. A scarred and dented Dumpster sat beside a big metal box brightly painted with the charity's logo.

"People can put clothing donations and toys and things through the slot there," the captain said, pointing.

Josh thought the part of the box that pulled out, the "slot," looked more like a hatch, but he wouldn't argue. To donate something, you had to grab the handle and haul it down and open, like a giant mailbox.

"A car seat's not going to fit through there," Agent Merritt said. "Not even an infant seat."

Josh glanced at him, wondering if Merritt had children of his own. He realized he didn't know anything about the man. But then, that was par for the course in his world. Once the case moved on, he'd never see the guy again, and that was fine by him. So why didn't he feel that way about Chang? He felt comfortable working with her, and was in no rush to move on to the next case or the next crime scene and leave her behind. *Weird.*

"The car seat wasn't in the donation box," the captain said. "An assistant manager found it between the box and the Dumpster. She wasn't sure if it was meant to be thrown away or had been left as a donation, so she took it inside."

"Isn't the store closed today?" Merritt asked.

"It is, but there are still donations. Either the manager or assistant manager makes at least one visit on the days they're closed to check the box and make sure it hasn't been filled with unwanted items or crammed full of so much stuff that there's not room for people to push things through."

"So, the assistant manager?" Josh prodded.

"Like I said, she went to take it inside. Then she remembered the Kowalik abduction and called us."

"You've confirmed it's the Kowaliks' car seat?" Chang asked.

"It's been taken down for forensics," the captain replied. "But it's brand new, and the same model as the Kowaliks bought. It would be an incredible coincidence if it isn't theirs."

A heavy silence filled the alley as they all acknowledged what it meant that al-Din no longer needed the infant seat.

"My people are looking along the riverbank," the captain said, gesturing toward the barrier and the river beyond.

"I've got agents on the way," Chang said, "and we need as many officers as you can get. State and local. I want every Dumpster, trash can, and alley back here searched. We've got to get someone who knows this river, and can figure out the current and where a body might end up. And I want all of these businesses canvassed. Someone must have seen something."

The captain nodded and turned to his state police counterpart, and they began making calls and issuing orders.

Chang turned to Merritt. "I want you on this, Ian. Stick with them and relay anything back to me."

Agent Merritt frowned. "Where are you going to be?"

Chang glanced at Josh, then pointed at the opening torn in the chain-link fence. "Out there. Looking."

Josh could feel the waves of anger and frustration coming off Chang. Either that, or it was his own emotion reflecting back at him. He had been convinced that the Kowaliks' daughter must be dead, but Chang had admonished him for that presumption. She had helped to kindle a small spark of hope in him. Now that spark had been extinguished.

He tried not to think of the Kowaliks, but he found he couldn't think of anything else. Barring a miracle, their baby girl was dead. He felt sick just thinking about it, and wondered if the newborn had been alive when he and Chang arrived in Bangor, or if al-Din had already done his terrible work by then.

"If I had him in front of me right now—" Josh began, as he and Chang walked toward the break in the fence.

"I know," Chang said. That was all. But it was enough.

As she started to climb through the barrier, Josh's phone buzzed. He let her go, pulling out the phone and glancing at it. Earlier today he had set up an hourly web search, looking for any references to child abduction. Now he opened the message on his phone, connected to the news site where his search had found a hit, and read the beginning of the article.

"What is it?" Chang asked, peering at him through the chain link.

"Someone tried to snatch a baby—seven months old—from a woman in Massachusetts today. Mother's name is . . ." He glanced at his phone. "Caitlin McCandless. Iraq War vet."

Chang arched an eyebrow. "You think?"

"I don't know what to think about anything these days," Josh said. "But I should at least make a call."

Chang nodded. "You'll catch up?"

"Two minutes."

For a few seconds after she turned away, he just stood and watched her go. He could hear loud engines up the street and knew more police cars would be arriving momentarily. The search was about to get much narrower, focused on these few blocks and a hell of a lot of riverside.

He called information and got the number for the police department in Medford, Massachusetts. A few seconds' wait and he was automatically connected, listening to the ringing of the line until he heard a click, and an answer.

"Medford police. This is Sergeant Bryce. Your call is being recorded."

Josh introduced himself. Homeland Security needed no introduction, but he had to explain the ICD unit. He offered to wait and let Bryce check him out, but the sergeant didn't seem to think that was necessary.

"What can I do for you, Agent Hart?" Sergeant Bryce asked.

"You had an attempted child abduction today. I'm working a case in Bangor, a newborn taken from outside a hospital here. You may have seen it on the news."

"How could I miss it?" Bryce said. "They keep showing that security video."

"What can you tell me about what happened there today?" Josh asked.

"You should probably talk to one of the detectives on the case. Monteforte and Jarman caught that one, but neither one of them is in right now. You want cell numbers for them?"

"That would be good," Josh said.

"Hang on," Bryce replied.

As he waited, Josh pulled out his pad and pen. He watched up and down the alley as more cops showed up and began to spread out, starting to search Dumpsters and doorways. Some of them found another opening in the fence down behind the Chinese restaurant and went through to the river's edge.

The sergeant came back and rattled off the numbers. Phone caught between his ear and shoulder, Josh scribbled them down.

"Thanks, Sergeant," he said. "I don't have any real reason to think there's a connection, but I figured it was worth a call. Do you have descriptions of the suspects?"

"Good descriptions, actually," Bryce replied.

He rattled them off, probably reading from a BOLO—a Be-on-the-Lookout Order—issued for the would-be abductors. Josh frowned as he listened. Two men, one Caucasian, one African-American. White guy had scruffy hair and blue eyes, African-American had a crew cut and a scar on his face.

"Thanks for that," he told the sergeant. "Doesn't sound like our guys at all."

"No problem," Bryce replied. "Let me know if you need anything else."

Josh ended the call, clutching his phone in his hand. He stuffed the pad and pen back into his pocket, trying to decide if he was relieved or frustrated that the McCandless case didn't have any connection to his. If the abductors had been Middle Eastern, they would at least have had somewhere else to start looking for al-Din. Right now, they were turning up nothing in Florida and Maine.

"Shit," he whispered.

Then he heard his name being called. He turned to see Chang approaching the cut in the fence from the river side. He started toward her, meaning to join her in the search, but as he got closer, he saw the expression on her face, the tightness around her eyes and lips.

At the fence, he reached up and pushed his fingers through the chain link, knowing without Chang saying a word. From the other side, she took his hand through the metal mesh, fingers sliding through the links above his.

"He threw her in the river?" Josh asked.

Chang nodded, her features turned to stone. "She's downstream. Not very far at all. Still wearing the plastic bracelet from the hospital."

Josh hung his head, tamping down his rage. When he could force his face to be as impassive as Chang's, he climbed through the hole in the fence.

In his career he had not only seen monstrous things, but encountered monsters. Gharib al-Din had just made himself the worst of them.

"We've got to find this son of a bitch," Chang muttered.

Josh reached out a hand and touched the small of her back. "We will," he said, knowing that he and Chang were both silently finishing the thought in the same way.

Before he does it again.

-27--

Herc stood in the office of his supervisor, Roger Boyce, studying the man's face, searching his eyes for some evidence that there was something Boyce was not telling him. The problem, he knew, was that Boyce had been a professional liar—working amongst the best professional liars in the world—for twenty-seven years. The man had a ruddy face caused by high blood pressure and snow white hair, along with a smile that might have belonged to Santa Claus, or Jeffrey Dahmer.

Boyce's eyes appeared blue thanks to colored contact lenses. In truth, they were brown. The eyes, people always said, were the windows to the soul, but for Roger Boyce, even those were covered in secrets and lies.

"Do you know anything about this business with Sean's niece?" Herc asked.

Boyce frowned. He did not like his subordinates asking questions that weren't pertinent to an assignment. There were, in fact, a whole host of behaviors that Boyce frowned upon. Normally, Herc attempted to avoid pissing his boss off, but today his natural sense of self-preservation had been overridden.

"You know as much as I do, Mr. Herskowitz."

Herc nodded. "Yes, sir."

Boyce had been sitting at his desk while Herc had placed the call to Cait McCandless on an anonymous secure line from within Boyce's office.

"When the girl contacts you to arrange a date for her brother's memorial service, inform me immediately," Boyce said, smoothing his purple tie. "Otherwise, return to your station."

"Yes, sir," Herc said again, not even trying to hide how unsatisfied this made him.

"You have something else to add?"

Herc blinked, surprised that Boyce had given him an opening. He pondered the question for several moments, considering the consequences that might come from answering it honestly. He held Sean McCandless's cell phone in his hands, turning it over and over almost unconsciously, as though it were a key to an unknown door he might open, if only he could find it.

The window in Boyce's office looked out onto acres of parking lot, a small duck pond, and then green woods as far as he could see. Above the trees in the distance there were cell phone towers and a white church steeple that thrust up from the heart of Croydon, Virginia, several miles away.

The sprawling complex with its enormous satellite dishes had been a fixture in Croydon for seventeen years—long enough for people to stop wondering what actually went on there. All anyone really cared about was that the facility provided a number of jobs for local people, even if they were mostly plant management and clerical positions.

The sign at the end of the long drive from the main road warned that it was private property, but the real sign—and the gate—was a quarter mile up the curving street, out of sight of people driving by. There, the warnings were more explicit, and the guard at the gate was armed. The complex was one of half a dozen major facilities run by the National Geospatial-Intelligence Agency. Once upon a time, it had been called the National "Imagery and Mapping" Agency, which Herc had always believed a far more useful name. He was of the opinion that things should carry names that indicated their true purpose, and if "Imagery and Mapping" did not give a clear picture of the agency's duties, it did at least imply the basics.

But they were the NGA now. Someone had obviously decided getting the word *intelligence* into the mix lent their work the appropriate air of gravitas, meant to put them on a par with other divisions of the Department of Defense that were jockeying for the same budget dollars. And Boyce, for one, clearly loved the idea of being part of the "intelligence community."

Sean McCandless had liked to say there was no such thing as intelligence in the community, or community in the field of intelligence. And he had known better than most. The guy had been incapable of setting his alarm clock, but his ability to interpret topographical images—to pinpoint the location of caves and gulleys and to identify man-made camouflage, no matter how artful—had been uncanny. The NGA had recruited him out of the Marine Corps's own intelligence division, and for more than two years, Herc had taught Sean everything he knew about satellite surveillance and the collection of geospatial intelligence.

And then the DoD had seen an opportunity. When the NGA identified areas of the mountainous regions of Afghanistan and Pakistan as possible al Qaeda bolt-holes, who better to insert into the region to infiltrate the enemy, investigate, and then lead a Special Ops attack squad, if it came to that, than a man who could tell just from looking at the side of a mountain where the caves and tunnels might be, how deep they would go, and where to plant the explosives to bring it all down?

Who better than Sean McCandless?

Herc and Sean had remained partners, in a sense, though they no longer reported to the same supervisor. They did the mapping together, made their reports together, and Herc was always in the mission control center, watching all the satellite and camera feeds, when Sean led a team into the shit. Sometimes they consulted Herc during the op, and sometimes they didn't, but he would be there, whether they needed him or not, because Sean McCandless had asked for him.

But now Sean McCandless was dead.

The hospital records would say that he had a rare heart defect that had gone unnoticed his entire life. Since his body had been cremated, no one would ever be able to call that data into question. No one outside of the NGA and the DoD would ever know that Sean McCandless had been poisoned, or the pain he had endured while lying on the sidewalk down the street from his favorite café in a puddle of his own vomit.

Up until now, Herc had just assumed that al Qaeda had taken him out. Not al Qaeda, really, because they were a

bunch of mad-eyed zealots who had never been very good at
blending in for very long. Sure, sometimes it was long
enough . . . but not long enough to get that close to Sean Mc-
Candless. Herc figured they had hired a professional to
punch Sean's ticket, and he had already started using back-
channel relationships to try to find out who had done the job.

Boyce would fire him if he found out. Herc didn't care.
Sean had been worth a hundred Roger Boyces.

Herc stood in Boyce's office, staring out the window.
Maybe five seconds had passed since the white-haired Via-
gra addict had asked him if he had anything else he wanted
to say.

Herc tore his gaze from the window. He made his expression as neutral as possible.

"I'm sorry, sir. I guess I'm having a difficult time with the
size of this coincidence," he said.

Boyce narrowed his eyes. "What coincidence is that?"

Herc tried not to clench his fists, knowing that Boyce
would notice. The guy might not be able to look in the mirror and see what an asshole he was—or maybe he could, and
didn't care—but he knew how to read just about everyone
else, and prided himself on it.

"You heard the conversation, sir. Someone driving a car
with blind plates tried to abduct McCandless's niece the
same morning McCandless himself is killed? Sergeant Mc-
Candless—"

"Sergeant?" Boyce asked.

"Caitlin, sir. She was a sergeant in the Guard."

Boyce held up a hand to silence him, lips pressed together
so tightly it looked like he might spit. "What kind of connection are you suggesting?"

Herc let out a short breath. "I don't know, sir. I only know
I have a hard time believing there isn't one."

"You think someone hated McCandless so badly they tried
to snatch his sister's child?"

"Maybe there's more to it," Herc said. "The aunt was beaten.
Maybe they wanted the child as leverage over McCandless
somehow, and killed him when the abduction attempt failed."

Boyce scoffed. "And who is *they*?"

Herc flushed, suddenly realizing how he sounded. "I don't know."

"Haven't I told you to stop reading those fucking *spy* novels?"

Herc could not hide how irritated this made him, nor could Boyce hide his smile of satisfaction at the sting.

"Look, Brian," Boyce said, patronizing him by using his first name, "you're very good at your job, but we both know you're no Sean McCandless. Neither one of us is an action hero, my friend. What happened to McCandless is tragic, and you better damn well believe there's going to be hell to pay. Hopefully, we'll play a part in that. But it isn't our area. All of that is going to be looked into, I'm sure. Until then, you need to return to your station."

Nodding slowly, Herc turned to leave the room.

"Herskowitz," Boyce said. "Leave McCandless's phone."

Herc glanced back at him. "If Caitlin calls . . ."

Boyce nodded, reaching out and gesturing for the phone. "If the sister calls to set up a date for her brother's memorial service, I'll deal with her. She needed a friendly voice to deliver the news, but you're too close to this. I'll handle any contact with her from now on. And if she attempts to get in touch with you via other channels, just refer her to me."

Herc hesitated.

"Herskowitz? Are you hearing me?"

"Loud and clear, sir," Herc said. "Loud and clear."

-28--

Leyla sat up on the carpet, playing with the rubber animals spread around her. She loved the panda the most, and smiled and beat her heels on the floor whenever she managed to knock it over. There were other toys, too—the big plastic car keys and the weird snake whose segments were different textures, each making a different sound—and she seemed content to play on her own, at least for the moment.

Cait sat tucked in a corner of her sofa, legs folded beneath her, and sipped at a glass of iced tea to which she had added too much lemon and not enough sugar. The modest flat-screen on the wall revealed CNN talking heads and scrolling headlines that crawled along the bottom of the screen like ants marching to a picnic.

The phone remained silent—both a taunt and a temptation. She had come home to more than twenty messages, some from friends teasing her about A-Train and others from newspapers and TV news producers trying to interview her about the incident. Cait had erased them all to free up space on the machine, but hadn't called anyone back.

Now the news had moved on. Washington politicians squabbled, undermining one another and the nation. A D-list Hollywood skank had survived an overdose that no one dared refer to as a cry for attention. Fires raged in California, consuming thousands of acres and millions of dollars' worth of real estate.

Worst of all were the two stories that involved children—the infant stolen from a hospital up in Maine and the string of crib deaths in the Midwest that Jordan had told her about, which the authorities were now admitting might actually have been murders. On weekends, the news seemed more than ever like an endless loop, and she had seen each report at least twice already. Add to those the family—including three-year-old twin boys—who had been killed in Fort Myers, Florida, and it had been a horrifying week in America.

She knew that such things happened all too often, but now that she was a mother, they cut her more deeply than ever. And yet she allowed the hideous news to wash over her in a constant drone. Whenever one of those stories came on, she sipped her iced tea and looked at Leyla, playing on the floor, and her heart clenched with fear and a love so ferocious that sometimes she thought the two emotions might really be just one.

Cait glanced at the time in the corner of the TV screen. Jordan and Sarah Lin ought to be arriving soon. That would be good. Being interviewed, telling the story of the attempted abduction—and of her brother's sudden death—would make her feel like she was doing something. She needed that. Reaching out to the television audience would be sort of like recruiting allies to her cause, and she needed allies right now.

Lynette's question from earlier in the day resonated. She had insisted that she had people she could call, and there certainly were such people, but what comfort could they possibly provide? The people closest to her in the world were Auntie Jane and Uncle George, who had dealt with enough today, and Sean.

Don't think about Sean.

Her friend Ronnie had left a message asking if she would be willing to beat him up, somehow making sexual innuendo out of the whole thing. Take away innuendo and Ronnie wouldn't have any conversational skills at all, but he was a good man. She and Jordan and Ronnie had been the Three Musketeers while serving in the Guard—one for all and all for one—and he had been one of the few who had never teased her about her relationship with Nizam. A blond tank of a kid named Stu Chadbourn had been the one to tell her about Nizam's death, though Ronnie was the first to say he was sorry.

But she'd see Jordan soon enough, and she didn't want to go through the process of explaining it all to Ronnie over the phone.

Then there were her two best friends from high school. Miranda and Nick were polar opposites still, one aloof and conservative and the other a portrait of laissez-faire, yet she had realized over the years that both had managed to set themselves apart from the world of ordinary people. Miranda had been privileged from birth and had crafted herself a life as both a prominent corporate lawyer and a Boston socialite. Nick Pulaski lived in a room over his divorced mother's garage and did just enough carpentry to keep himself in pot, beer, and gas.

She didn't really know them anymore. Or, perhaps more accurately, she knew them too well. But either of them would come if she called, even if only for old time's sake. Cait knew there was power in shared experience. She herself cherished the best of her childhood memories so fiercely that she would have been willing to do almost anything for Nick or Miranda if they needed her, not because they meant anything to her now but because of how much they had once meant to her.

There were others, from before, during, and after Iraq. Even Upstairs David would have offered her a shoulder to cry on and a sympathetic ear.

But what would she say if she called them? How insane would it all sound? Could she tell Miranda Russo that she thought her brother might actually be a spy, and that she feared he might have been killed because of it? Ronnie and Jordan would believe that, but Cait was not sure even she believed it. Sean vanished from the world for weeks at a time, his movements veiled in secrecy. Wasn't it possible all of this was another feint, a part of his work? She hadn't seen a body, and wondered if Herc had. This morning, her brother had been a voice on the phone, and now he was ashes in a jar, and his government employers wanted her to think those had been Sean's wishes?

Bullshit. He would never have wanted to hurt her, to deprive her of a chance to say good-bye, and that left only two possibilities. Either the whole story had been a lie and Sean was still alive somewhere, or he had been cremated so quickly in order to prevent an independent autopsy that would reveal the true cause of death.

Cait hated how much easier it was to believe the latter. After all of the hints Sean had dropped and the jokes he had made, it seemed all too likely. But the idea that he was gone, that she would never see him again, alive or dead, was too surreal for her to accept.

On the floor, Leyla began to fuss. She had flopped over and pushed herself up, as if she might start to crawl. Most of the time she seemed too lazy to put much effort into learning. Even now, she was trying to reach the plastic keys, which were her favorite thing to gnaw on, without actually crawling. The keys were just out of reach and the baby's face turned red with irritation.

"Come on," Cait said. "You have to learn to do these things for yourself."

When trouble came, the McCandless family had always circled the wagons. That hadn't changed, even if she and Leyla were the only McCandlesses left.

The doorbell rang.

Cait flinched, picking Leyla up and holding her close as she turned to look at the door. It took her a second or two to realize it must be Jordan and Sarah, and then another second to feel foolish.

Even so, she flashed on the locked metal box on the floor of her closet, and the gun that lay within it, nestled atop her life insurance policy, her bank bonds, and Leyla's birth certificate. An extra clip and a small box of ammunition rested in her sock drawer.

Cait put Leyla on her right hip and held her away from the door.

"Who is it?" she called.

"It's us," a male voice said.

"Jordan?"

"Yeah, Cait. It's me."

The restatement—from "us" to "me"—felt personal and intimate, and a rush of gratitude went through her. He was a good man, and he had always cared for her. He had been her friend before in times when she had felt incapable of reaching out for one, and here he was again.

But when she opened the door and saw the concern not just in Jordan's eyes, but in Sarah's as well, her heart began to break all over again. Cait had been forcing herself to be strong, to do without the support that friends might give her. Now she reached out and pulled Jordan to her, hugging him close with one arm even as she carried Leyla in the other.

"Oh, my God," she said. "Thank you so much for coming."

"Of course," he replied, his breath warm on her neck, his newly trimmed beard scraping her skin. She couldn't suppress the delicious shiver that went through her.

"When Lynette told me what was going on, I asked her for the assignment," Jordan added.

He seemed not to have noticed the reaction he'd gotten out

of her, and that was good. Her life was confusing enough as
it was without trying to examine her feelings about Jordan
too closely just now.

Cait stepped back, smiling at him. "I asked for you, too."

Jordan returned her sad smile, but then Cait turned to look
at Sarah Lin. They had only worked together a few times, but
Sarah had impressed her as friendly and smart and professional, much more open and human than some of the other reporters at Channel 7—especially sports asshole Mike Duffy.

"Sarah," Cait said. "I'm so glad you're here."

The reporter stepped inside, smiled at Leyla, and then
focused on Cait.

"We'll do everything we can. We're going to help you catch
these guys."

Cait faltered a bit, and she knew Sarah must have seen the
doubt in her eyes. But the reporter probably didn't know the
whole story yet. She didn't know about Sean.

"More than anything, I just want the truth."

-29--

Still stiff from her flight, Rachael Voss stood in the second-
floor corridor of the Comfort Inn in Bangor, trying to figure
out how to knock on the door to Room 227 while carrying a
cup of coffee in each hand. After a few seconds, she gave up
and just kicked the door a few times. The café across the road
brewed a decent cup, and the smell alone enticed her. She
took a sip, and then kicked the door again.

"Okay, okay!" came a voice from the other side.

"I hope you have your pants on," Voss said.

Her partner opened the door, his hair mussed from the pillow, still half-asleep. "Funny." But Josh didn't look amused.
His expression was grim, his eyes haunted from the discovery,

only hours before, of the remains of the Kowaliks' newborn daughter.

Voss glanced at the worn gray gym shorts he must have just tugged on and smiled, trying to lift his spirits. "Those will do. I take it I interrupted nap time?"

"Every cop in the state of Maine is out beating the bushes for this guy. If he's still here, they'll find him," Josh said, with what she knew was false confidence. "I knew I wouldn't be any good without some rest. It's not like we got any last night. I figured I'd get a couple of hours' sleep while you were in the air."

"Yeah," Voss said. "Me, too. Slept on the plane."

She and Turcotte had come directly from the airport. On the plane, knowing that al-Din was still in the wind, every minute had seemed like an eternity.

She handed Josh one of the coffees and moved past him into the room. He shut the door behind her and Voss crossed to the desk and slid into the chair. The bedspread had puddled on the floor at the foot of the bed and the sheets were in disarray.

"I wasn't sure you'd be alone," she said.

"What's that supposed to mean?" Josh picked up a discarded T-shirt emblazoned with a stylishly faded Batman logo. She wondered if this ensemble was a grown-up version of superhero pajamas.

"I don't know," she said, sipping her coffee. "I thought maybe you'd be with Chang."

"Really?"

Voss shrugged. "You're not laughing. And don't tell me you haven't thought about it."

"Of course I've thought about it. Nala's impressive. Smart. Smokin' hot. But no, I'm not having sex with her. Especially not today."

Voss nodded, her smile vanishing. "No, I guess not." She sipped her coffee. "So she's 'Nala' now?"

Josh sighed and looked at the clock. "Yeah."

Interesting. But now was not the time to discuss it. "Okay," Voss said instead.

A quiet moment passed, then she stood up, set her coffee

on the desk, and slipped her arms around him. Whatever they might one day be—or never be—Josh was her best friend.

"They finally named her," he said. "The Kowaliks."

"They gave the baby a name? Now?"

"They called her Grace."

Voss felt a sudden tightness in her chest. She exhaled, but it did not go away. "Are you gonna be okay?"

"I'll be fine." Josh stepped back from her, his expression hard. "Once we catch this guy, I'll be right as rain."

"Good," Voss said. "Go take a shower. You've got about twelve minutes before Turcotte and Nala get here."

"Here? As in, my room?" Josh said, looking around at the messy bed and the dirty clothes piled in the corner by the chair. "Why?"

"Eleven minutes."

Josh picked up his coffee cup, took a long swig, then went into the bathroom. When she heard the shower sizzle on, she picked up the bedspread, and covered the bed. Then she sat down and ran through the case in her head, trying to figure out what they knew and comparing it to what they could only guess.

Their research had turned up numerous other cases of presumed crib death that fit the m.o. of the murders of Michael and Neil Greenlaw. They had started linking the investigations together and had put in inquiries for copies of case files and evidence—which would take hours, if not days, to gather.

When Josh came out of the bathroom with a towel around his waist, he looked much more awake. He hadn't bothered to shave—the clock was ticking—but his eyes were alert and he'd run a brush through his hair.

"I see you stayed for the show," he said, trying for a levity neither of them believed.

"Don't worry, I won't look."

Something went through his mind, then. She saw it reflected in his eyes but couldn't decide if it was amusement or regret. Whatever it was, he chose not to give it voice, instead going over to dig clean clothes out of the suitcase, which lay open on the floor of the closet. Voss turned her back so he could dress.

"All right," he said after a minute. "You won't be blinded."

He was still buttoning his shirt when Turcotte arrived alone. Josh answered the knock and let him in. Turcotte had dark circles under his eyes, but his suit and tie looked crisp enough to be just back from the dry cleaners. If anything, the gray-brown stubble on his head looked shorter, as though he had just buzzed it.

"Chang on the way?" Voss asked.

"She's on the phone with the Florida State Police, listening to a pretty detailed report with a net result of absolutely nothing. But she'll be along. What's on your mind?"

Voss sipped her coffee, but it was down to cold dregs now, so she pushed the cup away. Turcotte would have to relay to Chang the conversation they were about to have.

"That *Rolling Stone* article," Voss said. "It might not be as crazy as it sounds."

"Either that," Turcotte added, "or someone took it seriously."

"It's always possible that whoever's behind this never read the article and doesn't know anything about the supposed history," Voss said, "but it sure as hell feels like these killers came to the same conclusion."

"Maybe not," Turcotte argued, frowning. "Maybe they just don't like half-breeds."

Josh ran his hands through his hair. "Maybe you guys could take a step back and tell me how we got here? As of a few hours ago, the Herod Factor was just some lunatic conspiracy theory."

"The 'crib murders' are all over the news," Voss explained. "The cases are spread out over five years, but they all have one thing in common. It isn't just the Greenlaw twins and Grace Kowalik. Each of the victims had one biological parent who was either Iraqi, Afghani, or Iranian."

"Wait," Josh said. "How do the Greenlaws fit in?"

Turcotte narrowed his eyes. "The twins were adopted from Afghanistan. The paperwork said the mother claimed the father was a U.S. aid worker who had married her, and then abandoned her when his company pulled out of the country. She gave the kids up specifically to be adopted by Americans, so they would have the life she'd envisioned for them."

Josh threw up his hands. "I'm more confused than ever. What is this? Are these guys terrorists or serial killers? This has been going on for years and the point of terrorism is to let the world know. Otherwise . . . no terror."

Voss sat back in the chair. "That, I can't help you with."

"So, we've got a serial killer murdering biracial children?" Josh asked.

Turcotte shook his head. "The media won't see it that way. Hate crimes. Someone's killing the babies of our enemies."

"You said 'one parent.' In every case, the other parent is American?" Josh asked.

"In every case," Voss agreed. "But I don't buy this Herod bullshit. The idea that children, just by existing, can alter the mood of nations . . . that's just nuts. And maybe it's not what this is about. Maybe Gharib al-Din and his buddies think of the babies as traitors. Obviously the spin will be that terrorists are killing their own, destroying any links between East and West, or something like that."

"None of it makes any sense," Turcotte said.

"There's something else," Voss replied. "I've been turning it over in my mind, and we need to talk about Norris. I'm not comfortable with the idea of Black Pine looking over our shoulders."

"Nothing I can do about it," Turcotte said. "I've got orders from the assistant director."

"It's possible I could help."

Turcotte eyed her suspiciously. "What do you have in mind?"

A knock at the door made Voss jump. The three of them glanced at one another, then Josh went to open it. Agent Chang stood in the corridor, eyes lit up like a rabbit on speed.

"They found al-Din," Chang said.

"What?" Turcotte asked. "Where?"

"The baggage compartment of a plane from Bangor to Boston. He's dead. Somebody cut his throat."

-30--

Detective Anne Monteforte sat at her desk, staring at a photograph of George and Jane Wadlow. In the picture, George wore a Red Sox T-shirt and his tool belt, while Jane held a screwdriver to his ear, nose crinkled and eyes narrowed as though she was trying to figure out how to fix him. It was a cute picture, from happier times. A picture today would have shown a very worried George tending to a Jane whose face was bruised and swollen, and whose confidence had suffered a terrible blow.

In frustration, she pushed the picture away. They had nothing.

The two events—the mystery vehicles watching the Wadlow house in the small hours of the morning and the attack in the Wadlows' driveway—had to be related. So the case created two jobs for the Medford P.D. The first was to figure out who these guys were and the second was to make sure they weren't coming back. The prevailing belief seemed to be that someone—sexual predators or human traffickers or someone who just wanted a damn baby—had spotted Jane out with Leyla at some point and had targeted her. Detective Jarman had suggested that, as an older woman, Jane might have seemed like she wouldn't put up much of a fight.

Surprise, assholes! Monteforte thought. *Good for Jane.*

Thought it hadn't really been good for Jane. Monteforte winced at the memory of the woman's injuries. She wanted to find the bastards responsible and hoped to have the opportunity to give them a few bruises of their own.

But as the day had progressed, Monteforte had begun to doubt the prevailing wisdom. If Jane and Cait's stories about the cars working surveillance on Badger Road had been accurate, there had been a team prepping for the attempted abduction of Leyla McCandless. That didn't sound like some pervert, kiddie pornographer, or baby black marketer. It sounded like someone who really wanted *this* child, which brought a slew of new questions to the table.

Monteforte had questioned A-Train herself. The guy was an asshole, no doubt, and the video of Cait kicking his ass had gone viral on the Internet and continued to be shown on the news all day, making its way onto national newscasts. He was pissed off and embarrassed, but he had an alibi and Monteforte had believed his denials. The guy was a dimwit, incapable of convincingly pretending to be mystified by her questions.

If it hadn't been random, that left only two possibilities— a custody-related kidnapping perpetrated on behalf of baby Leyla's Iraqi relatives, or something Monteforte and Jarman hadn't even considered yet. Her instinct told her it was the latter, which pissed her off. Anne Monteforte was a smart woman and she didn't like feeling clueless. There were pieces missing from the puzzle, and big ones.

None of the neighbors had seen anything helpful. Several had noticed the cars parked on the street, but either paid them little attention or developed their own theories about the presence of the unfamiliar vehicles. One old woman had thought the car must belong to a private eye out to catch a cheating spouse; Monteforte figured she watched too much television. The neighbors on either side of the vacationing DiMarinos, in front of whose house the cars kept parking, had not noticed more than one vehicle and had independently assumed it belonged to some friend or relative, there to check up on the house.

The supposedly untraceable license plate was a big question mark, but only if one assumed that Cait had written it down correctly. The woman had been a sergeant in the National Guard and spent more than two years in Iraq. She had been trained to pay attention, and her fight with A-Train showed that she was far more capable than the typical soldier. But that didn't mean she hadn't made a mistake about the plate number.

They had started to run down similar plate numbers, with one digit off from the number Cait had provided. Monteforte shuffled through a stack of papers on her desk, looking at the information they had collected on the owners of the cars with those near-miss plates. Thus far she had found only one potential suspect among them, a guy named Marcus Freiberg, who had two restraining orders against him and a sexual assault charge that had been continued without a finding. The sex assault beef had resulted in him violating a T.R.O. from his ex-wife, so maybe there was more to that story than the paperwork revealed. In any case, most of his ugly behavior seemed related to the ex, so the possibility of a connection to the Wadlow/McCandless case seemed slim. But they had to be thorough.

Nothing's going to come of it, Monteforte thought. *You're not getting anywhere.*

The thought infuriated her, but she couldn't deny it. Unless they got a major break, this case would go cold. Whoever had put the Wadlows' house under surveillance and then beaten Jane and tried to snatch the baby had left no trace behind. They were professionals, almost military in the execution of their crimes.

"Jesus," she sighed, and glanced at the clock, to find it ticking toward six p.m. Sunday afternoon was about to give way to Sunday night, and Monteforte just wanted to go home. Unless they caught a break, they had done all they could for today.

With a shake of her head, she dropped the file on her desk and stood.

As she did, Jarman came into the office, looking pissed off and more than a little scary. Her partner had a kind heart and a quiet wisdom, but he didn't smile nearly often enough and could be intimidating to people who didn't know him.

"What is it?" Monteforte asked, even before he could open his mouth.

"It's money. It's always money, isn't it?" Jarman muttered.

"What are you talking about?"

He sank into his desk chair and turned to her. "It's August, and the damn weekend. We're short-staffed and Hoffmeyer won't approve overtime for anyone. I asked Tagliabue to drive past Cait McCandless's place every hour or so—Parker's off duty now—but he just told me Hoffmeyer's asked him to sit on Wellington Station."

"So talk to Hoffmeyer," Monteforte said.

Jarman scowled. "I did. Where do you think I got the 'short-staffed' bullshit from?"

"So you're coming around to the idea that this might not have been random?"

The question took the wind out of Jarman. He exhaled, settling into his chair, and then shrugged.

"Just trying to keep an open mind. But something goddamn weird happened over there today, and the fact that neither of us has a clue makes me nervous."

With a deep sigh, Jarman stood up.

"You going home?" Monteforte asked.

Jarman nodded. "Just about to. Why? You want to get a drink? I sure as hell could use one."

Monteforte glanced at the papers on her desk. "Not yet. I want to run down this Marcus Freiberg guy. I'm sure it's a dead end, but I want to dot all the i's, y'know?"

"All right. Let me know what you find."

"Will do," Monteforte agreed. "Listen, though. If you're headed out, maybe you oughta take a drive past Cait Mc-Candless's place yourself. If we've got no one else who can do it . . ."

Jarman sighed, but then gave a firm nod.

"Yeah, you're right," he said. "I'm gonna go home, change my clothes, and then I'll go out for a drive. And if I happen to pass by the McCandless girl's apartment, well, the department doesn't have to pay overtime for what I do when I'm out driving around."

-31--

Cait watched the six o'clock news with horrified fascination. Sarah Lin had treated her gently in the interview, reported on the tragic irony of her brother's death occurring the same day, and delivered the televised version of the attack on Jane and the attempted abduction of Leyla with a grim air of consequence.

What horrified her was the way that watching the report changed her. She recognized the twisted irony of it, but seeing the story told on television made her confront it in a way she had not previously allowed herself to do. She watched herself sitting on the sofa in her living room, pale and ghost-eyed, talking to Sarah, and she felt pity for the poor little girl on the TV screen.

Vanity had nothing to do with it. Cait saw how awful she looked but, more, she studied her own eyes and saw someone who was *lost*. Perched on the sofa—first on her own and then holding Leyla—she looked sixteen or seventeen years old, if that. Her short hair, petite build, and almost elfin features nearly always made people underestimate her, which had sometimes been a curse and sometimes a gift.

But now she wanted to reach into the TV and slap herself awake. Her father had not raised her to rely on other people to provide answers. She and Sean had both been taught to search for their own solutions to problems. This might be an extreme situation, but the police had been awfully quiet today, and she'd placed very little hope in them to begin with, considering how little information they had been able to gather during their canvass of the neighbors on Badger Road.

She hoped the interview would help, that maybe someone had seen something they had yet to report to the police and would now come forward. But as she watched it, Cait realized it wasn't enough. Monteforte and Jarman had seemed competent, but they weren't family. They got to go home at the end of the day and stop thinking about Leyla, and untraceable license plates, and the sudden death of Sean McCandless.

Cait sat on the edge of the sofa, forking macaroni and cheese into her mouth as the commercials blared—why were they always so much louder than the regular programming? In minutes the weather forecast would come on, and then sports, and then what? The long night stretched out ahead of her. Even the idea of going to sleep made her uneasy. Sean had died shortly after she'd last spoken to him. If she slept, how would her life have changed when she opened her eyes again?

In her playpen, Leyla started to cry. It didn't start the way it usually did, with a fussy whimper. Instead, the baby wailed in what sounded like a strange combination of protest and sorrow. Cait set her plate on the coffee table, her already diminished appetite vanishing completely.

"All right, sweetie. Mommy's coming."

Leyla's face was red but there were no tears in her eyes. It wasn't that sort of cry. Cait plucked her from the playpen and held the baby against her chest, patting her back and humming a tired melody. In talking to other mothers, she had long since realized that she had gotten lucky with Leyla. Compared to horror stories Cait had heard, Leyla was a pretty easy infant, and she slept better than most. Even so, being the mother of an infant was draining, and most days she suffered from a kind of new mother exhaustion that had quickly replaced what had once been her normal life.

Now she did the slow dance around the living room that always calmed Leyla, and after a few seconds of complaint, the baby snuffled and went silent, trying to grab her face. Cait smiled tiredly.

"You're going to sleep with me tonight, baby girl," she said.

Leyla had eaten already. If Cait wasn't going to finish her own dinner, it was time for her to give the baby a bath, put her in her pajamas, and give her a bottle. They both needed to stick to their routine tonight.

Tomorrow, the routine would be shot to hell.

Cait knew that even if she went down to Washington, D.C., real answers about what happened to Sean would never be forthcoming, and pressing for them might endanger Herc and others. But she had to do something.

The phone startled her. She realized she ought to have been surprised it had taken so long to ring. Someone she knew must have seen her on the news and was calling now to tell her how sorry they were, to lend their support.

Cait wasn't sure she wanted to talk, no matter how sympathetic the caller might be. If she talked, she might cry again, and she needed to stop that shit. On the other hand, it might be someone calling for an interview, or even the police, phoning to tell her that they'd had a break in the case and knew why someone had tried to take Leyla.

On the fourth ring, she carried Leyla into her bedroom, but she paused in the open door as the answering machine picked up and her own voice filled the room.

"Hi, it's Cait. You know the drill." And then the beep.

"Cait, are you there? Oh, my God, pick up," Miranda Russo said, her voice on the edge of frantic. "Cait?"

She propped Leyla on her hip, picked up the phone, and hit the button to halt the answering machine's recording. "Hey."

"You *are* there. I saw the news. It's horrible. Are you okay? No, scratch that, of course you're not okay. Do you want me to come over?" Miranda said, the words coming out in a torrent.

Cait felt the muscles in her shoulders relax, just slightly, as she swayed back and forth to keep Leyla happy. She and Miranda might not have anything in common anymore, but the woman's frantic babble reminded her so much of the closeness they had once shared that suddenly it did not seem that long ago at all.

"No need," she said. "I've got to give Leyla a bath. I need to keep her on a schedule."

"Are you sure? I wouldn't get in the way," Miranda said. "I just thought maybe you could use some company."

Cait hesitated, all of her conflicting emotions about friendship clashing in the space of seconds.

"Maybe I could. If it's no trouble," she said quietly.

"Are you kidding? How could it be trouble? You need me, I'm there. We may not see each other much these days, but that hasn't changed. Have you eaten?"

Cait said that she had.

"All right," Miranda replied. "Give me an hour or so and I'll be over. Should I bring wine?"

"You'd better. And Miranda?"

"Yes?"

"Thank you."

-32--

On Sundays, the Northern Virginia office of the NGA operated on the equivalent of a skeleton crew. There were staffers there around the clock, watching satellite feeds and monitoring the equipment for glitches, but a lighter complement of analysts and administrative staff.

Brian Herskowitz had worked plenty of Sundays, hurrying to finish up a regional analysis or doing map overlays showing any topographical changes—sometimes to indicate geological events and others to reveal the appearance or disappearance of settlements and training camps.

Tonight, Herc had waited for Roger Boyce to leave the office and then let the clock tick off twelve full minutes—enough time for Boyce to get into his car and drive down to and through the security gate—so that he knew the asshole wouldn't be back until morning.

With a glance out into the monitoring room, which always reminded him of Mission Control at NASA, he closed and locked his office door. If Boyce ever learned what he was about to do, it would cost him his job, but his hesitation lasted only a second. Right was right and wrong was wrong, and Sean McCandless had been closer to him than his own brother.

Herc sat behind his desk, picked up the phone, and dialed from memory. The phone rang only twice before it was picked up.

"Stanovitch."

"Terry, this is Herc."

"Herc, you calling on a secure line?"

"I am. Did you hear about Sean McCandless?"

Stanovitch sighed. "Fuck, yes, I heard. I couldn't believe it, man. You like anyone for it?"

"Why, you don't think it was a heart attack?"

A second or two went by before Stanovitch replied. "That's not funny."

Herc leaned back in his chair and stared at the door to his office, watching the knob, paranoid even though he knew it was locked.

"No," he said. "It's not. There are a lot of people who would have wanted Sean dead if they'd known who he was, but he was not a sloppy guy, Terry. You know this. I hope we'll figure out who did it, and I hope we burn the fuckers down, but for now, I'm still getting used to the idea that someone got to him."

"I know what you mean," Stanovitch said. "But you're calling me, and I'm guessing it's not just to reminisce about Sean. What do you need, Herc?"

"I've got a license plate number, unregistered, though definitely from a vehicle that's on the street. Could just be a fake, but intuition says otherwise. I'm guessing covert surveillance, but I'd like to know who's running it and why."

"Simple enough," Stanovitch told him.

"Maybe not so simple," Herc said. "Once you've done it, I need you to forget you did it."

"You coloring outside the lines?" Stanovitch asked.

"Depends on who's setting the lines. But I can tell you it's for Sean. Does that help?"

"I'll be a ghost in the machine, brother. No one will even know I was there."

Herc smiled, nodding to himself. Stanovitch was CIA, but he was good people. Thanks to the synergy efforts of Homeland Security, they had worked together frequently, sorting out various intelligence reports and satellite analysis. Sean had been a part of most of those meetings.

"You want to ring me back?" Herc asked.

"Nah. Just give me the number."

Herc read it off to him and heard Stanovitch tapping away on his keyboard on the other end of the line.

"Got it," the man said. "Now let's see what we can see."

A few more clicks and clacks over the phone were followed by a low exhalation that might have been nothing, but made Herc frown.

"What is it?" he asked.

"Wow," Stanovitch said. "We're both pretending this call never happened, right?"

"Terry—"

"I'm covering my tracks right now, logging off, and going home," Stanovitch said, words punctuated with his keyboard.

"—talk to me," Herc finished. "What did you find?"

"Nothing. And that's the problem. This is definitely someone's op, but I couldn't tell you whose. The plate number is on a list I just found of 'blank slates.' Those plates are given out to field actives, sometimes to civilian contractors, for classified domestic ops only. Whatever questions you're asking, buddy, the answers are way above my pay grade."

"Terry—"

"Sorry, Herc. I'm going home."

The click that ended the call brought a terrible chill to the office. Herc stared at the phone in his hand for a second before putting it down. Terry Stanovitch had access to some of the government's best-kept secrets, things Herc himself would never know. If the holder of that license plate was above Terry's clearance level, that did not bode at all well for Cait McCandless.

Herc turned and stared out his office window as the summer twilight began to spread across the distant trees. He told himself that if Sean were there, he would know what to do.

And then he realized that there really was only one thing he could do.

But it would have to wait. If this went up so high that Stanovitch couldn't crack it, he didn't dare risk Boyce finding out. More than his job might be at stake. But now that he had started along this path, he couldn't turn back. Sean McCandless would have done anything for him. He knew that. And while Sean could not be there to take care of his little sister, Herc would be damned if he let anything happen to her.

He wouldn't be able to live with himself.

Detective Bill Jarman pulled his dented Saturn into the traffic at Powder House Circle with the same sort of aggressive daring that he imagined must fill the hearts of the fools who ran with the bulls at Pamplona. The traffic circle seemed to breed contempt in place of caution, filled day and night with drivers who seemed to approach the task as if it were a joust. And Jarman had never been one to back down from a challenge.

The worst of the various dings and scrapes on the Saturn had been earned in battle right there in Powder House Circle, courtesy of an attractive Tufts University history professor who'd nearly torn off his rear bumper with her pretentious purple PT Cruiser. But all he cared about was that the car ran, and pieces didn't fall off while he was driving.

Tonight, he managed to make it through the vehicular sparring in the circle without incident, heading up Boston Avenue. The university rose up to the left and he could see the peaks of its dorms and oldest academic buildings at the top of the hill. On the right were blocks of neatly kept older homes, most of which had long since been converted into apartment housing for Tufts students.

He drove slowly and with the windows open, letting the warm night air eddy around inside the car. The air-conditioning worked, though poorly, but he preferred fresh air whenever possible. His police radio crackled, keeping up a constant low muttering, but he had music on as well, a station called "The River," which played a little bit of everything.

Young guys, every one of them king of the world, laughed and taunted one another as they walked along the sidewalks with gorgeous girls of every conceivable shape and shade. Jarman wondered if girls had been that beautiful when he was in college, or if he had just come to see them with the eyes of age.

Like Cait McCandless. Now, there was a beautiful girl.

He mused on this almost wistfully. His interest in Cait had nothing inappropriate about it, except that he had taught himself to put some distance between himself and the people his job brought him into contact with every day. Most of them started out as suspects, victims, or witnesses, and if they weren't at first, they often became one of the three during the course of an investigation.

But he liked Cait McCandless. It didn't hurt that she was so damn cute, but mostly he respected her. She had served her country and fallen in love. She had a baby she obviously adored. And she could kick the shit out of a three-hundred-pound football goon without breaking a sweat. Jarman flat-out admired her.

None of that would have been enough to get him to do a personal drive-by, however. If she called and asked him, maybe, but to volunteer? No, there was more to this detour than his admiration for the former sergeant. Jarman did not like mysteries.

Thoughts kept trying to surface in his mind, but he pushed them away because they were simply absurd. The license plate number she had given them had to be wrong or fake; it wasn't difficult to make a fake plate, though it wouldn't hold up to close scrutiny. But a third possibility existed, which was that the plate was off the books for a reason, which meant . . . what? Secret government assholery?

That made no sense. Federal agents would not beat up a middle-aged woman in her driveway and try to steal a seven-month-old baby. But *someone* had attacked Jane Wadlow.

Cait McCandless and her baby might not be in any danger at all. But driving by every couple of hours for a day or two was the least they ought to be doing. It would take such little effort. No time at all, really.

Hoffmeyer obviously disagreed. He had canceled all drive-bys on Cait's apartment. Either he thought there was no danger—and maybe he was right—or protecting people in trouble simply wasn't as important to him as the bottom line.

Monteforte had been right to suggest he take a drive past the house. He was off duty now, and his time was his own.

So he watched the numbers going by as he drove past the houses on Boston Avenue. In the dark some of them were difficult to make out, but he slowed as he came to Cait Mc-Candless's block. A car drew up behind him, tailgating for a few seconds before the driver honked his horn. Jarman stuck his hand out the window and flipped the guy the bird, prompting the driver to gun his engine and swerve around him, speeding ahead toward a light that turned from yellow to red. Another night, he might have been tempted to put the bubble on top of his car and pull the guy over, put a scare into him.

Instead he pulled over to the curb across from Cait's apartment and killed his headlights. He was in a No Parking zone, but he wouldn't be there long. He let the engine idle as he studied the front of the house. There were two cars in the driveway and one of them belonged to Cait. The windows on the second story were dark, but the first floor was lit up, and after several minutes he saw a brunette woman move across what he thought must be the living room. He didn't see Cait, but nothing seemed out of order.

Killing the engine, he climbed from the car. If nobody else would be checking up on her, it wouldn't hurt to do more than just drive past the house, so he walked up and down the street a block in either direction, studying parked cars. If whoever had beaten Jane Wadlow really had been after Cait's baby, he wanted to be certain they didn't come back. At last, finding nothing suspicious, he returned to his own car, climbed in, and sat watching the house.

Jarman had been parked at the curb for nearly ten minutes when his stomach started to rumble. Much as he wanted to keep an eye on Cait, he knew he couldn't stay out there all night, and he hadn't eaten much of anything since breakfast.

He started up the battered Saturn and put it in gear. On Boston Avenue, on the other side of the hill, was a little joint called Sparky's that had the most extraordinary selection of chicken wing flavors he had ever encountered. Jarman stopped there at least a couple times a month and had been working up the courage to try their peanut butter and jelly wings.

The clock on the dash read 8:23. He'd hit Sparky's, put a little food in his belly, then make another swing by to check on Cait before heading home.

—34—

Voss had just gotten off an airplane, and now she was flying again. The small charter plane carried her and Josh southward, with Turcotte and Chang along for the ride. The FBI had plenty of pull, but it had been her Homeland Security contacts who had arranged this ride on such short notice.

Short notice? More like immediately.

If they'd driven, the trip would've taken four hours. Too damn long when there was a crime scene waiting. So instead they were flying, and she sat belted into her seat, wishing desperately for a margarita, a beach chair, and a beach to put it on. Ever since this case began, it had been getting uglier and uglier, and now she couldn't help letting her mind drift back to the days when she and Josh were working ocean interdiction cases for the FBI, headquartered on the island of St. Croix.

"You okay?" he asked quietly.

Voss nodded. "Sure. Some days, I just miss the Caribbean."

Josh smiled. "I know what you mean. But let's not forget how our last case there turned out."

Voss shivered. "You have to remind me?"

"There are all kinds of monsters, I guess."

She thought about Gharib al-Din and nodded grimly.

"We've got to catch one of these fuckers alive, or we're never going to solve this thing," she said. "Al-Din doesn't do us any good as a corpse."

"Sure he does," Josh said, eyes narrowed. "He saves the government the trouble of putting him on trial and the tax-payers the cost of keeping him in prison. Hell, he might have saved me the trouble of shooting him."

Voss glanced at him. She didn't think Josh would have killed al-Din, even after the atrocities the man had commit-ted. They both knew where the line lay and, so far, neither of them had stepped over it. Though if there had ever been a case that tempted Voss to mete out some private justice, this was it. But being tempted and committing murder were two different things.

At the front of the small charter, Turcotte and Chang were leaning into the aisle, talking quietly. Voss glanced at Josh, noticing not for the first time the way his gaze strayed toward Chang. A tiny, selfish alarm went off in her chest, but she pushed it away. No matter what she felt for Josh, they were partners first, friends second, and lovers not at all.

"She's on your mind, huh?" Voss asked instead.

Josh glanced at her, frowning as if he were about to deny it. Then he softened.

"I like her, but it's not what you're thinking. It's thanks to her, I think, that Turcotte's been playing nice with us."

"Yeah?" Voss asked, intrigued.

"She doesn't think he sees how capable she is, but he does. I got the feeling she thought sending her to Bangor—away from the hub of the investigation—was kind of a blow-off."

"Are you serious? He would never have put her in charge of something like that—a child abduction—if he didn't have faith in her," Voss said.

"I agree," Josh said, with a thin smile. "I guess they just have to learn to trust each other."

They sat in companionable silence for a few minutes, but she could sense there was something else on his mind . . . something that troubled him.

"What's buzzing around your brain? I can see something's eating at you."

"It could be nothing," he said with a small shrug, "but earlier today I got a report about an attempted child abduction just outside Boston. I called the local P.D. The witness descriptions said there were two guys, one white and one black. Non-Arabic."

Voss felt a strange tugging in her chest. "So you figured it wasn't related to our case."

"Right. We've been assuming that because these four guys are Arabic, if there are others in their cell, then they must be, too. But we don't *know* that."

"We don't even know if there's more to their cell than the four guys we're already aware of, and two of them are dead," Voss reminded him.

"I know," Josh said. "But now we're headed to Boston. If this DOA is al-Din, then someone killed him in Boston today. And the attempted abduction, not far from Boston, was this morning. At the very least, I think it warrants a closer look."

"Agreed," Voss said. "These guys are ghosts. Two of them are dead, but we haven't been able to come up with shit so far on the other two. Whatever their goals are, we're too in the dark to make any assumptions about what is and isn't connected."

Voss agreed with Josh's initial instinct, that the cases were unrelated. But if he had started second-guessing his gut, then she would gladly follow along. Instinct had kept them both alive more than once.

"We'll check it out as soon as we're done at the airport," she said. "If it's that close to Boston, we'll be over there and back before Turcotte even knows we're gone."

Josh frowned, patting his pockets as if just remembering

something. "Actually, I think I've got the investigating detective's cell phone number written down."

"Even better," Voss said. "We'll be on the ground shortly. You can give him a call, maybe save us a trip."

-35--

Cait set the phone down, feeling a little better for the first time all day. The horror had not receded at all, but the strange fog of surreality that had enveloped her did seem to have abated somewhat. She grieved for Sean, she worried that whoever had tried to take Leyla might return, and she fought a rising tide of panic that seemed ready to drown her at any moment—but she no longer felt alone, and for that she was grateful.

She came out of the kitchen to find Miranda standing by the bricked-up fireplace, holding the framed photograph of Nizam that usually sat on the mantel. A pang of grief touched Cait, but it was so familiar—always there, like an extra chamber in her heart—that it had become a part of her. Nizam had loved her, and she had felt a love and passion for him that astonished her. He'd somehow managed to be an ordinary man and a remarkable person, both at the same time.

Every night, when she closed her eyes, Nizam waited for her on the edges of sleep, as though he still wanted to protect her. She had always pretended to be amused by that—the taxi driver who wanted to keep the soldier safe—but it had also made her love him so hard that it hurt.

Nizam would want her to be happy. That was what people said to her all the time—Sean, Auntie Jane, Jordan . . . even the woman who cut her hair—and Cait knew it was true. She had always been astounded by the kindness in his eyes, and she knew that he would want her to fall in love again, to find someone to be the husband and father he had planned to be for her. Someday, perhaps, she would.

As she studied the photo of Nizam, Miranda wore a sad expression so open and contemplative that Cait thought it might be the most genuine emotion she had ever seen her friend display.

"Sorry," Cait said. "I told him I had company, but he wanted to make sure I was really all right."

Miranda smiled curiously. "But you're not all right."

"No. And he knows that. I guess there are levels of all right, aren't there? He wanted to know I was safe and reasonably sane. He lives in Hartford, but he was willing to drive up here, which is sweet."

"This is Ronnie, right? The guy from your troop?" Miranda asked.

Cait smiled. "My unit, yes. And before you ask, no, there's nothing going on there. He's just a stand-up guy who had my back when I needed it most. Without him and my friend Jordan, I don't think I'd ever have made it out of Baghdad."

Miranda pushed a lock of auburn hair behind her ear and glanced back down at the photo before carefully resettling it on the mantel.

"I wasn't going to ask," she said softly, turning dark eyes toward Cait. "I know you're still in love with Nizam."

Cait stared at her, oddly bemused. The war in Iraq had stripped away all of her pretension and given her new eyes with which to view the world. Miranda lived a life steeped in privilege and presumption, and her concerns were far removed from the things that Cait would normally have worried about. But maybe the girl with whom she had once been so close still lived inside of her after all.

"I am," Cait agreed, sitting on the sofa and picking up her wineglass. "I can't imagine a time when I won't love him. But you build rooms in your heart, you know?"

Miranda picked up her own glass from the mantel and moved over to join Cait on the sofa. "I guess I don't."

Cait took a sip of wine, then shook her head. "I don't know. It's silly."

"What is? Come on. It's just us," Miranda said.

The words took Cait back to another time, when the two of them had had sleepovers almost every weekend and shared all of the secret wishes they would never have dared tell anyone else. Miranda used to come into Sweet Somethings all the time when they were in junior high and high school, and Cait would always sneak her a few caramels—her favorite. Auntie Jane had known and never complained. When Cait got a little older, she'd often shared secrets with her friend Nick, too, but not in the same way. With Miranda there had never been any embarrassment, no shyness, just a kind of wonder.

"I just think you make space in your heart for people," Cait said. "I'll always love Nizam, and I miss him so much—especially right now. But when Leyla was born . . . I never knew how much love existed in one person until I had her. So, yeah, I think it's possible to fall in love with someone else someday without giving up loving Nizam."

Miranda clinked glasses with her in a quiet toast. "I'm really glad to hear you say that." She sipped her wine. "So, Ronnie?"

Cait laughed. She felt guilty, like she shouldn't be able to laugh. Then she thought of Sean and shrouds of grief wrapped tightly around her again, her smile slipping away.

"Not Ronnie," she said. "And not Jordan." She thought about that a moment and smiled. "Though he's really sweet, and those eyes . . ." She sighed theatrically. "Seriously, it's nice to know that they're looking out for me, even now."

Miranda grinned. "Jordan, huh?"

"Nah. We work together. He got me the job at Channel Seven."

"But . . ."

Cait gave a tiny nod. "He *is* a pretty amazing guy. I'd hate to ruin the friendship we have, but I guess I wouldn't say no if he wanted to take me out to dinner some night."

"And by dinner you mean . . . ?"

"Food!" Cait said, rolling her eyes and chuckling softly.

Miranda obviously wanted to lighten her spirits. Maybe allowing her to do it wasn't something she should be feeling guilty about. Whatever she could do to ease her mind had to be a good thing. Tomorrow, when Leyla was awake—or at least mobile—she could act. Tonight, she realized, she would have been driven mad with grief and frustration if not for Miranda's visit and Ronnie's phone call.

There had been loads of other calls, but Cait had continued to screen. A lot of them were hang-ups, which made her glad she hadn't answered. Some were acquaintances or co-workers or long-ago friends calling to offer words of comfort, and she felt bad for not picking up, but after the interview, and now talking with Miranda, she really didn't want to have to go through it all again. Then there were the media people looking for an update or a comment or an interview, and those she ignored for now. Someone had tried to beep in while she'd been talking to Ronnie, but she'd let it go straight to voice mail.

Now the phone rang again. Cait rolled her eyes.

"I can't believe Leyla is sleeping through all of these calls," Miranda said.

"She usually sleeps great for the first half of the night," Cait replied. "It's only in the wee hours of the morning that she sometimes has trouble. Anyway, I've got her door halfway closed, so it shouldn't be too loud in her room."

The answering machine clicked on and the two women paused to listen, but the caller hung up without leaving a message.

"God, give it a rest, people," Miranda said.

Cait sipped her wine. "I don't mind, really. If that many people watched my interview and want to talk to me, there's that much better chance someone saw something that could help."

"I'd jump out of my chair every time the phone rang."

"I kind of was, earlier," Cait admitted. "But then a friend brought wine over."

She smiled and raised her glass in a silent toast and Miranda clinked her glass against Cait's.

"Have you talked to Nick through all of this?" Miranda asked.

"He left a message, but I haven't talked to him. Honestly, I was pretty numb when you called. Doing that interview and dealing with the police . . . Nick called because of the thing last night, but after today that seems like it happened a thousand years ago."

That got them off on a tangent, talking about old times and old friends, childhood adventures and teenage romances. Most of an hour passed as they swapped stories, sometimes finishing each other's sentences, and drank more wine. Only two more calls came in, one another hang-up and the other from a reporter at the *Boston Herald*. But, like Leyla's sleep, their reminiscing could not be disrupted by the ringing of the phone.

Eventually, Miranda stood up, taking her glass with her. "I'm going to get a refill. Want me to top you off?"

Cait hesitated, but only for a second. She would pay for it with a headache in the morning, but right now the wine helped to untie the knots in her neck and shoulders, and the one in her heart.

"Yes, please," she said, offering her glass. "You're going to end up crashing on the sofa tonight, though. No way am I letting you drive home."

"A sleepover?" Miranda chirped. "I'd love to! Fair warning, though. That might mean a pillow fight later."

Cait shook her head, amused once again.

The apartment was small, rooms flanking a corridor that ran down the center, dining room, Cait's bedroom, and Leyla's bedroom at the rear on one side, and the living room with its two entryways on the other, plus the bathroom at the back. The only way into the kitchen was through the living room.

As Miranda went into the kitchen, Cait went through into the hall and peeked into Leyla's room. The baby still slept soundly, her exhalations softly audible there in the dark. The light from the living room cast a strange geometrical shape on the carpet and just reached the corner of the bed. Leyla looked peaceful in her crib, and that did more to soothe Cait than anything else could have.

Then the phone rang, causing her to flinch. She pulled the door almost all the way shut and hurried back, passing the doors to the bathroom and her own bedroom and then ducking into the living room.

Miranda stood just outside the kitchen entryway. "Unbe-lievable," she said. "It's almost ten o'clock."

Cait thought this was probably nothing, that she would get more calls after the eleven o'clock news. She didn't dare un-plug the phone in case the police called with news, but she could damn well turn off the ringer. She walked past Miranda into the kitchen, intending to do just that, when the phone ceased, mid-ring.

"Not bothering to leave a message?" Miranda said. "Some-one's unmotivated."

"They didn't even wait for the machine." Cait frowned at the phone, then walked into the kitchen, picked it up, and checked caller ID for the most recent incoming number.

She smiled and turned to look at Miranda. "It was Nick," she said. "Jackass. Should have left a message."

She thumbed TALK, but got no dial tone. Just to be sure, she pushed the button again, then just stood there a moment and stared at the phone in her hand.

"What's wrong?" Miranda asked.

"The phone's dead," Cait said.

Her thoughts, though muddled by wine, began to race. Nick had not hung up. Her phone service had cut out right in the middle of an incoming call. The night was neither stormy nor especially windy, providing no convenient excuse.

"But Nick just called," Miranda said.

Cait barely heard her. "Come with me," she said, her voice low.

She grabbed Miranda by the wrist and hauled her through the living room and into the short hallway. Cait felt the change in herself, a chill that had come over her. The sweet nostalgia that Miranda had managed to summon had departed now.

Only one thing mattered—Leyla. Maybe she was paranoid, but she thought she had reason to be.

"Cait, what the hell?" Miranda asked, her protest tinged with fear.

Without answering, Cait hustled her into Leyla's room. She put a finger to her lips to forestall any argument.

"Stay here. Watch Leyla."

Miranda looked frightened but gave a single nod, and then Cait raced from Leyla's room into her own, sneakers quiet on the carpet. She pulled out her keys, chose the small copper one, and dropped to her knees, hauling the lockbox out of the bottom of her closet. Her heart beat strongly in her chest, but she felt strangely calm. The key turned and she flipped open the box, snatched up her gun, and relocked the box so that she could withdraw the key.

Shoving her keys into her pocket, she ran to her nightstand, rattled open the sock drawer, and pulled out the box of ammunition. It caught on the edge of the drawer, spilling bullets onto the carpet, and she went to her knees again. Ejecting the clip, she loaded it quickly, her fingers having remembered the exercise all too well.

As she rose, she slammed the clip home and raced out of the room.

Cait had made it as far as the short hallway, face-to-face with Miranda—who stood in the open door to Leyla's room—when the first knock came at the door.

-36--

Jarman waited until he was a safe distance away from the front door of Sparky's to issue the mighty belch that had been building up for the last few minutes. He glanced around to confirm he was alone on the sidewalk, but felt embarrassed just the same. He'd grown up with a mother who frowned upon such things.

Sated and content, more than ready to go home, he piled himself into his car and started the engine. A quick pass by Caitlin McCandless's house and he could be reunited with the reclining chair in his living room.

Before he could pull away from the curb, his cell phone

buzzed. Grumbling, he managed to extract it from his pocket and glanced at the caller ID screen, which read *Private Caller.* A blocked number.

Jarman frowned, hesitated a second, then tossed the phone on the passenger seat without answering it. If Monteforte—or anyone else from Medford P.D.—had called him, he would have answered. But an anonymous call, hours after he'd gone off duty? If they wanted him, they'd call back or leave a message.

He had a date with his recliner.

On the passenger seat, the phone stopped buzzing.

Josh stood on the tarmac beside their charter plane. Voss came down the steps he'd just descended, looking around at the planes and terminals of Logan Airport like she had forgotten where they were.

"Start the day in Florida, finish it in Boston," she muttered.

Josh nodded, but didn't reply. He was listening to the electronic ring on the other end of his phone call, his cell pressed to his ear.

"This is Bill Jarman," said the Medford detective's recorded voice. "I can't take your call at the moment, but please leave a message and I'll get back to you as soon as possible. If this is a police emergency, please call 911, or call the Medford Police Department's main number at—"

Josh ended the call, frowning. He didn't want to leave a message. What would he say?

"No luck?" Voss asked.

Josh shook his head. "Nada. When we're done here, I'll try him again. If there's still no answer, we can call the Medford P.D., get the McCandless woman's address, and just drive there."

Voss nodded. "You got it."

-37--

Cait stood in the darkened hallway at the back of the house, holding her breath, gun clutched tightly in her hand. The lights from the living room illuminated two patches of the corridor ahead, but at the far end, the foyer was dark. The front door seemed to breathe with menace.

"Cai—" Miranda began, but Cait held up a hand and shot her a look that silenced her.

The dining room, which she used as a playroom for Leyla and a computer room for herself, was dark. From there, she could have gotten a look at whoever stood on her front stoop. But to get there she would have to walk the length of the corridor, and with the light from the living room spilling into the hall and the curtains open, anyone who might be watching from outside would see her.

Miranda came up close behind her and whispered low, "You're scaring me."

David entered his apartment from a set of stairs and a landing that had been built onto the outside of the house when it had been split into two apartments, but in Cait's kitchen there was a narrow door—locked from the other side—that led to an old secondary stairwell. David wasn't home, so it would be dark up there. If she could manage the lock, she would be able to get into his place and have a look outside.

The knock came again, more insistent this time.

"Come on. What the fuck?" Miranda whispered.

Cait glanced over her shoulder, looking past Miranda at Leyla's crib. Through the bars she could see the baby, still asleep, and she exhaled. No way could she break into David's apartment and leave Leyla down here.

"Dude!" Miranda said, a bit harsher now. "Overreacting

much? What if it's just someone checking on you? Or the cops?"

The possibility had occurred to Cait, which was the only reason she didn't snap at Miranda to keep her voice down. But the police would have phoned first, or so she assumed. And she couldn't think of anyone who would just drop by her place at ten o'clock to check on her. Maybe Nick would have done it, but he had just tried calling. It wouldn't be him. Then, of course, there was the small fact of her phone service cutting out, right before that first knock on the door.

Her fingers opened and closed on the gun's grip.

The third time, the knock was followed by a voice.

"Ms. McCandless?" a man said quietly on the other side of the door. "Federal agents. We know you're at home and we'd like to ask you a few questions."

Cait stiffened, thinking of untraceable license plates and tinted windows. Thinking of Sean dead on a sidewalk.

"Federal agents?" Miranda said. "Jesus, Cait."

But Cait remained frozen on the spot, torn between her paranoia and her suspicions about Sean's line of work. He had obviously been doing some kind of spy shit for the government. Maybe they had come to talk to her about their investigation into his death. The confusion made her want to scream, and then she remembered the dead phone line and that cleared her mind instantly.

She turned and grabbed Miranda's arm, stepping with her into Leyla's room. The shades were drawn so that the morning sun wouldn't wake the baby early, but it also meant no one could look in and see them. Cait grabbed Leyla's baby sling and slipped it on.

"Listen to me," she whispered, face up close to Miranda's.

Miranda wasn't looking into her eyes. The other woman could not tear her gaze from the sight of Cait's gun. Cait grabbed her friend's face and forced her to look up.

"Miranda, listen! We don't know who they really are, and they've cut the telephone line. Haven't you ever seen a movie? Look, if I'm being crazy, then they'll go away, maybe leave me a business card or something. But if I'm right, then they're not going to just—"

Whump!

Whatever struck the door then wasn't a fist. Someone had kicked it, or slammed it with a shoulder.

Miranda's eyes went wide with fear, but Cait had run out of time to reason with her or calm her down.

Whump!

She always kept the door fully locked, chained, dead-bolted . . . but none of that would last more than a couple more kicks.

A heartbreaking wail rose from the crib. All the noise had finally woken Leyla, and now the baby lay crying inconsolably.

"Pick her up, Miranda," Cait snapped. "We're leaving!"

Shaking, Miranda reached into the crib. Cait glanced again at the drawn shades in her daughter's room, then stepped into the hall. With the gun pointed at the ceiling, she motioned for Miranda to hurry, watching the front door. To her left, her bedroom door stood open, as did the bathroom door on her right. Both rooms were dark, but a breeze blew in from her bedroom. She leveled her weapon and scanned the room, then glanced at the windows, which she had left open. It looked undisturbed.

She turned right, into the living room, swinging the gun in an arc, ready to fire. Behind her, Miranda whispered comforting words and cooed to Leyla, whose crying had diminished.

Cait spotted a face outside the front living room window.

"Miranda—"

The next word out of her mouth would have been *Go*.

But just then the front door crashed open with a splintering of wood. She spun to see Miranda standing in the hall, brown eyes staring toward the front of the house in fear.

Miranda turned back toward Leyla's room, instinctively shielding the baby with her body. The first bullet struck her in the right shoulder and she went down on her knees and spun halfway around, but still somehow managed to hold on to Leyla.

The second bullet took her in the back of the head, kicking her forward in a spray of blood. She landed on top of Leyla, sprawled on the carpet.

All Cait could hear was her daughter screaming. Or maybe it was her own voice she heard.

A window shattered in her living room and a shot rang out, but she was already in motion. Whoever had shot at her from the window missed. She spun into the corridor, already taking aim, but she didn't stop. Instead, she let herself slam into the wall and pulled the trigger. Two dark-suited white men had come through the door. She shot the first one through the throat. Blood fountained from the wound as the bald man staggered, dropping his gun and reaching up to try to staunch the bleeding.

He fell backward into his partner, costing the other man two seconds and his life. As he tried to shove the bald man aside and get a clear shot, Cait put two bullets dead center in his chest.

Numb. Cold. They killed Miranda. They'd reaped what they'd sown. Still, it made her sick—and it wasn't over.

A third man appeared just beyond the front door, a tall black man who looked strong enough to break her into pieces. Cait took a shot at him, but he spotted her in time to jump aside.

That was all right. She wanted him outside the apartment.

Heart hammering in her chest, heat flushing her face even though the rest of her still felt cold, she flipped over Miranda's corpse without looking at her. Grief and tears would come later, when there was time. War had taught her that, and more.

Leyla's cries became shrieks. Red-faced and wide-eyed, the baby kicked her feet on the floor. Her pajamas looked wet, and the smell told Cait that her diaper had leaked. She only vaguely registered this as she scooped Leyla up and darted through the open bathroom door. If they became trapped in here, they were dead.

She poked her head out and saw the man in her doorway again. He took a shot at her and missed. The bullet pinged off the bathroom door hinge even as Cait fired back, blowing out his knee. Her aim had been for shit—she had intended to kill him—but at least it took him down for a second.

It was long enough for her to slip Leyla into the sling around her neck. Then she was up and good to go. Baby urine soaked through the sling and into her shirt, damp against her skin, and Leyla kept screaming, but neither of those things bothered Cait. Her baby was alive, and nothing else mattered.

She poked her head out again and spotted a skinny young blond weasel coming through the door. The guy dropped to the floor behind the huge bastard with the ruined knee, using him for cover. His human shield had regained his wits enough to start reaching for the pistol he'd dropped, despite the agony of his knee. Staring at her, fury in his eyes, he grabbed the gun and started to aim. She shot him.

The weasel darted into the darkness of the dining room. Cait didn't wait to see what he would do, or who would come through the door next. She had a moment's respite and she used it.

Left arm holding her screaming daughter against her chest, she ran back into the living room, head ducked low. A shot boomed, shattering a framed photo of her father on the wall as she ran past, and then she was in the kitchen and heading for the back door. Nobody had tried breaking that one down yet, but she wasn't fool enough to think that meant it was unguarded. They'd have to be total idiots not to have covered the rear of the house, but she had no choice. She had no idea how many guns were out there, and if the police didn't show up fast, she was a sitting duck inside the house. If she could get through the backyard alive and push through the opening in the neighbors' fence that bumped up against the property there, she would find someone home, someone who would let her in, hide her and Leyla, help keep them safe until the police arrived.

All she knew was that she had to get her baby away from the bullets.

Cait hauled the door open and kicked the screened storm door wide. Its springs creaked loudly, but no one shot at her. She hurled herself out into the night, gun hand sweeping the yard for targets, and nearly stumbled when she spotted two dark-suited men—they'd obviously been guarding her back door—sprawled in the yard with their throats cut, blood glistening black in the moonlight.

Beyond them were three others, olive-skinned men in street clothes who trained their guns on her. Cait aimed back, breathing hard, chest tight with fear for her baby, but nobody fired.

One of the men—clean-shaven and darkly handsome—put a finger to his lips to keep her from crying out.

"Give us the child and live, or die and we'll take her from your cold hands," the man whispered. They were the most hideous words she had ever heard, yet his voice was melodious, almost pleasant, and he spoke in an accent that was all too familiar.

He was Iraqi.

-38--

Jarman drove up Boston Avenue, pleasantly full of chicken wings. The Cajun rub were the best, but he knew he would regret them later, along with the huge order of fries dusted with Cajun spices. Already his belly had begun to rumble queasily. He imagined his breath must be hideous now—a combination of beer and spices that would wilt houseplants and humans alike.

Just a quick pass by the McCandless house, and then straight home. Tomorrow he would take a fresh look at the weird pieces of the puzzle surrounding the attack on Jane Wadlow and her niece's baby. In the light of day, with a good night's sleep and a fresh cup of coffee, maybe he would see something he had missed. Or maybe he would find it easier to accept that some mysteries were never going to be solved.

He doubted it, though.

Even as this thought crossed his mind, he spotted the car

parked just ahead—a black Lexus with dark-tinted windows. *Probably nothing,* Jarman thought, but the small hairs on the back of his neck stood on end and he let his beat-to-shit Saturn coast a little, slowing down.

The car parked right in front of the Lexus was a charcoal-colored Saab. Same tinted windows. Brand new. Both vehicles looked as though they had just rolled off the lot.

"What's this, now?" he muttered.

He had the radio up loud, '80s alt-rock playing on The River, but now he turned it down and tapped the brake, approaching Cait McCandless's house at a crawl, peering into the darkness between houses and the deeper shadows thrown by trees and cars along the road.

A block and a half from Cait's apartment, he heard the first shots.

"Son of a bitch," he snapped, pulling into a space between two cars, blocking a driveway. He killed the engine, silencing the Smithereens.

Jarman didn't have a police radio in the car. He grabbed his cell phone off of the passenger seat and called for backup. It took three rings, and when the line was picked up, he did not wait for the voice on the other end to identify itself. He snapped off his name and badge number and Cait McCandless's address.

"Shots fired!" he snapped.

"All right, Detective. Backup's on the way."

"Good. And someone call my partner."

Protocol demanded that he observe and report before taking any action. Screw that. He hung up the phone, jammed it into his pocket, and climbed out of the Saturn, closing the door as quietly as he could.

Jarman hustled into the cover of a pair of trees, trying to get a view of McCandless's apartment house, but he was too far away. In a house up ahead, a couple of stoner-looking college guys came out on their front stoop, apparently curious about the gunshots, maybe not really understanding what they had heard or too stupid to keep their heads down.

"Get your asses back inside," Jarman hissed.

They jerked back inside, probably more at the sight of his gun than because he'd ordered them to, but when he reached into his open collar and yanked out his badge—which hung from a chain around his neck—they stepped out again. They figured a cop wouldn't shoot them, too stupid or too high to realize he hadn't fired the shots they'd already heard.

More gunshots punctured the darkness. Jarman darted toward the front of the nearest house and raced across the yards, keeping close to cover. When he was two houses away from Cait McCandless's apartment, he ran low across the grass to take cover behind a car parked in the driveway, which would give him a better view.

A skinny little guy in a dark suit went up the stairs and through the front door, gun at the ready. Gunfire cracked in the air like fireworks—Jarman could feel the sounds echoing in his chest.

Two others stood outside the house, ducked down so they couldn't be sighted through the well-lit apartment windows. Jarman listened to the shots being fired inside and felt himself torn by indecision. The numbers were against him. At least three people were involved in a gun battle inside the house, and the two apes in the yard were obviously armed. Protocol and wisdom said he should wait for backup. They couldn't be far. He'd called it in at least a full minute ago. Any second he'd hear sirens.

Any second.

But he didn't hear them, and now the gunfire had fallen silent in the house. He cursed himself for waiting, hated the way his stomach churned—though he blamed Sparky's wings for that—and despised the little ball of cowardice that had curled up like a whimpering dog in his gut.

Cait McCandless had a baby.

"Screw it," Jarman whispered, and he started to run.

-39--

The guy was Iraqi. Maybe they all were, or maybe they were a hodgepodge of Arabic extremists. What the hell had she heard about terrorists killing a family? Something on the news, but she couldn't remember now.

Iraqi, okay. But what the hell that meant and how all the pieces fit together, she had no idea. The detectives—Monteforte and Jarman—had asked about Nizam's family, and if they might try to get custody of Leyla. That alone had been difficult for her to imagine, but this? Cold-blooded murder? Gunfire in her apartment—

Miranda. Oh, God, Miranda.

"Fuck you," Cait sneered, her aim not wavering. "One step and you're dead."

She had the gun pointed directly into the face of the man who'd spoken. Leyla went silent and still, but Cait could feel the baby's heart beating against her chest. A deathly calm had come over Cait. The war had given her the ability to kill when necessary. She had never wanted to learn that skill or to lose the part of her soul that it had cost her, but she had. Her government had demanded it.

"They'll kill you anyway, after you've shot me," said the one who gave the orders.

"But you'll be dead."

The man lifted his chin. "So be it."

Fuck. She hated martyrs. There was no way to get a fair fight with someone who didn't mind dying for their cause.

She shot him in the face. Even as the bullet snapped his head back, she swung the gun toward the third man, who still had his own gun out, but she knew she would not be fast enough. He had the drop on her. He would pull the trigger. This close he couldn't possibly miss. And then the other would stab her to death and they would take Leyla. They would . . .

These thoughts filled the space between two heartbeats. Her finger started to squeeze the trigger a second time, tracking the two survivors, the knife, and the gun, but knowing the bullet that would end her was on the way.

The gunshot made her flinch, resounding across the night sky. He had fired first, or so she thought until his gun hand drooped and he staggered aside, then crumbled to the grass and sprawled there, a bloody hole in the back of his shirt.

Leyla started wailing again.

Cait and the knife-man turned at the same time to see a pair of men in dark suits coming around from the front of the house. Only seconds had passed since she'd come out the back door. These two must have been on standby in front, but the gunshots had drawn them around back.

The knife-man dropped his blade, reaching for his gun.

Enemies. They were enemies.

Cait leveled her weapon at the men in suits, hoping the knife-man would shoot them before he'd try putting a bullet in her. *They want Leyla. Why do they want to hurt my baby?*

Her finger tightened on the trigger, but then she saw a third man coming around from the front yard—a black man in shirt and tie, no jacket. Him she knew.

Detective Jarman planted his feet and took aim, shouting. "Police! Drop your—"

Three shots rang out in quick succession and Detective Jarman spun around and fell, and only then did Cait see the skinny blond weasel hanging halfway out the broken apartment window, gun clasped in both hands.

Knife-man took aim at him, put a bullet in the window frame, and then the two who'd come from the front shot him dead, there in the yard, and the gunshots echoed into silence. The sounds drifted away like smoke.

"Get her, damn it!" the weasel in the window shouted.

Over the cries and choking sobs of her baby, she heard the distant banshee wail of police sirens, but by the time the cops came, this would all be over. She shot the one closest to her and ran, headed for the shed at the back of the yard. Shouts followed her, and so did bullets, one shattering the window in the shed, but though she braced for impact, none of the shots hit her.

A glance over her shoulder showed her the weasel using his gun to smash the rest of the glass out of the living room window. He crouched on the sill and jumped down, but the other guy had a twenty-foot lead on him, sprinting.

Cait knew then that they would catch her. The shed would block bullets, but offered no hiding place, and she would never make it through the backyards to the next street before they caught up with her. This wasn't going to work, which left her only one option—to be the last one standing.

She rounded the corner of the shed and stopped. Using it for cover, with Leyla's terrified shrieks filling her ears, she took aim at the black-suited gunman who was closing in on her. The weasel sprinted to catch up to him.

An engine revved, out on the street. Headlights swept the darkness of the yard and then the car's growl turned into a roar. The two men in suits spun around, silhouetted in the headlights as a silver, mid-'90s Cadillac El Dorado tore across the lawn, ancient Rolling Stones blaring on the radio. Weasel bounced off the front grill with a sickeningly wet crunch of bone and vanished underneath the car. The other guy lifted his gun, ready to fire at the Caddy's windshield, but the driver leaned out the window and shot him twice in the chest.

As the guy fell, she got her first clear view of the grim-faced old man behind the wheel, his hair as silver as the El Dorado's finish. He lowered his gun the moment he saw her—a comforting change of pace. But she wasn't in a trusting mood, and kept her own weapon trained on his face.

"Caitlin McCandless," he called, over the growing song of police sirens and Leyla's diminishing cries. "My name is Matthew Lynch. If you want your daughter to live through the night, you'd better get in."

"The police are coming," she said.

"They'll buy you a few hours, no more," Lynch said quickly. "You've got dead Feds and terrorists in your yard, honey. This is bigger than the Podunk P.D. Please, get in. For your daughter's sake, if not your own."

The sirens grew louder.

Lynch put his car in reverse, staring at her. "Decide!"

"Shit!" Cait snapped, and ran around to the passenger side.

As she climbed in, she kept her gun trained on Lynch, but he ignored her. She hadn't even closed the passenger door when he floored the car in reverse, tearing up the grass. He bumped over the sidewalk and into the street, jammed on the brakes, threw the car in Drive, and took off so fast the door slammed shut on its own.

Cait had made her choice. She put her gun on the floor and grabbed the seat belt, strapping it across her chest, holding Leyla in her lap. As she adjusted the belt, she caught sight of an empty car seat in the back, like Lynch had come ready to take the baby with him, and she turned to stare at him, wondering how different he was, really, from the other men.

Silent now, Leyla stared up at her, eyes wide with shock and probably exhausted from all of the crying.

Lynch reached Powder House Circle at the same time four police cars poured into it from three different directions. He slowed down, just an old guy in his well-preserved Caddy, and went around the rotary, headed for Route 16, or maybe Route 93.

As she stared at him, Lynch wrinkled his nose.

"Jesus, your baby smells like piss."

Cait laughed in disbelief. "I didn't have time to grab her diaper bag."

Lynch tapped the accelerator and shot through a yellow light. "I've got one in the trunk."

A terrible chill, growing too familiar by now, spread up Cait's spine. What the hell had she gotten them into now?

-40--

"I could do without the fucking entourage."

Josh Hart ran a hand through his hair—a nervous habit that showed up whenever he was in a crowd. Not that there were actually that many people in the baggage compartment of the plane. Him, Voss, Turcotte, a woman named Aria who was the mouthpiece for Massport security, and Special Agent Ben Coogan out of the FBI's Boston field office. The guy must have asked to be posted there because he was a local boy, South Boston Irish born and bred, with squared-off boxer's shoulders and a nose crooked from being broken in a bar fight. And that wasn't Josh stereotyping. Coogan had slipped the story into conversation within the first four minutes of their introduction on the tarmac.

"There's not much I can do about it, Agent Hart," Aria said, crouching down to glance out at the group gathered around the rear of the plane. "It's my people, your people, and the Boston P.D. It isn't like there are any media or civilians out there."

Josh and Voss exchanged a glance. Her eyes crinkled with amusement but she didn't quite smile. She didn't have to. They knew each other well enough that communication might as well have been telepathic. Aria worked airport security, and as much as she and her employees were a vital part of protecting the nation, for her to refer to *others* as civilians—as if scanning suitcases and patting down old ladies was the same thing as hunting terrorists and serial killers—made them both want to choke.

"I'm sorry, Ms. . . . ?"

"Fernandez."

"Ms. Fernandez," Josh continued. "I'm mostly referring to the various departments and agencies that we're accumulating on this case. It's snowballing, and you know what they say about too many cooks. Plus, I have some issues with crowds."

Aria smiled. "Everybody's got an issue with something."

Josh glanced around the compartment. The crime-scene team had been in hours ago. The body had already been removed and there was no blood, but the signs of a struggle were evident everywhere they looked.

"My issue's tight spaces," Agent Coogan said. "Can we get the hell out of here?"

Voss and Josh glanced at Turcotte. Unless they played their trump card, it was his case.

Turcotte nodded. "Absolutely. Nothing to see anyway."

Coogan made a beeline for the exit, stepping onto the platform that had been pushed up against the aircraft and hurrying down the stairs. Josh and Voss followed, with Turcotte and Aria Fernandez bringing up the rear.

On the tarmac, Nala Chang strode toward them accompanied by a pair of Boston police officers. Amongst the muddle of Massport, FBI, Massachusetts State Police, and Boston P.D. personnel were Lieutenant Arsenault from SOCOM and Norris from Black Pine. They had corralled a local detective and Josh didn't like the huddle the three men seemed to be in. Turcotte held the reins on this case; they shouldn't be speaking out of school to anyone without the FBI's go-ahead.

Don't jump to conclusions, he told himself. Easier said than done, though, considering how much Norris got under his skin. Arsenault seemed like a straight shooter, though. *Maybe they're just talking about the dead terrorist in the baggage compartment.*

"Cozy little tête-à-tête," Voss muttered as she joined him on the tarmac.

Josh nodded.

Turcotte headed straight for Chang. Josh and Voss held back, letting Coogan and Aria pass them. *Troubleshooter* had many meanings, but for now they were just helpful observers.

"What've you got?" Turcotte asked.

Chang glanced momentarily at Josh and one corner of his mouth lifted in a smile of greeting. Nala Chang seemed a formidable woman and, unlike so many he had encountered over the years, her sense of justice did not appear to have been corrupted or compromised by her experiences in the field. That was a rare commodity.

"Preliminary report from the medical examiner's office—" Chang began.

Coogan scoffed. "The body's only been there a couple of hours. No way the autopsy's done."

"As I said, preliminary," Chang said. "I pressed for something, and what the M.E. gave me is this: bruising shows the guy took a beating, ligature marks on the throat and neck indicate strangulation, but the neck was broken as well. Someone murdered Gharib al-Din with their bare hands."

"You made a positive ID?" Voss asked.

"Oh, it's al-Din. He'd altered his appearance recently. Haircut, shave . . . and the swelling and bruising doesn't help with an ID. But it's him."

Coogan puffed up like a rooster. "I told you it was your guy. What, you think my eyes don't work the same as yours?"

Josh opened his mouth to say something, but a glance from Turcotte silenced him.

"Agent Coogan, you made the right call, no question. But this isn't your first case. You know how it works. If we're going to put it into our files that our guy is permanently off the board, we need to verify that ourselves. You'd do the same."

Coogan grunted but didn't seem mollified. Turcotte clearly didn't give a shit.

"All right," Voss said. "We've viewed the scene. You've got a confirmed visual ID. Anything more from the witnesses?"

Before they had even arrived, Aria had gathered all of the airport and airline staff who had been in the area from the time the plane taxied in until the discovery of the corpse. Only about a third of the passengers had still been at baggage claim when the corpse had been discovered. They'd been interviewed by Massport and the Boston P.D., but the others had already scattered to the winds. The short flight meant most of the people on board were traveling only with carry-on luggage. For the last few hours, the Boston cops had been following up with the rest of the passengers.

"There are still three passengers unaccounted for," Chang

reported, dark eyes grim. "But unless one of them turns out to be our killer, we've got nothing new. A couple of them saw a mysterious white-haired man coming out from under the plane seconds after it rolled up to the gate. Statements don't vary much from the half-dozen employees who saw the same thing. Other than the hair and general height, weight, and race, it's all vague."

Josh noticed Norris edging closer to them, listening in. He wanted to tell the guy to back off, but if Turcotte wasn't going to stop him, it wasn't Josh's place to speak up. Chang went on, but the substance of her report had already been delivered. The white-haired man might have been an employee, but the rest of the staff on the ground didn't think so. It seemed likely that he'd come from the plane's baggage compartment, which meant that unless some unknown third person had been in that compartment—highly unlikely—the white-haired guy was the prime suspect in al-Din's murder.

Josh would have liked to pin a medal on him.

Norris's phone must have vibrated or beeped because he unclipped it from his belt and glanced down at what was apparently a text message. A ripple of disgust passed across his features before he composed himself and started keying a reply.

". . . should only be a few hours before we can pin down the last three people on the passenger manifest," Chang was saying, "but they're all female, so Mr. White Hair is not among them."

"Which means he had to have been in baggage with al-Din," Turcotte said.

"A short flight. I assume it doesn't hit extreme altitudes, or they would have suffocated," Voss noted, turning to Aria.

Turcotte's cell phone tweeted, but he ignored it, waiting for an answer.

"Agent Turcotte," Norris said, drawing their attention. "You're going to want to answer that."

Turcotte narrowed his gaze as the implication of this sunk in. As usual, it seemed Norris knew something they did not. Josh hated the guy, hated that Black Pine operated outside of the government's protocols, and he knew he wasn't alone.

"Ed?" Voss prompted.

Turcotte plucked up his phone and thumbed TALK, pressed it to his ear. "I'm listening."

His expression darkened then he shot Norris another withering glance. Moments later he ended the call, but he kept the phone clutched in his hand like he held a set of brass knuckles and had every intention of using them. Turcotte studied the people gathered around him and obviously came to a decision.

"Ms. Fernandez, I think we've got what we need. You can take it from here."

Aria blinked in surprise. "Of course."

"Wait, what?" Coogan said, flushing pink. "My office called you in as a courtesy, Agent Turcotte. You don't have the authority to turn my case over to anyone. We've got a dead terrorist and a murder suspect at large—"

"Coogan," Josh snapped.

His tone brought the other agent up short. Coogan looked like he might take a swing at Josh, but then he glanced sheepishly at Aria and the Boston cops, apparently realizing how out of line he was, talking like that in front of non-Bureau personnel. Arsenault and Norris were one thing—they were part of the federal investigation, at least the way Coogan must have seen it—but locals were another thing entirely.

Maybe there was an apology coming, but Turcotte didn't wait for it. He spun on his heel and headed for the cluster of vehicles that had been driven onto the tarmac, several of which had been arranged for them in advance. Chang fell immediately into step beside him, followed by Arsenault and Norris.

"After you," Voss said, gesturing to Coogan.

Lips pressed together in a tight line, he hurried to catch up to Turcotte, and Josh and Voss followed. Rachael looked like she wanted to kick Coogan's ass, and Josh couldn't blame her. When they were out of earshot of the local and airport police, Voss finally spoke up.

"You going to tell us what's going on, Ed?"

Turcotte didn't slow down. He reached the cars and a young agent from Coogan's team sat behind the wheel of the first one. The guy started the car, engine purring. As Turcotte opened the front passenger door, he turned to look at them.

"More than a dozen people were killed a short time ago at a house in . . . what was it? Medford."

Josh stared at him. "Caitlin McCandless lives in Medford. We were heading there right after this."

Turcotte nodded, standing inside the open door. "It's her residence."

"Son of a bitch," Voss muttered.

"A Medford detective is among the dead," Turcotte went on. "One civilian, female. The rest are apparently pretty evenly divided between what looks like two teams of professional hitters, half of them obviously of Middle Eastern descent, including, we think, al-Din's two buddies from Fort Myers."

Josh exhaled. "Holy shit."

Arsenault shot a dark look at Norris. "Is that what you meant when you told Agent Turcotte he would want to answer that call? You knew about this?"

Norris shrugged. "Not the details. A text I received from the home office."

Coogan stared at him. "How does that work? You know this shit before the Bureau?"

Josh began to adjust his opinion of Coogan. Right then, he could have kissed the guy. It was the question he wanted to ask, but they were all supposed to be playing nice with Black Pine.

"Not before the FBI," Norris replied coolly, almost smugly. "Just before Agent Turcotte."

"Maybe there's something you don't know," Turcotte said, glancing from Norris to Arsenault. "The woman the local police think was the target—this Caitlin McCandless— apparently escaped with her infant daughter in a car driven by a man with white hair."

"What the hell is this, now?" Nala Chang muttered, her eyes lighting up.

"If we're lucky, maybe the answer we've been looking for," Voss said.

They broke, hurrying to climb into three separate vehicles—

Josh and Voss together, Chang and Coogan getting into the backseat behind Turcotte, and Arsenault riding with Norris in a silver Lexus that clearly did not come from the FBI's motor pool—and Josh thought about Turcotte's words. *Maybe there's something you don't know.*

Norris had not seemed fazed by the revelation at all.

-41--

Cait's only comfort was the gun. When Lynch had pulled into a Burger King parking lot so she could change Leyla's diaper, she had taken it into the backseat and never let it get more than a few inches from her reach. Lynch had watched without comment, but the tension inside the Cadillac had a language of its own. Whoever the guys back at the house had been, they'd all wanted Leyla, and for the moment the only difference between them and Lynch was that he seemed content to get the mother along with the child.

Now the Caddy shot through the tunnel underneath Boston, overhead lights flashing over the windshield, flickering in the darkness inside the car. Cait held the gun across her lap as if she were in charge, like Lynch was her hostage, and he still made no comment. She glanced over her shoulder, relieved to see a fringe of Leyla's hair leaning out past the edge of the rear-facing car seat. Amazingly, and wonderfully, the baby had fallen back to sleep. After changing her diaper, Cait had strapped her into the car seat so conveniently supplied by Lynch, but she'd had to adjust the buckles. Along with the Cheerios and stains on the seat, that had made her feel better. This was somebody else's car seat, not something Lynch had bought just to carry Leyla McCandless.

Cait wrinkled her nose. When she'd been holding Leyla, the baby's diaper had already been leaking and Cait had a urine stain drying on her shirt. She wished for something else to wear, but right now baby pee was the least of her problems.

Lynch clicked on his right turn signal and slid the Caddy over for the exit onto the Massachusetts Turnpike.

"It's time, don't you think?" Cait said.

"Time for what?" Lynch replied as he guided the Caddy up the ramp and out of the tunnel, heading west.

"Time for you to tell me what makes you different from the men I killed tonight."

"At gunpoint?" Lynch kept both hands on the wheel, his own gun reloaded and stashed back in a holster he'd slid under his seat.

"I'm not pointing it at you."

"But you will if you have to."

Cait had no idea what to make of the guy. "Yes," she said. "If it means protecting my daughter."

She could see Lynch's jaw working, like he was chewing on the gristle of long-nurtured hate. He nodded slowly, then cut his gaze toward her.

"Good. The dead sons of bitches back there on your lawn make it clear you're willing to pull the trigger on your enemies, but you're gonna have to do a lot of thinking about who your friends are from now on."

"And you're one of them?"

The engine purred. Cars swept by in the fast lane but Lynch ignored them, keeping the speedometer pinned at sixty miles per hour, neither fast enough or slow enough to draw attention. In the glow from the dashboard, his silver hair made him look almost ghostly.

"No. I'm not your friend," he said at last. "But I could be. And I'm definitely Leyla's friend, whether you want me to be or not."

Cait lifted the gun from her lap, shifting to take aim. "Explain that."

"You won't shoot me while I'm driving. We'd all die."

"I can take the wheel."

Lynch risked another glance at her. He let out a long breath. "I'm honestly not trying to speak in riddles—"

"You're doing a hell of a job."

"It's just hard to come up with the words and make them sound like anything but madness."

Cait surprised herself by laughing. "This whole thing's been madness. By all means, let's not stop now. Talk to me, Mr. Lynch. Who the hell are all of you people and what do you want with my daughter?"

Cait glanced into the back again. Leyla's sleeping head tilted out past the edge of the rear-facing car seat. A rush of love and fear filled Cait as she realized that she herself would never sleep that deeply again. Whatever this was, it had altered the course of their lives.

"Have you ever heard the expression 'War's Children'?" Lynch asked.

"I don't think so. Maybe."

Lynch nodded, forging ahead. "My father was a GI during World War II. His unit was part of the Allied invasion of Sicily in '43, and that was where he met my mother."

"I don't—"

"You want an answer," Lynch said. "This is it. So are you going to listen?"

An eighteen-wheeler roared by, close enough to make her flinch. Lynch kept both hands on the wheel, stiff-armed, staring at the road ahead.

"Go on," Cait said at last.

"She was German, a secretary for the Luftwaffe. After the Allies defeated Rommel in Tunisia, they started bombing the hell out of Italy to soften them up for attack. My mother was injured in the bombing of the airfield where she worked. Half the building came down around her but she made it out with a broken arm and some busted ribs; ended up in the hospital. When the Allies hit the beaches in July, it wasn't long before the Italian and German troops beat feet for the mainland, but she was there in the hospital when the Allies rolled up, and that was how my parents met.

"I was born in September of '44, and the killers came for me on Christmas day."

A chill trickled down Cait's spine. Her fingers flexed on the grip of her gun.

"What are you talking about?"

Lynch still didn't look at her. "My mother died protecting me. When my father came home to bury her, he was approached by two men who talked what he thought of as a lot of nonsense. They told him that the birth of certain children could alter the fates of nations. 'War's Children,' they called them. In every significant military conflict in the history of the world, there have been children born of parents whose peoples were enemies."

The fates of nations, Cait thought. *Jesus, let me out of this car.*

As though he could read her mind, Lynch smiled thinly. He shot her a sidelong glance. "You killed a whole lot of people tonight. I thought you wanted to know why."

Cait looked back at Leyla, then shifted and stared out the windshield, studying the view ahead, the red lights on the backs of the cars that dotted the road in front of them. She thought of the Middle Eastern men who'd come after Leyla—Iraqis, Saudis—and the dark-suited bastards Lynch claimed were Feds. She thought of her brother, of Auntie Jane, of men trying to grab Leyla and dark sedans doing surveillance on Badger Road.

"You're saying this is all true?"

"Maybe it is. Maybe it isn't," Lynch replied. "It doesn't matter, really. The people who are after Leyla believe it. Or, hell, maybe some of them don't. Probably some are only hedging their bets just in case it's true. But they've murdered more than sixty children since the wars in Iraq and Afghanistan began, and those are just the ones I'm aware of."

Cait felt sick. "But why?" She hated how small her voice sounded.

"The Americans who came after you tonight work for very powerful people. I hate to use the phrase *secret society* because it sounds like something out of a Victorian mystery or a bad comic book. Cabal. Conspiracy. Over the years, my friends and I have taken to calling them 'the Collective.' I've also heard them referred to many times as the 'Herods.'"

"After King Herod—"

"Exactly," Lynch said. "Herod had been put in place by the Romans to rule over Judea. The Romans were an occupying force, the enemy. According to the story, Herod had been given a prophecy that an infant had been born who would one day rise to become King of the Jews. As he understood things, the only way for someone to be King of the Jews was if he himself was no longer King of Judea, and if Rome no longer controlled the region. This would require the withdrawal or defeat of Rome. To serve his own interests, and those of the empire, he gave the order to kill all newborn males so none of them would one day grow up to become King of the Jews."

Cait stared at him. "It's a Bible story."

"It's also history. And if you did the research, you'd find that there are scholars who believe early Christian leaders co-opted the story; that the slaughter of the innocents wasn't about a search for Christ at all. The infants killed all had something in common. They each had one Jewish and one Roman parent."

A trickle of dread ran down Cait's back.

"I can't say for certain if it was the first time a series of such executions was carried out, but it certainly wasn't the last. The Herod Factor has come into play during many of the world's major conflicts over the past two thousand years. The Napoleonic Wars saw the murder of hundreds of children born of parents from opposing sides. French and British. French and Spanish. French and Russian."

"Two hundred years ago," Cait said.

Lynch's grip tightened on the steering wheel. "And seventy years ago, during World War II, and forty years ago, during Vietnam. And on and on."

"And you're saying all of this has been done by this group? The Collective?"

"Their influence is enormous, but it's the same thing on the other side. Radical Middle Eastern extremists. We have the Collective and they have their own jihadist Herods. What they have in common is that, for various reasons, they don't want this war to end."

Cait couldn't listen to him anymore. "You're saying babies like Leyla could end the war? She's an infant!"

Lynch flexed his fingers on the wheel. "Who knows how long this war could last? It's not over territory, Cait, it's about ideology. It could be centuries before it's really decided one way or the other, and that's how they want it. They want to exterminate each other—except for the ones who are just in it for the money that war generates. But you're right. They're not really after Leyla because they think she'll be some great future diplomat. The whole mythology around War's Children suggests that they—that we—have a destiny bred into us. The power to bring about peace, to lend wisdom and understanding to both sides in a conflict. The Collective believes her mere existence is enough to lessen the hostility and aggression between the enemies without them even being aware of her. Like the wings of a butterfly in chaos theory, she will have a ripple effect on the war, an almost mystical influence—and so will the other children born of a union between enemies."

Cait lowered her gaze, staring at the floormat. The gun had gotten cold in her grip. "*Mystical?* Seriously?"

Lynch shot her a dark look. "Let me ask you a question. Have you run into people who look at you with disgust, or even hatred, when they find out your daughter's father was Iraqi?"

Cait hardened. "There are bigots everywhere."

"Absolutely," Lynch agreed. "But what about everyone else? What about people who are just afraid of the simmering potential for war to strike close to their hearts and their homes? What about people who are ignorant, and don't know any better than to be afraid or filled with hate toward anyone and anything related to the culture they've come to see as the enemy? When they meet Leyla, they see an innocent child. And when they understand what you have endured, and that you loved her father, some of them start to think differently. Tell me you haven't seen it. Tell me that you don't know exactly the effect she can have on people."

Cait started to reply, then gave a shake of her head. She wanted to deny it, to argue, but a chill began to spread through her body. How many times had she noticed people reacting to Leyla precisely the way Lynch described? Dozens, at least.

"You can say it means nothing," Lynch told her. "That one child can't change the fundamental beliefs of a nation or a culture. But that's not what we're talking about. It's about calming fears and making people think, and those things ripple outward, Cait."

She took a deep breath and let it out. "It's crazy."

"And yet . . ."

Cait said nothing. In her mind's eye she could see the thoughtful faces of people Leyla had affected, and a part of her did believe that such encounters could effect subtle changes on a community. Leyla was only one child, but the conflict between the United States and radical Muslim factions in the Middle East had been going on a very long time. How many children were there in the world now who had been born with one parent from either side of that conflict?

"You understand how hard it is to believe all of this?" Cait asked.

"I do," Lynch said. "But I'll tell you this much. *They* believe it."

A minute or more passed with only the sounds of the engine and the tires on the road and the soft breathing of her sleeping child to interfere with the silence between them. Her mind raced, trying to find a way to refute Lynch's story. True or not, if the warhawks and industrialists and religious zealots who thrived on this war really believed that babies born of parents from warring cultures could bring about the end of that war . . .

Could it be? How else to explain all that had happened to her and her family this week?

And friends. Oh, Miranda. I'm sorry.

Cait bit her lip and fought back tears. Her left hand shook, though her gun hand remained steady. It always had.

"So how come they didn't just kill Leyla? They could've done it almost anytime they wanted."

As the words left her lips, she knew that Lynch would take them as acceptance of his wild story, but she had to ask. Sean was dead and his friend Herc had been unable to help, but she knew that there were layers of secrecy behind the curtain of reality, which the rest of the world wasn't allowed to see. If the ruthless men who hid their actions behind that curtain believed this fairy tale, she would put nothing past them.

"You made them sloppy," Lynch told her.

"What are you talking about?"

"The Collective are usually careful and methodical. They cover their tracks so well that in most cases no one even knows a murder has taken place. But someone's finally figured out their m.o. If you've seen the reports about the crib deaths in the Midwest that are being investigated as murders—"

"I have."

"—then you know what I mean. How many children have appeared to have 'died in their sleep' but were actually killed by the Collective? I don't know the exact number, but there have been dozens. That's the sort of subtlety they usually operate with. But now that someone's connecting the dots, their usual procedure is unworkable. Right now the authorities think they're dealing with a serial killer. The Collective are in no real danger—they will point the investigation away from themselves, as they always have. But they need to figure out a new way of doing things, at least for a while."

"So coming after my baby in broad daylight, in my aunt's driveway, that's their new m.o.? They hit my house in force, Lynch, pretending to be federal agents. There's nothing fucking stealthy about that."

"Some of them might have actually *been* federal agents. As for the way they came after you tonight . . . that's what I meant about you making them sloppy. Even so, it wouldn't have been so hard for them to cover it up. You served in Iraq, and while you were there you became pregnant with the child of an Iraqi. How difficult would it be for them to spin that story for the public to make it sound like you were a traitor, working with terrorists?"

Cait wanted to be sick. "Nizam was no terrorist."

"You're mistaking the evening news for the truth. The two are not at all the same thing."

Cait shuddered. "They saw me on the news," she said.

"The jihadist Herods certainly did. They use Collective tactics with most of their victims in the United States— slipping into the children's bedrooms during the night, committing their crimes, and making their murders look like natural death. But they don't always play things as carefully and cleanly as the Collective. If they can make it look like a random child abduction, something the cops can attribute to pedophiles or lunatics or black marketers, they have no problem doing it ugly."

Cait frowned. "There was a newborn taken from its parents right in front of a hospital up in Maine."

Lynch nodded. "Bangor."

"That was them?"

"It was. And from there, they came here. It had to be ugly, and in a hurry. They had seen you on television, talking about the attack on your aunt and daughter, and the death of your brother. The news report played up that you're a single mother, that you fell in love in Iraq, and that Leyla's father is Iraqi. That set them off."

Cait could see it. If they thought that Channel 7 might continue to cover her story, that Leyla might appear on television in future reports, they would have wanted to put a stop to it immediately. So would the Collective.

"If the Collective really have the power you say they do, if they could make it look like I was a terrorist, then I get how they could come after me like this tonight and kill whoever the hell they wanted. But what about these jihadists? How are they going to spin the news?"

Lynch smiled grimly. "You're not thinking, Cait. They would try to make you and Leyla vanish, of course. But if they failed, if it got messy, or even if they succeeded and there was too much coverage on the local news talking about you and Leyla, well, the Collective are there to clean up their mess."

"They're enemies," Cait said. "Why would they . . . ?"

But she got it. Of course the Collective would clean up the mess. The extremists wanted to kill each other, but they also wanted to be able to *keep* killing each other. The Collective would cover up the jihadists' actions for the same reason they would cover their own. The Herod conspiracy had to remain a secret or the people on both sides of the conflict might demand an end to the war in such numbers that peace would result. And peace was the worst nightmare for the extremists on both sides. They needed hatred and fear.

No matter who killed Leyla, Cait would be painted as a domestic terrorist.

Or she would have been, if they had gotten away with it.

"If any of this is true, it still doesn't explain why this Collective had cars outside my aunt's house at two o'clock this morning, and why they tried to snatch Leyla about eight hours later. I made the eleven o'clock news last night for a skirmish I had with this football asshole, but there was no mention of Leyla during that report. That wouldn't have sent a flag up."

Lynch nodded thoughtfully, braking and checking his rearview mirrors as he took a corner.

"But, for some reason, it did," he said. "I can't explain it, but the timing is too close to be coincidental. That had to have been the trigger."

"And my brother?" Her heart felt like a block of ice. "He's really dead?"

Lynch frowned. "I don't know what you're talking about. Why would they go after other members of your family?"

Cait scowled, about to call bullshit, but either Lynch was telling the truth or he was a damn good actor. He didn't just look mystified by the question, he seemed greatly troubled by it.

As succinctly as she could, she filled him in on the events leading up to the massacre at her apartment. "How can you know so much about me and Leyla and nothing about the rest of it?" she asked at last.

Lynch's lips were a thin white line. He seemed to be struggling, trying to figure out how to answer her—or maybe if he wanted to answer her at all.

"I'm not a savior and I don't claim to know everything," he said at last, guarded and even a little ashamed. "I've spent my entire life fighting these people. There's a group—a Resistance, I guess you could call us—whose sole purpose is to stand against the Herods. All of them, in every conflict."

"To save the children."

Lynch hesitated. "I've saved some. But they're persistent, these people. You understand that? They have superior numbers and there are always more. At any given time, there are half a dozen or more significant conflicts going on in different regions of the world. The Collective are just the American end of things. Five years ago, I finally realized that I could never protect the children one at a time, that the only solution was direct action."

"Meaning?"

"I hunt them. I've been trying to infiltrate their organization, mostly unsuccessfully, but I've drained a certain amount of intelligence and have been eliminating those I can find, one by one. I've been able to track some of the jihadists as well. But in the past few months, both sides have gotten ambitious, like they are in a race to see how many of these kids they can track and kill. Maybe because tensions seem to be easing somewhat and they're afraid the war is starting to die down."

Cait stared at him, processing. "You're an assassin."

Anger sparked in his eyes. "Yeah? What are you? You left all those corpses—"

"I'm a mother, defending my child."

"And what about all the *other* children? What about the soldiers dying every day? When there are wolves in the woods, it isn't enough to guard the sheep. You can't watch them all, every minute. You hunt the wolves."

Cait studied the lines in his face, the crinkles at the corner of his eye. All her life she had considered herself a good judge of character, especially of men, but Lynch confused her.

"I caught up to one of them today," Lynch said, glancing at her. "You asked how I knew about you and Leyla? When the baby was stolen in Bangor, an Iraqi jihadist named Gharib al-Din—one of their baby-killers—showed up on the security camera. I tracked him down at the Bangor airport, on a plane bound for Boston, and persuaded him to tell me where he was going and why."

"You tortured him."

Lynch kept his eyes on the road. "He told me about you and Leyla. He didn't mention anything about your brother. The Collective probably took out Sean to avoid trouble once they had Leyla."

Cait squeezed her eyes tightly shut and tried to breathe. She had already begun to assume the same thing, but hearing it out loud made her feel sick. Again she thought of Miranda and a fresh wave of grief spread through her.

"You took a plane from Bangor. Which means you stole this car."

"From long-term parking at Logan Airport. Unless I'm very unlucky and the owner returns from his trip today, the car's safe for now."

"And Gharib al-Din? Where is he?"

"I sent him to Allah."

Cait shuddered. She swallowed hard and took a deep breath, then opened her eyes and turned to Lynch.

"So what's your plan?"

"We're fugitives," Lynch said. "All three of us. They could come after us quietly or go public, claim we're wanted for some crime. After the shootout on your lawn, I'd guess the latter. Within an hour, your picture's going to be everywhere, wanted for questioning in all those deaths. The Resistance has a safe house in New York. Four hours and we'll be there. If we can make it without you being spotted, we'll be okay for a while."

"For a while?"

"I didn't know you existed until a couple of hours ago," Lynch said. "Give me a chance to think."

Again Cait closed her eyes. Her body had started to come down off of its adrenaline high and at last she felt like she could focus. Matthew Lynch had saved her life as well as Leyla's. He might be a killer, but was he a soldier or a lunatic? She couldn't believe in destiny—in the birth of a single child changing the fates of nations—but people had killed one another for stranger beliefs. Countries had gone to war over less.

She only wished she could talk to Sean. Without a body, without a funeral, she could still not quite believe that he was dead and gone, and she really needed him right now. He would know what to do. He would raise hell in the secret corridors of D.C. to protect Leyla. But she didn't have Sean to rely on now. According to Hercules, all she had were his ashes.

Hercules.

She reached into her pocket and slid out her cell phone.

"What the hell are you doing?" Lynch demanded.

"Calling someone who can help," Cait said, and started to dial the emergency number for Herc that Sean had given her, in case she had no other way to reach him. Sean was gone now, but it was Herc she needed to talk to.

Lynch snatched the phone from her hand. Before she could protest, he ended the call. As she scrabbled at his hands, trying to get the phone back, he lowered his window.

"Stop! Give it back! Don't even—"

He tossed the phone out the window. She could picture it shattering on the highway but they were going fast enough that she didn't hear it hit the ground.

"Motherfucker!" she shouted, raising her gun and pointing it at his temple. "Whatever trust I might have been willing to give you just went out the window with that phone!"

Leyla began to whimper in the backseat, crying a little but not waking up. Lynch raised the window, one hand on the wheel. When he turned to look at her, his eyes were cold.

"Your brother worked with satellites, you said. Any idea how easy it would be for them to track that phone? If you want your daughter to live, Sergeant, you're going to have to be a lot smarter than that."

Cait's aim faltered. The barrel of the gun dipped and then she lowered it altogether.

"The guy I was calling might be the one person who could help us."

"You still don't get it," Lynch said. "You can't trust anyone."

"Except you," Cait said, practically sneering the words.

Lynch turned to stare at her with ice blue eyes, the Caddy gliding along the turnpike in the dark.

-42--

A voice startled Herc awake. He'd fallen asleep in the easy chair in the living room watching an old Clint Eastwood movie that he'd recorded on DVR. He looked around to find himself alone—his wife, Ellen, must have gone to bed—and it took him a few seconds to backtrack in his mind and figure out what had woken him.

The voice came again. "Hey, asshole! Answer the phone!"

His throat went dry and he stared over at a little corner shelf. Next to a tiny copper statue of an Indian—a replica of a famous Fredric Remington sculpture—a bright red cell phone lay charging. The Hot Line. Herc kept it charged, kept it with him, though it almost never rang. Today he had nearly forgotten about it.

"Hey, asshole! Answer the phone!" it screamed again.

Sean McCandless had recorded that message for Herc's ringtone. Now his voice was shouting from the grave. Herc spent a half a second longer trying to figure out who the hell could be calling him—only a handful of people had the number, including Sean and Terry—then he scrambled from the chair and raced for it.

"Hello? Terry?"

The line had a hollow tone. Dead, empty air. Whoever it was had hung up. He clicked over to check the number of his last incoming call and for a second the breath froze in his lungs. *McCandless, C.* In the space between blinks, he had let himself believe that somehow it had all been a huge mistake or some kind of cover-up, that Sean had been in deep cover and the corpse had not belonged to him, that he was calling now to apologize for putting Herc through the shock and grief.

But, of course, C stood for *Caitlin.* Sean had told Herc a

thousand times that he had given Caitlin the Hot Line number, just in case he went off the radar for a while and an emergency came up. Now Herc thought of Boyce and his insistence that he be the one to deal with Cait if she tried calling back. Boyce was an idiot. Why would she call that number when they had already told her Sean had died?

"Shit," he whispered, staring at the phone in his hand. It felt strangely warm.

If he called Cait back and Boyce found out, things could get very ugly. He would be disobeying a direct order. But his hesitation only lasted a second. Sean would have put his life on the line for Herc any day of the week. The least Herc could do in return was put his job on the line for Caitlin. He had made promises to Sean, sworn to look out for her if she ever needed help and Sean wasn't available. Boyce would never understand such promises, but Boyce was a prick.

Herc hit the callback button and put the phone to his ear, ready to talk. Ready to help. But the call went straight through to Cait's voice mail as if she had the phone off and he hung up without leaving a message. No reason to give Boyce any evidence; that would just be asking for trouble.

Half a minute ticked by while he stood there in the living room, his wife sleeping upstairs and Clint Eastwood dying on the television, poisoned by a crazy Civil War–era schoolgirl who thought she loved him. He tried the number again with the same result, then started to worry. Cait knew the Hot Line was for emergencies. Maybe whatever she was calling for counted, or maybe she just wasn't satisfied with the answers she had been getting and wanted a more private conversation with him, but it didn't matter. After his conversation with Stanovitch, he had already made up his mind to talk to her, but he had planned to do it a bit more surreptitiously, telling himself she would be in D.C. for some kind of memorial for Sean soon enough.

Apparently he'd been fooling himself with his definition of *soon enough*.

He ran it all through his mind again. According to Stanovitch, the cars watching her aunt and uncle's house had blank plates, which required a level of political clout that seemed almost mythical to Herc. He'd never known anyone who moved in those circles. But with Sean dead, it was obvious something major was going on, no matter what Boyce said.

Again he tried calling Cait. Again the call went straight to voice mail. Inside, he knew something awful had happened. The weight of that certainty seemed almost enough to suffocate him.

You should've moved on it immediately. Idiot. The self-recriminations came hard and fast. He had been frozen by Stanovitch's revelation, had told himself that whatever had happened had been focused on Sean. He'd been concerned for Cait, but not enough to act immediately.

Sean McCandless had been his best friend. In all the time they'd known each other, he'd only ever really asked Herc for one thing, and Herc had blown it.

The red phone felt weightless in his hand. He swore under his breath as he strode toward the small room at the back of the house that he kept as an office. Green banker's lamp over the rolltop desk. Original poster for *The Eiger Sanction* signed by Eastwood and George Kennedy over a bookcase. Next to the computer monitor, a black address book. He grabbed it, flipped through to *M,* found the number Sean had given him more than two years ago for his sister.

He dialed.

Someone picked up on the second ring. "Hello?"

Herc exhaled, thinking *Thank Christ.* "Cait? Caitlin?"

"Who's this?"

Shit. Not Caitlin. And as innocuously as the woman had tried to deliver the query, the tone had the air of authority, of someone used to getting an answer when she asked a question. *Cop.*

"I'm returning a call," Herc said. "Is Cait there?"

"Not at the moment. Maybe you'd like to leave a—"

Herc killed the call. He stared at the red phone like it would be able to help him somehow, trying to figure out what the hell to do next. The woman who had answered Cait's phone was either a cop or a Fed. Cait had called and hung up and now he couldn't reach her. The only thing he could think to do was wait until she tried to get in touch again.

He hung his head. "Fuck me."

He'd done enough sitting and waiting. It might already have cost Sean's little sister her life. And Cait had a baby, too. He'd practically forgotten about that. Sean's niece.

Jaw tight, knowing he might be throwing away his job, not to mention putting himself in danger, he scanned his contacts list until he found the one he needed, and then he made the call.

It rang a long time. Just when he had begun to think he would have to leave a voice mail, the ringing ceased.

"It's late."

"Yeah," Herc agreed. "Let's just hope it's not *too* late. We need to meet."

"This line is safe," Terry Stanovitch said.

Herc frowned. Stupid thing for a CIA man to say.

"No line is safe."

-43--

Detective Anne Monteforte set down the telephone in Cait McCandless's apartment and stared at it for a second before turning away. She stuffed the handkerchief she'd used to pick it up into her pocket and once again surveyed the living room. Crime-scene techs were digging bullets out of holes in the wall. Photographers were documenting every angle, every blood spatter, every corpse's profile. Damn, there were a lot of corpses.

Whenever doubt swam up into her head that Cait might be responsible for all, or even some, of this bloodshed, she remembered the video of the petite woman taking down A-Train. Nobody fought like that unless they had been specially trained.

The National Guard taught hand-to-hand combat, but not to the extent of Cait McCandless's skill.

The stink of blood and cordite filled her nostrils. She thought about pulling the handkerchief out again but knew she had to just stomach it. In addition to the crime-scene guys, a pair of uniformed officers were still in the house, not to mention all the cops milling about outside. Making detective had been hard enough. Every guy who ever took the exam thought they should have gotten the job instead, that she'd only been promoted because of her gender. Jarman had always kept after her about it, reminding her that she couldn't afford to look weak.

Monteforte swallowed hard. Her partner was dead, and she couldn't afford to cry.

A cop popped his head into the room. "The Wadlows are gone, Detective. Sacco took them home."

Monteforte nodded. "Good. Make sure he stays with them. They're going to want to come back at some point, but it's a bad idea for them to be here. This thing is going to haunt them every second until they know what's happened to their niece and her baby."

"You got it," the cop said before retreating.

She walked back to where two of the crime-scene guys were zipping a young woman into a body bag. Monteforte had found a small clutch bag on the coffee table with her ID in it—Miranda Russo. Given the wineglasses, she had been a friend of Cait's. The rest of these people, at least from what Monteforte could tell, had come to the party armed. They'd sprayed bullets all over the damn place. But Miranda Russo had just been keeping a friend company.

"What was up with the phone call?" one of the techs asked.

Monteforte glanced at him. "Why? You a detective now?"

The flinch was barely noticeable, but she saw it. She'd stung him. Tomorrow she'd care. Tomorrow, when she had to start training herself to think and speak of her partner only in the past tense.

"I don't know. Someone looking for Cait McCandless," she said, hoping her tone sounded less bitchy.

"Join the club, huh?"

"Yeah," Monteforte said.

It looked like a great many people were looking for Cait McCandless.

Monteforte tried to make sense of the weekend's events, to see how it had all come to this, and simply could not. There were too many pieces of the puzzle missing.

Glancing around, she satisfied herself that the rest was best left to the techs—at least for now—then went through the kitchen and out the back door, shoes crunching on broken glass. Lights had been set up on the back and side lawn and other officers and techs were working out there. Boston P.D. had loaned them some of their people and more were still arriving. As far as Monteforte knew, nothing like this had ever happened in Medford. Shit, it looked like the OK Corral. They'd had a major gang war spill out of Boston a few years earlier and a gunfight had gone down behind Meadow Glen Mall. Three dead, seven other gunshot wounds. That had been *West Side Story* in comparison.

And these weren't gang members. Two of the dead Arab-looking guys had already been ID'd as wanted terrorists, thanks to a federal BOLO for the pair of them. The men and women in tailored suits had the look of Feds or professional hitters.

Mystified, grieving, and wishing more than anything that she had not left it up to Jarman to swing by and look in on Cait McCandless, she glanced at the police and emergency vehicles that lined the street. Dark sedans were pulling up, officers moving the barricade out of the way to let them pass.

Monteforte frowned and moved in that direction. Then she saw the shimmering black bag that now lay, waiting to be carted away, where they had found Detective Jarman's corpse. Her stomach did a flip and her knees went weak and she nearly threw up right there on the grass.

Instead she went to her knees beside him, put out a hand, and whispered, almost like she thought his ghost could hear, "Help me, Bill. Where is she? Is the baby all right? What is all this?"

A minute or two passed while she knelt there with him, wanting to will him back to life, wishing so hard that he could be there to talk it out. He would have seen something she had not; he always did.

"Detective Monteforte?" a man's voice said. She did not look up, but he kept talking. "I'm sorry to intrude, Detective. I understand you must be grieving, and I'm so sorry for your loss."

Monteforte steeled herself, plastered on an emotionless mask, and turned even as she rose to greet him. The man wore a blue shirt rolled up at the sleeves and a red tie, but he wore them like a uniform. Half an inch closer with the razor and he'd be bald. His expression was intense though his sympathy seemed real enough, his demeanor professional but his eyes kind.

He flipped open a wallet to show his FBI identification. The entourage trailing him didn't bother.

"Supervisory Special Agent Ed Turcotte," he said. He glanced down at the body bag, his eyes gleaming with the glow of the work lights. "Once you get us up to speed, take the time you need to mourn your partner. We'll take it from here."

Monteforte's nostrils flared. She felt her lips peel back in a wide smile, but she made sure there was nothing friendly about it.

"Like hell you will."

Blue lights swept across darkened houses and flitted like ghosts through night-blackened trees. The crackle of static and voices came in bursts from a hundred radios clipped to the belts of cops and paramedics. Emergency vehicles crowded Boston Avenue, while other dark, nondescript vehicles prowled among them. Neighbors came out onto their front stoops only to be ushered back inside by uniformed police officers.

The whole street had been locked down tight. A reporter and cameraman scuffled with a pair of state troopers after scurrying across darkened yards trying to get to the scene. The susurrus of voices and static and car doors slamming became drowned out by the helicopter rotors high above, as local stations worked to get the story.

Rachael Voss took it all in. She sipped at her coffee and let her gaze wander a bit before focusing again on Detective Monteforte. It had been a long night, but Voss didn't really want or need the coffee. She only drank it so Monteforte wouldn't feel alone. Nothing made a law enforcement officer squirm more than having to answer the kinds of questions they would normally have been asking someone else. Voss knew this. Coffee wouldn't really make it better, but somehow it did make them sisters-in-arms.

"Had you been partners long?" Voss asked, breaking the silence between them.

The pain in the Monteforte's eyes sharpened a moment, then she cleared her throat.

"Three years. Long enough. He wasn't the kind of cop people want to see movies about, but he was the kind that people need. If someone broke into your house, stole the ring your mother left you, Bill would lose sleep over getting it back. If some girl reported her boyfriend for beating the crap out of her and then refused to testify—so many of them do—Bill would haunt them both."

After a moment's pause, they sipped at their coffees. Nothing Voss could say would leaven the detective's grief, and she respected that. Sometimes when people tried to help, tried to diminish someone else's pain or trauma, it was more about their own uneasiness at their inability to make the sufferer feel better.

"You know that Agent Turcotte was just trying to take the weight of this off you," Voss said.

Monteforte had seemed to be relaxing in her company but now the detective stiffened. "Bullshit. He wanted me out of the way."

Voss nodded. "That's part of it, sure. But he's also a halfway decent guy. Not that I'm his cheering section. We've butted heads plenty in the past and he's one of the most territorial guys I've encountered. I've seen him at his best and worst, though, and I can tell you he wouldn't know how to pretend to be sympathetic."

Monteforte leaned more heavily against her own car, a burgundy Honda Accord, and glanced at the people crawling all over the McCandless woman's yard like ants at a picnic. Voss knew what Monteforte saw—federal agents replacing local police, taking over her case. Hers and Bill Jarman's.

"You don't answer to Turcotte, do you?" Monteforte asked.

"No."

"So what are you doing here? Besides babysitting me."

"For now, just observing."

Monteforte shot her a curious look. "And then? When you're done observing?"

Before Voss could even consider her answer, she spotted Nala Chang and Ben Coogan striding across the lawn toward them. Voss slid off the squad car whose hood she'd been sitting on, spilling a bit of her coffee, and met them on the sidewalk.

"How many?" Voss asked.

Neither of the FBI agents had to ask what she meant.

"Three men of Middle Eastern origin, two of them al-Din's associates from the Fort Myers case. Seven others, not including Detective Jarman and the Russo woman," Chang replied.

"Twelve," Voss said. "Twelve people dead. Jesus."

Coogan glanced apologetically at Monteforte and cleared his throat. "One of Detective Monteforte's colleagues—an Officer Tagliabue—got something from a neighbor we hadn't heard yet. In addition to Ms. McCandless and our white-haired guy, a third person fled the scene."

Voss and Monteforte both perked up.

"Spit it out."

"Black male, forties, bald, driving a dark green or blue Lexus, limping. Blood spatter was found on the sidewalk where the car was apparently parked. Looks like he caught a bullet, but we don't know who shot him."

Monteforte nodded grimly. "Cait."

"Could've been the old guy who picked her up—" Chang started.

"Guy ran one of the shooters down with his car," Coogan added, interrupting. "Obviously he wouldn't stop at pulling a trigger."

Monteforte pushed off of her car and approached them.

"Any idea at all who these bastards were? I mean, okay, I get it, two of them were known terrorists, right? And you're figuring the third Arab-looking guy was on their side. I'm not going to argue profiling when two of these guys were already on your list. But who are the other guys? 'Cause if I read the scene right, it looks to me like one of them killed my partner, and they're too well dressed to be organized crime muscle. They look more like—"

Chang thrust out a hand. "Special Agent Nala Chang, Detective. I'm part of SSA Turcotte's squad. This is Special Agent Ben Coogan, out of the Bureau's Boston field office. I'm not sure if you've met. . . ."

"No. We haven't." Monteforte narrowed her eyes in suspicion but shook Chang's hand, and then Coogan's.

"I know this is a difficult time for you," Chang went on, "but I hoped you would tell us what you can about Caitlin McCandless. I spoke with several of the uniformed officers and I understand she's become something of a celebrity in the Boston area this weekend. We'd seen some of the news reports ourselves, even before all of this."

Voss listened, first only half paying attention, as Monteforte began to unspool the tale of Cait McCandless's run-in with an abusive football player. But when the detective related the story of the attempted abduction of McCandless's baby, Voss weighed every detail.

"Have you confirmed her story regarding the baby's father?" Voss asked, when Monteforte took a breath. "Talked to anyone in her National Guard unit?"

Monteforte frowned. "No. Why would I have done that? We had no reason to think she had been anything other than truthful. Hell, why would she lie?"

Voss gestured toward the house. "You've got suspected terrorists dead on the lawn over there, Detective. There's obviously more to the case than you assumed."

Monteforte exhaled. "I get it. But that was then, and this is now. If it helps, we spoke extensively to her aunt and uncle. You'll talk to them yourselves, I'm sure. They certainly back up Cait's version of things. I had no reason to doubt the baby was half-Iraqi." Voss could see puzzle pieces clicking into place behind Monteforte's eyes. "Your dead terrorists . . . you think they were here for the baby?"

"Maybe to save her. Maybe to kill her," Chang replied.

"Agent Chang," Voss said sharply.

Coogan stiffened, staring from one woman to the next and then to the next. "Maybe it's time you clued me in as to what this case is really about."

Voss glanced at him, then at Monteforte. "When we figure it out, we'll let you know."

As Chang started in on a question, they were interrupted by a shout. They all looked around to see Josh jogging toward them across the grass.

"Who's this?" Monteforte asked.

"My partner," Voss replied, before realizing it would sting.

Josh's eyes were alight with frustration and unburnt energy. Voss knew the look—he needed to hit someone or get laid. Instead he studied the faces around him, then turned to her.

"We need to talk. Now."

Voss glanced at the others. Josh and Nala Chang had started to get a little cozy, but he had doubt in his eyes, obviously wondering whether to include her. Chang saw it, too, and narrowed her eyes at the unintended insult. Whatever flirtation they'd been engaged in had just been polluted, big-time—but that was Josh's problem.

"Excuse me a second," Voss said to Detective Monteforte.

When she and Josh had put a dozen feet between themselves and anyone else, they stopped. Emotion rolled off him in waves but she couldn't read it clearly—was he angry or suspicious or excited?

"What couldn't you say in front of them?" Voss asked.

"Did Turcotte talk to you about the BOLO on the McCandless woman?"

"No. Why is that bad?"

"The BOLO identifies McCandless as a suspected terrorist."

"What?" Voss looked across a sea of cop cars and federal agents, searching for Ed Turcotte. Instead, her eyes alighted upon a figure standing to the side observing, hands clasped behind his back. Norris.

Cait McCandless's brother had died, at least according to the interview she'd given earlier in the day. Someone had tried to abduct her child. Two teams of armed men had shown up at her house, murdered one of her friends, and shot the hell out of the place and one another, and she'd obviously barely escaped with her life. Some of those men had apparently been terrorists. But to suggest that McCandless herself was a terrorist was not only a huge and irrational leap in logic, it might well make the difference between an arresting officer pulling a trigger or not.

"What the fuck is Turcotte thinking?" Voss muttered.

"No idea," Josh said. "But isn't it our job to find out?"

"Yes. Yes, it is."

Side by side, they started back toward the McCandless house.

-44--

By the time they reached the exit for Millbury off the MassPike, the clock on the dash showed it was after midnight. Lynch had been adamant about not stopping at a rest area on the Pike and was less than thrilled about the prospect of stopping at all. Considering he had landed at Logan Airport and stolen the first car he'd found with a car seat already inside, then stopped and bought all the things he thought he would need for Leyla while hurrying to try to keep Cait and her daughter from being killed or abducted, he had done fairly well in preparing for their fugitive status. But he hadn't counted on Cait's shirt being soaked with baby piss.

"This is a bad idea," Lynch said as he drove past darkened strip malls. The Target and Walmart were both closed, windows dark.

"Leyla needs something to wear that doesn't smell like pee. Plus, I need to get her some Cheerios."

"I have formula, jugs of water, baby cereal, and jarred food—"

"The jarred stuff is fine for the morning, but the easiest thing while we're driving would be Cheerios. They'll make her happy and keep her quiet. And I wouldn't mind a new shirt for myself, either. Plus I could use caffeine to keep me awake and something to eat wouldn't hurt."

"One stop only," Lynch said sternly. "We get what we can, and then we keep moving."

Cait hesitated. Keep moving. Right. To meet up with his friends in some secret location he would not reveal to her. But at least he had gotten off the turnpike and was willing to stop at all.

"I really do know people who can help," she said.

Lynch kept driving. Cait had figured in a place with so many fast-food restaurants and strip malls something would be open late. She was banking on it.

"My brother's friend Herc . . . I need to call him. And there are guys from my unit in Iraq who would march through hell to cover my ass—fuck, they *have*."

Up ahead, they spotted the illuminated sign for a 24-hour CVS pharmacy. Cait wished she could have felt some relief or gratitude, but all she wanted to do was scream. Not just at Lynch—the guy really did seem to be trying to help her the only way he knew how—but at the world, and at the sick freaks who thought the birth of a child could stop a war and killed babies to make sure that didn't happen.

"All of those people work for the government, or used to," Lynch said.

"My brother trusted Herc completely. And Ronnie and Jordan . . . either one of those guys would take a bullet for me, and me for them."

Lynch grunted; Cait had not known him long enough to interpret the sound. He pulled into the CVS parking lot and drove to a spot snug up against a Dumpster at the back of the store, where the light from the lampposts barely reached.

He killed the bypassed ignition on the engine, then leaned over and opened the glove compartment, which revealed a pack of Marlboro Lights and a few old CDs. Cait tensed, the gun comforting in her hand, but a moment later he pulled out a hard plastic eyeglass case.

"I thought I'd seen this in there," he said as he opened the case and donned a pair of nondescript spectacles. "Must be a backup pair, or he only needs them for driving." Lynch looked at her, squinting slightly behind the prescription lenses. "Wish I had a hat. Anything in particular you want me to try to get for you to eat?"

"At a CVS? It's snacks or snacks, basically. Coke. Pretzels. Some of those Goldfish if they've got them. Aren't you afraid I'm going to take off the second you're inside the store?"

His eyes darkened. "How far would you get with a baby in your arms at midnight? If you bang on someone's door, you risk them calling the police. If you try hitchhiking, you risk more than that. But if you think I'm completely out of my mind, that there's absolutely no truth to what I've told you—which would beg the question of how I found you in the first place—then by all means, make a run for it. I'm not going to shoot a woman I'm trying to help. And I'm not going to hurt a baby."

They locked eyes a moment, then Lynch climbed out, shutting the door quietly to keep from waking Leyla. That alone might have been the thing that kept her from running inside and telling the clerk he had kidnapped her, or trying to get to the pay phone she'd seen near the Bank of America kiosk a couple of parking lots back. She had no doubt the man lived on the fringe of lunacy; the look in his eyes was evidence enough. But she had to allow for the possibility that it was more fanaticism than insanity.

And he'd killed two men already to keep her and Leyla alive.

Cait glanced into the backseat. From around the edge of the rear-facing car seat, she could see that Leyla's head had drooped forward. She set her gun on the floor, unsnapped her seat belt, and got onto her knees to reach back and adjust the baby's position. A surge of love swelled inside her and she smiled. Leyla's mouth still hung open. Her lower lip trembled a moment and then she sighed, her breathing returning to the soft rhythm of sleep.

With a sigh of her own, Cait righted herself in her seat, which brought her gaze to rest on the open glove compartment and the package of Marlboro Lights in there. She hadn't had more than half a dozen cigarettes since returning from Iraq, but in the desert there had not been a lot to do to pass the time except clean the sand out of her weapon and smoke. The habit often disgusted her, but she could not deny its ability to calm her nerves.

She thought about Auntie Jane and Uncle George, and how worried they must be. At some point she would have to get a message to them, let them know she and Leyla were all right. But she had to be careful not to give them any information that the police, or anyone else, might be able to use to track her down. Whatever happened, she wanted to keep them as far away from this trouble as possible. They, and Leyla, were all the family she had left.

After a moment's reconnaissance—they really were parked in the darkest corner of the lot, near a half-fenced enclosure around the Dumpster by the pharmacy's back door—she pushed in the car lighter. As the seconds ticked by, she wondered how many people still used them to light cigarettes instead of to charge cell phones and other electronics.

A nervous glance back at Leyla, then she slid the Marlboro Lights from the glove compartment and tapped one out into her hand. Paranoid as Lynch was—and as paranoid as she needed to become—she knew she should stay out of sight. But she could easily keep an eye out for anyone approaching and jump back into the car. A quick glance out the window showed her the security camera up on the side of the building. From the angle she couldn't be sure if she would be within its range, but she could keep her back to it.

The lighter popped. No way would she smoke in the car with Leyla. She opened her door and lit the cigarette, taking a long drag to make sure it was burning before pushing the lighter back into place. Then she stepped out, cigarette pressed between her lips, and picked up the gun, which she slid into the rear waistband of her pants. They sagged, not made for this, but the gun remained in place.

She lowered her head and peered into the car to make sure she hadn't disturbed Leyla; the baby slept on. So much for the cigarette calming her; she felt more agitated than before, just being outside the car. Steadying herself, she took another long drag and let the smoke plume out of her nostrils. Then another. By the third, her pulse had started to slow and her mind began attempting to sort out the mess she was in. Grief tried to shove at the edges of her mind, but Cait shoved back. No time for grief—not when Leyla's life depended on how she handled herself from this moment forward.

A metallic creak made her jump. Biting down on the cigarette, she went to reach for the gun and then remembered the security camera aimed at her back, even as the back door of the CVS swung open and a young woman came out carrying two large garbage bags. Even in the dark, the moon provided enough light that the diamond stud in her nose glittered. Her features suggested India or Pakistan.

Breathe, Cait told herself. Her right hand, which had been going for her gun, relaxed and she let it fall to her side as the girl caught sight of her.

"Oh!" the girl said.

"Hi," Cait said, trying to look normal.

"Hi. Smoke break?"

"Yeah. My friend is taking a while. Figured I'd light up while I wait."

"This is where we always come to smoke on our breaks," the girl said as she tossed the lighter bag into the Dumpster and then hefted the other with both hands.

Cait wondered if she expected to be offered a cigarette now that she had made this revelation, but that wasn't going to happen.

"Must feel like forever, working the night shift," Cait said.

"Sometimes," the girl admitted. "But we get a lot of people who work nights coming in. Well, not a lot, but you know what I mean. Enough. That, and people who need medicine in the middle of the night, parents whose kids have fevers, that sort of thing." She seemed to realize she was talking a lot and grew sheepish. "Anyway, have a good night."

"You, too," Cait said.

The girl started to go inside, then paused thoughtfully and glanced back. After a second, a smile spread across her face.

"I knew I recognized you."

Cait froze, her stomach twisting. Lynch had been scanning radio channels for news stories on the shootings at her house, wondering if the police would bring the media into their search for her. So far they'd heard nothing, but maybe they had just missed it, like flipping TV channels trying to find the weather report. She plastered on a fake smile and dropped her cigarette, grinding it out with her heel.

"You do?"

She thought about the gun at her back and wondered if she could kill the girl if it meant keeping her daughter safe. But that would be murder. Cait could not commit cold-blooded murder. Not and live with herself. Which meant she had to think of another way to deal with this girl.

This smiling girl.

"Yes! I saw the video of you on TV kicking the crap out of that guy who was beating up his wife. A-Train? I watched it like ten times online. I posted it on my blog, even. That was just awesome."

Cait trembled as she exhaled. "Thanks. It wasn't . . . I mean, I didn't enjoy it or anything, but somebody had to do it."

"Totally." The girl shrugged. "I've got to get back in there, but it was nice meeting you."

"Yeah. Good night."

When she had gone back in, pulling the door shut behind her, Cait sagged against the car. From inside she heard a small mewling, which meant that Leyla was on her way to waking up, and she needed her to get as much sleep as possible on this long, insane night. The baby would need a bottle soon, but Cait was anxious and wanted to get back on the road first. So she slipped into the car and began to sing softly—an old James Taylor song that her father had sung to her when she was a little girl, and that Sean had sung once or twice when she was young, just to make her feel better.

This time she could not fight the pang of grief and it blossomed into something larger, something that began to fill her up inside. The summer night was warm, but she felt a kind of cold that she knew would never go away completely.

Lynch came out of the CVS and strode across the lot toward her, carrying several plastic bags. His eyes were narrowed in consternation, probably due to the fact that she had her door propped open, but when he got there he said nothing, only handed the bags in to her.

Oreos. Cheddar Cheese Goldfish. A box of plastic spoons. Four or five yogurts. Juice. A box of Cheerios. Lynch had done well. She tugged a pink Red Sox T-shirt out of a bag and held it up in front of her. At her size, there was no way it would be too small.

"Not the most inconspicuous choice," she said.

"It was that or an XXL Boston Celtics T-shirt."

Cait nodded. "Turn around."

When he obliged, his back to the car, she pulled off her shirt. In addition to Leyla's pee it had bloodstains on it. She dropped it on the floor and tugged the Red Sox tee over her head, finding it a little more snug than it had looked. Pink had never been her color, much too girly for her, and she wondered if she would have felt the same if she had grown up with a mother to look after her. A stray thought, filed away for another day, when such mundane things might mean something to her again.

She handed her soiled T-shirt out to Lynch, who walked over and tossed it into the Dumpster.

"You didn't run," he said.

"How far would I have gotten?"

He nodded in approval, took off the glasses he'd donned to go into CVS, dropped them on the pavement, then crushed them underfoot.

"Those things were hurting my eyes," he said, and then he walked around to the driver's side and got in.

Shutting the door quietly, he sparked a couple of wires together and the engine purred to life. As he put the car into Drive, he glanced over at her. "You didn't look in the last bag."

Curious, Cait dragged it onto her lap. Inside she found a pair of fashion glasses that people sometimes wore just for show.

They had clear lenses, but made you look smart. Also in the bag were scissors, a box of hair dye, and a hard plastic container that held a small black object.

"You bought a phone?"

Lynch pulled out of the parking lot and sped back toward the turnpike. The next exit up would put them on Route 84 toward Hartford, and New York beyond.

"It's a go-phone. Pre-paid. Your cell phone would have been easy as hell to track, but this is clean. Not linked to you. I'm more used to killing people than saving them, but I'm trying to work with you here. So you've got to think very carefully, Caitlin, before you use this phone. With your baby's life on the line, you've got to ask yourself, who can you really trust?"

As she stared at the plastic-encased phone, a cry rose up from the backseat and she turned to see Leyla fussing and licking her lips like she was hungry. The noise of the engine hadn't comforted her after all.

She just wants to be home in her crib, Cait thought.

But they didn't have a home anymore. Not for a while, at least. And not unless Cait could perform a miracle. Lynch's revelations had been sinking in. How long had ruthless bastards been doing this? Could it really be centuries? Millennia? How did one twenty-six-year-old woman fight that kind of history—that conspiracy—and keep herself and her child alive?

Cait felt her gun jabbing her in the back. She took it out and stashed it in the glove box, then picked up the phone again. After a few seconds she reached into the bag, drew out the pair of scissors Lynch had bought, and started cutting the phone free of its plastic.

Wondering who to call.

-45--

Josh hung back in the darkness beneath an oak tree while, across the yard, Voss ripped Ed Turcotte a new one. With the chopper noise overhead and the radio static and chatter on the ground, he was pretty sure that the assorted cops and Feds crawling over the grounds of Cait McCandless's house couldn't hear the exchange. Josh couldn't hear any of it, either, but he smiled to himself as he watched the two of them face off, circling each other like dogs about to go for the throat. Turcotte didn't stand a chance.

Nala Chang and Ben Coogan walked up to join him, both of them distracted by the confrontation, but neither of them daring to get close enough to overhear.

Voss and Turcotte stood at the corner of the house in a patch of shadow untouched by the crime-scene light setups and the strobing blue lights that swept across the house and yard. Their gestures and facial expressions were a visual staccato akin to the flicker of an old-time kinescope, and Josh didn't have to hear to know the gist.

Rachael wanted to know what the fuck the FBI had been thinking putting out a BOLO suggesting Cait McCandless was a terror suspect. Whatever the Bureau's rationale—and Josh couldn't wait to hear it—Turcotte would be bristling at the suggestion that he needed to get Voss's approval on anything.

"That doesn't look fun," Coogan said.

Josh shot him a dark look. "It isn't."

Coogan glanced at Chang, disapproval writ large on his face. "Isn't this Agent Turcotte's case? Why is he even listening?"

Chang closed her eyes and shook her head at the insult implied in the question. Josh narrowed his eyes, wondering what Coogan could be thinking to outright slam Josh's agency and partner with him standing right there. Maybe the guy was sick of being stuck in a field office and wanted a more dynamic posting, or maybe he just liked the way Chang's blouse clung to her breasts and wanted to swing his dick a little. Either way, it was a dumb move.

"You want to take that question?" Chang asked, glancing at Josh.

"No," Josh said. "You go ahead."

As Chang started to explain that Voss could take the case away from the FBI anytime she felt the urge, causing all the color to leach from Coogan's cheeks, Josh tuned out the conversation, watching his partner instead. He wondered if Turcotte would push back hard enough to make Voss burn the bridge, to force her to take the case from him.

"What do you think is going to happen?" Chang asked.

Josh blinked and looked at her, her face bathed in blue light. He had not noticed, but Coogan had marched off. Presumably he intended to try to make himself useful, though he might have come to the realization that he would not be on this case for long. That left just Josh and Nala standing beneath the branches of an oak tree by the sidewalk, waiting to see how it all shook out.

"That depends."

"On what?" Chang asked.

"On why." He looked at her. "Do you know why Turcotte had them word the BOLO that way?"

Chang seemed almost hurt by the question. "No. This woman sounds like a target to me. If people are coming after her child and she did this to them, she's my new hero. So, no, Agent Hart, I don't know. But I'd like to."

Josh found himself hoping Voss and Turcotte could keep from killing each other so he and Chang could continue this investigation together. He liked her smile and the way she did her job. Liked the way she could move from grim to amused with easy confidence. Over the past twenty-four hours or so, he had found that he liked her a great deal.

But you can't go there.

The dilemma of his job had turned out to be that while he

had made a rule for himself about not getting sexually or romantically involved with Feds or cops or anyone else who dealt with crime and punishment for a living, finding a civilian who could put up with what that life could do to a person—with the hours and the moods and the nightmares—had proven almost impossible. His blind date with Molly had gone well—right up until it had been interrupted by a quadruple murder in Fort Myers.

"What did you make of what Detective Monteforte was saying?" Josh asked.

"I think we've got to look into McCandless's brother," Chang replied. "If he's actually dead, that's a new wrinkle. None of the other child killings had collateral damage outside the household. And if he was really some kind of spy or whatever . . ."

"I know. It sounds crazy, right?"

Chang hesitated, then looked up at him. "Maybe not. If someone is really killing these kids because they're of mixed race and Sean McCandless had the kind of connections and training all this implies, he'd come after them. Taking him out first would be the smart thing to do."

Josh exhaled loudly. "We're not talking serial killers now. They'd have to know about him in the first place, be able to track him down, and then kill a government agent and get away with it."

Chang gestured toward the lawn, which had been turned into a killing ground. "This is way past serial killers, Josh."

He felt a pang of sorrow as he thought about Grace Kowalik, whose parents had named her after she was already dead. He didn't want Cait McCandless's daughter to end up the same way, on the bank of a river somewhere, or killed in her sleep like the Greenlaw twins and who knew how many others.

"I know. I just hate conspiracy shit."

"You don't think conspiracies happen?" Chang asked, eyebrows rising.

Josh surveyed the damage to Cait McCandless's apartment house. Bullet holes. Shattered windows. At some point the poor bastard who lived on the second floor would come home and find his place sealed off by the police. He might even be out there right now, kept back by the police cordon.

"Conspiracy's the wiring in the walls, Nala. It's always there. We're just not supposed to see it. And unless you're very careful, you're never supposed to touch it."

"We'll just have to be careful, then."

Her confidence made him smile but when he glanced at her, something else caught his attention. On the street, a cop bumped his cruiser up onto the opposite sidewalk to let a white box van get past. The van bore no insignia or identifying mark, but it had to be some sort of official vehicle or the cops wouldn't be letting it out.

"What's wrong?" Chang asked.

"Maybe nothing."

Curious, he crossed the sidewalk and moved between two cars into the street, and Chang followed. The van passed them, but Josh only got a quick glimpse of the driver—Caucasian, thirtyish, buzz cut—which told him nothing for certain. Maybe fifty feet farther up the street was a second box van, identical to the first. The rear doors were open and a quartet of men in dark jumpsuits were loading body bags inside. A few cops and a man wearing an FBI jacket stood nearby chatting, ignoring them. Gurneys that had been used to cart the bodies over from the yard were being rolled back to waiting ambulances and a black truck bearing the logo for Suffolk County on the side, obviously from the medical examiner's office. But the gurneys were going back empty. The M.E.'s truck and the ambulances would leave without their usual cargo.

"Any idea what this is?" he asked Chang.

"Let's find out."

They started toward the first white van, walking fast, dark suspicion rising in Josh's thoughts. "These guys look military to you?"

"My first thought."

"Shit."

As they approached, two of the guys climbed into the back of the van. Two others were about to close the doors.

"Hold on a minute," Josh called.

The two inside the van started shifting body bags around, but the men by the doors turned toward the interruption with guarded expressions. Other than the variance in skin color, they seemed made from the same mold: strong jaw, tightly cropped hair, powerful build, veiled eyes.

"Where are you taking them?" Chang asked.

The man on the left, African-American with coffee-colored skin, cocked his head as he studied them. Then he nodded to the other man and they slammed the rear doors and turned their backs, the white guy starting around the passenger side. The other was apparently the driver.

"Whoa," Josh said, anger flaring. He started after the driver. "A federal agent just asked you a question. You need to answer it."

As Josh caught up to him, reaching for his arm, the driver turned and stopped him with a look.

"You don't want to touch me, sir."

The *sir* confirmed all of Josh's worst fears. They were soldiers. On this case, soldiers meant SOCOM, and SOCOM meant Arsenault.

"Nobody wants this to turn ugly, soldier," Josh said. "It's a simple question. Where are you taking the bodies? And I'll ask another one: Who gave the order?"

In his peripheral vision, he saw Chang a few feet behind the van. The passenger appeared, edging into position in back of the doors, ready to act if something went down. The tension attracted immediate attention, several police officers and techs and a few FBI personnel gathering.

"We're going to get into the van now, sir," the driver said. "If you have questions about our orders, I suggest you take them up with your superiors."

Chang took out her ID, flipped it open, and stepped closer to the jarhead at the back of the van. "You will answer the question or you will be detained."

A restless shudder went through those who had gathered to watch. One police officer touched the butt of the gun hanging from his belt, eyes shifting back and forth as if he were watching a tennis match. Josh pulled out his cell, rang Voss, and she answered on the second ring.

"I'm kind of in the middle—"

"Come out on the street right now. White van. Bring Turcotte."

Voss didn't ask questions. She knew from his voice there was trouble. Josh killed the call, put away his phone, and looked around to find that every person in the vicinity seemed to be holding their breath. He knew he had to end this confrontation before it erupted into something they would all regret.

But the driver smiled, and it was almost a sneer.

"You don't have the authority to stop us," he said.

Josh didn't like that sneer. "The FBI doesn't have the authority? All right, then. I'm with ICD—"

"What the fuck is ICD?" the passenger muttered.

"A division of Homeland Security, moron," Chang said.

The passenger laughed. "So's the Coast Guard."

The driver silenced him with a look. Obviously his superior officer, and the one with the brains.

"Where's Lieutenant Arsenault?" Josh asked. "Let me talk to him and we'll sort this out."

The driver's nostrils flared in alarm—the only sign that he even knew who Arsenault was, or that he was troubled that Josh had figured them out. Now that Josh thought about it, he hadn't seen Arsenault or Norris for at least twenty minutes, maybe more.

"Sir, if you'll consult the officers around you, you'll find that the local authorities have received their orders and have released the deceased into our custody. And now I'm afraid we have to go. We're expected."

The driver turned again and started toward the front of the truck. The passenger smiled at Chang and did the same.

Josh drew his gun, the sound of it sliding from the holster strangely loud amidst the noises of the crime scene. Chang muttered a curse and followed suit, taking aim along the other side of the van, where the passenger must be.

"Don't take another goddamn step!" Josh said.

The driver froze, put up his arms, turned to face him, then slapped the side of the white van twice. The back doors popped open and the two soldiers who'd climbed in with the body bags held small semi-auto pistols aimed at Josh and Chang.

Cops swore and drew their weapons. Shouting erupted. Some of the onlookers couldn't seem to decide who they should be aiming at. The driver opened his door and slid behind the wheel, slamming it shut behind him.

"Fuck!" Josh snapped. He lowered his gun as he raced alongside the van. One of the soldiers crouched in the back tracked him with a sweep of his semi-auto but didn't pull the trigger, and then Josh was out of sight.

He tried the door, found it locked, then stepped back and aimed at the driver through the half-open window.

"Don't let this go any further!" he barked.

"Whatever happens is on you," the driver said, cranking the engine to life. "But it seems to me you've got a lot of people in the line of fire back there."

Then he put the truck in gear and it started rolling forward. Josh swore at him again, his finger twitching on the trigger, knowing there were a dozen armed men and women behind the van wondering if they were supposed to open fire, knowing a lot of them would get shot if any of them did.

Josh followed, running after the van. The cop who'd moved his car to let the first white van out hadn't moved it back into place. At the cordon down the street, they would have no idea what was going down and would let the bastards out. They had their orders.

"Goddammit!"

He stopped running, turned around to a sea of clueless expressions, and stalked over to the nearest Medford cop.

"Radio the cordon. Do not let that van get by them!"

The dough-faced, fortyish cop gave him a dubious look. "Why? I don't get it."

"You don't have to get it!" Josh yelled. "Those bodies are about to vanish—including your dead Detective Jarman—and then none of us will ever know what really happened here. Stop the fucking van!"

The bit about Jarman got the guy moving.

"Josh!"

As the cop whipped out his radio, Voss came running up with Turcotte and Chang. Monteforte and Coogan weren't far behind, and they were followed by a coterie of agents and cops. Josh started to shout to his partner, but he swallowed his anger and hurried to meet her instead. Too many people to overhear, too many potential leaks.

"We've gotta move!" Josh said, grabbing Voss's arm and running for their car.

"What the hell?" Turcotte called, he and Chang racing after them.

Monteforte kept pace, racing for her own car, blue bubble flashing on the roof. She flung the door open and shouted to them, "Get in!"

Josh didn't hesitate, diverting Voss to Monteforte's car. She ran around to get into the passenger seat and Josh climbed in back. Turcotte caught the door before he could close it.

"It's my goddamn case, Hart. Tell me what's going on!"

"It's being pulled out from under you, and not by us. Get in the car!"

Turcotte took an angry look around, then turned to Chang and Coogan, who were waiting behind him.

"Lock it all down," he snapped. "No one in or out. I'll call you in two minutes."

As Turcotte climbed in, Monteforte put it in gear and hit the gas, the car leaping forward. She swerved around the nose of a patrol car, nearly hit an unmarked FBI vehicle, and then they were rocketing up the street toward the police cordon.

Voss turned around in the front seat. "Talk to me, Josh!"

"Those guys were SOCOM," he said quickly. "Arsenault and Norris are gone. All of the bodies were just taken out of here in unmarked vans and the cops did nothing. They were all acting under orders."

"Orders we didn't get," Voss said, glaring at Turcotte. "Did you know about this?"

The fury in his eyes said it all, but Josh knew he wouldn't admit he had been made a fool.

"All the bodies?" Monteforte said, knuckles white on the steering wheel. "They've got my partner's body?"

"I don't think they made exceptions," Josh said.

"No," Monteforte said, pain ravaging her face. "No more of this!"

She floored it, hit the siren, laid on the horn. Up ahead a cop was just pulling his patrol car back into place—they had let the van through—but he reversed and pulled back out of Monteforte's path.

The detective skidded the car to a halt. "Which way?" she shouted out the window.

Several of the cops pointed straight across the traffic circle.

"Headed toward Route 16!" one of them called.

Siren screaming, Monteforte floored it, tearing through the traffic circle and nearly hitting a woman out walking her dog. The car hugged the road as it raced along a narrow street with cars lining both sides. The light ahead was red but Monteforte barely tapped the brakes before she shot through.

"This is insane!" Voss said. "SOCOM's not even supposed to operate on U.S. soil. Why would Arsenault do this?"

Josh glanced at Turcotte but neither of them answered.

Monteforte didn't hesitate. "Obviously he's got something to fucking hide!"

Turcotte had pulled out his cell phone, apparently to call Chang as he'd promised. Now he leaned forward.

"What's this direction, Detective? Where do you think they're headed?"

But even as he asked they came to another light, and beyond it they could see the interstate. Josh spotted the van off to the right on a road parallel to the highway.

"If they get on 93 going south, my guess is the airport!" Monteforte said.

Josh stared at Voss. "We can't let that happen."

"No," Turcotte agreed. "We can't."

-46--

In the dashboard light, Lynch looked almost cadaverous. He had to be exhausted. Cait figured something must be keeping him running and, given the absence of coffee cups or empty energy drink cans, she guessed pills. It frightened her to have her daughter in the backseat of a car driven by a guy this wired. She had offered to drive for a while but Lynch had grunted "No, thanks," and she didn't have a lot of options. At least his hands were steady on the wheel and, though the circles under his eyes had deepened and darkened, he stayed awake.

The guy turned purpose and determination into raw energy, and Cait would have to do the same. At least Leyla had quieted down again. When the baby had started crying, Cait had clambered into the back and given her a bottle of formula and a clean onesie that Leyla had chewed on for a few minutes before draping it over her face and falling back to sleep.

They were on Route 84 now, a few miles across the Connecticut border, but they had both gone silent. The engine hummed and Lynch scanned newsradio stations in search of any mention of her name or the bloodshed they had left behind in Massachusetts. She wanted to shout at him to leave it alone, to stay on one station, but the guy seemed fanatical about the radio so she said nothing. He had been on the run before, had killed people and had killers pursuing him. She had to trust that he knew what he was doing.

It was just that trust was so damn hard to come by right now.

"Watch the speedometer," she said. "The Connecticut State Police are brutal."

Lynch sniffed. "I've been driving longer than you've been alive." But he did ease up on the gas.

Cait had cut the go-phone from its plastic casing and put the detritus on the floor. Having decided she wasn't likely to shoot Lynch anytime soon, she had stashed her gun in the glove compartment next to the pack of Marlboro Lights. But the go-phone seemed to weigh more than the gun. She clutched it in her right hand, trying not to look at it, trying to tell herself it couldn't possibly weigh that much. Plastic and a battery—a few ounces, that was all.

But the weight of a gun came as much from possibility as it did from metal and bullets, and this phone was much the same.

Streetlights flickered across the windshield. Cars whipped by in the opposite direction, nighttime people with nighttime lives. There were only a handful of people she could even think of calling, and most of them would be asleep now. As much as she wanted them to know she was all right, she had decided that calling Auntie Jane and Uncle George might actually put them in danger, so that was out. She wondered about Hercules. Sean had made her commit the Hot Line number to memory. She had been calling him when Lynch had thrown her cell phone out the window, but now she hesitated. Sean had trusted him completely, but Herc had lied to her about the circumstances of her brother's death. She knew it. Maybe he had to be careful what he said—maybe others were listening—but could she trust him?

Despite the air conditioner whispering its chill, her hands felt clammy.

"Fuck it," she muttered. Doing nothing was no better than giving up.

And there was one person she knew she could call, who had always had her back. Lynch started changing radio stations again, voices mixing with the static, sports and L.A. gossip and weather and politics.

Cait held the phone in front of her and dialed Jordan's cell phone number. But when it clicked over to voice mail, she disconnected the call, heart pounding. Leaving him a message might be a mistake. The cops would have started interviewing people already—or maybe the Feds—and they would have found out how close she and Jordan were.

So who else could she call?

A smile flickered across her lips, and she dialed quickly, from memory. She needed him to answer, because there was no one else to call. Her pulse raced when it began to ring. She tried to get herself under control, tried to control her shaking hand. Then the answering machine clicked on and she heard Ronnie Mellace's voice, and she knew she had done the right thing.

"Ronnie, it's Cait," she said. "If you're there, pick up. Please, please pick up."

A beat. Then another. And just as she feared she would be cut off, a click.

"Cait? It's like a quarter to one—"

"I know. I'm sorry."

"No, no. Don't be," he said, his voice a familiar, comforting rasp. A nighttime desert voice, a whisper accompanying the hiss of blowing sand and the thunderous silence of dormant guns.

"What's wrong? Can't sleep?" Ronnie asked. And then, after a moment, "What phone are you calling from? Did you get a new cell?"

They had promised to watch out for each other, she and Jordan and Ronnie. But that had been in Iraq, where death had been their constant companion. Would it still hold true now that they were home? He'd said it would. He'd called to check on her earlier tonight. Now she would find out.

"Cait? Hello? You still there?"

"I'm here," she said, glancing at Lynch. The old man kept his eyes on the road but his knuckles were white on the wheel. "Ronnie, I . . . I need you."

She could almost feel him snap to attention.

"Tell me."

"Some people . . . I can't get into detail right now, but some people are trying to kill me and Leyla."

"Jesus!"

"There were guns. My friend Miranda, who was at my place earlier? She's dead."

"Cait, where are you? I'll come right now."

A soft smile touched her lips. Lynch was with her, but

Lynch was a stranger. Ronnie made her feel like she wasn't alone after all. Now she just needed Jordan. Just the thought of him eased her mind a little.

"I'm coming to you," she said. "I'm on 84 right now. There's crazy shit going down, man. You're gonna think my brains got mashed, but you've got to believe me. Conspiracy shit. I've got no one to trust."

"You've got me," he said, voice so strong.

"I know. And I need you to get Jordan, too. He knows some of this already," she said. "He's probably freaking out right now. I tried calling but got his voice mail. Track him down, Ronnie. Tell him I need him."

"I'll grab him and meet you. What's your ETA?"

She tried to read the signs flashing by outside. "Less than an hour. But that's a guess."

Ronnie rattled off directions to a Wendy's just off 84 east of Hartford. Easy enough. The mere thought of seeing them—especially Jordan—lifted her spirits. If the people hunting her baby found them again before Cait could vanish with Leyla, she wanted to know she had backup she could rely on.

"If I get Jordan in the next few minutes, we can meet you there in two hours," Ronnie said.

"Two hours. See you then," Cait said. "And Ronnie? Come strapped."

She hit END, but kept staring at the phone. More than anything, what she wanted was to know who she was up against, who wanted her baby. Lynch's rant had indicted everyone but ninja assassins, though she figured he would get around to them eventually. She had to know what was true, how widespread this really was, and if there truly was no help to be found.

Sean had trusted Herc. The question wasn't if she trusted Brian Herskowitz, but how much she trusted Sean. Making up her mind, Cait started to dial the Hot Line.

"I hope you're right about this phone being harder to—"

Lynch shushed her, turning up the volume on the radio. When Cait heard her own name, she forgot to breathe.

". . . instant debate over whether McCandless is a troubled

veteran who simply snapped or is actually working in conjunction with domestic terror groups. Police will say only that she is wanted for questioning related to two shooting deaths at her Medford apartment earlier tonight and that they would like to speak with her about her connections to domestic terror groups in Florida and the Midwest. A spokesman for Boston's Channel 7, where Sergeant McCandless is employed, has said the station will release a statement shortly.

"Meanwhile, the one person who is speaking about Sergeant McCandless tonight is former Boston College football star Aaron Traynor, whom the media has dubbed 'A-Train.' McCandless reportedly stepped in on Saturday night when, police allege, Traynor became violent with his wife, Alina. Worse than the broken bones he suffered, A-Train has endured days of humiliation over the YouTube video of the fight and has threatened to sue McCandless.

" 'I hope they track her down and throw her in jail. I've got issues I gotta get under control, yeah. I'm in anger management classes, all right? Tryin' to pick a rehab place right now, get the alcohol situation taken care of. But I ain't no terrorist. I'm not out shootin' folks.' "

Cait closed her eyes, sucking in a deep breath. People had tried to kill her and take her baby. Sean was dead, and they were calling her a terrorist. A-Train was whoring himself out to the media over beating the shit out of his wife and getting his ass kicked by a girl.

"Turn it down," she said.

Lynch obliged, but the radio voice droned on.

"Photos of McCandless are available on our website, along with the number for the police tip line—"

"Turn it off!"

He did. She clutched the phone in her hand and turned to gaze out the window. In the green glow of the dashboard she could see her face reflected in the glass, expressionless, bereft of all emotion.

"Oh, my God," she whispered.

She pressed her forehead against the glass, not bothering to try to wipe away the tear that slipped down her cheek, tasting the salt on her lips. With the hum of the engine and the hiss of the A/C, she could not hear Leyla breathing. She wished the baby would wake up, would cry, wished the morning would come and she could get out of this damned car and hold her little girl in her arms and feel the summer sun on her skin.

But where could she do such a thing, now that the whole country would recognize her face and think they were seeing a monster?

"Caitlin?" Lynch ventured.

"Drive," she rasped. "Just drive."

-47--

A rap on the glass made Herc jerk upright behind the wheel of his Camry. He tried flinching away from the window but was held in place by his seat belt. A figure loomed outside the car and it took a moment before he realized it was Terry Stanovitch.

"Christ!" Herc wheezed.

Hunched over, Stanovitch raised his fist to bang on the glass again. Pulse thudding in his temples, Herc cracked the door open.

"Get in, for fuck's sake. You scared the piss out of me."

"What are you, paranoid?" Stanovitch said, nervous irony draining the blood from his face. He glanced about, then skittered around the front of the car and slid into the passenger seat.

"You're a funny guy," Herc said.

Stanovitch pulled the door shut and both of them stared at the light above the rearview mirror, waiting for it to go dim and bathe them in the privacy of darkness.

"Nothing about this is funny," Stanovitch told him.

Terry had blue eyes and orange hair and freckles he inherited from his Irish mother. Not very inconspicuous for a CIA operative, Herc had always thought. But it just showed how little he really knew about the business he worked in. He gathered intelligence via satellite photography, but in truth he knew almost nothing about real espionage. Despite his friendship with Sean, how it all really worked remained a mystery to him. The number one thing Sean McCandless had taught him was that he didn't really want to know more than he already did. And if he had ever needed to be reminded of that, Sean's death had done the trick.

"What've you got?" Herc asked.

Stanovitch glanced around as though tempted to search Herc and the car for a wire.

"Come on!"

"Relax," Stanovitch said. "I'm here. Be grateful for that. I almost didn't come."

Anger surged up inside Herc. "What, you think you're doing me a favor? He was your friend, Terry. Saved your life once, and your career more than once. You told me that yourself, because Sean had too much class to ever mention it."

Stanovitch nodded. "Yeah, I know. And now Sean's dead and nobody—and I mean nobody—knows who took him out—"

"Somebody knows, because somebody did it," Herc snapped.

Eyes narrowed, Stanovitch glared at him. "No shit. Don't be a prick, Brian. You know what I'm saying."

Herc wanted to hit him, scream at him, but he knew it was just helplessness gnawing at him. He slapped the steering wheel and swore.

"I can't believe he's fucking dead."

That sobered Stanovitch. "He was one of a kind."

Herc stared at him, chewing his lower lip, contemplating. "Maybe not."

"You're talking about the sister?"

"Her name's Caitlin. Her baby daughter's name is Leyla. Sean talked about them constantly. You should remember."

"I do—"

"Their names, Terry. You should remember their names. Look, maybe Cait McCandless isn't the person her brother was, maybe she doesn't have his courage or his smarts or his loyalty—but maybe she does. We don't know. All we know is that Sean loved her and that baby more than anything else in the world, and he made me promise I would look out for them if anything ever happened to him. And now it has. So you need to tell me, man, what the fuck is going on up in Boston? Who posted a watch on Sean's aunt and uncle? Who tried to take the baby? Whatever you know, you've gotta tell me. You don't want to go all in, take care of this for Sean, that's up to you. You've got to sleep at night. But at the very least, you've gotta give me this."

Stanovitch stared at him, sort of twitchy, mouth working as he turned his palms up, like he hoped the right words would fall into them.

"What . . . I mean, did you think we were going to be like Butch and Sundance, going out in a blaze of glory? Because those are the odds," Stanovitch said.

Herc felt queasy. "No. Not at all. I'm not some action hero. I don't want to expose anything or even get in anybody's way. I just want to do what I promised and take care of Sean's sister and her baby."

"What if doing that leads to the other?" Stanovitch asked.

The question made Herc flinch. He hesitated, then shook his head to clear it of any doubt.

"Just tell me what you know. The rest isn't your problem."

Stanovitch took a deep breath. "Fine," he said, letting it out. "You wanted to know who's got the juice to blank those plates, right? I got your answer. But there's another question you should be asking." He glanced out the window again, as though afraid they were being watched.

"Which is?"

"Who owns the car?"

-48--

Monteforte drove without mercy, hitting the siren anytime some idiot on a cell phone didn't notice the dome light flashing in the rearview mirror. Rachael Voss liked her for that. The white box van had more under the hood than Voss would have believed without seeing it, but they could easily have caught up. Instead, they all agreed to keep a short distance behind. They didn't just want one truck and the armed soldiers it carried, they wanted both trucks and the person to whom the bodies were being delivered.

They had passed a state police patrol car, necessitating a quick radio exchange between Monteforte and her dispatcher, so now the state trooper roared along behind them on the way to the airport.

"We just came from the damn airport," Voss said, though mostly to herself.

Turcotte sat in the backseat, churning through cell phone minutes. He'd been on with Chang at first, snapping orders, making sure the local P.D. would be guarding the crime scene now that all the techs, investigators, and FBI were leaving. Once the police cordons were removed, the press would be swarming the place. It would remain an FBI investigation with Coogan in charge of the scene, but the Medford cops would keep the press behind the yellow tape, at least for tonight.

Now, as Monteforte concentrated on the road and Voss and Josh listened, Turcotte had moved on to his second call—to his boss. Voss noted the number of times Turcotte said "sir," and she wondered if he had always been that deferential or if this was a special case. The call lasted three or four minutes, and only ended because they went into the tunnel and Turcotte lost his cell signal.

"So?" Voss asked, turning to look into the backseat.

Turcotte's jaw was set, like he wanted to throw a punch. Then he uttered a short laugh of disbelief. "So he knew. He'd signed off on it."

"Without telling you?" Josh asked.

Voss heard the surprise and dismay in his voice and she shared those feelings. In the years that she had spent with the FBI, she had dealt with a lot of politics, a lot of shell games, but none of her superiors had ever pulled the rug out from under her the way Turcotte's boss had just done.

"It gets better," Turcotte said. "He's the one who issued that BOLO identifying McCandless as a terror suspect."

"For Christ's sake!" Josh said.

"Sounds like someone's got an agenda here that isn't about solving this case," Monteforte said.

The temperature in the car dropped twenty degrees. They all fell silent, staring at her. The engine roared and blue lights from the state police car behind them filled the interior of the Camry. Nobody wanted to respond.

"What was his excuse?" Josh asked at last.

"Wait," Voss said, before Turcotte could reply. "First up, who are we talking about here? This is Julius Andelman?"

Turcotte's face looked carved from granite. "Not for a while. Dwight Hollenbach. He's SSAC of CTD Ops II."

"All right," Voss went on. "So what did he say? Why is SO-COM operating on U.S. soil? Why did he let Arsenault take the vics from the scene? Where the hell are they going?"

For the first time she saw the tic at the corner of Turcotte's left eye. He reached up and ran a hand across his stubbled head.

"He told me that was not my concern—"

"It's your case!" Josh said.

"—and that I should focus on finding McCandless and her accomplice."

Voss scowled. "He used that word? *Accomplice?*"

"He did." Turcotte continued, "As for why the bodies were removed, SSAC Hollenbach informed me, 'Nobody wants the public seeing all of those body bags, or getting any ideas about who might be in them.' His superiors apparently decided this was the best way to keep the media in the dark."

Sickened, Voss could only laugh. "By making the bodies vanish?"

Turcotte lifted his chin, trying to catch Monteforte's eye in the rearview mirror. "Actually, Agent Chang just informed me that the bodies of the Russo woman and Detective Jarman were loaded into one of the ambulances at the scene. They're being taken to the morgue."

"And the others?" Voss asked.

The car shot out of the tunnel. They weren't far from the airport now.

"Let's find out," Turcotte said.

Voss glanced out the windshield, then at Monteforte. The detective must have exhaled at least a little when Turcotte had confirmed that her partner's body was not in one of the white vans, but she seemed no less determined to follow that van and get the answers they all wanted.

Voss turned again and looked at Josh, sharing a silent exchange. They were turning onto an access road that seemed to lead to hangars for overnight delivery company planes when she turned to Turcotte again.

"Ed," she said, "you know I have to take the case."

Turcotte's grimace was impossible to read. "By all means," he said. "It's yours. At least with you running the show, I know who's pulling the strings and why."

Voss looked at Josh. "Call in. Don't let Unger stonewall you. Get Director Wood on the line and tell her what's happening. Make sure she puts the call in to this Hollenbach herself, so there's no mistaking the chain of command here."

Josh nodded and pulled out his phone.

Monteforte swerved, tires squealing, and even as Voss looked up she saw they were racing around the nose of a dark sedan that had stopped in their path.

"That call might have to wait," Monteforte said.

Voss and Josh swore. Ahead of them, metal gates were rolling shut to block their entrance to an airfield. They were far from Logan Airport's passenger terminals here. The next airfield over, planes with Federal Express logos could be seen over the top of the fence, but this aircraft had no such branding.

Turcotte gripped the seat in front of him and leaned forward. "Don't stop."

"Easy for you to say. I'm still paying for this car."

But Monteforte floored it, the state trooper keeping pace behind her. Blue lights fluttered like ghosts all around them. Headlights filled the passenger-side windows and Voss looked to see two cars racing toward them.

Beyond the fence the white van kept going, not even slowing down. Other vehicles were in motion as well, dark figures running back and forth, but they were hard to make out in the dark and through the rapidly closing fence.

"Shit," Monteforte said, teeth snapping down on the end of the word.

The car shot through the opening, knocking the driver's-side mirror inward, and then they were inside the perimeter. Twenty feet in, Monteforte had to slam on the brakes. A military transport truck blocked their path, dark sedans on either side of it. Soldiers in T-shirts and fatigue pants leveled weapons at them. Men and women in suits pointed pistols at Monteforte's windshield.

The Camry skidded to a halt.

"Stay here," Voss said.

She popped the door and got out. The night had grown humid and she felt the air cling instantly to her skin. She started forward on foot and guns cocked, some of them tracking her while the others stayed aimed at the car.

A door opened behind her. Turcotte, she figured.

A glance back confirmed it, and revealed that the state trooper had skidded to a halt outside the gate. She could hear the crackle of his radio and see the flashing blue of his light rack, but this was out of his league anyway.

"I'm not going to bother to reach for my ID," she called to the soldiers up ahead. "I don't want to 'accidentally' catch a bullet. My name is Rachael Voss and I work for the InterAgency Cooperation Division. That's part of Homeland Security, for those of you who don't read the papers. ICD has situational jurisdiction over every other agency or department of the U.S. government."

Even as she said it, a chill went through her. The ones in suits didn't work for the government. Every single one of them looked just as cold and hard as Norris.

"I have taken over this case," she said. "Anyone who is still attempting to bar our way by the count of three will be up on charges before sunrise."

Nobody moved.

"Stupid, arrogant shitheads," Voss said, loud enough for them all to hear. "My authority comes from the President of the United States. Fucking *move!*"

One soldier, fortyish and grizzled, scar on his forehead, shipped his weapon and stepped away from the truck to approach her.

"I'll take a look at that ID," the officer said. "Nobody is going to shoot you."

"Do you speak for them, too?" Turcotte yelled, pointing at the Black Pine operatives on the left.

"Damn straight," the officer said, affronted by the question.

Voss pulled out her ID, feeling the clock ticking with her pulse, picturing the bodies being loaded onto a plane even as she handed her ID to the officer. He examined it for a few seconds, then seemed to deliberate.

"I have my orders, Agent Voss," he said.

"I've just given you new orders. You're SOCOM, soldier. You're not even supposed to be here, and Lieutenant Arsenault knows that."

Another few seconds and the officer handed her ID back, then turned to his troops. "Lower your weapons."

Voss spun and called back to the car. "Josh, go!"

Monteforte didn't wait. She cut the wheel to the right and started to drive around. A BMW—one of the Black Pine sedans—backed up into her path and the cars collided. Monteforte shouted and jumped out, and dark-suited cold-eyed bastards drew down on her.

"That's enough!" the army officer shouted. "Stand down right goddamn now!"

They did. Gun barrels lowered. Soldiers and operatives stepped back. But the damage was done. Beyond the truck and the cars a plane buzzed down the runway and took to the air.

Voss studied Turcotte's face. He had somehow made his features an emotionless mask. She couldn't hide her feelings that well.

"There's going to be hell to pay," she promised the officer.

Even as she did, a silver Lexus glided around the gathered vehicles from the direction of the runway. It slid to a halt and two men stepped out—Arsenault and Norris. Josh climbed out of Monteforte's backseat but Voss calmed him with a gesture. She walked to Turcotte and Monteforte.

"I've got it," she said softly, so only they could hear.

Monteforte nodded. Turcotte said nothing.

"You have a lot to answer for," Voss said as Arsenault and Norris approached.

Norris stopped and stood with his arms behind his back, military parade rest. Once he'd been a soldier or a Marine, that much was clear. He said nothing, deferring to Arsenault.

"Agent Voss—" Arsenault began.

Voss snapped, face flushing, nostrils flaring. "You are not even supposed to be here, Lieutenant! You were an observer. And your friend Norris here is a *consultant,* remember?"

"I received orders from my superior officer," Arsenault said. "Mr. Norris's organization offered their assistance. We were working with the full knowledge of the FBI—"

"Not of the agent in charge of the fucking case!" Turcotte snapped.

Voss silenced him with a look, then turned back to Arsenault.

"Listen to me, Lieutenant. From this moment forward, the ICD claims jurisdiction over this case. That means that any agency, military or civilian, taking part in the investigation must answer to me. So I'm going to ask you straight up, right now. Where are those bodies headed?"

Arsenault glanced at Norris, but it delighted Voss to see that the lieutenant was not looking to him for approval, but in irritation. Steeling himself, standing a bit straighter, Arsenault faced her again.

"Agent Voss, I am not authorized to answer that question. ICD will have to take it up with my superior officers."

She shook her head and gave a disgusted sigh. "You do know I could have you put in custody right now?"

But when she spoke, it wasn't Arsenault she was looking at. It was Norris. The slick son of a bitch just smiled. The Black Pine operatives—most of them ex-military—and the soldiers all stood by, listening intently. She almost expected one of them to speak up, but they were trained better than that. They waited like carrion birds for the outcome.

Arsenault met her gaze. "I'm not sure your authority extends that far, but I won't fight you if that's your move."

As Voss contemplated that, Turcotte's cell phone began to ring. At first it didn't seem like he was going to answer it, but once he glanced at the screen he took the call.

"Turcotte," he said, and then listened. Twice he said, "Go on," and then he thanked the caller and hung up, putting the phone back in its holster on his belt.

His smile spoke volumes.

Voss took a few steps toward him. Halfway between him and Arsenault, she stopped.

"What's up?" she asked.

Then Norris's cell phone began to ring.

Turcotte walked up to him, staring down at the smaller man, expression once again hard and cold.

"You're going to want to take that."

As Norris did, Voss caught Turcotte by the arm and led him back toward Josh and Monteforte. Arsenault had begun giving orders to disperse his troops, and the Black Pine operatives seemed to be following his orders as well, but Voss was only half paying attention to them.

"What was that?" she demanded.

Turcotte glanced at Monteforte and Josh, but only for a second before he forged ahead.

"We've got a line on where Cait McCandless is going to be,

about ninety minutes from now. It's in Hartford. Agent Chang is already arranging a plane for us. We've got to hustle."

Voss was already walking toward Monteforte's car, the others keeping up.

"I'm sorry, Detective," she said. "I hope you'll drop us off, but this is where we part ways."

"No problem. I want to look into some things from this end, see if I can figure out who this girl really is."

Monteforte got behind the wheel and they all piled in, slamming the doors.

"Thanks for understanding. If you'll keep me up to speed, I'll do the same for you," Voss said. "I know how I'd feel if it had been my partner out there tonight."

Monteforte said nothing after that. Turcotte directed her to Terminal A and they drove in silence for almost a minute.

"Rachael," Josh said, voice low.

Voss hated being called by her first name. Only Josh could get away with it. But tonight it seemed a very small thing.

"It's not enough to find this woman," Josh said. "Detective Monteforte wants to know why, and so do I. I think we have to find out why this is all happening, how it all fits. The brother, for instance. I want to head back to D.C. and see what I can pin down about his death. He worked for the government, right? Cait McCandless thinks he was some kind of spy."

Turcotte rolled his eyes a little at the use of the word.

"I've checked," Monteforte said. "Sean McCandless worked for the National Geospatial-Intelligence Agency. Satellite surveillance. I guess you could call that spying. But Cait thought there was more to it than that."

Voss took that in and turned to Josh. "You don't think a phone call to the investigating officer will do it?"

"Not if he worked in intelligence. Not if someone is covering up the circumstances of his death," Josh said. "Those people lie about what they had for breakfast. Look, if he really is dead, I'd like to know the circumstances. And I want more than the police file on it. I want to do some digging, ask around."

Voss nodded. "All right."

Turcotte shifted in his seat. "I'd been planning to get someone on that in the morning. There are only two of you, but you've got the whole Bureau to call on if you want them. Why not get someone who's already there?"

"No offense," Voss said, "but given that Hollenbach's screwing around behind your back, I'm having some trust issues."

Turcotte looked offended, so she hurried to continue.

"I'm not talking about you, Ed. Or Agent Chang. But unless it's someone you can personally vouch for, I'd rather Josh do it."

"I understand," Turcotte said, as Monteforte flashed her ID and drove them through the security gate and onto the tarmac of Terminal A. "I don't like it, but I understand. Any objection to me sending Chang along? I'd like to keep the Bureau a part of the investigation as much as possible."

Voss glanced at Josh, who gave her a small nod.

"No objection."

After that the car fell quiet again. Monteforte pulled over and Turcotte got out. He ran over to check on the status of the plane that would take them to Hartford. Voss glanced into the backseat at Josh.

"Never mind calling Director Wood," she said, pushing the hair out of her eyes. "I'll do it. I assume Chang will set up a plane for you to get back to D.C., but if not, call the office and get it done."

"Will do," he said.

Voss heard something, a soft sighing, and looked to see that Monteforte had begun crying quietly while they talked. Her heart ached for the woman.

She put a hand on the detective's shoulder. "I'm truly sorry."

Monteforte nodded. "Thanks. It's been a long night."

"It has," Voss agreed, turning to look out at the runway. "And it isn't over yet."

-49--

Cait snapped awake with a gasp and blinked, startled for a moment to find herself in a car instead of her bed. She had been dreaming that she and Sean had been in the stockroom in the back of Sweet Somethings. Leyla had been in the dream, but older—maybe four—and had pulled boxes of hand-dipped chocolates off the shelf, uncovering them and tasting each kind to see which she liked. Nizam had been there, too, standing in the shadows at the end of the aisle, a sad smile on his face as he watched them laugh over the faces Leyla made when she bit into chocolates she didn't like.

A little bit of heaven, she had said in the dream. Or maybe Leyla had said it, describing the taste of one of the candies.

Now, one glance at Lynch brought reality crashing back, and grim determination followed. They had pulled off the highway and parked in the short-term lot at a bus station, where other people waited to pick up arriving passengers. This late, there weren't many, but they blended easily amongst the others sitting in their cars, some of their faces lit by the green glow from their dashboards.

Now Cait whipped around to check on Leyla. The baby was still full from the bottle Cait had given her, but she wasn't likely to sleep all night in the car seat. For the moment, at least, there were none of the fussing and mewling sounds that would have accompanied her waking. Cait could hear her soft breathing, and it soothed her.

"You should have woken me," she said quietly.

Lynch shrugged one shoulder. "As long as the baby's not crying, I don't mind. You need the rest."

She studied the lines on his once-handsome face. "And you? Don't tell me you got eight hours last night."

"I'm all right. Anyway, we both need to be up now."

Cait glanced at the clock and saw that he was right. They were supposed to meet up with Ronnie soon. She only hoped that Jordan would be with him.

Lynch started the car and pulled out of the bus station, turning onto the ramp that put them back on Route 84. They rode in silence for a quarter of an hour, and then they were getting off the highway again. Lynch stopped at a blinking red light and put on his left turn signal.

"You're sure about those directions?" he asked.

Cait blinked, trying to clear the cobwebs of sleep from her mind. What had Ronnie said? Yes, left at the bottom of the ramp, under the highway, right at the second light, and Wendy's would be just past the Comfort Inn.

"If I got it wrong, I'll call him."

Lynch nodded and took the turn, following the curve as the road brought them south, beneath the interstate.

"Why are you doing this?" she asked.

"Trying to keep you and your daughter alive?"

"No," she said. "Why did you buy the phone? You said I couldn't trust anyone. Why are you taking me to meet Ronnie?"

Lynch half scowled. Cait figured she would get a scathing response, something about not getting in her way if she wanted to get herself and Leyla killed. Instead, his expression softened and he narrowed his eyes, keeping his gaze on the road.

"I'm not great at saving lives," he said, his voice a dry rasp. "I can keep you running for a while, maybe keep you hidden, but forever? I don't know. Quite frankly, you're up against something so big that the odds of you living through it are shit. I figure if you've got friends who can really help, not just be a liability—and the guys who watched your back in Iraq sure count—then you can use them. Who am I to stop you? To tell you who to trust? Hell, I don't trust *anyone*. I haven't had anyone to trust in a long time."

His words were steeped in pain.

"What about your people, the Resistance?"

Lynch's sadness deepened. The car rolled to a stop at a red light, surreal and absurd given the absence of other vehicles on the road. "The only one you can ever really count on to have your best interests at heart is yourself," he said. "And sometimes, not even that."

His despair felt suffocating, and she knew Lynch saw it on her face.

He exhaled. "Sorry. I'm not exactly a ray of sunshine."

The light turned green and he accelerated, but his words were resonating inside Cait. She'd called on Ronnie because she trusted him and because he could help. Jordan had been her first choice, and she hoped that Ronnie had managed to reach him. And she couldn't deny that, in the back of her mind it had occurred to her that it would be good to have them with her because they were soldiers. Because they knew how to pull the trigger and wouldn't freeze in a fight.

But she needed more than muscle. Lynch had come to save her life, and even he would bet against her chances of survival. Conflicting urges clawed at her, tearing her apart. Without Leyla, her path would have been so much clearer. Just try to vanish, head for Mexico or maybe Eastern Europe, disappear and hope they didn't catch up. But it would be so much harder to go unnoticed with a baby. She couldn't risk putting Leyla's life in the hands of anyone other than herself, but could they survive without taking risks? She didn't think so.

Who can I trust? she thought. And the answer came back clearly. *Sean.* No matter her fears or misgivings, she had to trust Sean.

Lynch turned right at the second light. Cait picked up the go-phone from the console and dialed the Hot Line.

Hercules answered on the third ring. "Who is this?"

The question was an accusation. Sean had told her only a few people knew that number, and none of them would ever give it out. It had been a secret fail-safe for Sean, just in case he ever got himself in too deep during a mission, or if Cait ever needed him while he was gone. Well, she needed him now, but he had gotten himself in much too deep this time, and had never had a chance to make the call.

Or had he?

"Tell me the truth, Herc," she said.

"Caitlin?"

Lynch had slowed the Cadillac to a crawl. Now he pulled up to the curb in front of a closed liquor store, neon beer signs in the otherwise darkened windows, waiting for her to finish. He studied her, then glanced out at the street, pretending to mind his own business.

"Yes," she said.

"Oh, thank God," Herc said.

Her mouth felt dry. He sounded so earnest and she so desperately wanted to believe him.

"Tell me the truth," she said again, her voice cracking with emotion. In the backseat, Leyla murmured in her sleep. "Is Sean really dead?"

"I'm sorry, Cait. He is. I'm very glad you called. I need to—"

"How did it happen?" she interrupted. "Did he call you? Did you know he was in trouble?"

"No. It just . . . he collapsed on a sidewalk in D.C."

"Collapsed? What, like a heart attack, or—"

"We think someone took him off the board, Cait. But you've got to listen to me—"

"Took him off the . . . He was your best friend, Herc, and you're talking like you're Jason fucking Bourne? Who did it?"

Herc sighed. "Cait, please listen. You and Leyla are in real danger."

She laughed bitterly. "No shit. What was your first clue? We need help, Brian. Sean always said I could call you."

"And I'm glad you did. I'll do whatever I can, but you're in real danger and my reach only extends so far. You wanted to know who those guys were, the ones watching your house?"

Cait straightened in her seat. "You have an answer?"

"I do. The cars are owned by a company called Black Pine Worldwide. They're a global security—"

"I know who they are. Mercenaries."

"Among other things." Herc hurried on, "The CEO is a guy named Leonard Shelby, former Marine Corps. His father was a war hero who served in the Senate. Anyway, what matters is that those cars were from Black Pine. The plates were originally assigned to them."

Now that she knew who to hate, some of Cait's fear evaporated. "The plates were supposed to be untraceable. Or fake."

"Neither," Herc said, "but they might as well be invisible. An order goes out from someone with enough power, and plates disappear from registries. They're only logged in the files of the people who are supposed to step in and clean up if one of those blank plates ends up connected to a mess."

"Like this one."

"Yeah," Herc said quietly. "Like this one. But you've got more than Black Pine to worry about. Leonard Shelby's a private contractor. He doesn't have the authority to order those plates invisible."

"So who did?"

"A guy named Dwight Hollenbach. He runs the FBI's domestic counterterrorism squad."

Cait let her head sag, bringing her free hand to her temple. "Are you fucking kidding me?"

"I wish I was. I don't understand any of it," Herc said. "I've got to be very careful, but I'm doing a little back-channel digging, trying to figure out what Hollenbach or Shelby might have had against Sean that would be so huge they wouldn't just kill him but go after you, too."

A terrible chill, the winter of despair, filled the deepest parts of her. "It wasn't Sean they wanted."

"What?"

"It wasn't Sean. It's Leyla they want."

"Leyla? Cait, what are you . . . what could any of this have to do with Leyla?"

With a shudder, she looked over at Lynch. The old man's granite features had softened and for a moment she thought she saw real empathy in his eyes. Then he frowned and tapped at the dashboard clock—they were late meeting Ronnie and Jordan—and she realized it must have been a trick of the light. Lynch lived for his war. His interest in her and Leyla was in denying the enemy what they wanted, nothing more.

"Herc, listen, I've got to go. Watch your ass. I don't want you to make yourself a target. But if there's anything you can find out for me about Hollenbach or Shelby, do it. I'll call you in the morning."

"Caitlin, wait. What's this thing about Leyla?"

"Tomorrow," she said, and thumbed END. She shook her head, whispered something that was half curse and half prayer, and glanced at Lynch. "Let's go. We need all the help we can get."

-50--

The private jet had seating for twelve, but Josh and Chang were the only passengers. He'd been on small planes before and usually they were loud, roaring things that left his ears with the same tinny buzz as a rock concert. Not this one. Aside from a low hum and a kind of distant whistling, the jet seemed almost silent—which spoke volumes about the vast sums of money that had probably been spent on it. Homeland Security had gotten it on loan, short notice, from a prominent Boston law firm. If there was one thing Josh had learned in the time since he and Voss had moved from the FBI to ICD, it was that there were always strings waiting to be pulled. You just had to find the right ones.

The cabin lights were dimmed, presumably to allow them to get some sleep, but Josh figured they would be in the air such a short while that a nap would only make him feel more tired by the time they touched down.

To his left, across the small aisle, Nala Chang dozed lightly. She'd put her seat all the way back and curled up sideways, knees tucked up to her belly. At peace, she had a beauty only hinted at while she worked. In the time they spent together, he had usually seen her full of purpose or troubled, intent upon something. But in repose, she had a tender sweetness that made her seem delicate, even fragile.

Chang would be furious if he ever expressed that thought aloud. Seeing her like this, though, together in that intimate silence, made him want to protect her. And that was a very dangerous thing indeed.

Josh forced himself to turn and look out the window, but there was nothing to see out there except darkness. *This is a bad idea,* he thought. He smiled to himself as he looked back at Chang. *Besides, Rachael would kill you.*

"What's funny?" Chang asked, gazing at him through half-lidded eyes. In the dimly lit cabin he hadn't noticed that she'd begun to wake.

"You. You've got a little bit of drool going, right there," he said, touching the corner of his mouth to demonstrate.

Chang made a face and reached up to wipe her mouth. Finding nothing, she shot him a withering glare.

"Nice. Make fun of the sleeping girl."

"I also shaved your eyebrows and drew on a funny handle-bar mustache."

Chang sighed, rubbing sleep from her eyes. "You do know I carry a gun?"

"It occurred to me, but too late."

"You're a riot," she said, turning the other way and closing her eyes again. In moments she was so still that Josh thought she had fallen back to sleep, and then she continued. "So, what's the story with you and your partner?"

The plane rumbled through a small pocket of turbulence. Josh stared at her back, trying to sort out the meaning of the question.

"The story?"

"Just wondering if you're sleeping together. You two have a vibe."

Josh glanced out the window, saw city lights below, and tried to gauge how long until they landed. Suddenly the plane's cabin felt even smaller.

"No," he said. "We're not sleeping together."

Twenty or thirty seconds ticked by in silence. Just when he was absolutely certain that this time she really had fallen back to sleep, he heard her speak again.

"Good."

-51--

The second the car stopped in the circle at the end of a dead-end residential street, Voss popped the door. She muttered a thanks to the Connecticut state trooper who had picked them up at the airport—he'd driven like hellhounds were on his tail to get them there—and then started for the hole in the fence. Turcotte hurried after her but did not call out. They needed speed and silence now.

A dozen cars filled the circle and lined the street. A handful of people, woken from sleep by headlights and the prowl of engines, looked out windows or stood on front steps, but nearly all of the duplexes were still dark.

Uniformed officers flanked the hole in the wooden fence where a four-foot segment had been removed. Voss and Turcotte produced their IDs—one of the cops squinted at hers, obviously clueless as to what ICD was—and were waved through. Beyond the stockade fence stretched maybe seven feet of trees and bushes, and then a chain-link fence that had been cut and rolled back, and past that was an alley that ran behind a dry cleaners. Uniformed cops lined the back of the dry cleaners and were scattered up and down the alley, along with Bureau agents wearing navy jackets with FBI emblazoned in yellow on the back. Times like this, they wanted to be conspicuous so the wrong people didn't get shot.

"Siegel?" she asked the nearest agent.

He pointed her to the left and she picked up her pace. She and Turcotte jogged to the corner of the building, where a cluster of agents stood with a cop wearing captain's bars. Two of the men seemed to recognize Turcotte and then focus on Voss. She figured the tall fiftyish guy with the mustache to be Siegel, but it was the shorter man—plump, pale, bald spot, a forty-year-old future department store Santa—who spoke up.

"Agent Voss?"

She nodded. "I assume we made it?"

"Supervisory Special Agent Siegel," the man said, holding out his hand. Voss took it, and then Siegel looked at Turcotte. "Hello, Ed."

"Todd," Turcotte said, nodding. He coughed. "Jesus, what's that smell?"

Siegel cocked his head. "Fish market, half a block down." He gestured for them to follow and walked to the corner. As he spoke again, he lowered his voice.

"You made it, but only because the McCandless woman's friends are late. She and her accomplice rolled up almost ten minutes ago. They parked in front of a small office building right next to the Wendy's, not in the lot. Obviously she's not stupid. The others probably won't park in the lot, either. McCandless and her partner are sitting in the Cadillac, apparently waiting for visual on Mellace and Katz. If they try to drive off, we'll take them. Otherwise we'd rather wait for them to get out and move a fair distance from the vehicle."

Voss nodded, glancing around. "What have we got on the other side of the street?"

Siegel looked at Turcotte, as though waiting for him to speak. When he didn't, the portly FBI agent continued. "We've got people at both ends of the block and on intersecting streets, ready to move in. There's a block of storefronts across from us—half of them empty—and we've got agents and state and local cops on either side of the building, but there's nowhere else for them to stay out of sight over there."

Voss caught his gaze and held it. "And what about Lieutenant Arsenault? Did you get word he was on the way to observe? Along with a consultant?"

Now Siegel really did look confused, but Turcotte still didn't jump in to rescue him. "We did. It seemed a little strange, but other agencies are always stepping on our cases."

"I know," Voss said. "I was FBI for years."

Trying to hide his disdain for her career choice, Siegel smiled. "You got a better offer?"

"Actually, yes," she said, and turned to Turcotte. "Whatever strings Norris or Arsenault may be pulling, they're not here yet. If they do show up before this goes down, I want them detained. Unless they have a goddamn army with them, I don't want them anywhere near this situation."

Turcotte did not smile, but she had the sense that he wanted to. He nodded. "Whatever you say, boss."

That got everyone's attention. Voss didn't have time to get them up to speed on chain of command.

"SSA Siegel, gentlemen, here are the rules. If Sergeant McCandless and her companion—not accomplice, because I can't think of a crime we know they've committed—attempt to drive off, they will be surrounded by police vehicles, so they cannot mistake our stopping them as anything but an official act. No weapon will be pointed at either of them unless they open fire first. Even if one or both of them does open fire, all of your people are to choose their shots carefully. There's a baby in that car, and I don't want to see her in my dreams for the rest of my life. Similar rules apply to apprehension if they do exit the vehicle. I want to talk to Caitlin McCandless without all of this getting out of control. I have a lot of questions for her, and I'm not going to be able to ask them if bullets are flying. Is all of that clear?"

The police captain and the agents stared at Siegel, who looked at Turcotte, who nodded once.

"The case belongs to ICD, Todd. Rachael's ex-Bureau. She knows what she's doing. And we don't have time for hesitation," Turcotte said.

Voss gritted her teeth at his use of her first name and fought the urge to kick him. "They know their job, Agent Turcotte." She turned to Siegel and repeated herself. "Is all of that clear?"

Stoic and grim, he nodded. "Crystal."

"Do it," she said.

Siegel lifted a handheld radio and rattled off her instructions, turning them into his own orders, leaving no possible uncertainty as to how they were all to conduct themselves.

While he did that, Voss turned to Turcotte. "No one calls me Rachael," she said, voice low.

"It makes you more human," Turcotte whispered, trying to reason with her.

"I can't afford to be human."

Seconds later, a radio crackled and the news came through. Mellace and Katz had arrived. McCandless and her companion were out of the car, the woman carrying her baby.

Answers were within reach.

At her first glimpse of Jordan and Ronnie, Cait felt a rush of relief greater than she could have imagined. Her problems were far from solved, but now she wouldn't be alone. She saw Jordan frequently at work, and elsewhere, but the sight of the two of them together brought her back to grim months in Baghdad and the way she had felt when the three of them had been together. A new courage filled her, along with a glimmer of hope.

"They're not stupid," Lynch said, his surprise evident.

"No, they're not," Cait agreed.

The guys had parked at the curb in front of the tanning salon next to Wendy's. They'd walked to the Wendy's parking lot but immediately slipped into a bus shelter, partially hidden by the dirty, scratched-up Plexiglas. Ronnie had a Red Sox cap perched on his head and a thin, dark scruff of goatee. Jordan had buzzed his hair short to match the stubble where his beard had been. They wore jeans and T-shirts they had probably pulled on in seconds when they'd learned she was in trouble.

"Let's go," she said, and climbed out of the car.

The dome light did not go on. Lynch had taken care of that during their first stop. Cait slid her gun into her rear waistband and the go-phone into her pocket, then she opened the back door and extricated Leyla from her car seat. The baby's eyes opened and she looked around, blinking dreamily, but the moment Cait held her close, she put her head on her mother's shoulder and sighed contentedly.

Lynch left the Caddy unlocked and they started along the sidewalk toward the Wendy's parking lot.

"Quiet," Lynch said.

"It's the middle of the night."

He said nothing more but they both glanced around cautiously, checking up and down the street, looking down a side alley, before picking up the pace as they headed for the Plexiglas bus shelter. Cait knew they were being too paranoid—no one knew they were here except for Ronnie and Jordan—but she had accepted paranoia as the only rational response to the ruin of her life.

The guys saw them coming. Ronnie stepped outside the bus shelter, face etched with concern.

"Oh, my God, thank you for coming," she said, hugging him with one arm as she cradled Leyla in the other. Ronnie bussed her cheek and then planted a gentle kiss on the baby's head.

"How could I not? Jordan's not the only one who loves you, y'know?"

As he spoke, Cait saw Jordan emerge from behind the Plexiglas. He smiled, and his eyes lit up when he saw Leyla. He kissed her sleeping head.

"If you wanted to come visit Ronnie, you could've just asked," he said. "We could have carpooled."

"Funny guy," Cait said.

Jordan's smile faltered and for the first time she saw the real depth of his concern.

"I guess now's not the time for funny," he said.

Cait took his hand and stood on her toes to kiss his cheek, clasping his fingers tightly. "It's the perfect time." She glanced at Ronnie. "So glad you're both here."

Lynch nudged her. "Get inside. We're too exposed out here."

Ronnie and Jordan both took his measure, trying to figure out who he was and what he was doing with Cait, but they obliged, stepping back into the bus shelter. Cait followed, but Lynch turned his back to them, on guard. He'd untucked his shirt to cover his gun, but Cait could see the bulge of it against the fabric. The guys were armed as well, Ronnie strapped at the ankle and Jordan carrying at the small of his back, like Lynch. They knew there had already been a fire-fight tonight and none of them were taking any chances.

There were two entrances to the shelter, one at the front and one at the back. The metal benches inside were engraved with graffiti, but otherwise it was clean. She sat on the edge of a bench, comforted by her friends and by the weight of her daughter in her arms.

"Talk to us, Sarge," Jordan said. " 'Cause on the news, they're saying some ugly shit."

It hurt her heart to even hear him say that. Quiet, handsome Jordan—a hell of a man, but still with the shy demeanor of a boy. When they had returned to civilian life and begun to work together, they'd had to learn to relate to each other on civilian terms. They had helped each other figure out how to live an ordinary life, complete with paychecks and office parties and watercooler gossip. Now all of that had been obliterated, and they were carrying guns again—at war, again.

"Please tell me you don't believe any of it."

Jordan arched his eyebrows in surprise. " 'Course not."

Lynch stuck his head in. "This isn't the place, Cait."

"I know, I know," she said, then turned to the guys again. "Look, we all know there're some devils in D.C. Some of them want Leyla, and they're not the only ones. I had al Qaeda or something on my back doorstep. Neither side has good intentions—"

"Listen to yourself, Cait," Ronnie said.

She froze, hating the tightness of his voice. "What?"

"All right, Washington has some shady bastards, but the whole government isn't corrupt. Not enough to hunt a seven-month-old baby. You never should have run. If you just talk to the FBI, go public, it will all get straightened out."

Cait stared at him.

Jordan ran a hand over his stubbled head, mystified. "Dude, are you listening? You saw the news. They're calling her a terrorist. People are after the baby. She's not talking to anyone until we can make sure they're safe, guaranteed protection or whatever."

Ronnie scratched at his arm, drew a hand across his mouth. "It's already guaranteed."

The words sunk in fast. Cait shot to her feet, clutching Leyla to her, stunned that Ronnie would betray her but knowing he must have been frightened and confused by the news stories and tried to do the right thing.

"Lynch—" she started.

The old man stepped into the shelter. "We've gotta move."

For a second she thought he was reacting to what Ronnie had said, and then she heard the roaring of engines and the squealing of tires and the static crackle of a distant radio. Ronnie started trying to tell them to calm down, that it would be all right. Jordan hit him so hard that his head snapped back and he staggered against the Plexiglas shelter.

"Son of a bitch!" Jordan shouted, grabbing a fistful of Ronnie's T-shirt and hitting him twice more.

Ronnie staggered and went to his knees. As he tried to rise, Jordan went to kick him but Cait caught him by the wrist and got him moving out of the shelter. She released him and drew her gun, saw Lynch do the same, and the three of them started running toward the Caddy—but too late.

Police cars tore out of connecting streets and shot from the alley beside a nearby donut shop, blue lights flashing but running without sirens. One by one they skidded to a halt, officers jumping out, weapons drawn. They'd boxed in the Cadillac—Lynch's stolen car wasn't going anywhere. On the roof of an office block across the street she saw several snipers taking position.

Squads of cops and FBI agents in bulletproof vests and flapping jackets ran from alleys and storefronts and hustled to join the party.

"Sergeant McCandless!" someone said over a buzzing bullhorn. "Think about your baby. Surrender now, for Leyla's sake."

Hate raged in her. They still wanted Leyla. It had been the very worst thing they could have said.

"She's *all* I think about," Cait whispered, starting back into the shelter. "This way."

Voss ran to a patrol car, her gun aimed at the sky. Turcotte slammed up against the vehicle beside her and leveled his own weapon, taking aim over the police car's roof.

"Goddamn bus stop," Turcotte snarled. "Nobody's gonna have a clear shot."

"Yeah," Voss agreed, but she didn't see that as a bad thing. She wanted an opportunity to talk to Cait McCandless and if that meant through the open door of the bus shelter with the woman and her friends still armed, that was all right.

She unclipped the radio from her belt. "Hold all fire," she said. "Repeat, hold all fire. Anyone puts a bullet anywhere near that baby, I'll shoot you myself!"

The whole street took a breath. Car engines rumbled and the Wendy's sign buzzed with electricity. The Cadillac that had brought McCandless and her baby here was completely hemmed in. This was good.

Voss turned to a police sergeant with a bullhorn and held out her hand. He gave it to her and she toggled the switch, getting a burst of feedback, then moved around beside the car to get a clearer view of the bus shelter, and to make sure that McCandless could see her.

She lifted the bullhorn to her lips, and a gunshot cracked the night sky. The bullhorn smashed into her mouth just as something slammed into her left shoulder and spun her around. Voss sprawled on the ground, blood quickly filling her mouth, and bright pain blossomed in her shoulder.

As shock began to set in, she tried to make sense of it all—the angle, the impact—and she knew the shot had not come from the bus shelter. Someone on the roof across the street had pulled the trigger on her, aiming for her head, not anticipating the bullhorn. The shoulder wound was a ricochet.

Tried to kill me, she had time to think, just before shock overwhelmed her and she sank into darkness.

The instant she heard the gunshot, Cait knew they had to run. If she was going to die, she would die trying her best to protect her baby girl, not standing still waiting for a bullet.

"Your car!" she snapped at Jordan. "Go!"

Lynch didn't hesitate. He darted out the back entrance of the bus shelter and ran low across the lot toward a small stand of trees. Cait held tightly to Leyla as a volley of shots rang out.

"Cait!" Ronnie said, drawing the gun he'd worn strapped to his leg. "Don't!"

She took aim at his left eye. "If my baby dies, you as good as killed her."

Jordan grabbed her arm. "Leave him. Run."

But before they could follow Lynch, Ronnie shouted Jordan's name. Cait thought he might shoot, but instead he tossed something to Jordan.

"You'll need these, dumbass," he said, a world of sorrow in his voice.

They were his keys. The car they'd arrived in had been Ronnie's. Cait looked at him, saw that he realized what a mistake he'd made, and then he made a break for it, racing out the front of the shelter onto the sidewalk and into the street. He took aim at the sharpshooters on the roof across from them and started firing. Before it even happened, Cait could see his death in her mind's eye.

She bumped Jordan and then the two of them were running, following Lynch, who raced from the trees toward Ronnie's pristine Ford Mustang. Leyla woke and started wailing in Cait's ear and her chest tightened at the sound as it always did. A Hartford cop ran out to try to stop them and Lynch shot him in the leg. The officer shouted as he fell, dropping his gun. Bullets flew, plinking the hood and sides of the Mustang, but by then Lynch had flung open the door and climbed into the back.

Cops and FBI agents came running. They hadn't blocked in the Mustang—presumably because Ronnie had been the one to call them—and now they were learning what a mistake that had been. Cait fired twice in the air, not willing to randomly kill people when she couldn't be sure who among them was an enemy. They fired at Jordan but no one even took aim at her. A bullet grazed Jordan's shoulder blade and he staggered forward, barely managed to keep his feet under him, and then dove into the Mustang through the door Lynch had left open. As Cait followed, Leyla screaming in her arms, Jordan scrambled into the driver's seat, jammed the key into the ignition, and the engine gave a lion's roar. He slammed it into gear and turned the wheel, spinning in a half circle that nearly threw Cait and Leyla out onto the street. The door swung wide. She had to throw her gun on the floor in order to reach out and grab the door to slam it shut, and then she snagged the seat belt and tried pulling it around them both.

"No. Get on the floor!" Jordan yelled.

"Screw that."

One of the back windows blew in, safety glass scattering everywhere. Lynch fired through the broken window and then rolled the other down. As he did, Cait strapped herself and Leyla in and plucked her gun from the floor.

By the time she glanced around, gun at the ready, looking for someone to fire at, Jordan had aimed the Mustang at a cluster of police cars blocking off the street west of the Wendy's. He jerked the wheel to the left and floored it, and she saw his target—the place on the corner where the curb had been cut and graded for wheelchair access. Half on the sidewalk, they shot past the cordon, the front right quarter of the Mustang slamming into the rear of a police car. The shriek of metal gave way to Leyla's shrieks, but they were through, tearing through the intersection and headed away from the scene. Unmarked cars—maybe FBI, maybe police—gunned out of parking spaces, but Jordan veered around them to cut himself a path, and a dozen police cars tried to navigate through the mess he left behind.

Gunshots chased them, plinked the trunk. A bullet came through the rear windshield, splintering it with cracks, and lodged in the dashboard in front of Cait. She glanced back and saw Lynch bleeding from a wound in his side. He'd caught one back there and the crimson stain on his shirt was spreading, but he looked all right for the moment.

Sirens blared. Engines roared. They were coming.

Jordan cut the wheel and as the Mustang shot into a narrow side street, she saw a sign that made her want to cry.

"Dead end, Jordan! It's a dead end!"

"I got it," he said, hands gripped tightly to the wheel. He glanced at her, eyes full of fear and love, and she understood for the first time that this sweet, shy man was not just her friend, that he cared deeply for her, and maybe always had.

It didn't help.

"Jordan—"

"I got it!" he said again.

The old apartment houses and duplexes were dark. A kid's tricycle lay overturned on the sidewalk. Cars too nice for the neighborhood were parked nose to nose with rusting heaps. But as they rounded a curve, she saw the dark, sprawling silhouette of an elementary school ahead. Its parking lot was the dead end.

Blue lights flashed way behind them, but the cops had not missed the Mustang's turn. They were following.

Jordan raced the car past the school and across the baseball field behind it, toward a chain-link fence. But just as she was about to speak again, she saw the opening in the fence, a path that came in from a neighborhood on the other side of the baseball field. The Mustang barely fit between two concrete pylons, which scraped the sides of the car as Jordan steered between them, and then they were past the fence and into a warren of old brick townhouses, narrow streets, and turns. Jordan took a right, floored the accelerator, and just when blue lights should have appeared behind them, he turned left and went down a hill, underneath some kind of highway overpass, and up into a road construction site on the other side.

Cait could barely breathe as she ran her hands over her crying baby, searching for any sign of injury.

Less than a minute later, the Mustang crawled along an alley running behind a pool hall, a liquor store, and a small Irish pub. Jordan's aged but well-loved Mercedes sat parked by a loading dock behind the liquor store. He pulled up next to it and killed the engine, exhaling with relief.

Cait felt a moment of almost hysterical elation. A car the cops hadn't seen. No broken glass. No bullet holes. She wondered how far they would get, if they could make it to the place where Lynch's associates, his Resistance, would be waiting.

And then she thought of Ronnie.

"I'm so sorry I got you into this," she said, taking Jordan's hand. "You and Ronnie."

He hid his grief poorly, but made the effort, squeezing her

fingers. "Don't be sorry. I promised you a long time ago I'd always be there when you needed me. And here I am. Ronnie . . . he thought he was helping."

"I know."

"It was stupid," Jordan said. "He should have trusted you more."

She searched his eyes, their gazes locked for a lingering moment.

"Let's get moving," Lynch muttered behind them, a hand pressed over his wound. "I try not to get shot more than once a night."

Somehow his gravelly voice seemed to comfort Leyla, who ceased her wailing. Cait looked at Lynch and realized what he had done for her—for them—and knew they would live or die together from this moment on.

She nodded at Jordan, and they all abandoned the Mustang. At some point they would have to stop and deal with the wounds Lynch and Jordan had sustained—the latter just a graze off his clavicle—but not here.

It occurred to Cait as she climbed into the Mercedes that she had nothing for Leyla now. No milk, no bottle, no car seat . . . nothing. They had the clothes on their backs and their guns. Until they could stop somewhere safely, that would have to be enough.

-53--

Voss woke up cursing, wanting to throttle the paramedic who was putting pressure on her wound. The copper stink of her own blood filled her head and she stared at him, this handsome blond kid forcing his weight onto her shoulder to staunch the bleeding.

"That *really* hurts," she rasped.

He smiled. "Pain means you're alive."

Smart-ass. But he turned to his partner and called for a needle full of something that sent a wave of blissful relief cascading through her in what seemed like seconds. They kept working, bandaging her, setting up a drip, and now that the pain had abated some, she saw that she was in the back of an ambulance, but it didn't feel like they were moving.

"What's going on?" she asked, licking her lips, which felt swollen, like she'd had Novocain or too much to drink.

The blond paramedic—the guy looked barely old enough to vote—shot her a worried look. "You were shot, Agent Voss. Do you remember?"

Her hand fluttered up, brushing the question away. "I got that part, junior. What happened to . . . McCandless?"

Motion at the rear doors drew the attention of the paramedics, the first time Voss had noticed the doors were still open, and she glanced over and saw Turcotte poking his head inside.

"You were supposed to tell me if she came around," Turcotte said.

"Give us a second," Blondie said, making sure the gurney wasn't going to be moving during transport. His partner climbed out to make room for Turcotte, who hoisted himself into the ambulance, drawing a dark look from Blondie. "You've got thirty seconds, Agent. Then you can follow us to the hospital if you want."

Turcotte gave him a look suggesting he get out and leave them alone to talk, but Blondie wasn't having it. Voss wanted to kiss him, but maybe that was the painkillers. It was nice to have someone watching over her, especially tonight.

"Someone took a shot at me," she said as Turcotte knelt beside her gurney.

"A pretty good shot," Turcotte replied, trying to sound light-hearted despite the glint of rage in his eyes.

"Better than that. If he hadn't hit the bullhorn, he'd have put that bullet through my face."

The bullhorn. Right. That's why my mouth is so swollen. She searched her teeth with her tongue and found a bloody vacancy, with a jagged fragment of tooth still jutting from the gum.

"You gonna live?" Turcotte asked.

"For now. Can you dig out my phone? I've got to call in. Does my voice sound funny?"

Turcotte nodded. "Like you had a stroke, but it's the drugs. Listen, Rachael, I called ICD already, spoke directly to Theodora Wood. She wants an update as soon as you're out of surgery, but otherwise, the case is going to your partner—"

"Josh," Voss muttered, the drugs thickening her tongue even further. "Thass good. Tell him . . . thissis a clusterfuck. Norris and wassisname, Arsenault, weren't even here. FBI shot me."

Turcotte flinched. "You think one of my people shot you on purpose?"

Even as fuzzy as her brain had become, she managed to narrow her eyes and glare at him. "Don't be an asss. You think so, too. They had . . . orders not to shoot. And when someone pulls the trigger, instead of at McCann . . . McCandless, the bullet's aimed at my fuggin skull? Thass not a accident."

Unconsciousness flowed in at the edges of her mind again. She blinked and when she opened her eyes, Turcotte had started to rise to depart.

"Ed . . ."

"I need to talk to Hollenbach," he said.

"Yeah. You do." She closed her eyes, then struggled to open them again. "One lasst thing."

Turcotte paused in a crouch by the ambulance doors, waiting.

"Don't . . ." she started, drifting. "Don't call . . . me . . ."

Then the world slid away. She felt the motion of the ambulance, but nothing else.

-54--

The remainder of the flight passed in silence as Josh contemplated his relationship with Rachael Voss. No one meant more to him than she did. But they had both agreed long ago that they could never be more than partners. So why did he feel hesitant to act on the attraction he felt toward Nala Chang? It wasn't as if he was contemplating cheating on a wife or girlfriend.

He stared at Chang's back for a while, admiring the curve of her hip and the gentle slope of her neck. When his admiration started to drift into lurid imaginings of what they might do in that private jet all by themselves, he forced himself to turn away again.

In spite of his vow to remain awake, after a while the hum of the engines and the darkness of the cabin lulled him and he drifted off, only to wake a short time later to the jerk of the wheels touching down on the tarmac. He woke to find Chang watching him, a sleepy smile on her face. They both glanced away, but the air inside the cabin felt electric with unspoken potential.

When they stepped off the plane in D.C., Josh wondered what would have happened if the flight had been longer, and was torn between relief and disappointment that he would never know. But it was for the best. The thought of Voss finding out he'd had sex with Chang mid-flight, during a case—or at all, for that matter—made him queasy.

Not for the first time, he considered the possibility that he would never be able to have a normal relationship. And, also not for the first time, it occurred to him that maybe he didn't really want one after all.

"So, what's the plan?" Chang asked.

Josh had put some thought into it. "No way there isn't someone on duty at the National Geospatial-Intelligence Agency, even at this time of night. Satellites don't sleep. But we want Sean McCandless's boss, so as much as I hate to wait, I figure we get there at eight a.m. so nobody can try telling us to come back tomorrow."

Chang nodded. "Sounds logical. And in the meantime?"

"Go home, get a few hours' sleep, get washed up."

"It'd take me almost two hours to get there from here, and the same to get back. There doesn't seem much point. But I would love a shower."

Josh hesitated, watched her watching him with a spark of mischief in her eyes, and he laughed. "I have a shower."

"You don't say."

"And a spare room where you can get some sleep."

She grinned. "Spoilsport."

Josh had turned his cell phone off for the plane ride. Now he turned it back on, watching it power up, the screen lighting. He'd expected a message from Voss, letting him know how the McCandless situation went down in Hartford, so he waited for the phone to beep, showing him that he had voice mail. When it didn't, he frowned, troubled, and started scanning his contacts list to call her, but then that familiar double beep came after all.

But it wasn't a voice mail. What he'd gotten was a single text message from Theodora Wood, the director of the ICD. Josh staggered to a halt in the middle of the terminal. His fear must have been plain on his face, because when Chang turned to see what had halted him, she reached out and laid a hand on his arm.

"Josh, what is it?"

He ignored her, trying to stave off the panic that tried to seize him. Director Wood tended to leave things like texting to her subordinates. Any message should have come from Assistant Director Unger or from his own partner—this was Voss's case after all.

He opened the message. *It's your case, Josh. Voss shot, in surgery now. WILL recover. Call me directly to report. Don't turn your phone off again. And watch your back.*

"Stupid," he whispered to himself, staring at the message. "What the fuck's wrong with me?"

"What do you mean?" Chang asked.

Josh looked at her, feeling himself come unmoored. "I'm so used to shutting my phone off for commercial flights, I wasn't even thinking. And such a short flight, I just . . . Fuck!"

"What *is* it?"

He handed her the phone and she stared at the open text message for a few seconds before giving it back. Josh slid it into his pocket, barely aware of Chang's hand returning to rest on his arm again.

"You love her," Chang said. It wasn't a question.

Josh looked into those lovely brown eyes. "Of course I do. She's my partner."

"It's more than that."

"She's been shot. I shouldn't be worried about her?"

Chang squeezed his arm, letting the subject drop. "Director Wood says Voss will recover. She's going to be all right."

"I never should have left her."

"And maybe you would have caught a bullet, too. I wouldn't have liked that very much."

Josh looked at her. Somehow she had managed to convey a dozen meanings in that one sentence, not just in words but in tone. She wanted to comfort him, wanted to understand him and reassure him, and yet her voice was playful, tapping into the bone-deep attraction that had been simmering between them since they'd first met. He knew she didn't want to confuse him, but for a few seconds all he could think about was how soft her skin would be under his hands, and that wasn't helping at all.

"Nala . . ."

"What was that about watching your back?" she asked, shifting gears.

Josh blinked, appreciating that she knew now was not the time. Troubled, he frowned deeply and pulled the phone out again to reread the message, wondering the same thing. He had been so focused on Voss being shot that he had barely paid attention to that cryptic warning.

Now he returned the call, glancing up at Chang. "Let's find out."

Shortly before dawn, the aging Mercedes made its way along narrow streets near the Hudson River. Following Lynch's directions, Jordan turned left onto an access road that ran past blocks of run-down warehouses in Yonkers,

New York. Beyond the hulking warehouses, Cait could see the Hudson River rushing by. The open window let in the stink of rotting fish.

Just getting to the Bronx had been an odyssey in and of itself. Cait had taken the loss of Lynch's Cadillac hard. In addition to the money and guns that Lynch had socked away in the trunk, they'd been forced to leave behind everything they needed for Leyla. At minimum, they needed a car seat, a baby bottle, formula, baby food, diapers, and something to change her into if she made a mess of herself. All they needed was to be pulled over because of a crying baby without a car seat.

Just off the highway, they had found a 24-hour Walgreens pharmacy. It had everything they needed, if they could get in and out without trouble. They had listened fervently to radio reports and no one had mentioned Jordan yet. Still, they had been cautious. A good soldier, Jordan had a first-aid kit in the car. While Cait sang softly to Leyla, trying to keep her calm despite the fullness of her diaper and the disruption of her sleep, Lynch and Jordan had been forced to doctor each other. Parked in the midst of the cars and vans of employees— hiding in plain sight—the two men had disinfected and bandaged each other's wounds. Lynch had been shot in the right side, just above his hip, so Jordan packed both entrance and exit wounds with gauze and taped them up. The bullet hadn't seemed to hit anything vital. He might still need to be stitched up, but he would be all right.

After Lynch had taken care of the graze on Jordan's right shoulder, Jordan had donned a clean sweatshirt from the trunk. If a BOLO had been issued for him, they could not afford for him to be recognized, so he put a baseball cap on sideways and slid his pants low on his hips so that his boxer shorts showed. He looked ridiculous and out-of-date, but anyone seeing him would notice the ridiculous look *of* him without really being focused on looking *at* him, or so they hoped.

The disguise had worked. And in addition to the things they needed for Leyla, Jordan had managed clean shirts for himself and Lynch, using crisp hundreds the old man had in his wallet. The shopping had left them with very little cash, but it didn't matter now.

They were here.

"Pull around back," Lynch said.

Cait felt a weird giddiness envelop her at the idea of rest. It wasn't just the lack of sleep—she'd endured far worse in Iraq—but the adrenaline hangover that had started to drag at her. Leyla had been awake for nearly two hours, alternately whimpering and playing with her feet. Cait had given her a bottle of formula, thinking that would put her out again, but it hadn't. The baby must be exhausted, too, and Cait hoped that would mean they could both get a little sleep now that they'd found a temporary sanctuary. The whole world seemed set against them and only tiny vestiges of hope remained within her. She knew she couldn't make any decisions about their future until she'd had some sleep.

Jordan drove between two old warehouses, their paint faded and peeling, and took a right turn. On the left was a short concrete wall, and beyond that, the river. There were piers up and down the Hudson here, places where ships would off-load cargo to be stored in warehouses—or where they would have done so in better times for the area.

"Right in front of the garage," Lynch said.

When Jordan pulled up, Lynch got out and walked stiffly—age and injury slowing him down—toward a small metal box beside the garage door. He opened the box, revealing a keypad beneath, and when he entered the code, the broad metal door began to groan and then to rattle upward.

Lynch glanced around suspiciously, then waved the Mercedes in. As Jordan drove into the warehouse, dim lights flickered to life high up on the ceiling of the garage, revealing some kind of delivery van and several other vehicles. He turned the car off, creating a single moment of silence before the garage door started rattling downward behind them.

Cait checked on her daughter—momentarily content to chew on her fist—then climbed out of the backseat. She stretched, nose wrinkling at the stale smell of her own body, and looked around. The garage took up a relatively small part of the warehouse. Two small doors led from it into other parts of the building, but they remained closed. Once the metal groan of the garage door ceased, the only sound was the ticking of the Mercedes's cooling engine.

Lynch pulled out a set of keys and strode toward the nearest door. Jordan stepped out of the car, careful not to startle the baby, and looked around.

"Not much of a welcome," Jordan said.

"Yeah. I was thinking the same thing."

A chill raced through Cait. Part of her wanted to jump back in the car with Jordan and Leyla, just leave Lynch and get the hell out. But the old man had already taken one bullet for her and had blown who knew how many opportunities to hunt down these baby-killers by coming out in the open. She had to give him the benefit of the doubt. He'd earned that.

She unbuckled Leyla and took her out of the car, carrying a plastic Walgreens bag with formula and bottled water, baby wipes, and a couple of tiny T-shirts Jordan had gotten her to sleep in. He grabbed the other bags and the package of diapers and followed her as she went to the door Lynch had gone through. It stood open, darkness yawing within.

"Lynch?" she called.

"In here," he replied.

From beyond the door, she heard a rustling and then a click, and the room lit up. Cait stepped through, Leyla tugging on a fistful of her hair, and stared around at the headquarters of the Resistance. Perhaps forty feet by sixty, this was clearly the nerve center of the operation. There were cubicles and computers around the edges of the room—in the middle, a conference table. To the left, Cait saw an array of various televisions—some flat-screen, others older—with cables snaking everywhere. To the right was a row of whiteboards covered with photographs of men and women who were clearly targets. Some of the pictures had been crossed through in red marker, presumably indicating that they were dead.

All of this had been done a long time ago.

"Oh, no," Cait said softly.

Months', maybe years', worth of dust lay over nearly every surface. The desk and black chair in a single cubicle and the television array seemed to have been used more recently.

Papers were spread across the conference table, stacks of files, and those also seemed to still be in use. The rest of the place seemed silent and abandoned.

"So where are they all?" Jordan asked.

Cait shot him a look of disbelief. Didn't he see? Didn't he understand? She held Leyla to her, wishing she could summon fury but only able to muster despair. Lynch walked over to the recently occupied cubicle and turned on the computer there. As she watched, he moved across the large room to a master control for the television array. A cacophony of voices echoed from the walls, CNN, Fox News, BBC, MSNBC, Al Jazeera via some kind of satellite uplink—and how the fuck did he do that?

Mesmerized, she could only watch as he crossed to the nearest of the whiteboards, picked up a red marker and drew thick X's through the photos of three men. He paused in front of two others, then drew question marks on them. Even from here, Cait recognized one as having been with the government agents who had tried to take Leyla from her last night.

Last night. By now the sun would be rising outside. Here in the warehouse, daylight—sunrise—meant nothing. There was only darkness here.

At last, Lynch turned his gaze on them. But he was back in his element. Preoccupied. Distracted. He gestured toward the rear of the room, past the television array.

"There are bedrooms and showers back there. You'll probably find something clean to wear if you poke around long enough. Clean sheets. There's food in the kitchen, but I wouldn't vouch for any of the dairy in the fridge."

Leyla nattered happily, bouncing in her mother's arms and tugging her hair.

Cait went to Jordan, kissed the baby, then handed Leyla to her friend. He scooped her up, staring first at Cait and then at Lynch, who seemed to have dismissed them.

Cait ran at him.

"No, Cait! We need him!" Jordan yelled.

"Fuck that," she growled.

Lynch saw her coming. The way he moved, she knew he had been well trained. He knew how to fight. His mistake was going for his gun. She gripped his wrist, stepped in, and launched a side kick at his armpit that deadened the arm completely. Tearing the gun from his hand, she tossed it across the room even as she spun around and struck the old man in the chest and gut. Even at his age, Lynch would have been a formidable opponent, but she brought him down hard and landed on his chest, pinning him with her knees, her hands on his throat.

Her tears splashed down onto his face. "You bastard," she said, choking on her sobs. "Crazy son of a bitch, you lied to me?"

"No," he rasped. "They were . . . The Resistance is real."

"Bullshit!" she screamed. "Then where are they?"

He clawed at her hands, unable to catch his breath, and she eased up enough for him to respond. Those steely eyes regarded her, full of loss and sadness, and she knew then that he was just as much adrift, just as terrified as she.

"Gone," Lynch said. "There were dozens of us once. Some were killed. Some bought. Some were too afraid to die. But I . . . I'm one of them, you understand? I'm a War Child, just like your little girl. I have to stop these bastards. I have to kill them, to save as many of the children as I can."

She sat back, feeling cold and hollow inside, the significance of it all settling in. She slid off of him, sat in a tangle on the carpet and stared at her hands for several long seconds while Lynch coughed and wheezed. Cait glanced over at Leyla and Jordan.

"Then there's no one," she said, shaking, breath hitching with the force of her tears. "We can't hide for long. They're going to get my baby. We're going to . . . to die."

She couldn't speak after that. Lynch tried talking to her but she didn't hear him. She could only stare at Leyla, her beautiful girl, and try to keep breathing as sobs wracked her body. Jordan brought the baby to her and Cait held her. She and Leyla lay together on the dusty carpet, the baby's head cradled in the crook of her arm, and she cried, staring in horror at the shadowed corners of the room.

Like death, sleep tried to claim her. Eventually she succumbed.

She dreamed of hollow-eyed Iraqi orphans, of dark-veiled Baghdad mothers with empty arms, and a burning taxi in the aftermath of a roadside bomb.

She dreamed of screaming.

-56--

Josh lay in bed with his cell phone tucked between his ear and the pillow. He had managed a little more than three hours of sleep and his eyes burned with the need for more, but it would have to be enough.

"All right," he said. "I've gotta hit the shower if I want to surprise the satellite geeks this morning. I'll call you when we're done there, check up . . . yeah. You sleep. Get some Z's for me. Right. Bye."

He moved the phone, ended the call, and lay there for a few seconds with it clutched in his hand. Reluctantly he forced his eyes open. He couldn't risk falling back to sleep. He'd brushed his teeth and showered before climbing into bed because he'd felt so grimy, but he wanted another shower and they needed to get moving.

"How is she?"

Startled, he turned to see Chang standing in the open doorway of his bedroom, and the sight of her made him catch his breath. She wore a faded Coldplay concert shirt he had pulled out of his closet for her to sleep in. Though oversized, the cotton fell just right, clinging wonderfully to her curves. Her legs were bare and shapely and her hair in fetching disarray.

Josh sat up in bed, sliding back to prop himself against the headboard, aware of how little they were both wearing. He was shirtless, clad only in a pair of boxers.

"Hospital-wise, she's doing all right," he said, trying to keep his cool, unable to take his eyes off of her. "She says she looks a little beat-up but they got the bullet out, no problem, no bone or muscle damage to speak of. She needs rest, but I give her until noon at best before she breaks out of there, guns blazing."

Chang came into the room, her bare legs, and the shape of her breasts beneath his T-shirt, making his mouth go dry.

"I'm glad," she said. "I know how worried you were."

"Case-wise, though, she's not so good."

Chang frowned. "What do you mean?"

"Voss says the shooter was FBI."

Chang's gaze shifted around as though searching the empty spaces of the room for an answer.

"Friendly fire," she said. "It sucks, but when things get chaotic, it happens."

"No," Josh said. "It was the first shot fired."

The corners of her eyes crinkled in pain. "She's sure?"

Josh nodded. "We don't want it to be true, either. The Bureau was our first home, you know? But she's sure."

Chang seemed to deflate. "Jesus." She sat on the edge of his bed, the hem of the T-shirt riding dangerously high. "SO-COM was bad enough. Who is this? Who's working against us like this? Who has this kind of reach?"

"Black Pine?"

"Maybe. They were in a hurry to move those bodies last night. But if so, they're not working alone. And what's it all about?" Chang asked.

Josh studied her face, his focus split between the case and her presence there, so close to him.

"Babies," he said.

Chang glanced away, then nodded. "The *Rolling Stone* thing—the Herod Factor—that's what you're talking about?"

"I know. Paranoid conspiracy bullshit," Josh said. "But what if it's not? All of the details here are pointing toward that article being dead-on. Someone is killing kids born of parents whose people are enemies, exactly what the anonymous source in that article was talking about. Then, once we start digging into it, people with more influence than God start interfering with our investigation, and now my partner's been shot."

"It adds up," Chang agreed. "I wish it didn't. Hell, it shouldn't. It's the craziest thing I've ever heard."

"I wish I could say the same," Josh said. He frowned deeply, then turned to her. "When we were in the state police barracks up in Bangor, I started looking into some of the claims made in that article. Back in the 1800s, the first time the French went to war in Indochina, it didn't last long, but the conflict didn't end then. War never quite went away, flaring up regularly, until the French finally left the mess to the Americans to clean up. That went on for about a hundred years, and there were plenty of times that peace seemed possible, but then something would happen to prevent it.

"There was a radical group in Indochina made up of people who wanted not only to drive out the French, but to exterminate them. They were ruthless and determined, and they called on the people to rise up. One of the other things they called for was the public humiliation of any woman who gave birth to a child with a French father, and the drowning of their children."

Chang stared at him, searching his eyes. "You didn't think maybe you should have shared this before?"

Josh shrugged and threw up his hands. "To what end?" He let out a breath and looked away. "I've been telling myself that it's all coincidence. It probably is. If you sift through history, you can find evidence to support almost any theory. Maybe the extremists in Indochina in the nineteenth century actually drowned babies who were half-French and maybe they didn't. But even if they did, that doesn't mean it's all connected."

He turned to find Chang studying him closely.

"But you think it is. Don't you?"

Josh scratched the back of his head and gave her a nervous smile. "It's not just the French in Indochina. It's the Carthaginians and the Romans, Napoleon and the Russians, and don't get me started on the Crusades. I assume you've heard of the Children's Crusade?"

"Of course," Chang said.

"According to one account, after a century of sending Crusaders to the so-called Holy Land, the Church rounded up the children who'd been born of European knights and Islamic women and marched them off to die."

"That's disgusting," Chang said. "I've never heard that version before."

Josh gave a small shrug. "Neither had I. But it's all history, which means no one agrees on what really happened, or why. That's what I'm saying. Unless you're dealing with who won a war or who controlled a region at a given time—when you're dealing with the *why* of things—you can make history say whatever you want it to."

Chang shook her head. "Now you're confusing me. Do you believe all of this, or don't you?"

"I think it's crazy," Josh replied. "But I think some of these guys—the ones whose entire worldview and business model is predicated on war—need it the way farmers need rain for their crops to grow . . . and then I start thinking maybe it isn't so crazy. And it only makes it worse not knowing who to trust."

Troubled, she gazed at him, face framed by sleep-wild hair. "Do you trust me?"

He arched an eyebrow. "I don't know. You're FBI. Are you going to shoot me?"

She whacked him in the arm, trying not to smile. "I think I might."

Josh laughed softly, aware of the way her hand came to rest on his arm, and the flash of pink cotton as the T-shirt rode up even higher.

"I also think we both need to clear our heads a little before we can really make sense of all of this," Chang went on.

"I know," Josh said, nodding. "Sometimes I get a little intense."

"This is a lot to take in, for both of us," Chang said. "But I like intense."

Their gazes locked, her hand still resting on his arm, and it seemed his heart had begun to beat so loudly that they should both be able to hear it. For long seconds they simply stared, then she crawled across the bed to him.

"Nala," he said, hesitant.

She straddled him, bent to brush her lips against his, slid

her hand behind his neck to kiss him more deeply, her body
so warm on top of him.

"Shut up, Josh."

He didn't argue.

-57--

Cait woke calling her daughter's name, terrified by the absence of Leyla's weight in her arms. It took her a second to
realize that sometime during the night she had been moved
to a musty-smelling bed in a windowless cubicle. Light
streamed in from the corridor. Still in her clothes from the
night before—the longest night of her life—she shot from
the bed, tangled in the sheets, and broke free to race for the
door.

The corridor showed her she was still in the warehouse,
the bedroom a kind of sleeping cube—a modular piece
amongst a row of similar cubes.

"Leyla!" she called, running down the corridor, glancing
into each room she passed.

"Right here, Momma," Jordan said from ahead.

She entered a kitchen to find him sitting at a small table,
holding Leyla cradled in one arm while he gave her a bottle.
Cheerios were spread across the table and scattered on the
floor, but Cait presumed some had made it into the baby's
mouth. A wave of relief went through her and she exhaled,
smiling at the sight of the strong, quiet soldier so comfortable with her baby in his arms.

"Sorry I panicked," she said, going to them. Leyla's eyes
locked on her but the baby didn't reach for her, which surprised, delighted, and saddened her all at once. Jordan's
warmth and the fresh bottle were apparently all Leyla needed.

"She's all right," Jordan assured her. "We thought we'd let
you sleep. Now that you're up, though, there's coffee."

Cait looked around, saw the coffeepot, and felt doubly grateful.

"What time is it, and where did you get this stuff?" she asked as she went to pour herself a cup.

Jordan glanced at her. "Not me. I woke up and Lynch was gone. Maybe fifteen minutes later he waltzes in with milk, OJ, and a box of Cheerios. He got some kind of baby oatmeal and some applesauce, too. I found a can of coffee in the cabinet. No idea how long it's been there, but it tastes all right."

Cait didn't bother with sugar or milk, just took a sip of the black coffee and relished its bite.

"Want me to take her now?" she asked as she returned to the table.

"No, just enjoy your coffee. Wake up first. The little princess and I are getting to know each other better."

Cait smiled and sat down. "Thanks. So, speaking of Lynch, where is the crazy fuck?"

Jordan must have heard the brittle fury in her voice, and he looked at her so kindly that it nearly made her cry. But she had done enough crying last night to last the rest of her life. She had been a soldier. She had seen friends and enemies and innocents die, had watched people bleed out, had watched life seeping from a young boy's eyes, had seen a father blow himself to pieces. And she had killed. Her daughter had needed her to leave all that behind, to open her heart again after working so hard to shield it. But now Leyla needed the soldier as much as she needed the mother, so for the first time, Cait would have to learn how to be both.

"He's watching all those news channels. He hasn't said much. I think he's embarrassed."

"That's something, at least. If he's got enough brains to be embarrassed, it means he's not as insane as I feared."

"Are you all right?" Jordan asked.

The moment the words were out of his mouth they both realized how ridiculous the question was, and Cait snickered.

"Not even close. Lynch saved my life last night, probably more than once. But the guy *is* delusional. Whatever organization used to exist is gone. Nobody's riding to the rescue. He's got his computer and his TVs and his list of baby-killers, but I don't know what any of that's going to do to keep us alive."

Leyla pushed the bottle away. Jordan tried to get her to take it again but she wouldn't. Cait took a long sip of coffee and then set down the cup and reached for her daughter.

"Come to Mommy, sweetie," she said.

Hoisting Leyla to her shoulder, she patted the baby's back until she was rewarded with a tiny burp. She closed her eyes and inhaled Leyla's smell, kissed her face and her neck, then just held her until the baby started to squirm. Then she sat Leyla on her knee and began to gently bounce her, eliciting a gurgling laugh.

She could hide her for a time, but it would be no life, always waiting for the moment when the doors would be broken down and the gunfight would begin again. They had been very fortunate last night, but she had no doubt that they would not get that lucky again.

"Poor Ronnie," she said with a sigh.

Jordan nodded sadly. "Don't beat yourself up, Sarge. I loved Ronnie, too. He was one of my best friends. But he should've talked to you first. What he did was stupid, and he knew it, or he would have told me about it before we got to you."

Cait wrapped her arms around Leyla and rocked her back and forth. "I'm still going to miss him."

"You and me both. But we can hurt over him dying after we figure out how to keep ourselves alive."

She picked up the bottle. "You're a good friend."

"You're not so bad yourself, Sarge."

She smiled as Leyla reached for the bottle, and guided it to her mouth. "You know I hate it when you call me that?"

"I'm aware," he replied, one corner of his mouth lifting in an amused grin.

Cait shook her head, forcing her smile away. "You haven't called me 'Sarge' for a really long time."

"We were home," Jordan said, his own smile slipping. "Now we're back at war."

Cait couldn't argue. It just seemed to be taking her longer to adjust to their new reality than it had taken Jordan.

"You're right," she said. "And it's time to start fighting

back. I'm going to need Lynch's computer. And I'm guessing he's got a whole lot of guns stashed around here somewhere. We're going to need those, too."

Jordan leaned toward her, brow furrowed, all seriousness now. "You saying you have a plan?"

Cait thought about that. What few traces of lightness she had mustered in her heart vanished.

"Not a good one. This thing is so big, there's no way to know who is and isn't a part of it. We could join Lynch's hunt, but my face has gotta be on every TV and computer screen in the United States by now. My life is over. And there's only one way I can think of to get it back and make Leyla safe."

Jordan leaned forward and gave the baby a little tickle. She kicked at his hand and he laughed softly. Then he looked up at Cait, his grim expression returning. "Just tell me what you need me to do."

"Let me think on it for a little while," Cait said. "I have to speak to Lynch and make a call, and then we'll talk."

Leyla pushed the bottle away and Cait set it on the table. She stood up, holding the baby against her shoulder, and bent to kiss Jordan on the cheek. He actually blushed a little.

"Thank you," she said. "Really. You being here helps me remember that the whole world hasn't gone crazy. Whatever happens next, I couldn't deal with it without you."

"You don't give yourself enough credit, Sarge."

"Hey."

"Sorry. Cait," he said, gazing at her. "Listen, I just . . . I'm here for you, okay? Like you said, whatever happens next. You and Leyla, you're not alone."

A long moment passed between them before Cait stepped back, holding Leyla close.

"Speaking of not alone, I should go talk to Lynch. I've got to break some bad news to him."

"What's that?" Jordan asked.

"All these years he's been hunting the people killing War's Children," Cait said. "It's time to tell him he's been thinking too small."

-58--

Detective Monteforte sat across the conference table from Sarah Lin, worried that she might be wasting her time. Sleep had been hard to come by and when she had called in just after seven a.m., the sergeant on duty had offered his sympathies about Jarman's death and then told her that Lieutenant Hoffmeyer had given the case to Teddy Sacco. Monteforte had nothing against Sacco, but she couldn't let that happen.

Jarman had been her partner. Policy dictated that she should have time off for bereavement or at least be riding a desk, and part of her wouldn't have minded that. There would be a wake and a funeral and a lot of pain. But she couldn't let the pain sidetrack her yet. Not without knowing who was really responsible for Jarman's death, and why he had died.

"And you're sure she didn't say anything about her brother's death that wasn't in the taped interview?" Monteforte asked.

Sarah Lin shrugged. "Nothing huge. When we got there, she prepped us with the rundown of what had happened to her brother, but it was more about the abduction attempt than her brother's death."

"And what about the cameraman who did that shoot with you?" Monteforte asked. She glanced down at the paper in front of her. "Jordan Katz. He served with Cait in Iraq?"

Sarah frowned. "I guess I knew that, yeah."

"Any idea where he might be at the moment?" Monteforte asked. "We're having trouble tracking him down."

The reporter shrugged. "I don't know Jordan that well. We haven't been paired up much in the past. So, no. Sorry, but I have no idea where he might be."

"There's nothing else that struck you, during the interview?" Monteforte asked. "Anything strange?"

Sarah Lin had a beauty and obvious intellect that were vital elements for anyone hoping to make it as a TV reporter, and the charisma and confidence that might make her an anchor someday. Despite the extraordinary nature of the things they were discussing, she remained cool and professional.

"I'm sorry, Detective," she said. "The whole thing was strange. Someone had tried to take Cait's baby. I've already shown you the unedited interview. Cait was pretty much at her wit's end, but she kept it together. What she said to us off camera was just more of what you saw on camera. She definitely thought someone had been watching her aunt and uncle's house, and there's no question she thought they were the same people who tried to grab her baby, but all this other stuff . . . I have no idea.

"But I can tell you one thing," Sarah added with a defiant glare. "Cait McCandless is no damn terrorist."

Monteforte took a deep breath and sat back. "I agree."

Sarah seemed surprised. "You do?"

"I do. I don't know who spun that bullshit, but it won't stick. I know people are always on TV saying 'She seemed like such a nice person,' but this is different. The people who tried to take Leyla . . . that was real. I'm convinced Cait is the victim here, but amazing as it may seem to you, there *is* some kind of terrorist connection. Maybe it has to do with her brother dying down in D.C. I don't know. But I intend to find out."

Sarah Lin tapped her fingers on the table. "How can I help?"

"I think the best thing you can do for your friend is keep telling her story," Monteforte said. "I'm going to be pulled off this case the second my lieutenant finds out I'm still working it, and then it's going to be in the hands of a detective who never met Cait McCandless and her daughter. None of this is going to matter to him, especially because we've basically been told by the FBI that we should butt out."

Sarah stared at her. "Are you saying all of this on the record?"

Monteforte smiled thinly. "Sure. But if you want to dig deeper, there are some other things you should know—*off* the record. Like how many DOAs there really were at Cait's house last night."

What are you doing, Anne? she thought to herself. But she knew what, and why.

"Why would you be pulled off the case?" Sarah asked.

Monteforte looked at the clock, wondering how long before the lieutenant figured out what she was up to and shut her down with a direct order.

"The detective who died last night was my partner. He and I were working the McCandless case together."

Sarah made a small sound that might have been surprise or sympathy. "I'm so sorry."

"Thank you," Monteforte said.

"No, thank you," Sarah said, wearing a sad smile. "Cait really needs people to believe in her right now."

Monteforte frowned. "Do you mean you've heard from her?"

Regret clouded the reporter's face. "No. I tried her cell—I mean, obviously she's not home. I've left a few messages, sent her a couple of texts." Sarah studied the detective. "Where's all this headed? Are they going to be all right? Cait and Leyla?"

"I honestly don't know," Monteforte said. "People are dying all around them. They're in a lot of danger. How they come out of it, I have no idea. But like you, I'll keep asking questions."

Sarah sighed. "I hope so."

Monteforte slid her business card across the table. As Sarah took it and began to rise, her cell phone rang. With a look of mild annoyance, she unclipped it from her belt and looked at the screen, frowning at what Monteforte assumed was an unknown name or number.

"This is Sarah," she said.

Monteforte knew immediately. The way her eyes widened with surprise and then narrowed in concern, she could practically see Sarah's heart leap.

"Hey," Sarah said, trying and failing to stay cool. "How are you? Are you okay? No, of course I didn't. . . . Are you kidding? I'm glad you called . . . no, it's not a problem. Whatever you need."

Sarah nodded as if to say good-bye and went to leave the conference room, pretending this was just another phone call, something she had to deal with. She gave Monteforte a little wave and then started to open the door.

"Ms. Lin," Monteforte said, and she put it all in those two words, in her tone.

Sarah froze, unsure, looking like she wanted to run. Monteforte rose and hurried around the table. She could hear the murmur of a voice from Sarah's cell phone.

"Let me help," Monteforte said. "Please. I *can* help."

"Cait," Sarah said. "No, listen. Hold on a second."

Monteforte reached for the phone and Sarah relinquished it. Her heart pounded as she lifted it to her ear.

"Cait, it's Anne Monteforte. Please don't hang up."

She heard a sharp intake of breath on the line.

"Please," Monteforte said. "I know you must be having a hard time trusting anyone right now. After last night, I feel the same. Everyone is lying, including the FBI. But the truth is being buried so deep, and I can't let that happen. I know you're not the bad guy, Cait. Please, let me help."

A sigh. "How can you help, Detective?"

"I don't know yet. I just . . . I want the truth."

"I'm sorry about Detective Jarman. He was a good man."

"He was," Monteforte agreed. She bit her lower lip to fight down the emotion welling inside her.

Another pause, and then: "How far are you willing to go for the truth, Detective?"

"Wherever it leads me."

"Then put Sarah back on."

Monteforte did as she was asked. Sarah took the phone from her, said "Hello," and then listened for perhaps a full minute, glancing at Monteforte from time to time.

"That's do-able," she said. "Is Jordan . . . I told you—whatever you need. I flatter myself that I'm a good reporter, Cait, and that means knowing when something smells like bullshit. Someone's after you—and your *baby,* for God's sake. The only thanks I need for helping you is for you to try to keep the bullets flying away from me, instead of toward me, if it comes to that."

Despite her brave talk, the reporter looked shaken. But she stayed on the line and Monteforte thought she would be true to her word. After giving Cait several more reassurances, she handed the phone back.

"I'm here," Monteforte said.

"There's something you can do. I was going to ask Sarah to try to pull it off by herself. It'll be the biggest story of her career. But it will probably work a lot better with you along."

"All right."

"You can't tell anyone," Cait said. "You can't trust anyone. And if you change your mind, if you fuck me over, then Leyla and I are as good as dead. Do you understand that? Do you understand that these people outrank you, and that there is nothing you can do as a police officer to make justice happen here?"

Monteforte felt a chill go through her. "I do."

"And you understand that I don't want anyone else dying, but that it isn't up to me?"

Monteforte thought about the pull it would take to make bodies just vanish from a crime scene, to play the FBI like puppets, to kill indiscriminately and have the government close its eyes.

"I get it, Cait."

"Have you eaten breakfast, Detective Monteforte?"

"No."

"You can pick something up on the way."

"Where am I going?" Monteforte asked.

"To Hoboken."

"New Jersey?"

"Get yourselves some coffee and something you can eat on the run. I'll call Sarah back in half an hour and give you the whole rundown. But if you're going to bail on me, do it now. Because I'm only going to have one chance at this."

Monteforte held her breath a moment, realizing what she was risking. Her future. Her career. Her life. But Jarman had been her friend as well as her partner, and he'd fought for justice for so many over the years. He deserved nothing less.

"I'm not going to bail."

"All right, then," Cait said, sounding tired but grateful. "I'll see you soon."

Monteforte handed Sarah the phone. A change had come

over the reporter. All of her confusion had evaporated. She bounced with a kind of nervous energy.

"You're really on board for this?" she asked.

"Are you?" Monteforte replied. "I mean, I know why I'm going along with it. But what about you?"

Sarah stared at her as if she hadn't understood the question. "These are good people."

"But you don't even know them very well."

"I guess I don't. But they don't have anywhere else to turn or they wouldn't be calling me. Someone's trying to kill Cait and her daughter, and now Jordan, and to paint them as terrorists. You told me yourself that you don't believe that's true, and I'm with you. I don't believe what's being reported, and that means someone is hiding the truth. Getting to the truth, finding the secrets the bad guys don't want the public to know and exposing them . . . that's my job."

Monteforte studied her. "But these people are willing to kill to stop you from doing that job."

"I get that, Detective." Sarah managed to muster a slightly nervous smile. "Must be some pretty big secrets."

"Okay, then," Monteforte said. "Let's get moving."

Sarah opened the door. As Monteforte walked through, she wondered how much of herself she had left behind in that conference room. But she kept walking. Jarman was dead. Cait and Leyla were being hunted and she couldn't just let that happen. There was no turning back now.

More than anything, Josh wanted to knock the smug look off Roger Boyce's face. The guy had an officious air about him that Josh suspected was not unique to this morning. From the way the other man in the room, Brian Herskowitz, looked at Boyce, he must be a joy to work with.

"Mr. Boyce," Agent Chang said, "I'm not sure you're clear on your position here."

Soft and bespectacled, Boyce did his best to smile, but it was almost a sneer. "We disagree on that, Agent. I think I've made my position very clear."

Herskowitz tried speaking up. "Roger, I think what she meant—"

Boyce shot him a withering glance. "I *know* what she meant."

Josh had been observing the dynamic between these two. Though Boyce had the authority in the room, it was clear that the subordinate, Herskowitz, was both smarter and more rational—and knew it.

"Look, I'm not sure what else you think we can tell you," Boyce continued. He spread his hands theatrically, as if to show he had nothing to hide. "I've told you about Sean McCandless's duties here, and Brian has very patiently answered all of your questions about McCandless's state of mind the past few weeks."

Herskowitz narrowed his eyes at the use of Sean McCandless's last name, as if offended by the callous tone.

Boyce sat behind his desk, trying to look in charge. He had been attempting to assert control of the situation since the moment just after eight-thirty when he had entered his office and found Josh and Chang waiting for him, drinking coffee the receptionist had thoughtfully provided and occupying the surprisingly comfortable guest chairs set before the desk. Boyce had been on edge at first, nervous, and had seemingly called in Herskowitz to bolster his version of the truth. Josh had no doubt that Herskowitz knew Sean McCandless, even considered him a friend. The man wasn't faking his sorrow over McCandless's death.

But Josh doubted everything else the two men had said.

"Agent Chang and I aren't running on much sleep," Josh said, and a flash of memory from their morning, the soft curve of Nala's breast, the urgency in her eyes, gave him pause. He smiled, not caring how Boyce interpreted that. "So let's not fuck around here, Mr. Boyce. Spin Sean McCandless's death however you want, but everyone in this room knows he didn't just have a heart attack, and that the government cremated him to hide that fact.

"I don't know what he really did for you people besides play with satellites, but the word *intelligence* is part of your agency's name. You spy with a satellite or you spy on the ground. Honestly, I don't give a shit about any of that. There isn't a shred of doubt in my mind, or Agent Chang's, that Sean McCandless's murder had nothing to do with his work for you and is instead connected to a larger threat to his family, and possibly to a lot of other American families."

Boyce glanced at Herskowitz, then looked at Chang. "Not to credit any part of this fantasy of yours, Agents, but if you're so certain of these assertions, why are you even bothering to talk to us?"

Chang shifted her legs in the seat and sat forward, drawing Josh's eye. From the moment they had showered and dressed and left his apartment, they had been working hard at pretending nothing at all had happened between them, but the air between them felt electric. Josh felt a prickling static at every nerve ending. They needed to have a conversation, but both of them knew where their priorities lay.

Yet when she moved, he couldn't help watching her.

"Why are we here?" Chang said. "That's your question?"

Boyce nodded, supercilious air firmly in place. "Essentially."

One corner of Chang's mouth lifted in a sardonic smile. "Maybe you really are as stupid as you look."

Boyce started to rise. "That's enough. Both of you can—"

"Sit the fuck down," Josh said. He spoke without raising his voice, but his tone froze Boyce halfway up from his chair. "Now, Mr. Boyce, or the next time your phone rings, it will be the director of Homeland Security on the line."

Herskowitz, properly chided, had been standing in the corner like a naughty schoolboy all this time. At last he spoke up.

"Roger . . ."

Boyce glared at him, but sat back down.

"Now," Josh said, taking both men in with a glance. "Once you confirm what we already know, then you can start telling us what we *don't* know. What do we want? Every detail of the investigation into Sean McCandless's death, anything that might lead us to the people who killed him, because those same people have been murdering babies and children all across this country, and we want to get to them before they can kill Cait McCandless and her daughter."

Boyce's arrogance finally shattered. "Babies? What the hell are you talking about?"

Josh and Chang exchanged a look but didn't answer, both choosing to let the question, and Boyce's confusion, hang in the air.

"The media's calling Cait McCandless a terror suspect," Herskowitz ventured.

Josh cocked his head, studying the man's face. Something was off about the tone of the question. He knew more than he was saying.

"You don't believe that," Chang said.

"No, I don't," Herskowitz said.

"Brian—" Boyce began.

"Fuck off, Roger," Herskowitz said, focusing on Chang again. "Sean was my friend. I've met Cait a couple times. I don't believe for a second that she's some kind of terrorist. And I'm getting the impression you don't believe that, either. Why is that?"

Again, Josh and Chang remained silent.

"Look, I appreciate what you're saying," Boyce said, "but if you have questions or concerns about the answers you've gotten here, you're more than welcome to go up the ladder and see if you get anything more to your liking."

Josh sighed, his patience at an end. "This is a whole different kind of cloak and dagger than you're used to, Boyce. Now, you *think* you don't have to tell us the truth. Maybe you think the truth is above our pay grade or our clearance, but the best thing about working for the InterAgency Cooperation Division is that my jurisdiction is what I say it is, unless and until my boss calls me off the scent."

"Josh," Chang said, "we don't have time to waste on this."

He nodded and pulled out his cell phone. "You're right." He looked at Boyce. "I'm not kidding about your phone ringing, Mr. Boyce. But don't worry about it. It isn't about screwing your career. I just want to expedite this whole thing."

"Hold on," Boyce said.

Josh started scanning his contacts list.

Boyce rose from his chair, pulling out his own cell phone. "I said hold on. Just give me a minute, all right?"

Josh nodded. "All right."

Boyce looked as though he expected them to leave the office to let him have a private conversation, but nobody moved. Finally he scowled and headed for the door, stepping out into the corridor and shutting the door behind him.

The moment it closed, Josh and Chang turned to Herskowitz. The man had been quiet and deferential with Boyce in the room, but now Josh saw a different person in his place. His gaze had hardened, his chin lifted in grim determination, and Josh realized that though he might work in an office, the man had been forged by his work in intelligence.

"Sean *was* murdered," Herskowitz said. "Poison. But we don't know a damn thing about who or why."

Josh glanced at the door, hoping Boyce didn't rush back. "You're sure there's nothing that would give us a lead?"

"Nothing," Herskowitz replied. He seemed to be studying them, gauging how much he could say. "Do you really want to help Cait?"

"Yes," Chang said, with a quick glance at Josh. "We really do."

"I take it you realize there are some pretty powerful people who don't want you to help her?"

"The people who are calling her a terrorist, for instance?" Chang said. "Yeah, we know. But we're here, asking the questions they don't want asked."

"Why?" Josh asked, sitting forward in his chair. "Do you know where she is?"

Herskowitz wrestled with the question for several seconds, obviously weighing the risks to himself, perhaps even to his life, if he answered truthfully.

"No," he said at last.

"Damn it—" Josh started.

Herskowitz stopped him with a look.

"But I know where she's *going* to be."

-60--

"Hoboken?" Voss said. "What the hell's in Hoboken?"

She lay in the hellishly uncomfortable hospital bed—made even more so by her attempts to stave off pain by remaining still—and held her cell phone to her ear. The hospital never slept, but it had quieted down enough for her to have managed to rest a little. Then Josh had called.

"Are you alone?" Josh asked.

Voss glanced at the door. "As I'll ever be while I'm here."

"How's your shoulder? Tell me the truth, Rachael. Are you mobile?"

"I'm fine."

She could hear him sigh over the phone.

"You're not fine. You took a bullet. But I know you, and I'm sure you're antsy as hell in that hospital bed. I also know that if the case is about to blow up, you're going to want to be here. So I'm asking you, bullet wound and painkiller haze and all, can you travel? Can you get out of there without telling anyone where you're going?"

Voss hesitated, considering the pain in her shoulder. The sling helped keep pressure off it, but didn't solve the problem.

"Yeah," she said. "It hurts, but I'm mobile. What about Turcotte, though? Aren't you with Agent Chang?"

"I am," Josh said, an odd tightness in his voice. "But if our information is correct, FBI chain of command is compromised. Agent Chang is following ICD protocol, taking directives from us."

"What, did you promise her a job? If she fucks over Turcotte, she's screwing her career."

"I disagree," Josh said. "She's protecting him by keeping him in the dark. He's not a fool. He'll figure that out."

"Talk to me, partner. What's in Hoboken?"

"Get moving, Rachael. Call me when you're rolling and I'll lay it out for you."

"Done. Twenty minutes. I need to find a vehicle."

As she ended the call, her thoughts were already racing ahead, solving that problem. Bracing herself against the pain, she sat up in bed and pressed the call button for the nurse. Painkillers had made the bullet wound a dull ache, but she would need more of them.

The nurse came in as she was pulling her pants and shoes from the closet, one-handed.

"Ms. Voss—"

"Agent Voss."

"I'm sorry—Agent Voss, what are you doing?" This nurse had just come on duty an hour or so ago. Short-cropped, bleach blond hair, and an almost military air about her, she seemed competent enough, and Voss had expected her disapproval.

"Signing myself out. I need a prescription for something for the pain and a shirt to wear. I assume mine is in the trash somewhere?"

Agitated, the nurse approached her. "Agent Voss, please—"

"I need a shirt. I assume they sell something downstairs that I can wear? Please tell me it opens at nine o'clock."

The nurse nodded. "I think it's nine, yes."

"Great. I'll leave the gown at reception," Voss said as she sat on the bed and tried to maneuver her way into her pants without using her left hand.

"Agent Voss, this is a very bad idea."

Voss stood up and buttoned her pants, then gingerly removed her sling and began the painful process of putting on her shoes. The nurse came a couple of steps closer, then backed up a little, obviously uncertain how to handle the situation.

"If you insist on leaving against your doctor's advice, there are some forms—"

"Get them, please. I'm in a hurry," she said, reaching into the drawer in the nightstand to retrieve her sidearm and strap on the shoulder holster she normally wore. Persuading the hospital to let her keep her weapon in the room had been a bitch, but logic and authority won out. Someone had tried to

take Voss out last night. No way was she going to be anywhere, including a hospital bed, unarmed. Turcotte hadn't
liked it much, either, but Voss was used to being a source of
frustration to him.

"There is a procedure for this, ma'am," the nurse said, getting strident now, trying to pretend she wasn't intimidated by
the gun and Voss's Homeland Security credentials. "You'll
need to be seen by a doctor."

Voss stood, pain flaring as she slid her arm back into the
sling. She went to the closet and pulled out the FBI jacket
she'd been wearing the night before . . . or so she had thought,
until she examined it now and saw no trace of bloodstains.
They couldn't have left a T-shirt?

"You want a doctor?" she said, putting the jacket over her
shoulders, partially covering the gun and the gown, thinking
what a vision of beauty she must be at the moment. "Go
ahead and get one. If you can catch up to me in the gift shop.
I'll be buying an 'I Love Hartford' T-shirt or something."

The nurse turned on one foot, not wasting any more time,
and rushed off to rat her out to someone in charge. Voss had
given up on the idea of getting a prescription from these
people. It would be an hour or more of sitting around, doing
paperwork, and waiting for a doctor. She would call in from
the road and have the office arrange a prescription for her to
pick up somewhere along her route.

She headed for the elevator. Another nurse tried to stop her
but Voss only smiled and stepped on, then pressed the button
for the lobby.

"Miss!" the second nurse cried in alarm.

"Sorry. Talk to my nurse. She'll explain it all," she said, but
even as she spoke the elevator doors were shushing closed.

In the lobby, two security guards were waiting for her.
They started to give her a hard time, but the FBI jacket and
her ICD identification with its Homeland Security stamp
made them fall in line, leading her to the gift shop and helping her pick out a T-shirt, even blocking the entrance to the
shop while she got rid of the gown and put the shirt on, pistol conspicuous in the armpit holster, even though it was
mostly covered by her sling.

The T-shirt offerings had consisted mostly of NEW DAD and BIG SISTER, but she managed to find a Boston Red Sox tee in just her size. She went out through the hospital's front door and hadn't gotten ten feet from the lobby when two FBI agents popped out of a car parked at the curb. She'd picked them out the instant she walked out into the sun—wondered, in fact, why she hadn't run into any of them inside, even guarding her room—and now headed straight for them.

"You guys aren't exactly inconspicuous, y'know?" she said as she approached.

"Agent Voss—" one, a cute Italian, began.

"I mean, the dark suits and sunglasses . . . it's all so clichéd. Never mind that you look more like Secret Service," she said as she walked over to the car.

"What happened to Agent Foran?" the Italian—the driver—asked.

Voss smiled, wincing at the pain in her shoulder. "So you did have someone keeping an eye on me up there? Must have been his bathroom break. Or time for a cigarette, maybe."

She went to the back door on the driver's side and opened it.

"What are you doing?" said the other agent. He was blond, with a linebacker's neck.

"Pulling rank," Voss said, no longer interested in smiling. "Please get in the car, gentlemen, and take me to the local airport. En route, I want to talk to Ed Turcotte, so if you could get him on the phone, I'd appreciate that."

"Agent Voss—"

"I'm getting sick of my own name today," she said. "Get in the car, boys. I won't say *please* again."

They exchanged a hesitant look. It was the driver who complied first, and the linebacker followed his lead. In seconds they were pulling out of the hospital parking lot as the linebacker handed a phone over the front seat to her.

"Hello, Ed," Voss said.

"What are you doing, Rachael?"

"Don't call me Rachael, Ed. I'm going home. I hate hospitals and I was getting claustrophobic. This is good for you, though. You don't have to have a team babysit me anymore. How's the case going?"

"You'd have to ask your partner. It's his case now, remember?"

"I know. But I also know that the Bureau is the Bureau, and no matter how much you're cooperating, there are other factors at work here. For instance, I assume there's an internal FBI investigation right now to figure out which one of your people shot me. Did you notice Norris and Arsenault didn't show up last night? Almost like they didn't want to be there when the ugly went down. Deniability, Ed. It's the new black.

"Where are they, by the way? Batman and Robin, I mean."

For the first time, Turcotte hesitated.

"Ed?"

"I don't know where they are. I'm told Mr. Norris has other consulting work that needs his attention, and SOCOM won't say where Lieutenant Arsenault is currently assigned."

"So now that ICD is in charge of the investigation and their observations and consultations are unwelcome, they've made themselves scarce. After they made all of those bodies vanish, swept a bunch of murdered children under the rug, and got the world thinking Cait McCandless is a terrorist—"

"That didn't come from them. It came from the Bureau," Turcotte said.

"Are you sure about that?"

Another pause, and then Turcotte said, "Where did you say you were going, Rachael?"

"Home, Ed. I said I was going home. We could all use a rest."

"You can say that again. Rest well, Agent Voss."

But she could tell from his tone that he knew she wasn't going to rest. That had been her intention. They had no choice but to cut Turcotte out of the loop—he had to report to Hollenbach, and Hollenbach seemed to be compromised—but he would get the message and understand that.

"You, too," Voss said. "Take it easy."

She tried to close her eyes and drift off on the twenty-minute ride to the airport, but every time the car went over even the smallest bump, the jar to her shoulder made her grit her teeth.

"Either of you guys got any Advil?" she asked as they pulled up to the departures terminal.

They didn't. Voss thanked them and the agents wished her a safe trip home. She waved as they drove off and as soon as they were out of sight, she went inside, checked in with airport security, so nobody started freaking about the woman in the Red Sox T-shirt with the gun, and started looking for the rental car desks.

"What kind of car did you have in mind?" the short Indian man behind the counter asked.

Voss smiled. "Something fast."

Cait sat on the edge of her cot, lacing up a pair of work boots she'd found in the extensive clothing supply room left behind when Lynch's old Resistance friends had given up the fight. In the shower, she had scrubbed her skin raw. Now she wore a clean tank top and her jeans from the night before, as none of the pants in the supply room had fit her well enough. She'd put her hair into a ponytail to keep it out of her eyes.

She stood, feeling good. Ready. Caffeine had her wired up tight, but she didn't mind. Today she had to treat her home soil like Baghdad, and she would need all the fuel she could get.

Despite the rattle of the air-conditioning units, the summer heat had already begun to make the air inside the warehouse feel close and sticky. All the more reason to get out of there, to put the plan in motion. Getting to the Resistance HQ had not gotten them any help in terms of reinforcements, but it had provided them beds and showers, clean clothes and sanctuary. More important, next to the supply room where the clothes and bedding were kept, the warehouse had an armory. Given its size she imagined that once upon a time it had held many more weapons than it now did. But how many guns did one woman need?

Cait clipped a pair of SIG Sauer nine millimeters to her belt at the small of her back—one for each hand. Then she slipped on a loose light-cotton shirt of a summery pale green that hung down far enough to cover the guns. But she could have been carrying an arsenal and no one would see the real weapon. Men looked at her and were distracted by her face, her smile, her body. They saw the cute, petite young woman without ever imagining how easily she could hurt or kill them.

The Collective—or whoever they were—had murdered her brother because they were afraid of him. They hadn't realized what it meant to be Sean McCandless's little sister, but they would learn.

Cait headed down the corridor into the main room, where the A/C unit sounded like distant applause and the television array continued its constant chatter of news. Most of the cubicles were still covered in dust, but a vacuum stood against one wall and someone had run it across the carpet. Jordan sat on a blanket that had been spread on the floor, playing with Leyla. He had the baby on her back and was letting her play with old remote controls and an empty plastic water bottle. These were what passed for toys in her child's life now.

Just for today, she thought. *I swear, baby, just for today.*

"Hey, Leyla," Jordan said, picking up his car keys and jangling them above her. "Look who it is. It's Mommy."

Leyla reached for the keys, staring in fascination. She raised one fist and thrust the knuckles into her mouth, seeming to forget about the keys until Jordan shook them again.

"You're really something with her, y'know?" Cait said.

Jordan glanced up at her, eyes shining. "*She's* really something. Like her mom."

The moment he'd spoken the words he dropped his gaze, focusing on Leyla, embarrassed by putting voice to the compliment. Cait watched him a moment, amazed that, in the midst of all this, she had finally seen the feelings he had for her. It helped, knowing there was someone who cared for her and for Leyla that the bastards hadn't managed to kill.

"You're wrong about this," Jordan said softly.

Cait knelt on the other side of the blanket and bent to kiss Leyla's forehead. She let the baby clutch at her fingers and swung her hand back and forth.

"What else can I do?" she asked, the question nearly breaking her.

"I don't mean the plan. You're right about that. They haven't left you any other options. Even if it works, you'll still have the jihadists to deal with. But all right, deal with that if you get the luxury. I'm talking about me." He gazed at her, and this time he didn't look away. "You shouldn't be leaving me behind."

She leaned over and kissed his cheek, then hugged him close, the two of them like a bridge over Leyla.

"I know you'd like to keep me safe. It means a lot to me. But I can't do what needs doing if I have Leyla along, if I have to worry about her, and you're the only person I can trust with her right now. The only person."

She withdrew, sliding her hands along his arms before letting go. Jordan had the pain of unspoken words in his eyes, but he nodded.

"You know I'll take care of her."

"I know," Cait said. She reached out and touched his face, then stood up. "I'll say good-bye to you both before I leave."

Jordan started playing with Leyla again. As Cait walked away, she felt a hook in her, trying to drag her back. How perfect a day could the three of them have had together, if only they'd had the freedom to leave this place without the fear of bloodthirsty men?

She passed by Lynch's cubicle. The computer was on, but abandoned. The chairs in front of the TV array, where they had spent a little time this morning, were empty. Then she came around the last cubicle and saw him standing in front of one of the whiteboards, studying the new photographs he had taped up—his new targets.

For a moment she just stood and took it in, this display of his work in progress. If what he had told her was true, Matthew Lynch was the last surviving War Child of the Second World

War. He had been involved in this fight his entire life, first surviving the killers who would have murdered him just for being born, then trying and mostly failing to save so many of the children of other wars, before finally giving in and becoming a killer himself.

Cait walked along the first two whiteboards, surveying the photographs of the men and women Lynch had marked for death—people he had confirmed were involved with the murder of War's Children. Many races were represented, but the overwhelming majority were photos of men who looked like Muslim jihadists.

"Why not more Americans?" she asked.

Lynch glanced at her, took in her appearance, and nodded in what she presumed was approval.

"The members of the Collective are harder to find," he said.

"That's a little difficult to believe," she said. "You're trying to tell me it's easier to track down radical jihadists who've infiltrated the country to murder children than it is to figure out who the Herods are in our own country?"

Lynch pointed to a photo on the board in front of him. "This guy? Saudi-born, living in Pakistan. Affiliated with loads of terrorist groups, wanted in Egypt for questioning in the beating death of a three-year-old girl. He's been in the United States a dozen times in the past five years that I know of, and if the information I have about his movements is accurate, you can trace the death of certain children to his presence. I know this because I have access to federal government databases that I should not have access to. Those same databases are not going to tell me who the Collective are using for similar jobs here. Those kinds of secrets are too well hidden. So, yes, I've caught up with a number of the American conspirators over the years, but the jihadists are easier for me to hunt. Unfortunately, I've never been able to track down any of the masters of the conspiracy on either side of this war. During Vietnam, we caught up to half a dozen American industrialists and politicians who were a part of it."

"You killed them?"

Lynch nodded, fixing her with a hard look. "And the war ended. Ugly, but it ended. Make of that what you will."

Cait shook her head and blew out a breath. "It hurts my head to even think about it."

"Unfortunately, it's your life now," Lynch told her.

"Not for long," she said. "I won't let Leyla grow up in the middle of this insanity."

Lynch smiled. Handsome as he was, somehow the effect was chilling. "Like me, you mean? You think I'm insane."

Cait considered lying. "With the life you've had, I don't think anyone would hold you to the usual standard for sanity."

The old man actually smiled. "Very diplomatic of you, Sergeant." He went back to looking at the photos. "In any case, things have changed. They got sloppy with you. Maybe they didn't understand how formidable a target you would be. However it happened, they've made a mess of things."

The photo Lynch had just taped up was of Dwight Hollenbach. Now he put up another, this one a blurry image of a dapper, dark-suited man wearing round glasses, and labeled it *Leonard Shelby*.

"Not as much as they will," Cait whispered.

Lynch nodded in agreement, and then turned to meet her gaze fully. "The Middle Eastern men we killed on your property last night were on my list of targets. As you know, I caught up to Gharib al-Din yesterday. Another of them was killed in a police shootout in Sarasota. That accounts for all of the jihadist Herods who were on my list for the eastern half of the country. There is another cell covering the West, but it's going to take them a while to figure out what the hell's going on here. And when they do, I believe they'll stand back and wait to see if the Collective can get the job done for them."

"So the Arabs are off the board for now," Cait said.

"Leaving the Collective. They're the immediate threat, obviously. And we still have no idea as to the extent of the conspiracy," Lynch said. "These men may be at the top, or just part of the hierarchy. But I do believe they'll be able to tell me a great deal more than the usual foot soldiers and assassins. I hope to be able to use that information."

Cait saw him as though for the first time, understood that these whiteboards, this work, was all he lived for. His whole life had been a tragedy caused by men like Hollenbach and Shelby.

"I hope you get the chance, Mr. Lynch," she said. "For all our sakes. Do you have the floor plan?"

"Already in the truck."

"And the rest of the guns?"

Lynch tore his gaze away from the whiteboard, fully focusing on her at last. "Also in the truck. We're ready to go, Caitlin."

"Good," she said, her mind running ahead. She didn't want to say good-bye to Leyla. She felt sick at the idea of leaving her baby behind. But their choices had all been taken from them. "What do you think?"

Lynch stared at her. "Oh, I think we'll survive getting in. But it's a terrible plan."

Cait pulled the photo of Leonard Shelby off the whiteboard, glanced at it once, then folded it and put it into her pocket before looking back at Lynch. "Only if we expected to get out alive."

-62--

Ed Turcotte felt like he'd been left swinging in the breeze, and he didn't like it one little bit. Worse yet, he had no one to blame. Voss had not been telling him the truth, and his number one agent had stopped answering her phone or replying to his texts. He had kept the messages simple because if he gave Chang a direct order to call him immediately and she did not comply, there could be serious consequences for her.

No matter how frustrated he might be, Turcotte did not want that. In a relatively short time, Chang had proven to be his squad's most valuable asset, and he could see no upside to letting her flush her career down the toilet. So he would

ive her plenty of room to run—to pry into places he could
ot go unnoticed, and pursue lines of investigation that
ould draw too much attention.

For now, he could truthfully say that he had no knowledge
f her whereabouts or activities and blame his ignorance on
oss and Hart and Theodora Wood, the director of ICD.
ight now they were giving the orders, and Turcotte had not
een made privy to all aspects of the investigation. Normally
hat would have burned him—even now it chafed something
ierce—but he knew they were all doing it for his benefit.

How long he would be willing to let them keep him out of
t was another question entirely. Terrorists and Black Ops
n U.S. soil, murdered babies and American war veterans
randed enemies of the state . . . the case had turned into a
lusterfuck of epic proportions. People were keeping abom-
nable secrets, performing hideous deeds, and the conspiracy
o try to make it all disappear included SOCOM, Black Pine,
nd Turcotte's own boss.

Current boss, he thought. Dwight Hollenbach had not al-
vays been his superior. The previous SSAC of CTD Ops II,
ulius Andelman, had moved into an advisory role fourteen
nonths earlier as a stepping stone to retirement.

Turcotte had been thinking about Andelman all morning.
Ie stood in the parking lot outside Hartford Police head-
juarters, where the FBI had set up an office through the
Iartford P.D.'s gracious hospitality, and flipped his cell
hone open and then closed, open and then closed.

Chang and the ICD were trying to keep him clear of the
hit, just in case it all went bad and he had to explain his ac-
ions to Hollenbach. But as much as Turcotte knew how to
ehave like a political animal, he could not close his eyes to
his. He wasn't stupid—he would tread carefully—but doing
othing would haunt him.

He opened the phone, scanned the contacts list for *DR. J,*
nd hit CALL. The phone rang five times, long enough for him
o second-guess himself and then reaffirm his decision. Just
vhen he thought he would have to leave a message, Andel-
nan answered.

"Agent Turcotte," Andelman said. "To what do I owe the pleasure?"

"Hello, Julius."

"My, aren't we informal today."

"We need to talk."

Andelman hesitated, recognizing the tone. "Where are you?"

"Hartford. If you're concerned about snoops listening in, let them listen. If things have gone so far that they're not as troubled by this as I am, then there's no hope for justice anyway."

"That's not like you, Ed. You were never prone to melodrama."

Turcotte glanced around the parking lot to make sure he was alone. A pair of uniformed Hartford cops were climbing into a cruiser at the rear entrance of the building, but other than that, he saw no one.

"It's not melodrama, Julius."

"Go on."

Turcotte told the story with as little editorializing as possible, sticking to the facts of the case, things he had observed himself. He kept it brief. "Agent Voss believes one of our agents was her shooter last night, and that it was no accident," he finished.

"I see," Andelman said. "And what do you think, Ed?"

"Given what's happened thus far—the cover-up at the McCandless woman's house, the way the public picture of her has been tainted—I think she might be right."

He heard Andelman exhale.

"You realize what you're saying?"

Turcotte glanced around again. "I called you, Julius. Hollenbach could burn my career to the ground, but I called you. Do you really think I don't realize how big this is?"

Andelman went quiet long enough to make Turcotte nervous. He started to wonder if he had made a lethal error in judgment.

"Julius—"

"I'm still here, Ed. Just thinking."

The purr of an engine made Turcotte turn and watch as a black Lexus slid into the parking lot, moving past the police

vehicles and toward him at a crawl. The car was too expensive to be federal or local law enforcement. He couldn't see
through the tinted glass, but the tight ball of anger forming in
his gut came from intuition.

"I've got to go," Turcotte said.

"Go," Andelman replied. "I'll ask the wrong people the
right questions. In the meantime, try not to do anything
foolish."

Turcotte closed the phone without replying and pushed
away from the patrol car he'd been leaning against. The
Lexus rolled up to him and stopped, smooth as silk, and the
passenger door opened.

Norris sat inside, staring at him. The son of a bitch didn't
even bother getting out.

"Agent Turcotte. I was told I might find you here."

"I thought you had another consulting gig to take care of,"
Turcotte said.

"A simple job," Norris replied. "Now that it's over, I thought
I'd see what help I can still offer."

Turcotte narrowed his eyes, knowing this guy was the enemy, or at the very least not his friend. He ought to keep his
mouth shut, but he could no longer manage it.

"'Cause you've been a ton of help so far."

Norris smiled, not even pretending to be startled or insulted. "I take it you're continuing your investigation of the
mysterious child killings as well as tracking Sergeant Mc-
Candless."

"I'm sure you'd have heard by now if we had found her."

Norris nodded. "I'm sure. Just as I'm aware of the BOLO
you issued for Jordan Katz. One of my people pulled a file together on him . . . He was in McCandless's unit in Iraq. But of
course you already know that. I take it he was the one along
for the ride last night with the ill-fated Private Mellace?"

Turcotte had had enough. "You do realize you're not involved in this case anymore, don't you, Norris? Nor am I the
one in charge. Yes, I'm following up on the avenues of the investigation that were assigned to me, but if you want in, you
should talk to Josh Hart."

A ripple of irritation passed over Norris's features. It

pleased Turcotte to see evidence that he had gotten to the man.

"Unfortunately, Agent Hart is not returning my calls."

"Have you tried his boss? You people have done such a bang-up job on this case so far, I'm sure Theodora Wood would be happy to hire you on to consult for the ICD."

Norris smiled again, all teeth, like a shark—and with the dead eyes to make the look complete.

"I'd think very carefully about who you choose as allies, Turcotte."

"I'll do that."

"And while you're thinking," Norris said, smile slipping from his face, "perhaps you know where I can find Agent Voss. I understand that Agent Hart is running the show while she recuperates from her injuries, but I'm hoping Voss can persuade him to accept my calls."

It was Turcotte's turn to smile. "Agent Voss went home to D.C. My people drove her to the airport."

Norris studied him. "Agent Voss did not fly home. In fact, after your people dropped her off, she rented a car. She's driving, Agent Turcotte. I'd like to know where she's going."

Turcotte frowned, genuinely curious. "Maybe she decided to drive home," he suggested, though he did not believe that for a moment.

Norris glared at him, shook his head at what he obviously perceived as Turcotte's foolishness, and shut the car door. After a moment, the tinted window slid down and Norris leaned over to look out at him.

"Perhaps I ought to have this conversation with your Special Agent Chang, since she's in D.C. with Agent Hart," Norris said. He looked thoughtful a moment, then continued, "I wonder, Turcotte. How does it feel to have the rug pulled out from under you after all the times you've done it to others?"

Turcotte laughed, wanting to throttle Norris, but happy to see the way his jaw tightened in anger. "Really?" he said. "You want to go there? I'm still working the case, asshole. You're the one on the outside. How do you like the view?"

Without waiting for a reply, Turcotte turned and walked toward the rear entrance of the police station. He wanted to be with real law enforcement people. The lowliest traffic cop was worth a thousand Norrises.

So much for Chang, Voss, and Hart trying to keep him out of it.

-63--

As Josh turned onto the New Jersey Turnpike, he caught Chang giving him a troubled look. The back of his neck prickled with heat and his body ached with the memory of their morning together.

She turned to watch the road ahead, her profile beautiful even when etched with gravitas. Josh told himself not to fall for her, that there were way too many complications.

"You all right?" he asked.

"Just worried. We should have flown."

"We're halfway there. By the time we'd arranged a plane and gotten into the air . . . not to mention the time it would've taken to drive from Newark . . . it didn't make any sense. Besides, with a plane it would've been damned difficult to conceal our movements." He frowned. "We've been through this."

"I know," she said, offering him a slim smile. "I'm just not a patient woman."

"You sure nothing else is on your mind?" he asked.

Chang shook her head with a grin, then whacked him on the leg. "You're so subtle. Seriously. Of course there are other things on my mind, but now isn't the time."

"No, I guess it's not."

Several minutes passed without any further conversation as Josh tried to find a decent radio station not fogged by static.

"So, Hoboken," Chang said. "What do we do when we get there?"

Josh left the radio alone. He glanced at Chang and then

focused again on the road. An old '80s pop song came on the radio—something he remembered from his childhood—and he turned up the volume.

"No idea. It'll depend entirely on what Cait McCandless does next."

-64--

Herc had spent most of the day in a kind of weird stasis, uncertain how to proceed. Boyce had been lurking behind closed doors ever since the ICD and FBI agents had left, but Herc couldn't decide if he was having phone conferences with the big bosses or just praying that whoever was trying to cover up this shitstorm actually succeeded. Meanwhile, Herc had gone about his business as if nothing were wrong, studying topographical scans on his computer and analyzing data. But he carried the Hot Line phone in his pocket and it seemed impossibly heavy. Cait had called several times already, and every time the phone vibrated, he jumped.

In addition to his other duties, he had been working on a special project for Cait, and it wasn't something he wanted to get caught doing. After the conversation he'd had with Agents Hart and Chang this morning, he had been waiting for the FBI to show up at his office door and charge him with conspiracy or domestic terrorism or the murder of Sean McCandless—any trumped-up charge that would allow them to throw him in a cell for the rest of his life and keep their secrets safe.

But hours had passed—it was after noon—and no one had materialized. Out in the corridor, people talked baseball and Hollywood scandals. His wife texted him to remind him they had dinner plans with Rich and Melinda Belinksy. Mundane e-mail kept arriving in his in-box. Andrea Ulman popped into his office to say she was going to get coffee, and did he

vant some? Herc thought he was jittery enough without caf-
eine but he could feel a headache coming on, so he said yes.

Satisfied that he had done all he could and praying that no
one in the monitoring suite would stumble across the new
ines of code he had keyed in, he closed all of the related
computer files and pushed away from his desk, just as Andrea reappeared in the doorway, holding two cups of iced
coffee from the second-floor café.

"You do take sugar, right?"

"Usually two, but one'll do."

"It will, yeah," Andrea said. " 'Cause I'm not going back
downstairs."

Herc took the cup from her and they stepped out into the
corridor, walking toward the monitoring room together. He
sipped iced coffee through the straw and savored the taste.

"I'm weird," he said. "Hot coffee I just take with cream,
but I need sugar in iced."

She arched an eyebrow. "And you think *that's* why you're
weird?"

"Wow. I'm guessing when you were a kid your parents
told you that you were funny."

"Absolutely."

Herc sipped again. "They probably also told you that you
were the smartest girl in the world, that you sang beautifully,
and that you'd be president someday."

Andrea grinned. "Nice. One jolt of caffeine just wakes
you right up."

They stepped into the monitoring room. Three rows of
terraced desks, each with its own personal monitoring station, faced walls of video screen that could be configured a
thousand different ways. Right now, two of the three video
walls in the hexagonal room showed familiar satellite views
of foreign topography, mostly but not entirely Middle Eastern. By the right-hand wall, however, half a dozen people
were gathered at the base of the screen, discussing what could
only be an American highway, with cars and trucks racing in
both directions, a shopping mall on one side and a sprawling
townhouse development on the other.

One of the analysts turned toward the first terrace of desks.

"We don't need this," he said. "Pull way back, put a map overlay up, and just keep track of the signal."

The woman at one of the desks gave him a thumbs-up and started tapping keys; the screen responded accordingly.

"What's going on?" Herc asked Andrea.

She rattled the ice in her coffee cup. "Orders just came in. We're tracking a cell phone GPS."

"Whose?"

Andrea cocked her head, maybe tipped off by his tone that this was not an idle question. Herc kept his face neutral.

"Phone belongs to an FBI agent. Something Chang. Why?"

"Just curious," he said, trying not to show his reaction to the name. He raised his iced-coffee cup. "Thanks for this, Andrea. Happy hunting."

He fought the urge to hurry back to his office, walking slowly and then closing his door without slamming it. Alone in the room he took a deep breath, cursing silently, and took out the Hot Line. *No, no, not that one. Your name won't come up. They won't know it's you calling.* Instead he used his own cell phone, the one with the account in his name. Both Hart and Chang had left him their cards, but he couldn't call the FBI agent if her cell was being monitored, so he called Agent Hart, listening in growing frustration as it rang without answer.

Shit. He had to warn them that their movements were being tracked, but he didn't dare leave a message. Herc killed the call and stared at the phone a moment. Then he set it down and picked up the Hot Line.

Herc searched the contacts list, pressed a button, and, on the third ring, Cait McCandless answered.

"It's Herc," he said, glancing nervously at the door. "Listen, they're tracking Agent Chang's cell. Once they figure out where she and Hart are headed, they'll know where *you're* headed. You've got to hurry."

"Thanks, Herc," Cait said, "but we don't need to rush."

"You're not listening—" Herc began.

"We're fine, Herc. We're already here."

-65--

Cait sat in the back of a truck, listening to the groaning engine and mourning lives she had yet to take. In Iraq, it had been simpler. And last night was even more straightforward than that—defending her baby, killing to survive. But this was different. It would still mean killing to survive, but she knew going in that some of the people she would have to kill meant her no harm and were not a part of the conspiracy. They were veterans, like her. In another life, she might have gotten out of the service and been hired by a firm like Black Pine, who scouted for personnel with exactly her skill set.

But they came for you last night, you and Leyla, and if these guys had been there, they would have followed orders, just like the others. No way could she be judge and jury for every Black Pine operative. *But you'll have to be executioner,* she thought, pain twisting in her heart. She told herself they were baby-killers, or worked for baby-killers. If the guards on the building had never done Black Pine's monstrous wetwork, they had done other hideous things.

It didn't help much. The only thing that soothed her at all was the little photo of Leyla she had brought. She sat on a box of copy paper in the back of the office supply truck, stared at the image of her daughter, and told herself she would do anything for Leyla—and for all the War's Children out there, still breathing, as well as those yet born. And if God existed and the blood she was about to shed stained her soul, she would just have to live with that.

The truck had come from what remained of a motor pool at the Resistance warehouse. In addition to the truck—the doors emblazoned with the name and phone number of a fictitious office supply company—there had been a battered taxi and a four-year-old Buick that looked brand new. The truck had been so perfect for what Cait had in mind that if it hadn't been there, she would have stolen one.

Now she listened to the engine grind as Lynch downshifted, then slowed to a halt. Considering he'd taken a bullet the night before, he must be in serious pain, but he had not complained about having to drive. Either the old man was even tougher than he looked, or he had good painkillers. Or maybe both.

With a low beeping, the truck began to back up. Cait kissed the photo of Leyla and slipped it into her vest, then ran her hands over her body, softly tapping each weapon to make sure everything was where it was supposed to be. When the truck halted again and Lynch shut the engine off, she heard him open his door and the creak of the shocks as he climbed out. Right now he would be walking to the back of the truck, maybe waving amiably to the guards that would be waiting on the loading dock.

She stood and pressed herself behind a pallet of boxes strapped to the wall. A newly oiled AK hung across her back, pressing into her hip. Her fingers opened and closed on the Sig Sauer in her hand. On the other side of the door, she heard muffled voices—Lynch talking to one of the guards. Her temples throbbed with the beat of her heart and sweat beaded on her forehead and trickled between her breasts. So damn hot in the back of the truck. An oven.

The click of a lock—the big padlock was a huge part of the illusion—followed by the ratcheting back of the handle, and then the door rattled upward on its tracks, splashing light into the rear of the truck.

"Sorry, my friend. Left the clipboard in the back, here. Getting old, y'know? Keep forgetting it."

The voice of a guard. "No problem, man. But you can't take anything out of the truck till we see the delivery manifest."

Cait held her breath.

"Sure, sure," Lynch said. "I gotcha. Lemme just . . ."

She felt the truck shift as he started to climb into the back.

"Oh," Lynch said, voice getting very small. "Oh, Jesus."

So claustrophobic back here in the truck. Too hot, no air, even with the door open. The smell of musty paper, sitting for years on those pallets.

"What the fuck, old man?" The guard, unsure, as Lynch crumbled to the pavement. "Are you . . . damn it. Billy!" he called to his partner, who'd be up on the dock still, in the little metal booth, trying to find something on the computer about a delivery from Spiral-Bound Office Supply. "I think the old guy's having a fucking heart attack."

Two seconds. The guard in the booth deciding whether to call the ambulance first or check it out; these guys would be trained to handle things themselves whenever possible. Four seconds. Billy coming out of the booth . . . Please, Billy, come out of the booth.

Sweat ran down the back of Cait's neck and she shivered, then wet her lips and prayed to a God she had never truly believed in to forgive her.

She heard the zap of the Taser, and the first guard's grunt as Lynch shoved it against his throat, turned up to brutal voltage. Before the guy could even hit the ground, Cait stepped out from behind the pallet and the whole picture spread in front of her in vivid colors—Lynch on the ground in his oversized yellow company shirt, the guard in navy blue with the Black Pine logo in red and white on the shoulder, bright sunshine, green weeds growing wild where the pavement met the concrete base of the dock, and here came Billy down the side stairs from his silver metal booth, just realizing that they had fucked up, eyes widening, reaching for his gun.

Cait set her feet, took aim, tracked him as he moved, and shot him in the head. Billy fell down the last few steps as Lynch zapped the other guard again to make sure he was unconscious. *One life we won't have to take today,* she thought. If they were fast and lucky, there would be others.

Lynch ran up the steps to the metal booth, fishing into his pocket for the one piece of tech they had brought with them. They both knew their way around a computer, but neither was any sort of hacker genius. Half of the tech Lynch's old comrades had left behind mystified them both, but he knew what this particular item did. There were at least a dozen of them in a plastic bag back in the warehouse. It wasn't subtle, but it didn't need to be.

Cait kept her gun trained on the building's rear entrance

while Lynch ducked into the booth and popped the cap off the little black plastic that looked like an ordinary flash drive. He plugged it into the computer's USB port. She heard a crackling noise, and then he turned and gave her the *go* sign.

Cait jumped down from the truck, almost landed on the discarded Taser, and ran for the stairs. Every computer in the building would be fragged and all the cameras down, but the scanners on the doors would still be active. They were separately wired, not a part of the computer grid. Right now, everyone inside would be trying to figure out what had shorted out the system, and if fortune was with them—if no one had looked at the delivery dock surveillance camera in the seconds between Lynch faking a heart attack and fragging the computers—they would have two minutes, maybe three.

She knelt by Billy, took his key card, then raced up onto the dock, where Lynch waited. He tore off the yellow shirt, revealing a Kevlar vest that matched Cait's and a pair of guns at the small of his back. He drew one as she slid the key card in, and covered the door as she turned the knob and pushed it inward. Lynch went in low, Cait high, and suddenly she felt like she was in Baghdad again—clearing rooms, every doorway holding the potential of a bullet or a bomb, or hostiles with intent to kill.

Swift and silent, they hustled down the short, wide corridor. It jogged left, and she knew from the plans that the service elevator lay around that corner. Lynch stopped, pressed himself against the wall, and waited. They could have tried a ruse of some kind, but every second counted. She stepped around the corner.

Two guards—one male, one female. Cait shot the woman in the thigh and the man in the throat even as Lynch came around the corner and put a bullet in the female guard's left temple— an extraordinary kill-shot. It made Cait want to vomit. But Leyla's picture was tucked inside her vest, right against her heart, and she knew there could be no going back now.

The silenced guns had done little more than whisper, but they couldn't risk one of the guards getting a shot off.

Cait handed Lynch the key card as she watched both ends

of the corridor. He ran the card through and punched the call button, and they heard the elevator start to hum as it descended toward their level. It would be more difficult from here on out. No one would invest the kind of money required to have thumbprint or hand scanners on every door, but Lynch seemed certain there would be tighter security inside.

How long now? How much more time would they have before the cameras came back online? Every second they stood in front of the elevator felt like an eternity.

The doors shushed open and they stepped on. Cait punched the button for the top floor—seven—and pointed her gun into the blood-spattered corridor they'd left behind as the elevator doors closed. This was their most vulnerable moment. If the camera system rebooted now, they would have a deadly welcome waiting for them upstairs.

The elevator opened on an ugly service corridor lined with doors the floor plan had identified as maintenance and storage closets and restrooms. They turned right, walking fast, not wanting to run for fear their urgent footfalls would rouse suspicion.

Again, Lynch put his back to the wall while Cait walked around the corner, weapon at the ready. There was only one guard this time—a big bastard. Two shots to his chest knocked him off balance, but still he tried to shoot her. Lynch put one through his forehead, then did it again to stop him twitching.

"Should've been another," Cait said quietly as they both holstered their weapons. "No way they'd leave this to one guy."

Together they hoisted him up, pressed between Lynch and the door, and Cait took the dead guard's hand and pressed his thumb to the print scanner. The light above the unit turned green and she reached out and turned the knob. The big man's weight pushed the door open and he slumped to the floor, blood immediately pooling beneath him.

Cait stepped over him, running now, past the time for stealth. A slick-looking suit, fiftyish but still with the military clinging to him, came out to see what the noise had been. Unlike the guards, he didn't have body armor. She fired one shot to the chest—maybe not enough to kill him, but she didn't need him dead. Just out of her way.

Lynch closed the door behind them, shot out the thumbprint scanner, then dragged a coffee table over to block the entrance. Cait hurried on. The rest of the offices she passed were empty, coffee mugs and paperwork abandoned, phones ringing. The second the cameras and the computers went down, all the executives would have been rushed to the safe room, taking it seriously only because they were professionals, not because they actually thought they were in any danger—which explained why the guy she just shot had remained in his office. He hadn't taken it seriously—which meant no one had seen their work at the loading dock. No one had reported intruders yet.

Or maybe they were doing that this very moment; maybe that was why the phones were ringing like crazy.

She reached her destination. A plaque on the door read LEONARD SHELBY, CEO. The door was closed, with no illumination visible through the faux transom window above it. Cait rapped lightly—two short, one long, two short—and the door clicked and opened.

Detective Monteforte stood on the other side, her back to Cait, already moving across the room with her gun out, never wavering in her aim. All this time Cait had told herself Monteforte would be here, that it would go smoothly, but she had never really believed it in her heart.

"Is that guy dead?" Monteforte asked without turning around.

Cait glanced back into the executive suite, watching as Lynch darted in and out, making sure they were the only people left, then focused on the suit sprawled bleeding on the carpet.

"Might be," she said.

"Clear!" Lynch called. "I've got the door."

Cait gave him a nod, then followed Monteforte into Leonard Shelby's office. Shelby looked just like his picture on the website—just as polished and soulless. He sat at a chair drawn five feet back from his desk—far enough that he couldn't set off a hidden alarm.

Monteforte held her gun on Shelby. After today, the badge she wore clipped to her belt would be a useless piece of tin.

"Strange," Shelby said, looking coolly at Cait and then at Monteforte. "This doesn't feel like an arrest."

"You didn't tell me you were going to be shooting people," Monteforte said, with an edge of panic in her voice.

Cait aimed her weapon at Shelby, steadying her right hand with her left. "I'm doing what has to be done, Detective. This is the guy who gave the order that cost your partner his life. He might as well have pulled the trigger himself."

Shelby didn't flinch. "I don't know how many of my people you killed getting up here, Sergeant McCandless, but they won't be the only ones dying today."

Cait smiled, ignoring Monteforte, focused only on Shelby and the thought of everything he had taken away from her.

"No," she said. "No, they won't."

-66--

All along, Monteforte had thought someone would stop them, that somehow Shelby would know she was lying when she called him to arrange a brief meeting. But that hadn't happened. Detective Monteforte had put in a call to Black Pine, claiming that she needed to speak with Shelby on what she had referred to as a delicate matter involving a former employee. She insisted that she required his opinion and a brief consultation, and then expressed reluctance to go into further detail over the phone. They had arranged a time— one p.m.—and when Monteforte had arrived, the guards had ushered her through security without difficulty or delay.

Monteforte's end of the plan had been simple but troubling. During that meeting, she was to restrain Shelby, either physically or at gunpoint, so that when security went on the fritz and the rest of the executives were hustled into the seventh-floor safe room, Shelby would be unable to go with them. And with the door locked and the lights turned off, everyone would assume he was already out of his office. Monteforte had originally planned to cuff Shelby and duct tape his mouth, but the chaos had begun before she could get around to it. With those hard eyes and grim features, he did not seem as if he would be intimidated by her gun, but its presence—aimed at his chest—was enough to prevent him from crying out when a security guard knocked. But Monteforte thought half the reason the CEO of Black Pine played along had less to do with self-preservation and more to do with his desire to discover who had the gall to arrange for him to be taken hostage.

Of course he had guessed before Cait's arrival.

And even now, with Cait holding her gun on him as well, he behaved like he was the one in control. Monteforte stared at Cait, wondering how long it would be before Black Pine security blew open the doors to the executive suite and killed them all. Any law enforcement agency would have to follow certain protocols to safeguard the lives of any hostages—*Oh, my God, I took a hostage!*—but Black Pine did not have to follow any protocols but their own. Would they worry about the life of one executive if it meant the humiliation of having their offices breached?

The only thing that allowed her to breathe was the knowledge that Shelby was rich and powerful and had probably been one of the people who wrote Black Pine's protocol, and she didn't think he would have instituted rules that would allow anyone to throw his life away.

"Cait, what have you done?" Monteforte asked. "You didn't say . . . you told me you knew how to get through their security."

"We did get through," Cait said, as if it meant nothing. But Monteforte could see the truth in her eyes. "We got through the only way we knew how. And now we're here, Detective."

Monteforte swore. She looked at Shelby, who seemed smug and amused. She had agreed to this insanity because her partner had been murdered and people in power were trying to protect the identity of his killers. She had known when she signed on to Cait's plan that she would probably be razing her career, not to mention risking her life, but she believed that Cait and Leyla would be killed if she didn't step in somehow, and she couldn't let Jarman's killers go without consequence. He deserved more.

Now she ran it through her mind, trying to figure out what Cait could have done differently, how she could have saved herself and her daughter from people whose reach seemed unlimited. She could think of no other option, but somehow that didn't make her feel any better.

She wiped at a bead of sweat on her brow, though the room felt cool.

"Cait," she began quietly, "Shelby's right. There's no way his people will let us out of this building alive. You told me you just wanted the truth, wanted someone else to know, so they would leave you alone."

Emotion contorted Cait's features and then she nodded toward Shelby, keeping her gun trained on him. "You really think these people would ever leave me alone? Ever leave Leyla alone? They murder children. I know it, and they know it."

"So what are you—" Monteforte began.

"Going to do? I'm going to kill him," Cait said, almost wistfully.

"You're going to make me an accomplice to murder?"

"I'm going to do to him what he did to my brother, and to who knows how many babies and children!" Cait snapped. "What he did to your partner, Detective. These people have got to be stopped, starting with Shelby. And when this all hits the media, the truth will come out."

Shelby sighed as though bored and clapped his hands in mocking applause.

"Really, Sergeant McCandless, the passion is admirable," he said, "but the truth is what *we* make it. When the smoke has cleared, it's quite likely that all of us in this room will be dead—or, at least, all of you—and Black Pine will still control the message. Tell me, though, who is your accomplice out there? When I received reports about him, he intrigued me."

Cait ignored the question. "I called the police and texted the TV and print media people just before we got here."

Shelby shook his head. "You're not listening."

"You wanted my baby dead!" Cait screamed, leaning over

his desk to point the gun at his face. "You and your goddamn Collective."

"We did," Shelby agreed.

"You admit it?" Cait said, staring at him in shock.

Shelby sighed. "It was regrettable, but necessary. Actually, it should have happened much sooner. All of this might have been avoided if we had acted when you and your daughter first came to our attention. But when our people performed the requisite background check on you, and we learned about your brother—"

Cait flinched. "I knew it. You killed Sean, too."

"It took time to arrange," Shelby said. "A man like Sean . . . only subterfuge would work. We had to find the place where he would be most at ease. It was our only chance of getting him while his guard was down. And we considered it inadvisable to eliminate your daughter while he was alive.

"Of course, even then, you forced us to move our agenda forward more quickly than we wanted. When your encounter with that football player put you on the news, it seemed inevitable that the media would turn you, at least briefly, into a celebrity. We couldn't risk the possibility that they would begin to focus on your personal story, on your life as a single mother/soldier with a half-Iraqi baby. That sort of thing always leads to fluffy news pieces where gentle-voiced narrators ask us all why we can't follow the example of the American soldier and the Iraqi taxi driver who fell in love." Shelby actually laughed in derision.

"We couldn't have that," he added, "so we had to speed things along. Fortunately, the plan to remove your brother was already in place."

Cait leaned against the wall, using it to prop her up. "That video with A-Train? That's what started it all?"

"That's overstating it," Shelby said, almost admonishing her. "Granted, the Arabs who came after Leyla probably had no idea she existed until they saw the news reports about you, but you were on our list. Another few weeks, and we would have been paying you a visit anyway."

"How can you be so fucking cavalier about this?" Monteforte asked. "What kind of monster are you?"

"The practical kind," Shelby said. "You seem to think my friends and I take some pleasure in what we've had to do over the years. Trust me, we don't. Neither have any of the Herods before us."

"Herods?" Monteforte asked.

"Baby-killers," Cait whispered, shaking with rage.

"It's all necessary," Shelby said. "Don't you see? We can't allow the war between Western culture and radical Islam to succumb to exhaustion or to the cowardly nature of the tenderhearted who cannot stand the body count. We've got to see it through, to obliterate our enemy, or we might as well surrender."

Cait sneered at him. "You kill mixed-race children because you believe that, just by existing, they might make people want peace instead of war. And you're trying to justify that?"

Shelby froze, staring at her. "There is no 'might' here, Sergeant. War's Children have a real and measurable influence on international and even tribal conflicts. We have a century's worth of statistics tracking the drop-off of public support for war in direct correlation with a rise in the number of War Child births."

"My God, you really believe all this?" Monteforte demanded.

"Of course I do. Could I bear the weight of it on my soul if I didn't?"

"Make him stop talking, Cait. Please?"

Cait shot Monteforte a dark look. "No. I came for the truth. And for blood."

"The fucker is gloating," the detective replied. "There's only one reason he'd ever admit to any of this stuff. He knows we're not getting out of here alive."

Cait gave her an apologetic look. "I'll do what I can. I swear to God I will. But he might be right."

-67--

Josh pulled up at the curb and got out, standing and staring at the marble and glass of the Black Pine building. But his focus was less on the architecture and more on the quiet tension growing on the street in front of the building. Half a dozen Hoboken police vehicles had already parked there, and others were creating a cordon on either end of the short block on which the building sat. People were being evacuated from neighboring buildings.

But the most peculiar and disturbing element of the growing chaos was the line of Black Pine operatives and security spread along the sidewalk in front of the building, blocking every entrance. The ones on the sidewalk, guns held across their bodies, were not concerning themselves with the situation inside their headquarters.

"You getting the same read off this that I am?" Chang asked him over the roof of the car as she got out.

"If you're thinking those guys aren't out here to keep the trouble from escalating, but to keep the police from interfering with Black Pine business, then yeah."

Chang slammed her door. "They certainly don't look like they're in the mood for company."

Josh started across the street. His and Chang's federal ID had gotten them past the cops who were setting up a roadblock, but still he wanted to be careful not to get them shot. He held his ID up and Chang did the same as they jogged toward a cluster of cops standing in the V between two patrol cars. There were several higher-ups there and, though he couldn't make out their ranks immediately, it was obvious the others were deferring to a heavyset man with Asian features. Josh approached him without hesitation and held up his ID.

"Excuse me, sir. Agent Joshua Hart, InterAgency Cooperation Division. This is FBI Special Agent Nala Chang—"

"Captain Albert Koh," the man replied, brow furrowing deeply. "What's ICD want with this? Better yet, how the hell did you get here so fast?"

"We were already on the way," Chang said.

Koh looked at her. "Meaning you could have called ahead and warned us some shit was about to blow up in our city, but didn't bother?"

"We didn't know the nature of the shit, Captain," Chang replied.

Any other day, Josh would have smiled. Instead, he changed the subject. "Can you give us the rundown?"

"We got a call that people were going to die here today," Koh said, hooking a thumb toward the building. "We arrived to find the place locked up tight. The asshole militia over there are denying anything's going on inside, and say they won't let us in without a warrant."

"Oh, there's definitely something going on," Josh said. "I just wish I knew exactly what it is."

"What about the call we got about people dying?"

Josh glanced at Chang, then back at the police captain. "That wouldn't surprise me in the least."

"Then maybe you'd better start at the beginning," Koh said.

Josh stared at the Black Pine operatives in their uniforms and thought about Cait McCandless and her baby, and wondered how far a woman would go to protect her child. But he didn't really need to wonder. He knew Cait would do whatever it took.

"If you don't mind, Captain, Agent Chang will catch you up on the details. I'm going to go over there and figure out who's in charge of the 'asshole militia.' "

"You taking charge of this situation?"

Josh frowned and turned to the captain. "I am. I hope that doesn't ruffle your feathers too much."

Koh shot a look of disdain at the Black Pine hard cases lining the sidewalk. "You kidding? You're welcome to it. Just tell us how we can help."

-68--

Gunshots rang out in the executive suite. Cait kept the Sig Sauer aimed at Shelby's face but glanced over her shoulder to see Lynch withdrawing from the foyer. The old man pressed himself against a wall, gun clutched in both hands, ready to fire again.

"Lynch, sitrep!" she called.

"Someone snaked a camera under the door, so I put a few bullets through it."

"Camera still there?"

"What do you think?" Lynch called, but she noticed he darted his head around the corner to check the door into the suite, just in case.

The man might not be entirely sane, but she could not help admiring him. At his age, most people were either retired or planning for it. Instead, Lynch had spent the past twenty-four hours running a dangerous gauntlet.

"Hang on a minute," Cait called to him.

The phones had been ringing constantly since she and Lynch had arrived. She'd been so focused on the task at hand that they had been only a mild irritation.

"Keep him covered, Detective," Cait said.

Monteforte didn't like it. Cait could see the panic in her eyes. But it was obvious that the detective hadn't come up with a way out of the situation as yet. For the moment, they were allies. She felt awful having dragged Monteforte into this, but Monteforte had wanted answers and vengeance almost as much as Cait had.

Cait snatched up the phone on Shelby's desk. Others out in the suite kept ringing, but for the moment, this phone went still.

"Hello?" she said.

"Caitlin McCandless?" a clipped, grim male voice asked.

"Stupid question. Try anything like that stunt with the camera again, and this will end immediately—and not in Mr. Shelby's favor."

"What is it you want?" the voice asked. "What do you hope to gain?"

"I want an ending," she said.

The voice began to talk, trying to reason with her, to negotiate how it would all end, and she hung up the phone. Shelby's grin had settled into a supercilious smile, eyes lidded with disdain as he watched her. She almost shot him right then.

"They'll probably try gas next!" Lynch called from out in the suite.

"Cait," Monteforte began, but Cait gave a shake of her head that silenced the detective.

Monteforte went to the window, glancing around warily.

"Be careful," Cait said.

Cait hoped she would, but also figured she would be all right. Thus far they had stayed clear of the windows. There were thin curtains, but she did not bother to draw them. The buildings across the street were all a couple of stories shorter than Black Pine, so it would be difficult to get an effective sniper shot on anyone who wasn't right up close to the glass. And even if they did, she was sure the glass was reinforced. Nothing was bulletproof if you had a big enough bullet, but they hadn't reached that point yet. They weren't going to be firing anti-tank weapons into the CEO's office with Shelby still in there.

"There are tons of cars down there now," Monteforte said. "Not just police, either."

"That'll be the FBI. I suspect we'll get plenty of them."

Shelby laughed at the tough-girl tone of her voice. "I really am curious about your next move, Sergeant. Truly. The FBI aren't going to help you. They're not even going to get a chance. The last minutes of your life are ticking down, and you're going to leave your daughter an orphan. But don't worry. We'll take good care of her when you're gone."

Cait steadied her breath, forcing herself not to pull the trigger. "You'll never find her."

He shook his head, giving her a look of profound pity. "Of

course we will. You really don't understand any of this, do you? Even if I let the FBI into this building, I only have to give the order and they would execute you themselves. We have Herods everywhere. Everywhere that matters."

"One guy." Cait scowled. "Dwight fucking Hollenbach. And the FBI aren't going to kill babies on his say-so."

"Hollenbach only needs his people to *find* Leyla. Black Pine will do the rest."

"And if she's no longer in the country, what then?" Cait asked, feigning a confidence she didn't feel.

Shelby's eyebrows went up. "Don't you know who we are? Black Pine is everywhere. And the Herods . . . the chairman of the Senate Foreign Relations Committee is one of us, Cait. The combatant commander of SOCOM—"

"Bullshit!" Monteforte said. "I can't . . . That's bullshit."

Shelby stared at Cait. "I tell you this because I want you to know there is nowhere she will be able to hide. And I want you to know what is going to happen to your little girl once you're dead."

Monteforte pressed her gun to Shelby's head. "Motherfucker."

Cait watched it all, Shelby's words filling her with icy hatred.

-69--

"I'm here now," Voss said into her cell phone, putting the car in Park. She pulled out the keys and opened the door, standing up to look around. "Where are you?"

"In the middle of the shit," Josh said. "Where else?"

Voss slammed the door, pocketed the keys, and transferred the phone to her right hand, maneuvering her left arm back into the sling. Her shoulder throbbed, and she could barely imagine how much worse it would have been without the painkillers, which gave her a pleasantly detached feeling.

She had called in to the office and arranged to pick some up on the road, a brief diversion to a CVS just off the highway that was more than worth the trouble of stopping. The pain hadn't gone away, but it seemed separated from her consciousness by a layer of cotton.

She wanted more drugs, but for now she would have to turn the pain into adrenaline. No more blunting of edges; she needed to be sharp.

"I'll meet you at the front door," Voss said, hanging up and clipping her phone to her belt. She looked past the vehicles that were arranged in a kind of semi-circle in front of the building. There were many more farther along the street in both directions, police and FBI—not to mention ambulances waiting like vultures for the inevitable.

As Voss walked toward them, a pair of cops standing behind their cruiser turned to confront her, their gazes fixed on the gun at her hip. It took her a second to realize she didn't have her ID out. A cute blond with a gun was a fantasy for a lot of guys, but never for cops in the middle of a standoff.

She identified herself, pulling out her ID. The officers let her pass but she kept the ID out, making her way through a maze of vehicles and personnel. She spotted Josh and Nala Chang with a cluster of cops and FBI agents, and made a beeline for them. Something about the way Chang stood so close to Josh made her take notice. The corners of her mouth tweaked upward, but even to herself the smile felt brittle and false.

Josh glanced around expectantly, saw her coming, then broke away from the others. As she walked up, he shook his head at the sight of the sling.

"I leave you alone for twelve hours, and you go and get yourself shot."

Voss laughed, forcing herself not to reply with a quip about what happened when she left *him* alone for twelve hours. She might be jumping to conclusions anyway. And all the assholes with guns in front of the Black Pine building were slightly more of an issue at the moment.

"I'll try to avoid it in the future," she said, then nodded toward the uniformed operatives lining the sidewalk. "Who's speaking for them?"

"You'll never guess," Josh replied, the words dripping with sarcasm.

"Don't tell me."

He nodded.

"Where is he?" Voss asked.

Even as she spoke, they heard the staccato chop of a helicopter and looked up to see it appear over the top of the Black Pine building, the wind and noise battering the street as it descended. Police and FBI took cover, tracking the chopper's arrival with dozens of guns, but the Black Pine logo on its door made clear that whoever was inside the machine had not come for a fight.

Voss fought the downdraft from the helicopter as she started toward it. Josh fell into step with her and, as they passed, Chang and a heavyset police official joined them. Over the roar of the chopper, Josh introduced her to Captain Koh, but she couldn't do more than nod. The noise of the rotors set her teeth on edge.

At last the rotors slowed, and as they stopped twenty feet from the helicopter, the door opened and Norris emerged. He dropped to the ground, bent slightly, then ran over to them.

"Agent Voss!" Norris called amiably. "Excellent to see you still among the living."

Voss wondered if Norris had personally given the order to take her out. If not, he must know she suspected it. Either way, his amiable greeting had to be intended as mockery. Josh, Chang, and Captain Koh all looked at her, awaiting her reply. Technically the case was still Josh's, but she was the senior partner and he would defer to her now. The pain clawed at her shoulder. She could feel the scowl on her face and did not try to hide it.

"Where's your friend Lieutenant Arsenault?"

"He has other duties to attend to," Norris replied.

"More likely, his puppet-masters yanked him back since they're trying to cover their asses in any way they can."

"I don't know what you're implying, Agent Voss," Norris said, with a scowl to match her own, "but I can tell you this much, I have been authorized to speak for Black Pine's board of directors. You and your people are impeding our ability to do business. There is no reason for you to be here—"

"Other than the goddamn gunshots, you mean?" Captain Koh said.

Norris waved this away. "We have a practice range in the building. If you'd care to check, you'll see that all of our permits are in place."

"That wasn't—" Chang began.

Voss cut her off. "You actually think we're going to leave?"

Norris lifted his chin. "One way or another, yes. For now, you're to draw back at least one block from our property. Shortly, your people will be called away. A court order could do the job, but I'm sure it won't come to that. Already the media are arriving. I saw news vans and cameras and reporters as I flew in. The damage you are doing to the reputation of Black Pine Worldwide—the very idea that we cannot maintain our own security—"

"So this is fucking P.R.?" Josh scoffed.

Before Norris could reply, Voss stepped in so close to him that he backed up, head whipping back, to stare at her in astonishment. Voss reached out and tapped his forehead, hard, with her index finger.

"Listen to me, asshole."

"Who do you think you—"

"Twenty minutes from now, I'm going to have forty Homeland Security agents on the ground. New Jersey State Police are a hell of a lot closer than that—I'm told we have nearly a hundred officers responding from various locations. But looking at your fucking jarheads over there on the sidewalk, I don't even care if we wait for that backup. There are a lot of police and FBI right here already. And no matter who you think you are, or who you think is in charge of this situation . . . Right now, they answer to me.

"Just before I got here, I was on a conference call with the director of the ICD and her boss, the director of Homeland Security. I received my orders directly from them. I hope you're following this."

Voss turned to the others. "Captain Koh. Agent Chang. Pass the word along to your people. Ten minutes and we go in. And if Black Pine operatives attempt to bar entrance to the building, to interfere in a Homeland Security action in any way, you are authorized to treat them with extreme prejudice."

She relished the horror on Norris's face. "You can't do that. You don't understand the people you're fucking with!"

Voss poked him in the chest, backing him up another step. "No, it's you who doesn't understand. Your powerful friends stay in power only as long as their secrets are safe. It's over, Norris. The only thing you get to decide is how many people are going to die here today."

"It's going to be a bloodbath," Norris said, still staring at her like she was the monster.

The standoff continued as Chang and Koh pulled out radios to pass along the orders.

"Mr. Norris," Josh said, "there's another option."

"Yeah? What's that, junior?"

"Cooperation," Voss explained. "Stand down your men and let me send two people in to bring us up to speed on what's really happening inside."

Norris appeared to consider the suggestion, but she could practically read his mind. He would go along with it because he had no other viable option. What worried Voss was what would happen once Josh and Chang got inside. It could all go very badly very quickly. If Black Pine had a chance to wipe the slate, they would do it—even if that meant killing her partner.

One way or another, Black Pine needed Cait McCandless dead—but Rachael Voss needed her alive.

-70--

Cait leaned against the wall, gun still aimed at Shelby, who had wisely stopped smiling.

"Cait?" Monteforte ventured. "You said you had a plan. Please tell me there's still a plan!"

"I'm sorry."

"Sorry?" Monteforte asked, voice rising.

"For bringing you into this. I needed help, and when Sarah put me on the phone with you . . . I'm sorry."

Monteforte swore, shaking her head in dismay.

Shelby let the whole situation ride for a few seconds and then he seemed to settle back into his chair, more than comfortable. He stared at Cait's gun and then at her face.

"You surprise me, Sergeant McCandless. Your service record indicates a highly capable soldier. But you come into something like this without an exit strategy?"

Cait laughed. "Sweet of you to worry about me, but I'm not concerned about an exit. Neither is Lynch. We're here to put an end to you and your whole Collective and we never expected to get out alive."

"Jesus, Cait," Monteforte whispered.

"His name is Lynch," Shelby said. "Good to know. What I wonder, however, is what you intend to do now. How are you planning to, as you say, *end* the Collective? If you were going to kill me, I imagine you'd have done so already. Maybe you've found you're not much of an executioner. Killing an unarmed man in cold blood isn't your style?"

Cait stiffened, finger tightening on the trigger. "Maybe. And maybe not." She looked at Monteforte. "How're you doing, Detective?"

"Terrified," Monteforte said. "There are too many ways this could all end in bullets."

"I know. And I'm sorry about that. But you've done your part, and very convincingly, too," Cait said. "I liked how freaked out you seemed just now. Don't worry, though. It's time to lower the curtain on our little show. No one else is going to die today."

Cait glanced at Shelby, saw the confusion in his eyes at the sudden change in her demeanor, and she relished it.

Shelby started to rise from his chair. "What are you talking about? You're trapped in here, girl. You're not walking out of this room alive."

Cait smiled at him. "We'll see." She glanced at Monteforte. "I hope Sarah got this right."

For once, Monteforte smiled. "Me, too."

Cait went over beside Shelby's desk and aimed her gun at his head. "Detective Monteforte, if you'd do the honors?"

Monteforte did not smile. With her left hand, gun still steady in her right, she pulled her badge off her belt and tossed it onto Shelby's desk.

"Pick it up," Monteforte said.

Shelby did, studying the badge.

"Cait works at Channel Seven News in Boston. Her friend Sarah Lin is a reporter there. The cameramen all love her. And those guys can rig a camera into anything," Monteforte explained.

"Bullshit," Shelby said, holding the badge up in front of him. "You expect me to believe you managed to get a camera through my security?"

"Actually," Monteforte said, "it wasn't that hard. That pinhole camera's one-thirty-second of an inch wide, less than half an inch thick. Sarah had a guy drill a hole in the badge. Your scanners couldn't have picked it up."

As she spoke, Shelby tore the badge off the leather clip Monteforte had used to affix it to her belt. He turned it over and stared at the chip on the back, maybe the size of a postage stamp. He could barely contain his fury, but Cait watched him tamp it down, stifling the tremor in his hands and the flare of his nostrils.

"You'd have to have a receiver for this," he said, almost hopeful.

Cait nodded toward the window. "Right out there. My friend the reporter drove the detective down here in a borrowed Boston news van. It's parked out there, set to receive the signal and transmit it live."

-71--

Herc sat in his office with the door closed, tapping away at his keyboard. He kept refreshing his search, waiting for it to come up, knowing it would but still terrified that somehow it would not, that it hadn't worked. Before he hit the final key, he had taken the time to consider how many laws he would be breaking and what prison would be like. Then he had thought about Sean, who wouldn't even have hesitated.

"Come on, you bastards. Use it," he whispered, hitting RE-FRESH again, his heart thumping loudly in his chest. He was aware of the personal risk he'd taken, but right now his main concern was what would happen to Cait if he'd screwed up.

The live feed from the news van Sarah had borrowed from her employers had been transmitted to the local TV tower, and Herc had ripped it from there into his own system. A few keys to execute his previously prepared program, and the video file had been filtered through all of the satellites he could access, down to cell phone towers, and then out to every single customer within range of those towers . . . probably eighty percent or more of the cellular phones in the United States and a percentage of the phones in Canada and Mexico as well.

Two minutes ago. Three. How long did it take for the file to transmit and then show up on those phones as a message? He wasn't sure. *Millions of phones,* he thought. *Tens of millions. More.* There would be politicians and journalists receiving that video file, but more important, there would be all those ordinary people who had seized control of the national and international dialogue through the Internet.

He tapped the keys again, stared at the search results. A smile spread across his face.

"Yes!"

The blog was called SleepAllDay and the latest entry had been titled "Feds and Black Pine in Crazy Baby-Killing Conspiracy?" *Holy shit,* the blogger began his piece, *can this delusional prick actually be for real? No question it's Black Pine CEO Leonard Shelby, and we always knew his mercenary forces were evil, not to mention that the company shakes down the government for billions every year to provide "security" in places our military isn't enough or shouldn't be in the first place. But who the hell is Sergeant Kate McCandies, and are officials at the FBI and the army really involved in sending assassins after children? Really? WTF? This guy and his friends are monsters! Watch for yourself!*

Herc did not bother watching the video. Instead, he went back to the search window and refreshed, and his smile broadened as he saw that the coverage had truly begun. Within half an hour, the video would be everywhere. The media would not be able to ignore it. Social networking sites would be talking about nothing else.

And there was the true power of the people.

-72--

Josh and Chang rode the elevator to the seventh floor surrounded by Black Pine personnel. Tension filled the silence. The guns remained pointed at the floor, but that was cold comfort. Josh had no doubt they were in enemy territory. Norris had consented to let them into the building only to give his people more time to fix the problem in their own way, which meant Josh and Chang would have to be extremely careful not to get "accidentally" caught in a firefight.

The doors slid open on the seventh floor. Two Black Pine guards stepped off and Josh and Chang followed. He pulled out his radio.

"We're in. Seventh floor."

"Go 'head and make contact," Voss replied.

"Check."

Josh turned to one of the guards and the man gestured down the corridor to the left with the barrel of his gun. Along the hall there were nine or ten other Black Pine employees— some women but mostly men—all dressed in the company uniform. Guards and standard ex-military security. The fact that they hadn't already rushed in and killed everyone showed how much Black Pine valued its CEO. But from the way they huddled in conversation around various schematics and reports, that wouldn't keep the situation calm forever.

"The door to the executive suite is just around the corner," the lead guard said.

Josh nodded to Chang as they neared the end of the corridor. She drew her gun slowly, so as not to present herself as a threat. The idea amused Josh. How could dozens of mercenaries with the best guns money could buy see Nala, or even the two of them, as a threat? Still, he moved awfully carefully as he drew his own gun.

At the corner, they received suspicious glares from a number of Black Pine operatives, but after a moment the cluster of people in the corridor parted to let them pass, and a space cleared at the corner. Josh leaned against the wall there and took a quick look at the suite door. There were bullet holes in the wood. Exit holes.

A noise coming along the hall behind them drew his attention, and he glanced back to see four men carrying metal canisters with rubber hoses attached. Josh shot an inquisitive look at the man beside him.

"Gas?"

"You've got two minutes to try to talk them out of there," he said, his tone perfunctory. "The gas is our next move."

"What if she kills your man in there?" Chang asked, pushing her hair behind her ear.

"If she intends to kill him, he's probably not getting out of that room alive anyway."

Josh shook his head. He felt very exposed, as if he had painted a target on his skull. Dread crawled up his spine. He

looked at Chang again and she gestured for him to hurry
They could have used a phone to call inside, but according to
Norris, Cait had only picked up the phone once. And even
from out here, Josh could hear ringing within. She was not
going to answer.

Josh holstered his gun, feeling more vulnerable than ever
and went around the corner. Light shone in the gloomy corridor through the bullet holes in the door.

"Don't knock," Chang whispered behind him.

He almost smiled. Of course he wasn't going to knock
Startling the people on the other side of the door would only
get him shot. Kevlar vest or not, he had no interest in being
shot. He'd lived through that once, and had no desire to repeat it.

"Sergeant McCandless, please don't shoot!" he called.

"Don't even try the door, jackass!" a gruff male voice
shouted from the other side. It had to be Lynch, the man
Brian Herskowitz had told them about.

"I won't!" Josh said quickly. "I'm not touching the door. I
just want to talk."

Silence from within.

"I want to speak with Sergeant McCandless." He waited
ten long seconds and still no reply came. "Look, obviously
you have some vested interest in keeping Cait and Leyla, not
to mention yourself, alive. So do I."

The gunshot made him jump aside and plaster himself to
the wall. Every weapon in the corridor came up, ready to return fire. Chang and Josh both signaled for them to relax.
There were no new holes in the door. The shot had been for
effect only.

"Got your attention now?" said the man in the executive
suite.

"You've always had it. But you don't want to do that, sir.
You've got a lot of grim bastards up here who'd like nothing
better than to return the favor, but with better aim."

"You want to keep anyone else from dying, you'd better
back away from that door and keep them away, too," Lynch
shouted, and now Josh could hear the exhaustion in the man's
voice.

"Mr. Lynch, please just listen. Tell Cait it's Josh Hart from he ICD."

Josh glanced at Chang, then at the Black Pine men around iim, who were already eyeing him suspiciously.

"The one Herc said would come?" Lynch called.

"That's me. I'm with Agent Chang from the FBI. If you've iccomplished what you set out to do, we're here to place you n custody and make sure you get out of this building alive."

"Son of a bitch," said the Black Pine operative right next to osh. The man raised his gun, and pointed it at Josh's temple. 'What the fuck do you think you're doing?"

The man flinched as Chang put the barrel of her gun igainst the back of his head. Guns cocked up and down the corridor, but now they were aimed at Chang.

"Before you do anything stupid," Chang said, "you should know that both of our radios are transmitting. Everything we've said, everything transpiring up here, is being heard by he cops and federal agents down on the street."

The man swore and turned away, tapped the phone piece in his ear, and started whispering as he retreated a few steps, obviously trying to figure out what the hell to do next.

"Mr. Lynch, I think you can open the door now," Josh called.

"Would you bet your life on it?" Lynch shouted back.

Josh glanced at Chang, throat dry. "I think I just did."

-73--

When Voss's phone beeped, she ignored it, focused on lis- ening to what was transpiring up on the seventh floor. But hen a cascade of beeps went up and down the street, nearly ill of the officers and agents receiving a message within sec- onds of one another. Sunlight glinted off cell phones as seven or eight people nearby checked to see if the messages hey were receiving were anything important.

Voss turned up her radio, trying to hear not only what Josh and Chang were saying, but the responses that this Lynch guy was shouting through the door. It was nearly impossible to make out, however. Lynch's voice was muffled, and there was too much static.

She heard Josh on the radio. *"Mr. Lynch, please just listen. Tell Cait it's Josh Hart from the ICD."*

Things were about to get hot up there, but she could barely make out the words because of all the growing chatter around her. Irritated, she glanced about and saw more and more officers and agents checking their phones, watching something on the tiny screens. Captain Koh stood perhaps ten feet away, with a junior officer holding a cell phone up for him to view.

Revulsion and amazement competed for control of Koh's expression. He glanced up at the top floor of the Black Pine building as though he wanted it to explode.

What the hell? Voss thought, unclipping her phone. She had one message, and she opened it. Immediately, video began to play, the sound crackling but the words mostly audible. The grainy image showed a man seated behind a desk, and beneath the picture a single line of copy—*Leonard Shelby, CEO, Black Pine Worldwide*.

She understood immediately, and couldn't believe Mc-Candless had pulled it off. But another grim certainty seized her and she knew she had to act. Voss saw Norris out in front of his muster-line of stormtroopers, staring at his cell phone, clutching the side of his head with one hand and looking like he wanted to run six directions at once.

She slid her arm out of the sling and plucked her radio from the hood of the patrol car in front of her. *Quickly,* she thought, watching as Norris pulled out his own radio—knowing that it no longer mattered if Leonard Shelby lived or died. In fact, it would be better for Black Pine if he did not survive the day.

Holding her cell in her right hand, she lifted the radio. "This is Agent Voss to positions thirteen and fourteen. On my signal, take out the windows on either side of the seventh-floor corridor."

"Position thirteen, ready."

"Position fourteen, ready."

She saw Norris barking an order even as she glanced at her cell phone, scanned through to Josh's name, and hit the button to call him. Voss counted to three, pushing her phone into her pocket, then lifted the radio again.

"Thirteen. Fourteen. Go."

Shots from sniper rifles cracked the air in a brief volley. Norris started shouting at the Black Pine men lining the sidewalk, startling them all. Voss ran toward Captain Koh and a group of FBI agents, speaking into her radio.

"Go! Go! Take them!" she shouted, drawing her gun.

-74--

Josh and Chang stood in the little alcove that led from the corridor into the executive suite, their backs to the door. Half a dozen Black Pine guards glared at them. The one who'd aimed his gun at Josh a few seconds ago—his name tag identified him as Hewitt—seemed to be in charge, so Josh focused on him.

"If Mr. Lynch opens the door for us, we'll go in and talk to them," Josh said. "Mr. Hewitt, remember that the FBI and local police are monitoring this conversation and will be able to hear whatever transpires here. Homeland Security is officially guaranteeing that if Sergeant McCandless and her associates surrender to me, personally, they will be taken into custody without any harm befalling them."

Hewitt's upper lip curled in disgust, but he radioed for instructions. Josh looked at the uniformed goons along the corridor to the left. They were adjusting black hoses on canisters full of some kind of gas that would knock everyone in the executive suite unconscious, but probably not fast enough to prevent bloodshed.

Then Hewitt's orders came back, and it was very clear that he did not like them.

Josh blinked. "Are we clear on this now?"

"Just do your job, asshole," Hewitt sneered.

Josh rapped loudly at the door behind him. "Mr. Lynch, go ahead and open the door. We've settled our differences out here."

For a moment, there was no reply. Josh and Chang brushed shoulders. He breathed in her scent and wondered if there was any way to avoid this whole thing blowing up in their faces. Then he felt the door jerk against his back. The thumbprint scanner had been destroyed, making it impossible to open the door from the outside without breaking it down. But it could be unlocked from within.

The door clicked, slid open two inches. Josh watched the eyes of the men and women from Black Pine, worried that one of them might not care that the FBI were listening in.

"Mr. Lynch?" Chang said.

Music filled the alcove, Josh's cell phone playing Ozzy Osbourne's "Crazy Train." Everyone in the corridor froze, staring at him. Josh stopped breathing. Hewitt actually started to smile, but not Josh. The ringtone was personalized—it meant Voss was calling him. And he could only think of one reason for that.

Hewitt's radio crackled, someone shouting his name. Josh heard the word *kill* in there somewhere, but he was already in motion.

The windows at either end of the hallway shattered, thick glass flying. Operatives turned away to protect themselves from the shards. Josh shot Hewitt in the side of the head, knocking the man back against the wall in a spray of blood. Before Hewitt even began to fall, Josh shot a second man, in the shoulder, and a blond woman in the leg. Still, her finger clenched on the trigger and bullets punched the carpeted floor before Chang shot her in the face.

Josh felt a bullet clip his right shoulder and he slammed himself back against the door behind him. It swung inward. Black Pine guards stepped over their fallen comrades in a fury. Chang took a bullet in her right thigh and staggered to

he right, blocking Josh's view of the shooters, and he had a
plit-second nightmare of her body dancing with the impact
of a hundred bullets.

Then Chang aimed to the left, right at the tanks of pressur-
zed gas, and pulled the trigger. The explosion blew both of
hem through the door into the executive suite, where they
anded in a tumble of bloody limbs and guns as a cloud of
gas filled the corridor and ballooned into the suite after them.

Josh looked up into the grim face of a white-haired man he
knew must be Lynch.

"What the hell did you just do?" Lynch asked.

A ripple of gunshots came from the corridor and tore up
he receptionist's desk, shattering the computer and framed
family photos. Lynch, Josh, and Chang all returned fire into
he blossoming fog of knockout gas.

"Not me," Josh said, firing as he nodded toward Chang.
"Her. And what she did is buy us another sixty seconds."

-75--

Shelby used the chaos in the executive suite to make a
move for Monteforte's gun. Cait caught the motion in her peripheral vision, and she ran at them both, holstering her gun.
If she shot Shelby, no one would believe that she had not
come here to kill him.

Shelby had Monteforte's wrist and they struggled for control of her gun. The detective showed grit, headbutting
Shelby and trying to knee his crotch, but Shelby had been
someone's Special Ops bastard once upon a time. Keeping
Monteforte between himself and Cait, he twisted the gun in
her hand and started punching her in the armpit and breast.

The gun came free. A look of triumph lit up his face before
Cait yanked Monteforte out of the way and launched a kick
at Shelby's chest that knocked him back against the wall hard

enough to shake a painting off its hook. As the frame crashed
to the ground, Shelby brought the gun up, aimed at her face,
but Cait had already moved. She slid to one side, grabbed his
gun hand, and broke the wrist even as she drove her other elbow into his chest.

Twisting the gun from his hand, she tossed it back to Monteforte, who barely managed to catch it as she stared at Cait
in grim wonder. Cait bounced Shelby off the wall and started
raining blows on his face and chest and gut.

"Cait!" Monteforte yelled.

Cait spun to face her, breathing heavily, feeling the flush of
blood in her cheeks. Then she nodded and backed away, willing her pulse to slow down.

"I guess you've lost a few steps after spending all this time
killing people from behind a desk," she said to Shelby, who
had slid down the wall and now sat nursing his face.

Another burst of gunfire came from the executive suite and
she turned, seeing just how large the cloud of gas swirling toward them had become. She could make out the dim forms
of Lynch and two others in the fog.

"Look!" Monteforte shouted, pointing at the window.

Cait spun in time to see black forms swinging toward the
glass. She dove to the floor even as gunshots boomed and the
windows spiderwebbed with a million tiny cracks, then shattered as Black Pine operatives swung into the glass, crashing
into the room. Three of them landed on their feet, but two
lost their footing on the glass and stumbled to the carpet.

Cait drew her Sig Sauer, slammed in a fresh clip, and
started firing. There were so many now that it would take too
long to try to disarm them. Kill-shots were all that counted
now. She shot one operative on the floor to her left in the narrow opening between his helmet and armored vest, put four
shots into the vest and legs of the one farthest to the right,
then reached out with her free hand and grabbed his assault
rifle by the barrel, dragging it forward—and him with it,
since it was looped around his neck. She jammed her gun
against the visor of his helmet and pulled the trigger twice.

The second of the two who'd landed on the ground fired,
strafing her with gunfire that slammed into her back and sent

her staggering forward, but her vest kept her alive. Cait started to turn, aware in the space between heartbeats that she was about to die, if not by the hand of the man on the ground then by one of the other two operatives still drawing breath.

Then a single shot rang out above the others. Monteforte had put a bullet through the helmet of the man who'd been firing at Cait. The only operative still standing swept his gun around and fired at Monteforte, but his aim was off.

Cait launched a chest-high kick that sent the Black Pine killer pinwheeling backward through the shattered window. He tried to reach for a handhold on the window frame, but the strap of his gun got in the way. His scream was muffled by his helmet as he tumbled through and fell.

Fresh air had thinned the cloud of gas, but Cait felt disoriented. She saw Shelby, propped against the wall and smiling at her in spite of his bloody face and broken wrist. Monteforte covered him with her weapon. Gunfire popped in the diminishing mist in the executive suite, but then it ceased, the echoes of the last few shots then dying away.

Something wasn't right. Cait wracked her brain, running the whole thing through her head, wondering if any more of them were going to come down from the roof and swing through the shattered windows. Were there really only five?

Five. Blinking away her daze she turned to see one of the operatives inching across the carpet. When she'd shot him, he had somehow lost his weapon. His legs were bloody and the left looked broken, but his vest had taken the other shots. She put a bullet in his arm as he reached for the gun and he screamed, cradling the bleeding, now useless arm against his chest.

"You don't have to die," Cait told him.

The man took a shuddering breath and closed his eyes, though whether in surrender or unconsciousness, she didn't know.

"Cait, you all right?" Lynch called from out in the suite.

"We're good."

Only traces of the gas remained, but Lynch looked very unsteady on his feet. He blinked as though he could barely stay awake.

"Thank you for your help, Agent Hart," Lynch said, glancing back into the suite.

The federal agent who appeared behind Lynch might have been handsome another day. This afternoon, he looked a wreck.

"That's what they pay us for," he said, pulling out his radio. Static squealed from it but he started talking, telling someone on the other end that the executive suite was clear and they should send a team into the building. "And tell them to put cuffs on any sorry Black Pine motherfucker they run into on the way up."

Agent Hart turned away, and now Cait saw a third person in the suite—a beautiful Asian woman he seemed to be helping to stand. At first Cait thought the woman had just succumbed to the gas but then she saw the blood soaking the right leg of her trousers.

"Just a graze," Agent Hart said when he saw her watching. "Agent Chang will be all right."

"Easy for you to say," Chang said, holding a hand against her wound.

Cait started moving. Monteforte looked up, frowning at her.

"Caitlin, get down!" Lynch shouted.

She dropped to her knees just as half a dozen bullets struck the far wall of the office. Cait rolled and came up, gun aimed at the broken windows, but she saw no one.

"They're starting to get control of things down below," Lynch told her, "but the kill order went out. Once those snipers figure out it's really over, they'll beat feet, but for now, stay away from the windows."

Monteforte still had her gun on Shelby. "What about him? This son of a bitch is responsible for everything. Who gets him? FBI? ICD? I know you're not going to put him in my custody."

Shelby said nothing, but he gave a soft grunt that might have been a laugh and shook his head almost imperceptibly.

The two federal agents kept their focus on the entrance to the executive suite, just in case some fanatical Black Pine operative decided to make a last-ditch attempt to carry out their orders. But Agent Hart glanced quickly over at Shelby with a look of disgust.

"I'm going to let my boss make that call," he said, "but he's done. Finished. Now the real fallout starts."

"And it wasn't just him," Cait said. "The others he named . . . who knows how many more of these fucking *Herods* there are. We've got to take them all down, make sure their quest is really over."

She pointed her gun at Shelby, on her knees amidst the shattered glass. "As for you, Leonard, you get to face the world as a baby-killer."

Glass crunched underfoot. "No," Lynch said. "He knows the secrets of too many powerful people."

"What, you think he'll get off?" Monteforte asked, horrified. "After what we just exposed to the whole damn world?"

"He won't go free," Lynch said. "But they might make him vanish, just to be sure their secrets go with him. They might cut a deal."

Cait turned to stare at him. "Come on, Lynch. You seriously think he can get away with this?"

Lynch shook his head. "No."

He emptied his gun into Shelby's chest. The second bullet probably killed him, but Lynch kept firing, the man's body jumping with each impact, then listing to one side in a spill of blood when the shooting was done.

"What the fuck was that?" Agent Hart snapped.

He and Chang aimed their weapons at Lynch, both looking wary, afraid of what he might do next. They swayed with the lingering effects of the gas, unsteady on their feet. Their guns wavered in their hands and Cait wondered if they would be able to hit their target, or if she and Monteforte would end up getting shot instead.

"Drop your weapon!" Chang said, her tone steadier than her aim.

Lynch turned to Cait, searching her eyes. It seemed like he wanted to apologize, but couldn't decide what for.

"I'm happy you and Leyla will be all right," the old man said. He squinted a little, deepening the crow's-feet around his eyes. "But stay vigilant. No matter how many of Shelby's friends they might arrest, remember that the other side, the jihadists, are still out there."

Cait nodded. "I'll remember."

Lynch smiled and turned his back on the people in the room.

"Goddammit, Lynch, keep still and drop your weapon!" Agent Hart shouted.

Lynch stepped in front of the shattered windows and pointed his gun down at the crowd of police and federal agents below. Monteforte shouted at him to get back, Chang yelled for him to put his gun down, but Cait could see the determination and a strange sort of contentment in his eyes. And though a deep sorrow filled her, she did not try to argue with Lynch's choice.

The snipers made him dance. Four bullets, each one hitting home. He jerked back from the broken windows and spun around, arms outflung, then he sprawled on the floor. He had managed to hold on to his gun, perhaps by instinct, but as life flowed from him, Lynch released his grip on the weapon and used his fingers to push it away—a refutation of the violence into which he had been born and upon which he had been weaned.

Lynch twitched once, then his eyes glazed and he went still.

A child of war had at last found peace.

"Stupid son of a bitch," Agent Hart said. "What the hell was he thinking?"

Agent Chang leaned against him, weakened by blood loss. They both stared at Lynch's corpse in confusion. Monteforte stepped over Shelby's corpse and retrieved her badge, then sank into the dead man's chair, her eyes round and glazed with shock.

Cait sat alone on the floor, surrounded by the dead. Her family had been torn apart, and her brother was dead. But she knew that her baby was alive and well and waiting for her back in the Bronx. Her arms ached to hold Leyla again, and soon they would.

After what the world had seen today, via cell phone and

Internet and probably television by now as well, the lunatics and murderers who believed in War's Children wouldn't dare come after her.

The thought made her smile vanish and her heart grow cold.

Of course they will. Unless they were all caught, someone would come for Leyla again. But next time, Cait would be ready. And in the meantime, she wouldn't allow her daughter to grow up the way Matthew Lynch had, knowing nothing but survival and death. They would learn and laugh and play together.

They would live.

-epilogue--

Finnerty's had been established in 1956 by a legendary Washington, D.C., police sergeant who had been shot three times, stabbed twice, and electrocuted once in the line of duty before riding a desk for the last few years of his career. Shortly after he opened the pub in the fall of that year, he'd had a heart attack while having sex with the wife of his former precinct captain. It was this last more than his reputation as being unkillable that made him a hero to legions of D.C. police officers. Bert Finnerty had died in his sleep in 1980, at the age of seventy-four, but his legend lived on.

Voss sat at a booth in the back, where the wall was papered with vintage photos of local girls who had posed for the annual Finnerty's Heart Attack Calendar, which raised money for the widows and children of D.C. police officers killed on the job. Her shoulder still hurt, but Josh had teased her mercilessly. Less than a year earlier, he had been shot in almost the same place and she had mocked him for not moving a little faster. Now he tormented her for catching the bullet. Her doctor had called her lucky, said the damage had been minimal, but she still felt like pieces of her were tugging themselves apart anytime she shifted position.

She knew she was already healing, and quickly, but she promised herself she would dodge better next time.

Several televisions were bolted to the wall behind the bar. Two of them had sports running in silence, but the nearest one showed CNN. An image of the Black Pine building flashed by, and then the anchor appeared with a photo of Dwight Hollenbach behind her. The words *King Herod?* were superimposed beneath the picture. With Shelby dead, the media needed a villain to be the face of the conspiracy, and Hollenbach fit the bill nicely. General Barnes from

SOCOM—Lieutenant Arsenault's boss—was an older man, balding and jowly, and looked too much like someone's kindly grandfather. The chairman of the Senate Foreign Relations Committee, John Graham of Florida, had taken his own life only hours after the standoff in Hoboken had come to an end. Dozens of participants in what was now being called the "Herod Conspiracy" had been uncovered, but Hollenbach was being painted as the man behind the curtain.

Voss knew it was bullshit, and she suspected the media knew it was bullshit, too. If anyone had been pulling the strings, it was either Shelby or someone they hadn't gotten to yet. But the American public needed a villain as much as they needed a hero.

Nobody would dare pitch Matthew Lynch as the good guy; his final act had been to aim a weapon at police officers and federal agents, provoking FBI snipers into killing him. The investigating agencies were still trying to figure out if any of those shooters were the same guys who had fired at Cait through the broken windows of Shelby's office, or who had shot Voss in Hartford. But, for the moment, Lynch's death was considered a righteous shooting.

Detective Monteforte had become a media darling. She had been suspended from duty with the Medford Police Department pending the conclusion of an investigation into her participation in the events at Black Pine, but Voss felt confident that she would be cleared and fully reinstated. Homeland Security's official report would reveal that the plan executed by Cait McCandless and Detective Monteforte had been conducted in cooperation with the ICD and FBI agents working to expose the Herod Conspiracy. The media dissected the hell out of the irony involved in Black Pine taking part in acts that could be construed as domestic terrorism.

Monteforte had already hired an agent, who was shopping a book about the case, though she had agreed to let the ICD vet the manuscript before she delivered it to her publisher. With the money she would get for the book, it didn't really matter if she got her job back. But Voss knew Monteforte didn't really care about the money. Writing about what happened was the detective's way of dealing with the death of her partner and the shock of what happened in Leonard Shelby's office. All the media interviews were a kind of therapy, as well as a way to continue to report the version of the story they had all concocted.

What the media wanted most, of course, was Cait McCandless. That was the real story—the soldier mother who had done whatever it took to keep her baby safe—but Cait was nowhere to be found. And that was the way it would stay.

Voss slid her empty beer glass around on the scarred wooden table and glanced back at the TV above the bar. CNN was showing the video of Cait beating the shit out of that football player in Boston for the millionth time. That video would be the bane of the young woman's life. It had gone viral online even before the rest of this had happened. A lot of people would recognize Cait McCandless's face, and that was a dangerous thing—both for her and for her daughter.

Josh stepped back from the bar with a glass of beer in each hand. Careful not to spill, he navigated his way through tables and chairs occupied mostly by cops. Voss noticed a couple of guys give Josh a dirty look. He was in street clothes—jeans and brown shoes and a decent shirt—but they had a sixth sense in Finnerty's and had sussed him out as a Fed. The local police were not warm and welcoming to federal agents of any stripe who came among them when they were off duty.

"Ice cold," Josh said as he set down the two frosty beer glasses and slid into the booth across from her.

Voss thanked him and smiled, lifting her glass. Josh did the same and they toasted, clinking glasses quietly.

"To Cait McCandless," Voss said.

"To luck," Josh replied.

They drank. The beer went down smooth and cold enough that Voss took a long second gulp before setting the glass back on the table and studying Josh's face.

He frowned. "What?"

She had a lot on her mind, but some of it she didn't want to talk with him about.

"Do you believe it?" she asked.

Josh frowned. After a second he raised his glass and took another sip of beer. "You mean the whole War's Children thing?"

Voss cocked her head, arching an eyebrow. The whole point in coming to Finnerty's was so they could relax over a beer and talk about things in a place where they could be sure no other federal agents would overhear them.

Josh took a long drink, and when he put the glass down it was halfway drained.

"I ran across all sorts of things when I was digging around in this case, a lot of small, pretty much forgotten bits of history—"

"Footnotes," Voss said.

"Exactly. Footnotes," Josh agreed. "I found enough of that stuff—about kings and governments ordering the killing of children, officially or in secret, or sprees of unexplained child killings—that it's hard to ignore. But learning something like this can change the way you look at the world. This is the lens I'm looking at that research through. So maybe I'm seeing things that aren't there. But I keep thinking about that *Rolling Stone* article."

Voss nodded. "Me, too." She took a sip of beer and glanced away. "The guy who wrote that article is dead. But the editor—the guy who commissioned it, and who was the only other person to know the name of the source—he's still alive. I put Turcotte on it. Took a while, but we found him."

Josh stared at her. "You're shitting me."

"I shit you not," Voss said.

"What was his name?" Josh asked.

Voss arched an eyebrow. "Matthew Lynch."

For several long seconds, Josh just stared at her. Then he laughed.

"Still, that doesn't make it true, does it? I mean, we've pretty much established that Lynch was a lunatic."

"He was right about the Herods, though. On both sides of this conflict," Voss reminded him. "Obviously that doesn't mean it's *all* true—the mystical stuff—but he sure as hell believed it."

"People believe all sorts of crazy shit," Josh said, glancing around to make sure no one was paying them any special attention. "Whole groups of nutjobs believe the Holocaust never happened, or that the moon landing was a hoax. I don't know what to believe anymore, but does it really matter if any of it is true? From our perspective, the only thing that matters is that there are a lot of dangerous people out there who believe it enough to kill for it, and we have to stop them."

Voss ran her thumb over her glass, wiping away a swath of condensation. "I'm not sure you're right about that."

"How do you mean?"

She smiled sheepishly. "We'll never catch all the Herods. And the other side has their own crop of killers who believe this shit. From what little we already know, it goes back a very long time. Maybe hundreds of years, all those generations of people who believed it enough to commit abominable acts."

"People murder for their faith every day, Rachael."

Voss nodded. "Yeah. They do. And I know you can't judge the truth of something by how many people believe it. Hell, you can get the public to believe almost anything if you want to badly enough. Modern politics is based entirely on that truism. But what if they're right?"

"The Herods?" Josh asked.

"Yes. What if the mere fact of these kids' existence somehow alters the cultural consciousness or whatever? What if just by being born, they change the world on some metaphysical level that can undermine war?"

Josh held his beer like he wanted another sip, but didn't raise the glass. "You believe that?"

"I'd like to."

"Why?"

Voss laughed dryly. "Seriously? Aren't we all looking for some evidence of a higher power at work? I mean, I can't tell you if I believe in God, but it would be a comfort to know there's something more than this. We spend our lives fighting to be right and do right, and to find a little love and kindness. Wouldn't you like some reassurance that we're not alone?"

Josh gave a small shrug. "It wouldn't hurt my feelings any."

"I'm serious, Josh."

He seemed troubled by the question, joking to make light of it. Voss sipped at her beer while he contemplated. After a few seconds he leaned forward, reached out with his glass and clinked it against hers again.

"You're not alone, Rachael."

Voss merely stared at him, unblinking, barely breathing. A loaded silence had descended upon them and she was afraid to break it for fear of saying something that would lead them into confusion. Josh seemed to be studying her, searching her eyes for something he wasn't even sure was there. They had always been direct with each other; this awkwardness was new.

She broke the tension by lifting her glass and taking another sip, then glancing away. When she glanced back at him, she managed to smile.

"Shouldn't you be going? You don't want to be late for your first proper date with Nala."

Josh seemed like he wanted to say something, but instead he pulled out his cell phone and checked the time. She could tell by the look on his face that it was later than he'd thought.

"You'll be okay getting home?" he asked.

Voss arched an eyebrow. "I'm not an invalid."

He laughed and nodded. "All right. Just wanted to be sure."

"Besides," Voss went on, "who says I'm going home? Maybe I'll pick up some young boy in blue and play the handcuff game."

"Have fun with that," Josh said, downing the rest of his beer before he slid out of the booth. She liked the fact that he did not seem completely certain she was joking.

He reached for his wallet, but she waved him off.

"I've got it," she said. "Tell Agent Chang I said hello."

Josh hesitated and, for a second, Voss thought he might break their new, unspoken rule and start the conversation they'd been avoiding. Then the moment passed.

"I'll do that," he said. "See you tomorrow."

She watched him leave, weaving through the tables toward the door. When he had gone, she signaled the waitress for the check, paid, and left without even finishing the rest of her beer. Perhaps another night she would be in the mood for picking up a strange man in a bar, but that didn't seem likely. Regardless of Josh's assertion otherwise, tonight she would be alone.

As for Josh and Nala Chang, well . . . the idea of the two of them dating seemed not to sit very well with Turcotte, and anything that bothered Ed Turcotte was all right with her. Or so she kept telling herself.

Cait lay on her belly on the warm tile floor, sticking out her tongue at Leyla and blowing raspberries. The baby was on her hands and knees on the thick playmat her mother had put out, a set of plastic keys in her hand, but now she pushed her legs out behind her, going down on her stomach like Cait. Leyla grinned, drooling, and laughed at her mother's antics.

"Silly girl," Cait said, stretching forward to press her forehead gently against her daughter's.

She pulled herself into a sitting position, bracketing the playmat with her legs, then propped Leyla between them. She grabbed the tower of multi-colored plastic rings that the baby seemed to love. The idea was for Leyla to put the rings onto the conical tower in order of size, but it had quickly become obvious that throwing them was much more fun. Fortunately, she didn't usually manage to throw them far.

"Baseball is not in your future," Cait said, nuzzling her daughter's cheek.

A familiar sorrow seized her. Baseball really wasn't in Leyla's future. America wasn't in her future. This was home now. And it was going to take some time to adjust.

With a sigh, she picked up Leyla and rose, propping the baby on her hip. Leyla still had the green ring and she bopped her mother on the head with it, making Cait smile. Then the baby started slobbering all over the plastic ring and Cait could only shake her head in amusement. It would take some getting used to, yes, but as long as she had Leyla with her and safe, nothing else really mattered. Wherever they could be together, that would be home. They would build a life together, the two of them.

Cait went to the window and looked out at the cobblestoned street below, the whitewashed buildings just across from hers, and above their orange-tiled roofs, the view of the harbor afforded by her second-story window. Brilliant blue, the sea glittered in the sunshine, dotted with the white sails of pleasure craft and a handful of the village's fishermen, getting a late start.

As new beginnings went, it truly was a beautiful one. Fifty miles north of Dubrovnik on the Croatian coastline, the village was small and quiet enough not to attract a large number of tourists—just enough to help the economy, and nearly all of them from elsewhere in Europe instead of from America. Even so, Cait had to be careful. She'd dyed her hair a very boring brown and would keep it that way, and she was letting it grow. Remembering her nightmarish ride with Lynch, she had suggested glasses, and Agent Hart had agreed. An optometrist would know they weren't prescription just by looking at them, but no one else would think twice.

The American government had financed her relocation, but only Agent Hart and his partner, Agent Voss, knew where she was. The building she and Leyla lived in belonged to her, free and clear. No mortgage. Although as far as the locals knew, her name was Catherine Shaughnessy. The small but well-kept row house was on the village's cobblestoned main street, where most of the shopping was done. She and Leyla lived on the second and third floors, while the first floor would become her shop.

It wouldn't be enough for her to simply live here. An American mother who did not need to work to support her baby would invite too much speculation. Better to define herself than to give others cause to wonder. As a girl, she had spent far too much time in her aunt's chocolate shop, and so Catherine's Candies would open within the month.

This was a beautiful village. It would be a good life, for both of them.

Leyla laughed at some sort of babies-only joke and pressed the drooly plastic ring against her cheek. Cait nuzzled her and the baby laughed again. If anything had happened to Leyla—

She stopped herself, unwilling to allow herself to consider it. Everything and everyone else in her life had been stripped away. Her job had been interesting, but not something she loved. Nick Pulaski had been calling her, but she did not return those calls. She felt badly for that, but other than her aunt and uncle, there weren't many other people she felt she owed a good-bye. Most of the people she loved were dead.

Miranda had been buried four days after her death. Cait

had not been able to attend the funeral. Agent Hart even refused to allow her to send flowers. Anything he thought might lead someone to her and Leyla, she would avoid.

She had wished that Auntie Jane and Uncle George could have come with her, but they had Tommy, and a life in Medford. Josh Hart had promised to pass a message to them for her now and again. She missed them horribly—both Auntie Jane's warm chatter and Uncle George's contented silence. Other than Leyla, they were all the family she had left.

Hart and Voss had done a great deal for her, but the real miracle they had performed had been acquiring Sean's ashes. Cait kept them in a ceramic jar on a bookshelf in her bedroom. Her brother's ashes were all that she still had of the life she'd left behind.

And then there was Jordan. She had thought of him constantly since arriving here, hoping and wondering.

Leyla started babbling, then went back to gumming the ring.

"You hungry, baby? Time for lunch?" she said, thinking that afterward Leyla would nap and then she could get some work done down in the shop, where she was putting up shelves and painting.

Only the noise and the paint fumes had convinced her to let Leyla out of her sight, but since their arrival here she had not been farther from her daughter than the baby monitor would reach.

She glanced once more at the picturesque view out the window, then looked down at the people moving along the cobblestoned street below. Just before she would have turned away, she noticed someone approaching her door and an icy ripple of fear went through her. Then he stopped and glanced up at the number above the door, and she saw his face.

"Oh, my God," Cait whispered, stepping back from the window. She looked at Leyla, pressed their noses together, and felt elation fill her. "He's here!"

She rushed down the stairs with Leyla on her hip. At the bottom, she unlocked the dead bolt and the chain, then pulled the door open and stepped out.

The building had two doors—one for the apartment upstairs and one for the shop. Jordan stood with his face against the shop window, one hand shielding his eyes from the sun as he tried to peer inside.

"You came," she said.

He turned, and that boyish grin spread across his face and lit his eyes.

"How could I not?" he said, looking sheepish and almost embarrassed. "When Agent Hart gave me your invitation . . ."

Cait glanced around to make sure no one was watching them. "You're really here? I mean, *here*?"

His smile faded. "That was the deal, right? I mean, Agent Hart said the only way he could tell me where you were, even after he gave me the note, was if I was gonna . . . y'know, *stay.*"

Still she couldn't accept it, couldn't believe it. "You're not going to want to go home?" she asked, as Leyla began tugging on her hair.

Jordan shrugged, unable to meet her gaze. "I never really had much of a home, Cait. Not anywhere." He glanced around. "It's beautiful here. As good a place as any to find out what home feels like."

Her heart hammered in her chest. It had taken her a long time to figure out exactly what she wanted to put in the note she had written for Josh Hart to give to Jordan. She'd written twenty or more versions of it before she had realized what she really wanted to say. He had always been there for her, in the desert and afterward, and he had kept her daughter safe when the rest of the world had shown her its ugliest face. There was no one alive she trusted the way she did Jordan, and she knew that he had feelings for her. She knew she cared for him, and that it could be more if they had a chance to find out.

She went to him now without another second's hesitation and kissed him, Leyla on her hip, still tugging her hair. When the baby hit Jordan with her goopy plastic ring, he laughed and kissed her head, just the way Cait always did.

"I missed you, little lady," he told Leyla, eyes alight as he raised his gaze to meet Cait's. "Almost as much as I missed your mom."

Cait kissed him again.

"Home's going to be good," she said. "Really, really good. I just hope you like chocolate."